The Procedure

A Novel

Terry Brown

Chapter 1

The scream from the back seat penetrated his eardrum and ripped through to his very soul. The piercing sound of his daughter screaming uncontrollably ricocheted off of the glass windows of the car and scarred him forever.

"Daddy, it hurts so bad," she cried from the back seat. He glanced over his shoulder and noticed that there was blood everywhere. His daughter's beautiful blond hair was matted against the side of her face. He pushed the gas pedal down a little farther and drove as fast as he could, even though the hospital was only a few blocks away. The lights of Hot Springs were a blur as he raced down Central Avenue.

"Daddy, my stomach is killing me," his daughter cried out. "Please make it stop."

"Aagh!" Another scream cut through the air. He couldn't bear to hear that sound again. The desperation and helplessness was like nothing that he had ever felt before.

"Just hold on a little longer, baby," he said with all the encouragement that he could muster. "We're almost there. When we get to the hospital, they'll make you feel better."

"Daddy, will they make the hurt go away?" Her voice was straining now. She was struggling to get it out.

"Yes, baby. They'll make the hurt go away." He glanced back again and saw that his daughter's blood was staining the gray fabric of the back seat a deep, dark red. He couldn't believe how much blood there was. His daughter was curled up in the seat and the blood was accumulating in pools, on the seat, and unto the floorboard.

"Oh Daddy, Daddy, Daddy! Make it stop. It hurts!" The scream came again.

"Help me...e...e...!"

He gripped the steering wheel tighter and a look of determination covered his face. He could see the hospital up ahead.

* * * * *

"Daddy, I'm pregnant."

Sheriff James McLaughlin would never forget the day he heard those words. His daughter had come into the den of their house, when he and his wife had been watching TV. He had been sitting in his favorite chair, large and overstuffed, with an ottoman. They had already commented that she had been acting differently as of late.

He had acted very predictably. After being stunned and speechless, he then got angry. He had never before been angry with his daughter. Pacing all over the floor, ranting and raving, he wanted to kill whoever had done this to his baby.

Finally, his wife quietly said, "Dear, you've got to settle down. It won't do us any good now to get upset and make threats. Besides, our daughter has some fault in this too."

He stopped in his tracks. His wife was right. He turned and looked at his daughter sitting on the couch. She had her head buried in her hands. He could tell that she was crying.

"That's right Daddy," she sobbed. "It's my fault too. I knew better, but I did it anyway. I'm so sorry, Daddy. I'm sorry that I've embarrassed you and Momma. People all over town are going to be talking about me. I'll never be able to go anywhere in this town again."

She stopped and looked up at him.

"Daddy, I can't have a baby now. I want to go to college. I just can't have a baby, not now. Please help me, Daddy."

* * * * *

His hands were trembling. It must have been a thousand times that he had wiped his palms off on the legs of his pants.

He wasn't really comfortable asking other people for favors. He hated to think that he might owe somebody something, especially this guy. A county sheriff in south Arkansas was more accustomed to handing out and collecting favors, than asking for one for himself.

After his daughter had come to him and his wife and told them she thought that she was pregnant, he had been able to confirm this by quietly calling in a favor with one of his buddies, a local physician. The physician had run a pregnancy serum test on his daughter's blood. However, his ability to call in favors ran out as he considered the options for his daughter. In this day and age, the options for respectable people were few.

One of the local physicians in town, a family practice physician that he had known forever, had laid out the options for him, adoption or parenthood – the only choices his daughter had.

He couldn't imagine his daughter with a baby right now. His daughter had so much potential. She would be graduating from high school in a few weeks. If everything worked out just right, she would soon be valedictorian of her class,. He had hoped that she would be the first in the family to go to college, but that dream would go right out the window with a baby. They wouldn't even let her finish high school, if they found out that she was pregnant. That was one of the rules that the local school district had. You just didn't do that in a small Bible Belt town - nice teenage girls didn't get pregnant.

How could either of those two options work for her or for his family? He had to have another choice.

That question led him to the pursuit of the third option. It was an option that he had only heard about through rumors. The rumors generated from back room discussions were that there was another way to take care of this problem.

He had heard that there was a place downtown, where a girl could go after dark to take care of a pregnancy. It was outside of the regular medical community. It was outside of his regular contacts. That was why he had to approach "The Boss."

The Boss had been around town for a long time. He had no apparent means of support, at least none that anyone knew about. The talk was that he was retired from the Chicago Mafia. His reward for a job well done was to have his "retirement" setup in this resort community.

His "Family" had a long history in this town, particularly since this had been their regular vacation stop since the Thirties. In fact, the head of the Family himself had made the Arlington Hotel his vacation headquarters during his glory days.

Although this had been a so-called neutral zone for several rival gangs that vacationed here, it was rumored that they did bring some of their more lucrative and convenient activities to town. Whether this particular service was of the lucrative or convenient type, McLaughlin didn't know. He had been told that this particular business had been introduced to Hot Springs so that the "boys in the family" would have a way to eliminate any mistakes that they had with the local girls.

His baby girl had become one of the mistakes people hear about in whispered conversations - the conversations that resulted in those "holier than thou" looks from the ladies at church. How would his family ever be the same? This mistake was going to change everything, unless he could fix it.

Still, he couldn't believe that he was about to ask The Boss for a favor. How could it have ever come to this? He had managed to keep from being indebted to these kinds of people during his entire career. He had been free from the influence of the criminal elements of Hot Springs and the people of the community knew it. However, now that was about to change.

All these years, he had always been the one in control. Now his daughter had ruined everything. He wasn't sure that he could bear the embarrassment of a pregnant daughter and an illegitimate grandchild.

He had to gain control over this situation. He needed an answer and The Boss looked like the only one who could get it for him. "The Boss" was the only one that he knew of who could arrange for his daughter to get the procedure done quietly. And maybe, just maybe, no one would find out about it.

He rethought his options one last time. Were there any others?

* * * * *

He followed his instructions to an apartment downtown, in one of the alleyways off Central Avenue. McLaughlin knew Hot Springs like the back of his hand. The apartment that he had directions to was a block north of the Arlington Hotel and owned by The Boss. It was on the second floor above a nondescript shop that sold local crafts. Access to the apartment was up a rickety metal staircase that led to an old wooden door.

The doctor was a retired guy from Chicago. It was rumored that he had run into some problems with the local medical society in Chicago and had come close to losing his license. He had been able to keep his license only through some major string pulling. He had come to Hot Springs to continue his work for the Family.

When the Sheriff arrived at the apartment with his daughter, he knocked softly, looking carefully up and down the alley. Immediately, the door was opened.

"Please come in," the man answering the door said. "I've been expecting you. I'm Doctor Hamner."

Dr. Hamner extended his hand and the Sheriff shook it. The doctor had small, soft hands. He looked to be about sixty-five. He had white hair that flowed back and just touched his collar and he wore small, round wire-rimmed glasses. Oddly, he had a comforting look about him.

"We're kind of nervous about coming here tonight," the Sheriff said.

"Most of my patients who come this time of night are very nervous. But we can take care of this little procedure in about 15 minutes and then you can be on your way," Dr. Hamner said.

He looked at the young girl and said, "Darling, don't worry about a thing. Come with me and we'll get this over with quickly. Sheriff, if you'll just take a seat out here, we'll be back in no time. Please make yourself comfortable."

As the doctor and McLaughlin's daughter walked through the door to the back room, she looked back at him with blue eyes filled with confusion, fear and shame. Then the door closed and he was left alone. A shiver went down his spine. Looking around, he could see that he was standing in the living room of the apartment. He walked over to the one window in the room. He looked through the dirty streaks on the panes of glass down into the street below. It was very quiet in the streets of Hot Springs tonight.

He turned and examined the rest of the room. It was a small apartment that was beginning to show its age. The hardwood floors needed to be refinished and some of the paint was beginning to peel off the wall around the window. The room was painted a drab white and was turning yellow with age in the corners. Apparently, the doctor was not much for home maintenance.

The furniture in this cramped makeshift waiting room was a little frayed also. McLaughlin sat down on the faded green couch and felt the springs shifting underneath him. His palms were sweating, so he rubbed them on the stained arm of the couch, and then he checked his watch.

It had been over 15 minutes. What could be going on? Was something wrong? He stood and paced back and forth across the living room. He tried to relax by breathing deeply and examining the pictures on the walls as he walked around the room, trying to take his mind off his daughter in the next room. The Sheriff noticed that the doctor had no personal pictures or diplomas hanging in the room.

What could be possibly taking so long? He looked at his watch again. Twenty minutes. He kept pacing, noticing the dirty smell that the room had. He stopped in his tracks and stood stock-still. He thought he heard noises in the next room. Twenty-five minutes. The noises were getting louder and McLaughlin was straining to distinguish what they were. They began to have a frantic sound to them. He looked at his watch, 30 minutes, but it seemed like an eternity.

A scream stopped him dead in his tracks. As he rushed to the door of the adjacent room, he heard Dr. Hamner calling out to him.

"Sheriff, get in here, I need your help!" Hamner was yelling. "Something's wrong."

The Sheriff burst into the room, sending the heavy wood door crashing into the wall. He saw his daughter lying on a table in the middle of the room, facing away from the door. Her head was propped up on several pillows at one end of the table. When he moved to her side, what he saw at the other end of the table made his blood run cold. His daughter's legs were propped up in a spread-eagle position at a ninety-degree angle from the table and blood was everywhere. The doctor's gloved hands were covered in blood. As sheriff of Garland County, McLaughlin had seen many gruesome sights in his career. Realizing the blood had most recently been in his daughter's body, his knees almost buckled beneath him.

Dr. Hamner shouted at him, "Hurry, Sheriff, we've got to get her out of here. Your daughter's had some complications and needs to get to the hospital right away. I've used a little anesthetic to numb her, but it's already wearing off. This procedure has taken much longer than I expected."

McLaughlin was standing beside the table in shock, unable to move. His daughter was writhing on the small, Formica-covered table and moaning.

"Sheriff! Sheriff!" Hamner was practically screaming. "Come on, we've got to get her out of here. For both of our sakes, she can't be found here."

McLaughlin finally snapped out of his daze and moved over to help Hamner.

"You grab her under her arms and I'll get her legs," Hamner barked. "Where did you park?"

"I…I…I'm right downstairs," the Sheriff stuttered.

"Let's go then," Hamner yelled. "We don't have any time to waste!"

They picked up his daughter and began to move her through the apartment and down the narrow stairs to the street. The door at the bottom of the stairs opened to the alley, where he had parked his car.

Dr. Hamner yelled at him, "Can you open the door to the car?"

"Yes, I think so," the Sheriff said, straining under the weight he was carrying.

He propped up against the car and reached over and opened the door. They slid his daughter into the back seat. She moaned from the pain.

"Hurry, Sheriff!" Dr. Hamner insisted. "Get her to the hospital! You don't have a second to lose. She's already lost a lot of blood."

* * * * *

His daughter's scream jolted McLaughlin out of his trance just as he was speeding up to the hospital. Wheeling into the ER entrance, he jumped out of his car and ran to the door.

"Please, someone help me! My daughter's bleeding. Please hurry!"

Two nurses moved quickly out to the car with a stretcher and opened the back door. The Sheriff could see over their shoulders into the back seat. Blood was everywhere. The nurses dragged his daughter out of the car and loaded her onto the stretcher. They rushed her into the ER and immediately took her into a treatment room.

The Sheriff staggered into the hospital and collapsed into a hard plastic chair in the waiting room, just steps away from the room where they were working on his daughter. He could hear her screams and moans, although with each passing second, they seemed to get weaker and weaker. A doctor and several other medical personnel rushed into the treatment room. He could hear the sounds of furious activity coming from the room. He could hear the shouts from the medical staff as they worked on his daughter. With the activity going on around him, McLaughlin felt as though he were suspended in space, every movement around him in slow motion, every sound and smell amplified. He wanted to reach out and stop this horrible ride. The sounds from his daughter had almost stopped. The urgency of the work in the room seemed to intensify.

After what seemed like an eternity, the room was suddenly quiet. He was alone in the waiting room. One by one, the hospital personnel began to shuffle slowly out of the room where his daughter was. McLaughlin had seen this before, in fact many times, he had been the one coming out to talk to the family. It was the nature of his job.

At last, the doctor came out of the room and walked directly over to the Sheriff and sat down beside him. He knew the doctor well, as he knew most of the people working in the ER.

"I'm sorry, Jim. We did everything we could," the doctor began, with moist eyes. "She'd lost too much blood and was in shock by the time we could do anything for her. We tried everything, but it was no use. I'm so sorry."

They were sitting together, alone in the ER waiting room, a moment of grief shared between them.
The doctor, McLaughlin's friend, had placed his arm around the sheriff. They both sat there with tears streaming down their faces.

The Sheriff couldn't believe what he was hearing. Surely this was a bad dream. This kind of thing didn't happen to good people. Maybe he was just having a terrible nightmare. This couldn't happen to him.

He looked up at the doctor. He could tell by the look in his eyes. He had seen that look before.

Sheriff McLaughlin looked down at his watch. At precisely 11:59 p.m., his baby girl, his only daughter was dead.

Chapter 2

Thirty-five Years Later, 1999, in Little Rock, Arkansas...

Martin Smith, MD, was sitting on a metal stool in front of the operating room table. He placed the Auvard speculum in his patient after prepping the area with antiseptic solution. He looked up around the stirrups to see the face of the young girl lying on the table. "Are you OK?" he asked her. She nodded groggily and very unconvincingly.

"We can wait a few minutes if you need us to," he told his patient, pausing from his work.

"No," she replied, "let's go ahead and get this over with."

Dr. Smith grasped the patient's cervix with two tenacula and injected a solution of pitocin. This drug would firm up the uterine wall, so he would be able feel the limits of the uterus and avoid perforating it. The drug would only take a few moments before it took effect in his patient. Dr. Smith reached over to the instrument tray and picked up the sound, which was a long, thin steel instrument. Using the sound, he could tell how far the other instruments could be safely inserted into the uterus. He then proceeded to dilate the cervix with the shiny steel dilators. When he had dilated the cervix to the necessary diameter, Dr. Smith placed the hollow plastic cannula into the interior of the uterus. At this point he usually had the nurse turn on the suction machine, but they were a little short staffed today and he didn't have much help. He reached over and switched on the suction machine. The sound caused his patient to jump.

"Just lie back and relax," he told her. "This will be over in just a few minutes."

When the gauge on the machine reached fifty-five millimeters of negative pressure, he began to move the cannula around the interior of the young patient's uterus. The sound of tissue and fluid being caught in the vacuum of the machine created a sucking noise, which varied depending on the size of the tissue as it made its way into the plastic suction containers. It was kind of like using a vacuum cleaner at home. Anything of substantial size made a horrible noise as it passed through the tube. As he watched, Marty could see the bloody pieces of tissue flowing through the hollow, clear cannula on their way to a small cheesecloth sack inside the clear plastic container.

The noise from the suction machine turned into a steady swooshing sound. He looked down at the cannula and saw that there was no longer any fluid flowing into the suction container. A couple more sweeps with the cannula for good measure and this one would be history. After the last two sweeps around the uterus, Dr. Smith turned off the suction machine and withdrew the instruments from the patient. He unscrewed the plastic container marked "POC" and removed the cheesecloth sack. He took the sack over to the surgical tray and spread the contents out on the sterile blue towel. This was the last step of the procedure. He was required to view the "Products of Conception" and account for the major anatomical parts of the fetus. After taking an inventory, he could be certain that he had completed the procedure and thereby reduced the patient's chance for complications. As he viewed the uterine contents, he was able to identify the tiny scapula, ribs, legs and the arms with a little hand. This girl was at least ten weeks into her pregnancy.

The doctor got up and walked to the head of the bed and took his patient's hand.

"It's over now," he said. "You did just fine." She smiled a tight, strained, little smile and nodded her head groggily. A tear trickled down her cheek.

Marty walked out of the operating room, stripped his latex surgical gloves off, and threw them at the hazardous waste box. He missed, as usual. Moving into the hallway, he noticed that the other two OR's had charts in the racks outside the big swinging doors. That meant that he was really running behind. As he walked through the hallway, he grabbed a Diet Coke out of the refrigerator and stopped at the dictation station. He dictated the details of the procedure on his last patient, Kristen Dunlop, but after completing the dictation, instead of moving on to the next room, he ducked out the back door. He went around the corner, leaned up against the side of the brick building, and looked out over a small grassy area behind the clinic. The rain had been steady all day, but this was his first chance to notice. Since he had come in this morning, he had been going from one procedure to another. Marty barely had time to catch his breath between procedures. This place was his one escape during days that seemed to get busier and busier.

He leaned closely against the wall. He knew that if he stood under the eave just right, he could manage to stay dry. He tried to count the number of procedures that he had performed already today. As best as he could remember, it must be around twenty-three. He looked at his watch. Only 2:15. How could that be? It seemed that he had been at the clinic forever today, even though he hadn't started until nine. According to what he could remember from the schedule, there must be at least ten more cases on the books for the afternoon.

"They weren't kidding when they told me that they would keep me busy," he mused aloud. It was especially busy when he was the only doctor working in the clinic. "I wonder what the clinic record is for the most procedures performed in one day. I must be getting close. I wonder if they give out an award for that," he said to the rain.

He could see it now, a plaque with an inscription.

> Presented to
> Martin R. Smith, M.D.
> Daily Production Award
> Most Procedures in One Day

He had always been a hard worker – he had to be. Marty certainly had the grades to get into medical school and survive, but they had not come as easy for him, as they had for most of his classmates. Marty's roots were not the roots of privilege. He grew up in a lower class neighborhood on the east side of North Little Rock. His neighborhood was not on the circuit for the rich and famous.

His parents had not been able to help him with the cost of his education. He had worked and borrowed his way through four years of college, four years of medical school and four years of residency. Everything that he owned, which wasn't much, he had worked and struggled for. Nothing was given to him. He knew nothing of the good life. He was still waiting to taste it.

The back door opened, breaking his trance, and the OR supervisor, Janet Rawls, stuck her head around the corner.

"I thought I'd find you here," she said with a look of disgust. "I've got all three rooms ready and waiting for you. Any time you're ready, Doctor."

"I'll be there in a minute, Janet." He hated it when she came out and did that. She could be so condescending.

Marty stood there purposefully another few minutes sipping his Diet Coke and watching the rain. It seemed to be coming down a little harder now. The air also seemed to be getting colder.

The weather in Arkansas could be so unpredictable. One day it could be seventy degrees, and the next day it could be snowing. Today the gray skies made it look like winter was here. Well, it was the first of December. It was about time for the weather to turn cold.

"I'd better get back to work before the Nazi Nurse comes looking for me," he said to himself. "I sure don't want to get in trouble with her." Janet Rawls seemed to pull a lot of weight around here and this wasn't the time for him to rock the boat. He really needed the money that this job was providing. His financial situation was pretty dire at the moment, and the money that they offered him to do these procedures was beyond belief. The offer had exceeded the only other opportunity that he had received after residency by $100,000. It was a tough market to be a male ob-gyn physician. The best jobs were reserved for the female residents. Oh well, he would just have to make do with the genetic cards that were dealt to him.

He tossed his empty Diet Coke can into the trash receptacle and strolled back inside.

Marty wandered over to OR 2 and met the disapproving stare of Nurse Rawls. Janet was a tall, thin woman. With her frosted hair, it was hard to judge her age, but Marty had pegged her for late forties. She was all business.

He looked at the patient and saw that it was another young, white female. Glancing at the chart, he noticed that Abigail Peterson was just seventeen years old. Looking at the clothes she had changed out of, young Abigail would fit into the upper middle class of the socio-economic rankings. As Marty was closing the chart and replacing it on the end of the bed, the notation of "PIF-Cash" was indicated at the bottom of the information page. PIF, paid in full. It was amazing that so many of these girls came through the clinic with that notation on their charts. He had often wondered how much cash came through these doors every day, but as a hired hand, he had no concept about the business of the clinic.

"Dr. Smith, I hate to disturb your daydream, but we do have several patients waiting for you," Janet said in her most annoying voice.

"Ms. Rawls, I certainly appreciate your concern for operational efficiency, and I will certainly try not to let my daydreams disrupt the clinic's workflow in the future," Dr. Smith said in a slightly sarcastic tone.

"Doctor, I've got Tammy Hawkins working with you the rest of the afternoon. If we're going to get everything done today, we'll have to get moving and you'll need some help."

Well, Janet was right about that. He would need some help to get through the rest of the schedule and get the staff out at a reasonable hour. As far as the potential for help, Tammy was probably the best choice. Tammy Hawkins was an LPN, Licensed Practical Nurse. She had good patient care skills and a pleasant personality. She also could anticipate a physician's moves and provide the right instrument at just the right moment. Tammy was really good help. Maybe this afternoon would improve after all.

Janet Rawls shoved the OR door outward and left the room. Before the door could even stop swinging, Tammy Hawkins came into the OR.

"Hi, Dr. Smith," she said cheerfully. "I hear that you need a little help this afternoon. Well, I'm here to serve."

Marty smiled beneath his surgical mask. Tammy was always so bubbly.

"Hello, Tammy," Marty replied. "I could use a little help. The front desk has booked me pretty heavy this afternoon and this patient looks like she may be a little more complicated than normal. By the way, how many times do I have to tell you, call me Marty?"

"I know, I know Marty," she said. "It's just so hard to remember when everyone else around here is so formal and stuffy."

"Speaking of stuffy, are they trying to save a little money by keeping the air conditioner off?" Marty was wiping his forehead as he spoke. "It's unbelievably stuffy in the OR's today."

Tammy moved around to the head of the table to check the patient's vital signs. As she was writing the information in the chart, she commented.

"You know, I didn't think that I would ever get Janet to agree for this patient to have a general anesthetic. You'd think that the cost for the anesthesia was coming right out of her pocket. Anyone in their right mind could tell by the size of this girl that it would take a general to do this case."

"Yeah," Marty mused, "I've noticed that it takes a lot of effort for these guys to sign off on anesthesia. They usually want these patients to get by on a local anesthesia and a little something to calm their nerves."

Dealing with the anesthesia issue had been difficult for Marty. During his training in residency, he never even considered the possibility that he would be administering anesthesia on his own patients. He couldn't believe that a clinic would operate in this manner. He caused a major scene during the first week he was working at the clinic. Marty still remembered that day. He had a patient that needed anesthesia and he requested that a nurse anesthetist or an anesthesiologist be called to assist. The nurse that was working with him in the OR chuckled to herself and stepped into the hallway. A few moments later Janet Rawls entered the OR and explained to him that the clinic did not use anesthesia personnel. It was too expensive, she said. After much yelling and cursing, Marty threatened to go over her head and get the appropriate personnel to work in the OR with him. She explained once again in a patronizing manner that it would be impossible for him to go over her head, as she had the support of the clinic owners in this matter.

Marty calmed down and quietly checked Janet's story. It was true. The clinic had never used trained personnel to administer anesthesia. He was amazed and realized that he had just experienced his first professional disappointment. It would not be his last.

"Well, Tammy," Marty quietly called, "let's get busy and get this one done before the Nazi Nurse comes checking on us again."

As Marty reviewed the chart one last time, he noticed that Janet Rawls herself had done the pre-abortion counseling with this patient. She was extremely thorough, and she was sold one hundred percent on the procedure. He had heard her spiel before. Marty knew that she focused hard on the patient's rights as a female to take control of her womb. Since this girl was only seventeen years old, Janet had probably covered the choices that she would never get to make if she became a mother.

Tammy had the instrument tray unwrapped and ready to go. Marty grabbed a weighted speculum off the tray and began the procedure. Within ten minutes, the procedure was complete, and Tammy was beginning to recover Abigail Peterson from her anesthesia.

Marty walked outside the OR door and began to dictate a note on the patient's procedure.

Operative Note

Patient: Abigail Peterson
Patient Account #: 34895
Date of Service: 12/03
Physician: M. Smith, M.D.

Procedure: D&C

Operating procedure and findings: Under good general anesthesia, the patient was prepped and draped in a routine sterile fashion for vaginal procedures. The bladder was emptied. Weighted speculum was placed in the posterior vault. The cervix was grasped with a single tooth tenaculum, serially dilated to admit a size 8 curve suction curette. Suction curettage was carried out with substantial POC's obtained. Further curettage with sharp curette was productive of no further tissue. Post curettage hemostasis was good and the patient was taken to the recovery room in stable condition. Estimated blood loss was less than 50 cc's.

Marty tossed the chart into the out-box at the dictation station and moved on to the next room.

By 5:30, they had completed the thirty-first procedure of the day. Marty sat down in the dressing room and took the sterile footies off his Nike tennis shoes and threw them at the trashcan. He missed again. As usual, he left the clinic still dressed in his scrubs. It seemed like that was all he wore these days. He went out the back door of the clinic and crawled into his old Mazda RX7. He had bought the car while he was in high school with the money that he saved from working 40 hours a week. As he pulled out of the clinic parking lot, he didn't notice the man in the white Chevy Malibu parked across the street. He had been parked there every afternoon for the past two weeks.

Chapter 3

He sat at his desk slowly turning and admiring the new plaque that his staff had recently given him upon the completion of his doctoral program. Dr. William H. Roberts. Man, that "doctor" sounded good next to his name. It had been a long time coming. He had spent four years during his last two pastorates working to complete this degree. A Doctor of Divinity degree. This was something that he had been waiting for, for a long time. How sweet it was to have that accomplishment behind him!

His plan was coming together nicely. Not many people could say that they had come so far, so fast. From his humble start in rural Georgia, to pastoring one of the largest non-denominational, evangelical churches in the South at the age of thirty-five, man, what a ride this had been!

He had endured all of the typical bumps and bruises that most pastors experience. Previous congregations had questioned his authority. They had given him grief over the amount of time that he had taken off to get his doctorate. He had endured threats of termination and had even been terminated twice. He had suffered through restrictions on his financial control of the church.

Not anymore. He finally had the right church and they didn't ask questions. They were ready to be led. Over the last two years, he had been putting the perfect staff together. He had managed to chase one off by insinuating to the church personnel committee that he had been having a relationship with one of the women that worked in the church office. He had convinced the youth minister that he would never be capable of making it big in church work, unless he went back to school and obtained his master's degree from the seminary. Both of these staff members had the tendency to question him. He had known from the very first meeting that he had with them after he began work at this church. He knew they would have to go, for him to implement his plan. Having the right staff in place would be critical if he was going to sway his congregation. And they were his congregation now.

It had taken several confrontations to get the congregation on board. In fact, he had found it necessary for some of the people to leave the church, in order to begin the core part of his plan. But now, he had a congregation that would do anything for him.

Now for the next step in the plan, he needed an issue that would get him recognition outside of this church. He needed an issue that could propel him to statewide or regional recognition. He was ready to move beyond the confines of a church.

And he had just the issue. Right to life.

He was going to use this issue to make his name known, and he had a plan for this too. He was finally in the perfect location to get himself involved in the issue, Hot Springs, Arkansas.

He had learned that Hot Springs was right in the middle of the Bible Belt, ideally situated for developing the evangelical congregation base that he needed to enthusiastically support the issues he wanted to pursue. But, Hot Springs had a unique history of being unusually tolerant for a small Southern town in the Bible Belt. Gambling and gangsters had been status quo for this town in its early history.

The only gambling that had ever been legal in this town was wagering on thoroughbred horses. Since 1903, horse racing had been legal in Hot Springs. That in itself was somewhat of an anomaly. In recent years and on several different occasions, well-organized supporters of casino gambling had made attempts to legalize their business interests in the state. Each time the voters of Arkansas had defeated the proposals. It was as if they were saying, "We don't care if you gamble in Hot Springs, but you can't do it anywhere else."

The natural hot springs that bubbled up in downtown had been the drawing card that had given the city international acclaim. This had been the attraction for the gangsters that began to come to Hot Springs in the 1920s. With the gangsters had come many other activities in addition to the gambling. Prostitution. Extortion. Public corruption. These activities had been either allowed or tolerated for years in this town.

With such a rich history, it made perfect sense to make this the time and the place for his next big move. What made it even more perfect was the political climate that Hot Springs and Arkansas had generated over the last few years. The previous Governor of Arkansas had grown up in Hot Springs. During the ten years that he had been in office, he had instituted a very liberal slant to state government. This included the state's policies that dealt with abortion.

The state had begun to pay for a wider range of services related to abortion procedures. The court system was now taking a very progressive approach to prosecuting the protesters that seemed so prevalent around abortion clinics these days.

Roberts had spoken to the new Governor. He knew that he could count on him for support on his right to life campaign.

The intercom on his phone buzzed and disturbed his thoughts. He reached over and pushed the button so that he could respond. "Yes?"

"Brother Bill?" It was his secretary, Betty Baker.

"Yes, Betty, what can I do for you?"

"Well, I hate to disturb you, but I knew that you would want to know about some of the calls that you had received. First of all, the chairman of the deacons called and wants to talk to you about several issues."

"Well," Bill thought, "that one can certainly wait."

"Anything else, Betty?" he asked.

"Yes sir. The Governor's office called and he would like to set a meeting with you to discuss your plans for the coming rally."

"Is that it?"

"No sir, I've also got Mike Hanks on the line. He says that it's very important that he talk to you."

"Well, why didn't you say so?" Bill said raising his voice slightly. "I've told you before that I always want to talk to him, when he calls. You didn't keep him waiting long, did you?"

"No, Brother Bill. He's on line one."

Mike Hanks had been a godsend, quite literally. He was one of the first church members to really get the big picture of his vision. Mike had come forward early and made himself available for anything.

"Mike, is that you? I hope I didn't keep you waiting long."

"Yes sir. It's me, Brother Bill. I didn't have to wait too long. I'm just glad that I was able to catch you. I was afraid that you might not have time to talk to me."

"Mike, you know that I always make time to talk to you. The project that you're working on is vital to our plan," Brother Bill said earnestly.

"That's what I wanted to discuss with you. I've spoken to our guy," Mike replied.

Bill's heart skipped a beat. "Any news from him?"

"Yeah, it looks like everything is coming together," Mike said. "He told me to get the final payment together, because it wouldn't be long now."

"That's great news. How's he holding up?" Bill was having a hard time containing his anticipation.

"He sounds great, Brother Bill," Mike observed.

"Do you anticipate any problems with him?" Bill wanted to make sure that everything was perfect.

"I don't think so," Mike said thoughtfully. "He sounds stronger than ever. It was almost like he had a new commitment to the cause."

"That's great, Mike. Let me know if there are any changes. I appreciate your call."

"You bet. You know I'm committed to making this happen." Mike had conviction in his voice. "Oh, and by the way, congratulations on your doctorate. That's quite an accomplishment."

"Thanks, Mike. I appreciate the support. You can't imagine how important it is to have church members like you who are supportive of my efforts."

"You have a great day, Brother Bill, and I'll keep you posted. I'll call you as soon as I hear anything."

With that, the phone line went dead. A smile came across Bill's face. This was coming together very nicely. Mike was performing like a true follower. When Mike had first come to talk to him, he had made it very plain that he would do anything to make Bill's plan a reality. Anything. Mike had very subtly explained that he had connections that would allow him to get almost anything done. He also told Bill that he understood that drastic measures might be necessary to achieve the goals that they were planning.

Bill placed the phone back in the cradle. With a few more people like Mike Hanks in place, this plan would work.

He had to finish the preparation for his next sermon. He already had the outline formed in his mind. He just had to find the right Scriptures that would bring his people along with him. He had to get them focused on the Right to Life issue. He wanted them to hurt over the death of millions of babies each year from abortion. He wanted his congregation to become so obsessed with abortion that they would follow him anywhere to fight it. He had already planted the seed in several sermons that he had given to his congregation. In fact, Mike Hanks and his contact had both been swayed by one of his earlier sermons. Now it was time to turn up the heat.

It was easy for him to get his people to oppose abortion. The Bible had many references to God "knowing us before we were born." It was also easy for him to link the procedure of abortion with murder. The tricky part of his next sermon was to develop an intensity among the congregation that would incite them to a new level of activism. He needed them to be ready to take the next step of the plan. They couldn't just agree and sit in the pew. They needed to agree and move out into the community in a wave of protest. They needed to be prepared for the harsh reality of the measures that it would take to make real change in abortion in America.

Now, if he could just get a few more of the right people in place, he could use the prestige of this church and his position to get the true recognition that he deserved. Not many men had the ability that he did to really understand what God wanted for his people. But he did. Not many had the skill to move people to action beyond their comfort level. But he did.

He knew that he had the gift. He knew that God had chosen him for this moment.

He was ready.

He would lay out this issue for his church members and they would never know what hit them.

They would have to follow him. He knew that his gift of persuasion would be much too overwhelming for anyone to stand against him. He would set the stage and make the case for this new movement, and "his people" would be obligated to do his bidding.

He had heard the whispered criticism. He had heard the jokes from those who doubted about drinking the Kool-Aid, but he had carefully weeded most of those people out of the congregation. Now, it didn't matter. These people were ready. He had already seen two come forward and move beyond their comfort level to accomplish the goals of the plan. He knew that there would be more. They wouldn't be able to resist. He would have them swarming down the aisle after this sermon. He would have the emotions so high that no one could justify sitting passively on the sidelines.

He knew the time had come.

Dr. William H. Roberts would be the new spokesman for the unborn. He would take this fight to a new level. He had been waiting for this moment. He had prepared himself for this time and place. By the time his plan was in full swing, the people of this state would be begging him to be their leader on this issue.

This would give him power that he could only dream about as a pastor. The recognition he received from this would increase his influence far beyond Hot Springs. Power and influence. That's what it was all about. It's what he deserved. He had paid his dues and suffered through those miserable little churches in podunk little towns.

As he had discovered early in his career, without power, a person amounted to nothing. Roberts promised himself that he would never be in that position again. He would never again put his family in the position of being bounced from church to church, community to community, just because the people disagreed with him. He was never again going to take orders from a church member, or anyone else for that matter. Dr. William H. Roberts was God's man and no one would tell him what to do! It was time for a change.

He was ready. It was time to build his kingdom. It was time for him to take control and exert the power and influence that he had been patiently waiting for all these years.

It was time.

Chapter 4

The pecking of the rain on the roof of the car had gone on for hours. The droning sound made it hard to stay awake. The hours of watching the raindrops running down the windshield was about to drive him crazy. How much longer would this miserable weather go on? It had already been raining for several days.

Kevin McLaughlin had been sitting in the car for hours, waiting and watching. The white Chevrolet that he had rented for this last part of the mission was very nondescript and very uncomfortable. He didn't know that they even made cars anymore without CD players. Had it not been for the commitment to his mission, he would have gone stark, raving mad from boredom hours ago. He had been watching this building for months. He had been here in the early morning hours, just as the sun was coming up, before any other activity on the entire block. He had been there at midnight, when a full moon had kept the rear portion of the building light enough to see every detail of the structure.

He had been in the clinic during office hours, pretending to need directions. He had even worked inside the building for a brief period of time with the janitorial service that cleaned the place after hours. That move had been a stroke of brilliance. Working with the old man who ran the cleaning service had allowed him to learn the entire layout of the building. Since the old man was usually half drunk, he had been able to get a copy of the key to the building and learn how to operate the security system.

He turned the key over slowly in his hand. Sometimes he turned it end to end. Sometimes he turned it side to side. Sometimes he didn't even realize he had it in his hand.

He liked the feel of the key in his hand. It was a heavy key, one of those bulky brass types.

It reminded him of his mission.

He had been looking for an opportunity for several years to get involved in this fight. As far as he was concerned, he had been called to this battle. Most people wouldn't understand it. But God had called him, just like a preacher. He knew he would someday be involved. He just didn't know how until he had heard the preacher at his church talking about it.

Brother Bill had preached a sermon encouraging people to get involved in issues in the community that went against God's word. It was that sermon back in the spring that had renewed his interest and sparked this new aspect to his efforts. He knew then and there, that he would get involved in this fight at a new level. He had reasons that went back a long way. After that sermon, he began to hear the calling stronger than ever. It was shortly thereafter that he met Mike Hanks. It had been very exciting for him to find someone else who shared a similar calling. Mike had been a great help to him. Mike had helped him bring his thoughts and ideas together. Mike's convictions didn't have the same long history that his did, but he was still equally committed. Over the last few months, Mike had helped him understand that no action was too extreme to stop the horror that occurred in this building every day.

He looked down at his hand, where the cold, metal key was turning slowly from side to side.

He couldn't believe how perfect Brother Bill's sermon was this past Sunday. The message in the sermon had been for him. He knew now that he was on the right track. After listening to Brother Bill, it was obvious that he needed to complete his mission. It was almost as if Brother Bill was speaking directly to him. It was unbelievable. He wondered if anyone else felt the same way. Although he was ready to complete the next step, he knew for the real change to occur, the change that Brother Bill was talking about, it would take a groundswell of people with a passion for this issue. Now there was a great man who really understood the call. Brother Bill could really bring out the emotion of the people. He had people moving all over the sanctuary. By the end of the sermon, the congregation was at a fever pitch. Kevin thought they might all march down to the closest clinic and burn it to the ground.

His attention came back to the task at hand. Kevin looked up at the rain running down the windshield. His breath was fogging the inside of the car window. Through the car window, he read the sign in front of the building, "Women's Health Inc." He was always amazed at the benign names that the owners gave these businesses. As he had researched these types of clinics, he had discovered that not one single clinic identified itself for what it really was.

He knew what it really was, an abortion factory. It was like entering a manufacturing plant. Walking through the building, each step of the process was laid out in vivid detail. The first step on the assembly line was the preparation of the raw materials. This was the counseling stage. The pregnant women were given their options regarding their current situation. Practically always, 99.9 percent of the time, the choice was made to terminate the pregnancy. At the end of the assembly line, you could find the end product in the Clean-up Room. You could see the rows and rows of jars labeled "POC." Kevin still had a hard time referring to the jars of babies as "product of conception." The process was amazing. He couldn't imagine that it would have been any more productive, if you were making cars, or computer chips, or widgets. It was fantastic that they were able to do this so efficiently. Or at least it would have been fantastic, had the product been anything else.

He had been in front of many of these types of clinics. It galled him to think of these places as clinics. He preferred to think of clinics as places where people were cured and sent home. These "clinics" had healthy pregnant women walking in and when the procedure was complete, they sent emotional wrecks out the front door and jars of dead babies out the back.

The key was turning slowly, always slowly, in his hand.

Kevin's real involvement began three years ago. He had known since he first went to college that he would become a part of this issue. It was too personal for him to ignore. He had been involved in all of the activities of the typical pro-life worker. He had marched in front of clinics. He had marched in rallies. He had counseled girls at crisis pregnancy centers. He had even chained himself to the front door of a clinic in Jackson, Mississippi. All this work had been great, but it was not making a very big impact for real change. People still thought abortion was a personal choice. Didn't they know what God had done to nations in the past that allowed the murder of innocent people to continue? God had punished entire nations for a complete generation for this kind of stuff. If America was ever going to wake up to criminal activity allowed in the name of civil liberty, someone had to do something. He knew he was supposed to do this. He knew it was his turn. It was time for him to move on to the next step. It was his calling.

The layout and location of this building should work perfectly. He had studied several different locations over the last three years before settling on this one. The selection of the right clinic was critical. He had to make sure that all of the variables would work in his favor. His work was too important to be stopped or delayed by the authorities. He had to consider all of the details. He had checked escape routes. He had checked the building structure. He had checked the traffic flow on the street. No detail was too small. He had checked them all. It had to be perfect.

The building was a two-story brick structure with the clinical space located on the first floor. A reasonably sized waiting room was located in the front corner of the building, along with the reception desk and the file room. Just behind that space were the consultation rooms. The remainder of the space on the first floor was sterile space considered part of the surgical suite. The entire top floor was dedicated to the administrative functions of the clinic.

The key was turning slowly from end to end in his hand.

He had watched the staff come and go. He knew each of their names. He knew where they lived. He knew what cars they drove. He knew what bumper stickers they had pasted on their cars. He knew which employees were the counselors. They were the ones that made sure each girl that entered the clinic made the right decision. He knew which ones worked in the rooms with the doctors, helping to terminate life. He knew which ones collected the money, mostly cash. He had seen Tammy Hawkins, one of the nurses, leave the building a few minutes ago. Kevin knew that she drove a Toyota Camry that her parents had given her after a recent divorce. He knew that she originally had been very committed to the pro-abortion movement. She had become very active in Planned Parenthood. He knew that her commitment level had waned and she was now in it for the money, especially since her divorce. She was now a single parent, struggling to make ends meet.

He was rubbing the key between his index finger and his thumb, very slowly. He had been sitting out in front of the clinic later in the evening and knew that the OR supervisor, Janet Rawls, was always one of the last to leave the clinic. He was still a little puzzled about Janet. Kevin knew that she was totally committed to this clinic. He knew that she was making a lot of money and that was what puzzled him. The amount of money she was making did not add up to the type of position that she had. There must be something else that he was missing. He made a mental note to do a little more research on Ms. Rawls.

He had monitored the patient flow through the clinic. He knew the busy days. He knew that many of the patients liked to have the procedure on Friday to give them some extra time to recover before work or school on Monday. He had watched the girls come and go. He knew that most of them came from middle and upper class families. You could tell by their clothes and their cars. People always talked about making sure that the poor had access to this procedure. He didn't know for sure, but he didn't think the poor could afford the procedure at this clinic. He had picked up a copy of their price list and payment policies one night when he was cleaning the place. They were awfully strict about paying at the time of service. It was plastered all over the counter inside and there was certainly no doubt about it in their printed policy. As far as he could tell, this clinic served mainly white women with money.

That was the funny thing about the debate, Kevin thought to himself. They always made you think that the purpose of all of this fanaticism was for the rights of women. Most of the pro-life people liked to talk about the rights of the baby. That was fine with him, but what about the women who went through those doors? He had seen many women walk into this clinic with a look of anxiety and fear on their faces, but the look on their faces as they walked out later in the day was just downright spooky. They had the look of an actor in Francis Ford Coppola's *Apocalypse Now* film about Vietnam, kind of distant and soulless.

He had once positioned himself close enough to look into the eyes of the women as they left the clinic. The vacant gaze from their empty eyes gave their faces a lifeless expression. It was hard to imagine that this experience had been good for these women, or that it promoted their rights in any way.

The white Mazda roared out of the parking lot, or at least as much as a fifteen-year-old Mazda could. Dr. Martin Smith was leaving for the day. Kevin looked at his watch, 5:45 p.m. Right on time. He knew which physicians worked each day. He had already checked the background of each of the providers. He knew the ones who were committed. He knew the ones that needed the money. And he knew the ones that wanted the money. Marty, as he liked the staff to call him, fit into the category of needing the money. Kevin had been astonished at the amount of debt Marty owed. He knew that Marty was doing his best to work his way out of debt. t appeared from the information he had obtained on Marty that he was pretty ambivalent toward the politics of abortion. Kevin wondered how a doctor could feel ambivalent about killing babies.

It was this thought that brought the past rushing into his mind, filling it with painful memories. The memories of his personal loss made this mission so important to Kevin.

He felt the key turning in his hand. Slowly.

He liked the look of this place. This street did not have a lot of drive-by traffic. The street was a cul-de-sac. The only types of businesses on this street were medical clinics. Most people knew that doctors' offices closed by 5:00 p.m. during the week and didn't even open over the weekend. Behind the buildings across the street was a wooded area that stretched over to Kanis Road. This road would give him two different means of escape. The landscaping around the building gave him plenty of cover to get in unnoticed. If he timed it right he would have plenty of time to put his equipment in place without being seen. This place was looking better all the time.

Most of the other places he had considered for this mission were in storefront locations. Those types of locations made for a challenge in executing the mission. The military called it collateral damage. It was the loss of civilian life as a result of an attack on a military target. He really did not want to cause any harm to civilians. It was okay to refer to innocent bystanders as civilians. He had begun to think of this next phase of the project in military terms. After all, he did consider this a war. This was a holy war, with a holy purpose, that he had been called to serve. And he was a soldier, a commando in this war. He was on a mission, a mission from God.

The rain was still coming down. He watched the drops of rain accumulate just at the top of the line where his windshield wipers reached. The drops would get bigger and bigger, until they welled up over the line and rolled to the bottom of the windshield. It was probably a good thing that it had been raining. Everyone was in too much of a hurry to pay any attention to him. They were too anxious to get out of the rain. He noticed that Nurse Rawls was just leaving the clinic. She was pulling her Lexus onto the street. He looked at his watch and saw that it was 8:00 p.m. Her concentration was obviously on the rain that had just started to come down a little harder. She didn't even look over at him.

He flipped the key in his hand, turning it around, slowly. The key was slowly turning from side to side now. He could feel the weight of it on his fingertips.

The key would make it so much easier to pull this off. Everything about this place was coming together. All he had to do was decide on the correct timing. He had to make sure that he got the maximum impact out of this mission. This one was going to work. This one was going to make the world stand up and take notice.

He knew that it was his destiny and he accepted it with zeal. He was really getting excited about this place. He would get to complete another piece of his mission here. Maybe this would finally take some of the pain away. Maybe this would help heal some of those very old wounds. He had tried many things through the years to resolve this for him and his family, but somehow, it was never quite enough. Maybe he had finally found the right mission that would change things forever.

And it was a mission. Maybe, just maybe, it was the right one.

Chapter 5

Marty rolled over in bed at the sound of the alarm. He stretched across to the nightstand to slap at the alarm and turn off the loud, obnoxious noise. It was all he could do to open his eyes.

Swinging his legs over the side of the bed, Marty rubbed his eyes. Only then did he hear the sound of the rain pecking steadily on the roof of his condo. How exciting! Another rainy day. When was this rain going to stop? It was getting a little depressing. At least the rain wasn't interfering with anything he had planned for the day. All he had planned was work. What could interfere with another day in the OR, doing procedures?

Marty stood up and stumbled to the bathroom. After ridding himself of last night's Diet Coke, he headed for the kitchen to start all over again. He could see that Allison had left the coffee maker on for him. At one time, he and Allison had been dating. Now, they were just roommates. He wondered if she would ever notice that he didn't really drink very much coffee. He ignored the coffee and reached into the refrigerator for a Diet Coke. As he opened the can and took his first drink of the day, he noticed the note that Allison had left for him on the kitchen counter. The note said that she would be home late again tonight. She would be studying late at the library, and then she had a function with the Bar Association. It also reminded him that he had committed to go with her to a party tomorrow night for the third-year law students and the clerks for the State Supreme Court. The party was going to be at the Chief Justice's house.

He was already regretting that he had told Allison that he would go. He really hated those parties. He knew that the only reason she asked him to go was that she needed to have a date. Otherwise, she would have gone by herself, and immersed herself in all of the legal talk, and been perfectly content. Now, when she arrived at the party with him in tow, she would make all of the proper introductions, excuse herself somewhere near the food table and disappear with her legal buddies and catch up on the latest gossip in the legal community. He would be left to make do with the incessant small talk of people he didn't know and hoped he would never know any better. He hated parties. They were bad enough even when he liked the people. Maybe he could polish up some of his old lawyer jokes and become the entertainment for the evening.

Allison would be mortified.

He couldn't believe that he had gone to school all those years for a career doing one procedure with no apparent end in sight. The misery of the unknown was beginning to settle in on him with a weight that he had difficulty bearing. Allison had become totally absorbed in her quest to become a lawyer.

Marty met her two years before, while he was a third-year OB resident and she was a first-year law student. They used to see each other all the time at a little bar in downtown Little Rock. After dancing and drinking together several times, they started dating. He had to admit that it was the physical attraction that brought them together. Initially, they had loved each other, or at least that's what each told the other. The love they thought they had and the things they thought they had in common led them to move in together six months later. After that, they were never really physical again.

Now Marty was struggling to remember even one of the things they had in common. Oh, they tried in the beginning to share time together. He learned very quickly that being around lawyers was not very interesting. He had been to a few of the Bar Association functions with her, but his interest waned very early in the relationship. Allison had never even tried to fake it by going to any medical functions with him. Her total focus was the law and those who engaged in the practice thereof. She was working full-time to make all the right grades and all the right social connections to get an offer from one of the old-line law firms in town. He never could remember which one. All he could remember was that they had dozens of lawyer-sounding names down both sides of their letterhead. At first, he had received ongoing invitations from Allison to join her at all of the legal parties. That was before he had become involved with the procedure. Although most of the lawyers he had met in Little Rock were social liberals, it was still not quite acceptable to socialize with an abortionist. He had certainly received calls from a number of them to perform the procedure on their daughters, wives and girlfriends. However, socializing with an abortion doctor had not made the leap up the social ladder yet. Now when he got an invitation, it meant that Allison had to have a date for social reasons.

He dug around in the clothes dryer for a clean pair of scrubs. He couldn't believe that he didn't even wear real clothes to work anymore. He pulled out the top to the surgical uniform. It had two socks, a blue one and a black one, attached to it with static cling. Marty peeled the socks off the scrub top and put it on. He stuck his hand back into the dryer and fished around for the pants that matched. Pulling them out of the dryer, he gave the pants a quick shake. Only one pair of panties fell to the floor.

Panties were the worst offenders for sticking to other clothes in the dryer. Every time he shook a pair out of his scrubs, it reminded him of the time he forgot to go through his now routine shaking procedure and didn't find the panties clinging to his scrubs until he was already at work. How embarrassing! He would never forget the smug look on Janet Rawls' face as she pulled the panties from under the edge of his scrubs.

"Will you be needing these later?" she asked sweetly, as she held them up for everyone in the OR to see.

Marty had blushed and walked away.

In the short time that he had been at the clinic, he had already fostered a great dislike for Janet Rawls. Marty considered himself a people person and there were not many people that he disliked. He had given it a good attempt to find some common ground with Janet, but there was something about her that just didn't fit. He really couldn't put his finger on it, but he didn't really trust her. As that thought rolled around in his head, he walked back into his bedroom and sat down at a makeshift desk – a couple of sawhorses and a piece of plywood from Home Depot. He turned on his computer and entered his login and password.

The computer had been the only extravagance that he had allowed himself. During his time in medical school and residency, Marty had become very proficient with a computer. He was excited when they had given him access to the system at the clinic. It had become part of his morning ritual to log on and check his schedule for the day. After maneuvering his way through several security screens, his schedule for the day rolled up on the computer screen.

Marty scrolled down the list of patients scheduled and noticed that it was going to be another busy day. Marty found it amazing that he could stay so busy just performing abortion procedures. He had planned to go into private practice and do the full range of services that he was trained to perform. Delivering babies, hysterectomies, D & C's, routine pap and pelvics, he had planned to do them all. He truly loved the variety that his specialty offered. But he was a guy. The problem with that was everyone wanted to hire a female. Somehow along the way he had become the minority. Now most of the OB programs were filled with female physicians. He had become an exception. He had interviewed with several great OB groups, but in the end, they all wanted to hire females. One group had even told him that if he could wear a skirt, they would hire him. That interview had been the low point in the job search process. It was then that he realized that his career as an obstetrician would not begin as he had planned.

By the time the interview with Women's Health Inc. came along, Marty was really desperate. During medical school and residency, he had accumulated almost $120,000 in debt paying for his training and living expenses. He knew that he wouldn't be able to pay back those loans working at the public health clinic, which was his only other option at the time. He had to have a decent income or the interest on his loans would keep him in debt forever.

Brad Giovanni originally contacted him about the job. Brad said he had obtained his name through the residency program. When Marty first heard about the job, he was completely turned off by the prospects of working in an abortion clinic. But Brad had been very smooth in his presentation. He seemed to know everything about Marty. He knew exactly the right buttons to push. By the time Brad was done, Marty was hooked. Also, it didn't hurt that about the same time, Brad introduced him to J. Peterman Straun, MD. J.P., as he liked to be called, was the other physician that worked in the clinic. But J.P. was more than that, he was Brad's top physician in the region. Apparently, the payoff for J.P. was huge. J.P. drove a brand-new red Porsche convertible. He always dressed immaculately and that was unusual for a physician in this day and age. While most of the guys Marty knew dressed just like he did, in scrubs, J.P. dressed more like one of the elite plastic surgeons in West Little Rock. It was obvious to Marty that there was money to be made in abortion. And more than anything, money was what Marty needed right then.

Since J.P. had responsibilities in several other clinics, he was only in the Little Rock clinic a few days a month. At first, it had been fun for Marty to have another physician around. He had enjoyed the opportunity to have a little collegial discussion. However, he soon discovered two things. First of all, J.P. was not interested in collegial discussions. J.P. was there for business and business only. It was obvious that his other duties for the clinic had become much more important to him than the practice of medicine. The second thing that Marty noticed was the reaction of the staff to J.P. On the days that J.P. was working in the clinic, the tension level among the staff was unbearable, and J.P. seemed to thrive on the strife he caused. It was not uncommon for him to throw instruments, belittle the nurses and curse at the front office staff. It was almost as if he felt that it was his job to keep the staff off balance.

Marty scrolled through the appointment scheduling system on the computer and saw that J.P. would be working in the clinic today.

"Great!" he said aloud to himself with a trace of sarcasm. "It'll be another terrific day in the OR."

It looked like J.P. would be there all day and he had twenty-two procedures scheduled. Marty could tell by looking at the procedures that J.P. would be generating quite a bit more money than he would today. Although Marty was scheduled for twenty-five procedures, they were all first-trimester procedures. Almost all of J.P.'s cases were over fourteen weeks, which were identified by the dates entered into the computer for the "last menstrual period" (LMP). These procedures were more expensive for the patient. J.P. also had three procedures on his schedule that were just over twenty weeks. Procedures at this stage of pregnancy could sometimes cost more than three times that of a first-trimester procedure.

Marty glanced at his watch. It was almost 7:15. He would have to hurry to get to the office in time for his first procedure. He logged off his computer and got up to finish getting ready.

* * * * *

The nurses were finishing the case in OR 2, as Marty walked out into the hall and began to dictate his note on the patient. Within a minute, he had completed the dictation. That's when he heard the screaming. It was coming from OR 1 and it wasn't the typical patient screams either. It was J.P.

J.P. had been there all day, and the morale among the employees had been miserable. He had already berated the front office staff for "screwing up his schedule." The tension among the staff had been so thick that even the sharpest scalpel couldn't cut through it. Marty heard a thud on the door of the OR and knew that J.P. was throwing instruments again. The door swung open and Tammy walked out with tears in her eyes. While the door was still swinging, Marty could hear J.P. screaming about the idiot nurses around this place. He never gave them a break. He was always riding them.

From the dictation station outside OR 2, Marty could see that Tammy was ready to break and run. He called over to her.

"Hey, Tammy, can you give me a hand in room three?" Marty was always quick to be the peacemaker in the office. She nodded and they both moved over to the door of OR 3. Marty held the door for her and followed her into the room.

"Looks like J.P. is up to his usual tricks today," Marty commented. "Don't let him get under your skin, Tammy. You know how he can be. You shouldn't take it personally."

"I don't know why he has to be such a jerk." Marty could tell the fire was coming back into her eyes. "He's such a pompous little thing."

As Marty was listening to Tammy, they were moving to their places around the OR table.

"Well, you know how he likes to be in charge. He doesn't want anyone threatening his authority as a physician."

"Oh, I certainly know that he's the one with MD behind his name. I can't tell you how many times he's told the nurses that. If I had a nickel for every time I've heard that, I would never have to work again."

As they were beginning to start the procedure, the patient groggily looked over at Marty. "Are you the doctor that's going to take care of me today?" she asked.

Marty motioned for Tammy to get the patient's chart. "Yes, I'm Dr. Smith. I'll be taking care of you today. We're going to be performing a procedure on you today that will terminate your pregnancy."

Tammy handed him the chart, and he saw that this patient's name was Cassie Clancy. "Are you Cassie?"

Cassie blinked her eyes slowly and said very deliberately, "Yes, that's me. What did you say your name was again?"

"My name is Dr. Smith. I'm your doctor today. Are you ready to get started?"

"Uh, I dunno," Cassie mumbled groggily. "I thought that maybe they might talk to me a little about my choices first. I'm not sure I really want to do this. Will it hurt?"

"Cassie, if you would like to talk about this first, we can do that," Marty said. "You need to be sure that you really want this procedure before we get started. Why don't we talk about some of your other options?"

It became very apparent that Cassie never had a chance for any option other than "the procedure." To have a real opportunity to hear the patient's perspective was refreshing to Marty. Several times he had suspected that these patients were never given an opportunity for anything other than a procedure. As the shot of Demerol began to wear off, Cassie became more vocal about her need to think about this a little more.

"Cassie, we can get you more information regarding your choices," Marty explained. "As soon as you can get up, Tammy will take you into one of the consultation rooms and I'll be down to talk to you in a few minutes."

"Doctor, thank you for listening to me," Cassie said. "I would really like to wait and think about the options before I go through with this. I hope this won't mess up your schedule too badly."

"Making sure that you make the right choice is much more important than my schedule today," Marty said, as he gave her shoulder a pat. "I'm glad that we were able to talk about it."

Twenty minutes later, Marty left the consultation room. He knew he had taken longer than he should have with Cassie, but the counseling that he had been able to do had been professionally fulfilling for him. Marty walked out into the hall and saw Janet Rawls staring at him. He smiled politely at her. He could tell that she was seething inside, as she spun on her heels and hurried into OR 1.

"Well," he thought to himself, "I'm sure I'll hear from her later today." But, for the moment, he dismissed his dread of the confrontation.

* * * * *

Marty had just finished the dictation on his last case, when J.P. walked up to him. "I need to talk to you," J.P. said tersely.

"Sure, J.P., what can I do for you?" Marty asked pleasantly.

"Well, for one thing, you can stick to your job," J.P. said in obvious anger.

"What do you mean?" Marty was caught off guard. "Did I do something wrong?"

"Do something wrong?" J.P. snapped. "You bet you did. You cost this clinic money today. You let a done deal walk out the door this afternoon. Your 2:30 case in OR 2 was a sure thing and you talked her out of a procedure. When you do stuff like that, you cost us money."

"I'm sorry, J.P., but I thought that it was appropriate patient care to talk to her about her options," Marty explained. "She asked me a question, and I provided counsel. What more can I say?"

"Look, Marty, we don't pay you to think. We don't pay you to provide counseling to patients. And we don't pay you speak out of turn." J.P. was fuming. "What we pay you for is to do procedures and that's it. Nothing more and nothing less. If you have a problem with that, I need to know right now. I don't have time for someone going around screwing up the process. Do you understand that, Marty?"

Marty was humiliated. He couldn't believe what he was hearing.

"Sure, J.P., I understand," he lied.

"Good. Just don't let it happen again."

With that, J.P. turned and walked away. Marty slumped against the dictation station. He was devastated. The fact that another physician would talk to him like that blew him away. So much for collegiality.

It was a miserable end to a miserable day in a miserable existence. Marty couldn't wait for tomorrow, until it started all over again.

Chapter 6

Kevin had been in front of the clinic since mid-afternoon. He noticed that they had a full house today. Dr. Straun's red Porsche was in the parking lot. With both doctors working today, there would be more than fifty babies murdered.

He peered out of his car window into the gray sky. He couldn't remember when it had rained this much in December. It had been raining for over a week now. It felt like it was getting colder, too. Kevin made a mental note to check the weather for the next few days. If he were going to pull this off soon, he would need to pay attention to the effect the weather might have on his plans.

It was almost 5:45, and most of the staff was gone. As he was watching, Dr. Smith came out of the clinic and moved slowly, very deliberately to his car. It caught Kevin's attention, since Dr. Smith was usually in an upbeat mood when he left the clinic. Dr. Smith opened the door to his old RX-7 and slid behind the steering wheel. Then, he just sat there, slumped deep into the bucket seat.

Other than Smith's car, only four other cars remained in the lot. The clinic secretary would be leaving in a few minutes. Dr. Straun would be there another hour. The OR supervisor would be there until at least seven o'clock and the last to leave would be the clinic administrator. The order was almost always the same. Some nights it was almost eight o'clock before everyone was out of the building.

He saw the brake lights of Dr. Smith's car glow red in the distance. The doctor must be leaving. Something seemed to be troubling the good doctor. Kevin wondered what had gone on in the clinic today. He would have to check his computer tonight and look for any problems that might be occurring. He could sometimes gather information by monitoring the flow of email in the clinic.

Kevin felt the key in his hand. A smile crept slowly across his face when he thought about the key. The key had certainly been a terrific benefit from the time he had spent working on the cleaning crew for the building. But it had not been the most important benefit. He could have picked the lock, if necessary. He had done it before and this lock would have been no challenge. No, the most important benefit of spending time on the cleaning crew had been the time he was able to spend alone with the network server for the clinic's computer system.

Kevin had developed a keen interest in computers at an early age. He had pursued a degree in computer science at Texas A & M. By the time he graduated and had spent innumerable hours with all the other computer geeks, he could hack with the best of them. There was almost nothing that he couldn't do with a computer.

He had made the most of his time spent alone in the clinic. Well, practically alone. The old man who owned the janitorial service usually staggered in, with the scent of alcohol on his breath, and collapsed on one of the sofas in the waiting room. Within minutes, he would be snoring. Kevin would hurry through the cleaning and spend the rest of the time working on the computer. He had been able to prowl around in the drawers at the nursing station and find a password to the system. Like most businesses, the employees here did not work very hard to conceal their passwords. Once he was able to get into the system, the rest was easy. One night, he installed software on the clinic's server that would allow him to monitor the activity on their network. He could do this on his laptop from anywhere. He had monitored their email. He had looked through the payroll system and knew exactly how much each employee was paid. Since the clinic used direct deposit for their payroll, he had easily been able to get in and look through their bank accounts. The amount of money that flowed through the accounts of the clinic was amazing. It had also been interesting to see the variety of locations money came from and went to before it settled in its final destination.

Kevin smiled again as the key turned over again and again in his hand. He watched as the little Mazda sports car pulled out of the parking lot. Yes, Dr. Smith looked very troubled tonight. He didn't even look around toward Kevin. It was amazing how much people failed to observe when they were stuck in their daily routines. He had been out in front of this clinic every day for two weeks, and he was sure that no one had noticed him. Truly amazing.

Yes, Kevin would be looking through the system tonight to see what had gone on in the clinic today. Smith was obviously disturbed, and Kevin wanted to know why. He was too close to completing his mission to let anything unexpected surprise him. The time was drawing near for him to execute the next portion of the plan. Kevin had checked Dr. Smith out and he seemed to be a decent guy. He couldn't figure out why a nice guy like him would be working in a place like this. Even for the amazing amount of money, it would seem to be asking a little too much.

The key felt good in his hand. The time was coming. He would finally have an impact. His voice would be heard. He would be speaking for the millions who had died in places like this. He would be speaking for those who couldn't.

Chapter 7

"Ms. Sharkley, is there anything that I can get you before I leave for the day?"

"No thanks, Patsy, I'm just winding things down for the day. You have a good evening."

"Thanks, Ms. Sharkley. If you need me to work on anything first thing in the morning, just leave it on my desk and I'll get to it right away. See you tomorrow."

"Good night, Patsy."

Carla Sharkley really liked her secretary. Patsy was so efficient. They had been together for eleven months and Patsy was already beginning to read her mind and anticipate her moves. Several times recently, Patsy had been waiting with the information she needed, just when she was asking for it. The only thing that was even the slightest bit negative about Patsy was her religion. Every now and then, she could get a little too preachy. All in all though, she was probably the best help Carla had ever had.

Carla was a confident woman and it showed in the way she moved around the clinic. She had a fair complexion and short hair that she wore in a pixie cut. Her clothes were always in a professional, business style and never included pants suits.

Carla had felt very lucky to have the opportunity to take on this job. She first heard about this chain of clinics when she began working for them as a consultant. She had been hired to help them work through some personnel issues. As she had come to the completion of that project, the regional director for the company had come to her with a job offer to run their Arkansas clinic. When Brad Giovanni had first mentioned the idea of employment, she wasn't sure that she really wanted to run an abortion clinic. She had never been a real fanatic about these kinds of women's issues. She initially thought that she would turn down the opportunity and then Brad told her about the money. Carla had been floored. In addition to a lucrative salary and benefits package, they had even moved her to Little Rock and made the down payment and financed her new home for her. This had allowed her to buy a home in the nicest neighborhood in which she had ever lived. She had purchased a home in Chenal Valley. It was the neighborhood for the up-and-coming wealthy of Little Rock. With this new position, she certainly fit in with the neighborhood standards. As the end of her first year with Women's Health Inc. was approaching, she had the potential to get a bonus based on the performance of the clinic. If everything held as it was, she was likely to get over $50,000 in bonus for the year.

The turn of events was unbelievable. Just eighteen months ago, she was struggling, trying to make it with her own consulting business. Now, she was in the big time. She had dreamt of this kind of opportunity for her entire career. It was perfect. As a single parent, she was finally able to support her son financially. Her career had taken a monumental leap with this job and she was enjoying the challenge.

The clinic put her through an excellent orientation program covering everything from the history of abortion to training on the clinic's computer system. Although this was the first time that her career path had led to an abortion clinic, she was able to use her management skills, honed through the years, to excel in this job as well.

Carla was reviewing the clinic's financials, as she did at the end of every day. She had been running this clinic for eleven months and was still overwhelmed by the amount of cash that came through the clinic. In her past experience with medical clinics, the amount of cash collected was miniscule. In this clinic, the amount of cash approached 90 percent of daily collections. That suited Carla just fine, since part of her bonus was tied to the amount of cash that was collected during the month. She thought that incentive was a little weird, when she first heard it. Brad had explained to her the clinic's efforts to reduce costs by eliminating the billing process. Collecting at the time of service was great, if you could get away with it, and this clinic could. It had a lot to do with supply and demand, and access to abortions was limited in this state. It also had a lot to do with confidentiality. Most of the women and girls that came through the clinic certainly did not want a bill for an abortion showing up in their mailbox for their family to see. They also didn't want it to show up on a credit card statement, so most of them came to the clinic with cash in hand. They paid in cash at the front desk, had the procedure performed in the OR and walked out the front door a few hours later.

It was funny. The people working at the clinic typically referred to an abortion as the procedure. Carla really couldn't remember the last time that she had heard the word abortion mentioned in the clinic. The doctors and nurses always referred to it as the procedure, never as an abortion. It really was odd. The patients that came to the clinic talked about their desire to have an abortion. However, after they spent time with the counselor, even they didn't use the word again.

As Carla reviewed the month-end numbers, it really was amazing. The clinic had averaged almost 700 procedures a month during the last eleven months. The clinic was on track to generate close to $6 million in revenue this year. If that happened, she would maximize her bonus potential for the year. She still felt like she was on a whirlwind. With her performance in producing cash flow and profits for the clinic, she was expecting Brad to boost her compensation package for the next year. This job was great. At this pace, she and her son Thomas would never have to worry about money again.

The cash flow still boggled her mind. They had collected almost $440,000 in cash this past month. Out of the total revenue there would be over $5 million in cash for the year. Not many businesses this size generated that kind of cash flow.

Carla was scheduled to meet with Brad in a few days to begin her performance evaluation for the year. There were several issues that she wanted to address with him. She was hoping to be able to get some additional responsibilities with Women's Health Inc. Although her office generated numerous reports on production, collections and expenses, Carla never got to see any of the final reports. The central accounting office in Chicago, the headquarters of Women's Health Inc., produced all of the final monthly reports.

She thought that this was a little odd. In all of her previous jobs, she was always required to produce monthly financial statements. In fact, it had been a big deal to keep the physicians informed in every clinic that she had ever worked in before. Not that it really broke her heart to skip the financial meetings with the physicians. The meetings were pure misery. The physicians typically wanted to haggle over every last nickel and dime spent for overhead.

Now, her office didn't even balance the checkbook. The people in her business office just sacked up the cash and credit card receipts at the end of the day and the courier service took it away. The accounting office in Chicago called every month to give them a beginning balance for the checkbook. They really didn't need a lot of money in the account, since most of the regular bills were paid out of Chicago and the payroll came out of an entirely separate account. Oh well, it made her job a little easier and gave her something to negotiate with Brad.

Carla spun around in her swivel-based executive chair. She stared out of her office window watching it rain. She loved to watch the rain roll down the glass of her windows.

She could see the hills of western Little Rock in the background. Carla really was not all that sure about Brad. He was nice enough, sometimes almost too nice. He had been especially attentive to her during her move and start-up with the company. It was just that he was a little too slick. He always seemed to have an answer for everything. There was something about him that made her a little uneasy. She had never met anyone else with the company other than Brad and the employees that worked with her in the office. She had almost no contact with the home office. Everything went through Brad.

She spun back to her desk. Looking at the month-end reports, Carla noticed that there had been an increase in ultrasounds and procedures performed after seventeen weeks of pregnancy. This trend was helping her numbers tremendously. Procedures done after seventeen weeks increased profitability dramatically in the abortion business. These procedures jumped from a base charge of $850 and went up rapidly to $1,850. She had not spent much time learning the difference in the types of procedures, from a clinical standpoint. To Carla, they were just dollars, and rightly so. Her job was the business of the clinic, not the clinical details.

The cash still amazed her. As the volume had increased during the year, Carla had implemented a number of new policies in the business office to insure the proper handling of all that cash. She had checks and balances at every point at which people touched the cash. Her policies were all designed to ensure that all the cash made it directly into the proper account. Carla knew that they had to be impressed with this in Chicago. Brad had even commented on it, although he was not nearly as excited about it as Carla thought he would be. It was almost as if he didn't care about the improvements that she had made in the cash handling policies.

She had also given her employees incentives to encourage the patients that came through the clinic to pay with cash. And it was working. Cash collections had risen steadily since she had taken over this clinic. This was something that Brad had been pleased with and noticed right away. He had commented on the positive impact she had made on the cash totals. He had even commented that the people in Chicago were pleased. She was planning to follow up on that comment with Brad during her performance review. She still wanted to know who the people in Chicago were. When Brad hired her, he had explained that Women's Health Inc. was a private company that was owned by a small group of investors in Chicago. The investors, Brad explained, had a wide variety of business interests that spanned many different industries.

Carla reviewed the clinic expenses for the month, as part of her normal routine. It galled her to see the cost for security and legal fees paid each month. The security costs were directly proportional to the level of militant activity outside her clinic each month. It cost her a fortune to hire the armed escorts for the patients and staff. After the rash of violent attacks against clinics in Birmingham and Atlanta, she had been forced to purchase bulletproof vests for the physicians that worked in the clinic. The vests cost her $750 apiece and she had yet to see one of the physicians wear one. Carla also had to install a metal detector, a door buzzer and surveillance cameras. These items had set the clinic back almost $15,000 this year. It had been an expensive year to maintain the security of her staff and patients.

On the other hand, the legal fees were for all of the nonviolent activities that she had to address. Although these were not dangerous to her or the staff, they were terribly time consuming. The clinic attorney prosecuted the guy who had chained himself to the front door – three times before a restraining order could be filed and implemented. The lawyer defended the clinic from the multitude of frivolous lawsuits that the militant anti-choice groups continually filed. Lawsuits drove her crazy. She hated spending clinic money for attorneys.

She had never really thought much about the pro-choice debate before she took this job. Now this debate was driving her crazy. She was developing a strong hatred for those radical groups that caused her so much grief. She hated the time that she had to spend dealing with depositions and all the other legal crap.

Her thoughts shifted from the legal mess to her current task at hand. At the end of each day, it was her custom to review the procedures that were performed during the day. She would call the daily status report up on her computer and review it online. Women's Health Inc. had a fairly sophisticated computer system. Carla used the system constantly to keep up with the business. There were so many functions available on the network that Carla tried to spend 20 to 30 minutes each night before she left the office learning some new facet of the system.

As she looked down through the daily status report, Carla noticed that something weird had happened with Dr. Smith's schedule. She could see that one of his patients in the afternoon did not appear to have completed her procedure. Carla was doing a little research on this patient when her computer sounded, indicating that a new email message had arrived. She minimized the reporting screen on her monitor and clicked with her mouse to the email program. She saw that the new message was from Dr. Straun. Carla knew that he had left the clinic about 40 minutes ago, and he had a habit of sending her email as he traveled between clinics. He carried the latest technology and used it extensively.

Carla clicked on the new email message to open it. She could see from the subject of the email that Dr. Straun already knew about Dr. Smith's patient this afternoon. The time required for her research project had just been greatly reduced. Dr. Straun's email was as follows:

From: Straun, J.P.
Sent: Thursday, December 2, 1999 7:25 PM
To: Sharkley, Carla
Subject: Dr. Smith

This afternoon Dr. Smith became involved in the counseling of a patient. This patient subsequently left the clinic without having the scheduled procedure performed. Dr. Smith knew when he took this job that he was to avoid patient counseling. I am concerned with Dr. Smith's willingness to follow this directive. You need to watch him very closely. If he is allowed to proceed on his own, he may become detrimental to our operations. As you are aware, the collections for our clinic are very important. We cannot have some idealistic physician subverting our plans and efforts. Please keep me posted with your thoughts on Dr. Smith. If we need to take any immediate action, you know how to reach me.

JPS

"Wow!" Carla thought to herself, "this is a big deal." She knew that Dr. Straun had a temper, but she was not prepared for this. The focus on running the procedures through the clinic was intense, even for the physicians. She had been involved in several discussions with Dr. Straun regarding the business of the clinic. However, when it came right down to it, Brad was the one who called the shots. Straun's focus was on physician performance, and he tolerated very little deviation from the established norm.

Marty Smith, on the other hand, was a different story. He was one of those rare cases of a physician that had great clinical skills, a true concern for patients and a terrific personality, and could put all three characteristics to use at the same time. Marty would be the one who would put a halt to all business functions and procedures just to meet a patient's request. She had always liked Marty. He had started working at the clinic five months after she had. He was a hard worker, and really easy to get along with. All of her staff loved him and jockeyed for a chance to work with him.

As Carla scrolled through the reports for the day's business, she found the patient in question. She could see by the report that the patient had left without the procedure, and with her money. No wonder Dr. Straun was after this one. Carla didn't know for sure, but she suspected that Dr. Straun had incentives to increase procedure volumes in the clinic. She hoped that Marty was ready for the pressure he would receive for bucking the system on this case. She was sure that both she and Marty would hear from Brad.

As the thought of Marty went through her mind, she used her computer mouse to get out of the daily reports and move into the human resource part of the clinic system. The clinic stored biographical information on each employee in the system. For the non-physician employees, these were resumes. For the physicians, the information was stored in a curriculum vitae, or CV. Marty's CV listed all the information about his education and training. The CV also contained a good deal of personal information. Since Carla was responsible for the clinic payroll every other week, she was quite familiar with each employee's file.

Marty was a good-looking guy. One day he was going to have a great ob-gyn practice. He had a way with people that put them at ease, and she envied that in him. Carla struggled to relate that easily with people. She always wanted to get right down to business. She tended to think that all other efforts at conversation were a waste of time.

She was still thinking about Marty, as she moved back into the accounting portion of the computer system. Carla needed to review some of the current financial information of the clinic before she left for the night. She was reviewing the cash collections for the past week, when she accidentally clicked onto the confirmations from the bank on the electronic transfers for the month. She had never been in this part of the system before and she wasn't sure how she had gotten there. Since Chicago balanced the books at the end of the month, she typically did not have a need for this information. But since she was there anyway, Carla just scrolled down through the screen.

The first thing that caught her attention was the rather large discrepancy in the cash deposits for the month. If she was not mistaken, the deposits recorded in the electronic transfers were several thousand dollars greater than the amount they had collected in the clinic. Carla took her pen and wrote down the daily cash deposits that were listed on her screen. She then scrolled back to the daily reports for the month. She was right. So far this month, the electronic deposits were almost $340,000 more than the totals on her daily reports. That was almost double the amount of cash that the clinic had sent to the bank!

Carla sat back in her chair and stared at the screen. "How could that happen?" she thought to herself. If she was reading the screen correctly, someone was putting extra cash deposits in the clinic account on a regular basis. She began to rock slowly back and forth in her chair. Her elbows were propped up on the arms of the chair with her chin resting in her hands. She was thinking about the information she had just seen on the screen.

"Where was that money coming from?" she thought to herself. "Why would someone be putting money into this account?"

This was the first time that she had ever seen this information. Carla began to look closely at the path she had taken to get to this part of the system. She turned around to her desk to get a pen and a pad of paper to make notes. When she reached over to her desk, she saw the clock on her desk and noticed that it was seven forty-five.

"Oh my gosh," she said aloud, "I've got to get home to Thomas." The neighbors had taken him to basketball practice and he would be home in the next few minutes. Carla quickly jotted down the information necessary to find this screen on her computer again. She would make sure to come back to this and investigate it a little further.

Carla logged out of the system and shut down her computer. She was really confused by the information she had discovered. She would have to ask Brad about it tomorrow.

She grabbed her coat and briefcase. As she turned off her office light and closed the door, her mind was racing to consider the possibilities. She stepped into the parking lot and the rain sprinkled on her face. Carla looked up at the grayness of the sky. Winter was finally bringing its frosty breath to Arkansas.

Chapter 8

Kevin had been sitting in front of his computer for several hours. The computer was on a small desk that had been in the cabin when he moved in. He had rented this cabin after accepting a job with an engineering firm in town. The cabin was a small lake house that was owned by a family who lived in Dallas. They rarely vacationed in Hot Springs anymore and had been renting the cabin out for several years.

From the street, a long driveway led to the front of the cabin – at least it was considered the front of the cabin by anyone who did not live on the lake. For those who lived on the lake, or spent any significant time there, it was known that lake homes should be viewed from the water. Therefore, the part of the house that faced the road was obviously the rear. When entering the cabin from the driveway, the door opened into a small kitchen. The kitchen had beautiful yellow pine floors and cabinets. From there, the cabin flowed into a cozy living area. Kevin had placed the desk against the far wall by the windows looking out across the lake. The other interesting thing about this house was in the laundry room off the kitchen. The laundry room was so small that you could hardly turn around in it. On the wall closest to the washing machine was a door that opened out of the laundry room onto a small landing at the top of a flight of stairs. These stairs led down to a small basement.

Kevin was using a laptop that he had recently purchased with all of the latest technological advances. The laptop sat on the desk by a desktop model that he used to complete work from the office. When he had first moved into the cabin, he had a high-speed Internet line installed. He was using this connection now to get into the Women's Health Inc. computer. Kevin had been reviewing the day's business. He noticed a discrepancy on Dr. Smith's schedule. By following each of Smith's patients through the process for the day, Kevin had identified the patient who failed to have her scheduled procedure done. He also noticed that this patient had paid cash in advance for the procedure and had received a refund from the clinic by check.

Kevin sat back and rubbed his chin with his fingers as he thought about the reasons that this patient left the clinic without an abortion. While this event made him happy, he knew that it was an aberration. He knew that his mission would still need to be completed. Maybe this event caused some problems for Dr. Smith with the people who ran the clinic. Whatever the problem was, Dr. Smith was obviously distressed when he left the clinic tonight.

The key to the clinic was lying on the corner of the desk. The reflection of the light was shining off the smooth surface of the key. As he looked at the key, he began to wonder about the people who ran the clinic. He certainly knew a lot about the people who actually worked in the clinic, but he realized that he knew nothing about the owners of the clinic. Originally, he had thought that Dr. Straun might be the owner of the clinic. However, he soon discovered that the clinic was part of a chain and Dr. Straun was just a hired gun. He was an expensive hired gun, but still just a hired gun.

Kevin now knew that Brad Giovanni was responsible to some larger organization for this clinic and several others. But, he still had not figured out anything else about this company. Kevin had decided that he would try to dig a little deeper this evening and make sure he had covered all his bases. He didn't want any surprises in his mission.

He moved through the different software programs by clicking his mouse. He left the scheduling portion of the package and moved to the part of the system that processed the accounts receivable. This was the function where most medical clinics spent the majority of their time. Almost every clinic in the country handled their billing and collections in the same manner. As patients received services in the office, a charge ticket was generated. Typically, the patients would either pay their bill on the way out of the office, or the clinic would bill the patient's insurance company. The latter of these two paths was the direction that the majority of most patients expected their bills to take. This was the unique thing about the Women's Health Inc. clinic. They didn't do a lot of billing. In fact, 90 percent of all their charges were paid for at the time of service with cash, or a credit card. The 10 percent of charges that did generate bills went almost exclusively to Medicaid. Kevin had thought that these percentages seemed a little unusual. After he did some investigation, he found that most clinics collected practically no cash and had minimal payment in full at the time of service. While most clinics depended on their accounts receivable software as their lifeblood, Women's Health Inc. seemed to use theirs mainly for tracking the business. They sent out very few bills to their patients.

Several weeks ago, when he was searching through the clinic's system, he discovered that the local server was networked with another server that appeared to be off site. As he thought back to his time in the clinic with the cleaning crew, this seemed to make sense. As he recalled the equipment that was housed in the computer room at the clinic, he could only remember one machine that could have functioned as a server. He also remembered that the room also contained a router configuration. This would indicate a connection to the outside world. He couldn't believe that he had just realized this.

"Where were they connected to?" he spoke aloud to himself. Tonight he was going to attempt to find the trail to the other server.

Kevin was moving into the communications software of the system, the clicking from his keyboard and mouse the only audible sounds competing with the ticking sound from the old clock in the bookshelf. As he followed the trail of IP addresses, he soon found himself communicating with a new server. According to the information that he was now looking at, this server appeared to be part of an organization referred to as GFE in the system. He had no idea what or where GFE was. But, he did know how to find out. The easiest way for him to find this information was through his network of old college buddies. They had a chat room that they frequented and that was the quickest way for him to get in touch with them.

He minimized the screen he was looking at and clicked on his Internet icon. When the connection was made, he clicked on his Favorites folder. He scrolled down and found the site he was looking for and clicked on it to enter. He was now in the chat room that his friends frequented. He sent out a general greeting to see who was online.

"Hey guys, it's KayMac and I'm looking for some info. Anybody out there?" KayMac was the nickname the guys had given him back at A & M and he still used it as his screen name.

"Hey KayMac, it's Wheels, how are you doing? It's been a long time since I've heard from you."

Wheels was the only one of Kevin's college friends that had a car while they were in school.

"I've been doing great, Wheels. Are you still building code for the corporate machine?"

"Yeah, it gets a little old. The corporate types don't want me to be too creative. They're afraid I might set their standards too high. You know how that works – if we get too good, someone higher up might expect too much."

Wheels was the typical computer geek, pocket protector and all, that went to work for regular corporate America. He thought that no one else in his company was as smart as he was. The funny thing about it was that he was probably right. He had to maintain his programming creativity within the confines of the strategic direction of the company. Unfortunately for guys like Wheels, the strategic direction was usually not very exciting or challenging. Wheels had to get his kicks from his after-hours work, hacking and searching on the Internet.

"Hey Wheels, I'm doing a little project and I'm trying to find some information. I'm looking at a server that's registered to something called GFE. I think that it might be a company name, but I'm not sure. I'm trying to find out who they are and what they do. Any ideas?"

"I'm glad you asked. I was getting a little bored anyway. I've been doing my day job in my sleep and
I'm out of interesting evening projects. Can you get me an IP address and the other info you already have? I'll try to get in touch with Rooter for some help."

A smile came across Kevin's face. He hadn't thought about Rooter in a while. Rooter was another member of the old gang. He had gotten his nickname from that old commercial about clogged drains. He could root out any trouble or problem on a computer or network and send it down the drain. Some of his antics from college days were legendary.

"I'll send you an email with the info I have on GFE. Are you still at the same address?"

"Yeah, still there. I'll try to get something going tonight on this info. Stay online for a while and see if I can get anything. Rooter is almost always working on his box this time of night."

"If you get anything significant, get back to me by email. This may end up being a little on the confidential side."

"You bet, KayMac. Thanks for the opportunity. A mind can be a terrible thing to waste, especially on the corporate world. Catch you later."

With that, Wheels moved out of the chat room and was off working on the project. Kevin really missed those guys. Their college days had been a blast. He knew that Wheels would attack this project with a vengeance, just like he did every other challenge that was put before him.

Kevin sent the information that he had on GFE to Wheels. Then remembered that he was going to check the email at the clinic for any traffic that would give him a clue about what was happening with Dr. Smith. With minimal effort, he was soon reviewing the email traffic that had gone through the clinic during the day. Within a few minutes, he had spotted the email from Dr. Straun to Carla Sharkley.

"Wow!" he said out loud. "No wonder Dr. Smith was upset. He really stirred the pot this afternoon."

The email made Kevin wonder about the incentives the physicians had within the clinic. Straun was sure high strung about the loss of one abortion today. By watching the activity in the clinic, it appeared that Dr. Straun's motivation went way beyond patient care concerns. The way he was reacting to Dr. Smith's patient this afternoon was highly unusual. He knew from watching and researching other abortion clinics that there was a tendency for tensions to run high among the staff. But, he had not seen any of that with this clinic since he had been watching them. He would have to monitor things more closely over the next few days to see if he could detect anything out of the ordinary building up.

He looked over at the clock and noticed that ten minutes had elapsed since he had last chatted with Wheels. Depending on the sophistication of the network and its trail, it could take Wheels and his friends a while to make any progress with the information that he had given them. Since he was already in the clinic system anyway, Kevin decided to spend a little more time searching for information. He moved out of the email program and into the daily activity report for the clinic. The report listed a total of twenty-two procedures for Dr. Straun and twenty-four for Dr. Smith. He remembered from the schedule that Cassie Clancy was the patient that would have made twenty-five. At the bottom of the report, the totals for the day were listed. They had collected another $36,720 in cash. The cash flow through the clinic was impressive. He had seen the armored truck pull up in front of the clinic every afternoon. He knew that the guards came in and picked up the deposit and took it to the bank. Too much cash came into the clinic to leave in the building overnight, or to send with an unarmed employee to the bank.

Since the clinic's payroll was handled electronically through direct deposit, Kevin had also been able to get into that program and scroll through the clinic bank account from his computer. The bank had given the clinic a program to use for electronic banking activities. It had really been easy to get around in the system once he had a password. Regardless of who actually owned the clinic, they were sure not paying a lot of attention to the security of the local system. Kevin clicked through several screens and was soon looking at the account history at the bank. He finally scrolled over to the deposit record. As he looked at the day's deposit that had just been posted, it caused him to do a double-take. The day's cash deposit was $58,220. He clicked back through the system to look at the daily activity report again. Sure enough, there was a discrepancy in the cash deposit. He made a quick calculation in his head. There was $21,500 in additional cash that made it to the bank. Kevin kept looking around to see if he had missed anything, but he couldn't find any other reason for the extra cash. He pulled his HP 12c calculator out of the box stashed under his desk and made the calculation again. As far as he could tell, his calculations were correct. For some reason, more money was being deposited in the account than was being collected in the clinic.

"How could that be?" he said to himself. He spoke to himself frequently when he was working on the computer.

He started scrolling back through the records and he was stunned. Almost every day the cash deposits at the bank were showing a higher total than the cash collected at the clinic. He went back to the first of the year and totaled up the difference. For the current year, it looked like over $5 million in extra cash had been deposited in the clinic's account. He sat back in his chair and stared out at the lake.

"Where is all that cash coming from?" he said aloud. "That's a lot of money!"

As Kevin was thinking through the possibilities, the email alert on his laptop sounded. He minimized the program he was in and brought up his email. He saw that Wheels had responded. He clicked on the email and opened the communication from Wheels.

From: Wheels
Sent: Thursday, December 2, 1999 11:56 p.m.
To: KayMac
Subject: Info Search

Sorry it's taken a while to get back to you. This one looks like it may be tougher than most. I followed the initial info that you gave me and I've run into several dead ends. But don't worry, I got in touch with Rooter and we're after it. You know us – always up to a challenge. Keep checking, we'll get a break soon.

Kevin laughed out loud. Wheels was still using that little symbol for his sign-off signature. He had started that in college soon after they had given him the nickname.

It was good to hear that Rooter was on board. With those two working on it, nothing could be hidden for very long.

He looked at the key. It was still on the corner of the desk. He didn't like the way this was shaping up. He had worked too hard and had planned too well to have significant variables come up now. He wasn't sure of the exact timing of the mission. But, he knew that it would be soon.

The money discrepancy at the clinic had him worried. It made him wonder even more about the owners of the clinic. How could the owners not know about the cash difference? Why did the local people not know anything about the cash? If the local people knew, why wasn't it reflected in their accounts receivable system? If they were the ones making the deposit, where did the money come from? How did it get to the bank?

These questions began to make Kevin nervous. He originally thought knowing the ownership of the clinic would be a nice extra. Now he was beginning to think that it was crucial. He thought this clinic was just another abortion mill. But now, what did all of this mean?

He looked down at his hand. He had instinctively reached out and grabbed the key. He had it in his hand and it was already turning from side to side.

"Yeah," he thought to himself, "I have to get some answers." He couldn't let this interfere with the mission. It was too important. The plan was already in motion. He couldn't let anything stop it now. Not anything!

Chapter 9

Carla walked into the clinic a few minutes after 8:00 a.m. She took the stairs up to her office on the second floor. As she walked into the administrative area, her secretary greeted her.

"Good morning, Ms. Sharkley. Happy Friday to you."

"Good morning, Patsy. Did you have a good evening?"

"I sure did, Ms. Sharkley. I'm looking forward to a great weekend also."

For some reason, it always amazed Carla how happy and perky Patsy was. Patsy acted as if she never had a bad day. That was certainly a good thing for this office, because Carla's days were filled with highs and lows. It was nice to have Patsy's uplifting persona to even out the rough spots. She had asked Patsy about her positive outlook before and Patsy had told her it was because of her Christianity. That had stopped Carla cold. She had never asked about it again. Carla could talk about many things, but talking about religion made her very uncomfortable.

"Anything new going on this morning?" Carla always checked for any new developments. Patsy usually knew what was happening around the clinic.

"Well, Dr. Smith has already been by looking for you twice this morning. He seemed very anxious to talk to you."

"Dr. Smith? He almost never comes up here. Wonder what he wants?" Carla thought she knew exactly what was on Marty's mind. She thought that she would spare Patsy the details of what she knew for now.

"He didn't say what he wanted. He did say that he would be back. My guess is that you have about ten minutes before he comes back, if he stays on his same schedule."

"Thanks, Patsy. I'll be in my office when he gets here, just send him on in. It looks like we're going to get off to a running start today."

"Yes ma'am, but it'll be a good day."

Carla set her briefcase on the desk and sat down. She turned to the credenza behind her and pushed the power switch on the computer. It was part of her morning routine to check her email and any other activity on the system before she started working on any hot issues for the day. As she was getting into her email, she wondered what Marty's spin on yesterday's events would be. She scanned down through the list of new email messages that had come in since last night. She could see that most of the communication was routine. Maybe the event yesterday would blow over without becoming a major deal.

She had just finished reviewing her email, when Dr. Smith came into her office.

"Come in, Marty, and have a seat. What's on your mind?" she said waving to the chairs in front of the desk.

"Did you hear what happened yesterday with one of my patients?" Marty said taking a seat.

"Yes, you really irritated J.P.," Carla replied. "I got an email from him last night. What are the details? He didn't give me any specifics."

Marty jumped up and started pacing around Carla's office. "Well, I was in the OR about to start a new case, when the patient began to talk to me. Her name was Cassie Clancy. It was obvious from the questions she had that her pre-procedure counseling was pretty weak – plus the fact that she was scared to death. I couldn't go through with the procedure without talking to her. It just wouldn't have been good medicine."

"I know, Marty," Carla said. "Sometimes these things happen. Just give it a couple of days. You know how tightly wound J.P. is. He'll settle down. He won't be back here till next week anyway."

"Yeah, I know that. It's just that I've never had that kind of encounter with a colleague. The last time that I was chewed out like that, I was in medical school, being humiliated by a professor. I wasn't expecting that in the real world."

"Welcome to the real world, Marty," Carla replied. "J.P. has a lot of pressures on him other than the clinical stuff."

"I've been meaning to ask you about that." His curiosity was raising the question in his mind. "Does he have some incentive for this place to produce a certain number of procedures? He seems awfully intense about the business of the clinic."

"I can't go into the specifics of anyone's compensation with you. You know that, Marty. In fact, I don't even know all the specifics of his package. The details of that are handled out of Chicago."

"Well, Carla, maybe it's time that you found out about some of those details. There's something funny going on around here." Marty had stopped pacing and was leaning over Carla's desk with his hands on the edges.

"What do you mean, Marty? Just because J.P. blows up over one patient, you think something is going on? Isn't that being a little paranoid?"

"It's not just that, Carla," Marty explained. "I came in early this morning to work on some charts and found some strange stuff."

"What do you mean?" Carla was puzzled.

"Well, for one thing, some of the documentation in the charts of my patients seems to have been altered."

"How could they have been altered? And maybe more importantly, why would they have been altered?"

"I was trying to follow up on a case that I had done about six months ago. The patient had some mild complications and I wanted to make sure that we had followed up with her. When I pulled the chart, I found documentation for a procedure done in the twentieth week of pregnancy."

"What's so unusual about that?"

"It's unusual because this patient was only thirteen weeks pregnant," Marty replied.

Carla stared at him. "How could you possibly remember that? Maybe you made a mistake. Maybe you're remembering a different patient. After all, it was six months ago. That's a long time to remember the specifics of every patient."

"I don't have to remember the specifics of every patient, just this one," Marty responded. "Besides, I made a note on my computer to follow up in six months. I'm not mistaken. My note was very specific regarding the details of this patient."

"Why would someone do that?"

"Maybe for the money," Marty said. "People do strange things when money's involved. What's the price differential between a procedure in the thirteenth week and one in the twentieth week?"

"What are you suggesting? Are you saying that someone is altering the documentation, so that the clinic can get more money for the procedure? That's a pretty serious accusation."

"I'm not accusing anyone of anything. I'm just saying that something weird is going on that I don't understand. By the way, you didn't answer my question about the money," Marty persisted. "What's the difference?"

"Well, it depends on several factors, but it can more than double the price. Sometimes the difference can be well over a thousand dollars."

Marty finally quit pacing and sat back down in one of the chairs across from Carla's desk. He leaned back in the chair, closed his eyes and ran his hands through his hair.

Carla studied him as he sat there, not realizing that she was staring. His hair was a very light brown color with a certain unruliness to it. He really didn't look old enough to be a doctor. He typically had such a happy-go-lucky demeanor that any change from that had a profound impact on him. Right now, he was more troubled than she had ever seen him.

"Do you think there could be some mistake, Marty?" Carla was trying to find a logical explanation. "Maybe the wrong information was placed in the chart by one of the clerks."

"Maybe, but I don't think so," Marty said, his eyes still closed. "The chart included an ultrasound with the patient's name on it. Since almost all the patients that I take care of are less than fourteen weeks pregnant, they don't require ultrasounds. I bet I can count on one hand the number of ultrasounds that I've seen in charts since I've been here."

"There must be some mistake. I don't think that this one incident indicates that something sinister is going on, do you?"

Marty quit rubbing his head and opened his eyes.

"I don't know what I think, Carla," Marty said. "Listen, I'm sorry that I've barged in on you like this. Maybe I'm a little edgy since my encounter yesterday with J.P. I'm usually not like this." A smile finally creased his face.

Marty looked at his watch and stood up.

"I've got to get down to the OR, but I'd like to spend some time looking through old charts and see if I can find anything else. I'd like to be able to do that when the Nazi Nurse is not around. I don't think that she would be too crazy about me looking through any charts around here."

"I'll be happy to help you, when would you like to start?" Carla asked.

"The sooner, the better."

"Well, how about this evening after work? We could come back after everyone is gone and have the place to ourselves."   ·

"I can't tonight. I'm stuck going to some party with all of the great legal minds in the community." Marty was not very enthusiastic. "How about tomorrow?"

"Oh, okay." Carla felt a tinge of disappointment that they wouldn't be able to meet tonight and it surprised her. "I'll meet you here at 10:00 tomorrow morning. That should give us plenty of time to find out if something is going on with our charts."

"Okay, 10:00 tomorrow it is. Now I've got to get to work." Marty was already heading out the door. "Call me if you get any great revelations about this stuff."

With that, Carla was alone in her office again. She felt like she needed to catch her breath. It wasn't even 8:30 yet and she already had dozens of thoughts running through her head looking to occupy her time today and distract her from the work at hand. She thought that she was prepared to talk to Marty this morning, but he had thrown her a curve with that bit about the charts. Surely there must be some mistake. Charts didn't just get randomly changed and who would want to change them?

As Carla was thinking about the information that Marty had dropped in her lap, she remembered that she had also found some interesting information last night on the computer. Maybe she needed to spend the day doing a little research to resolve some of these questions.

The intercom on Carla's telephone buzzed. It was Patsy.

"Ms. Sharkley, you have a call. Would you like to take it?"

"Yes, go ahead and send it through."

With that, the day moved forward. Carla made herself a note to come back before the end of the day and find some answers.

Chapter 10

Marty had just gotten out of the shower and was standing in front of his closet, trying to decide what to wear. Allison had told him that he needed to wear a coat and tie to the party tonight. He knew that most of the lawyers at the party tonight would have on suits. He, however, did not own a suit. He did own one sport coat, blue of course. And he did own two oxford dress shirts, one white and one blue. And he thought that he still owned a tie, although it had been a number of months since he had seen it and a number of years since he had actually worn it.

He could hear Allison in the next room getting ready. He could tell that she was excited about the party. She, on the other hand, had yet to figure out that he had no interest at all in socializing with the legal elite of Little Rock tonight.

It had not taken very long at all for he and Allison to transition from dating to roommates. The transition from roommates to acquaintances was taking a lot longer. Marty was ready to move on to something else. But what would he move on to? He thought back to earlier this morning, when he was talking to Carla Sharkley. He realized that he had enjoyed the time with her, even though it had been kind of stressful for him. At least, they had something in common.

Allison called out from the next room. "Marty, are you almost ready? It's 6:45 and we need to be there by 7:00."

"I'll be ready in a minute," he called out.

Marty threw his sport coat on the bed. He grabbed the blue oxford cloth shirt and put it on. He pulled on his trusty khaki pants. He loved these pants because they would go with anything. Marty recognized that he was fashion challenged, and because of that, most of his wardrobe was versatile and low-key. He rummaged around in the back of the closet until he came across his tie.

"Oops," he said to himself. "I should have hung this tie up. I've never seen a tie this wrinkled before."

As he was looking around the room for some way to get the wrinkles out of his tie, Allison came to the door.

"I thought you said you were ready."

"I am. All I have to do is put my tie on."

"Is that a new tie?"

"No, I've had it for a while."

Marty watched her walk into the living room of the condo, as he tied the tie around his neck. He continued to be totally amazed at the little ways that she demonstrated her absorption in the law and her role in it. She never noticed anything else, but the law. He wasn't even sure that she had ever seen him wear a tie, but that never crossed her mind.

He followed her into the living room, as he finished securing the knot of the tie around his neck. He took one last look at his hair in the mirror over the sofa and tried to brush down one of the unruly waves with his hands.

"That's it, Allison. I'm ready to go."

* * * * *

The party was at the home of Richard Stanley. Stanley was the Chief Justice of the Arkansas Supreme Court and one of the most respected lawyers in the state. He lived in one of the Old Money neighborhoods of Little Rock. He lived within walking distance of the Little Rock Country Club in an exclusive area known as the Heights.

Marty parked the car about half a block away from Judge Stanley's home. It was obvious that the party inside was already under way. Cars were parked down both sides of the street leading away from the Judge's home. The rain that had been falling for most of the week had momentarily stopped.

As they walked down the street toward the party, Marty commented to Allison, "It looks like this is going to be a large party. Every lawyer in town must be here."

"Yeah, it's hard to do anything for the third-year students without getting everybody in town involved. They either want to show off their new hires, or see the new competition."

They stepped around a puddle of water and turned off the street onto a brick sidewalk. The Judge lived in an old colonial style home with four tall white columns on the front porch. The home was set back from the street almost 200 feet. It was a large two-story house with dormer windows in the attic.

"Man, this place must be worth a fortune." Marty whistled.

"It probably is," Allison commented. "This house has been in the Judge's family at least two generations. His family goes way back in this town. He's got connections like you wouldn't believe. You know the old saying, 'It's not what you know, but who you know?' Well, the Judge has both. He knows everybody and he's one of the smartest guys you'll ever meet."

They had reached the front door and Marty rang the doorbell. An older woman in a simple black dress with a starched white apron answered the door.

"Welcome to the Stanley's' home. Please come in and make yourself at home. If you would sign the guest book," she said pointing to a book on a small table in the foyer, "so that the Stanley's may have a record of your visit to their home. You will find food and drink in the family room through that door, straight ahead."

After signing the guest book, Marty and Allison walked into the family room and saw a large congregation of people around a long table of food. The table was set up in front of French doors that led onto a brick patio in the backyard. Over to the right, a bar was set up in the corner of the room. Marty and Allison moved over to the bar and placed their orders with the bartender. Allison ordered a glass of white wine and Marty got his usual. A Diet Coke.

As they turned from the bar and faced the crowd in the room, Allison immediately saw one of her fellow students across the room. She leaned over to Marty's ear, to be heard above the noise of the crowd, and said, "I see someone that I need to talk to about a case we're working on. Do you mind if I go talk to her? I'll be back in a few minutes. You can go ahead and get something to eat."

"Sure, Allison, go ahead. I'll be fine."

With that, she was gone. Marty had been to enough of these functions with her to know the truth. She wouldn't be back until the night was over and she was ready to go home. Knowing that made it easier for Marty to mingle with the crowd. He didn't have to worry about Allison, because he knew she wasn't worrying about him.

He wandered over to a table that was loaded down with food. He picked up a plate and began to circle the table making selections from the choice of appetizers. After he filled his plate, Marty stood off to the side and watched the people come and go, as he ate his food. The room was crowded with people. It was obvious that most of these people knew each other. The conversation had risen to a dull roar. After several minutes, he was engaged in conversation by one of the local trial attorneys. Pretty soon, he was just a part of the larger conversation of the party.

Marty needed a refill on his Diet Coke. As he wandered over to the bar, he glanced at his watch and realized that he had already been at the party for over an hour. He had only seen Allison once since they first separated and that was from a distance. He was standing in line at the bar, when someone came up and grabbed his elbow.

"Hey, Marty Smith, I thought that was you!"

Marty turned to his left to see a woman with jet-black hair holding his elbow. At first, he didn't recognize her. Then it dawned on him.

"Teresa! Teresa Madison. It's been forever since I've seen you. How have you been?"

Marty and Teresa went way back. They had dated back in high school, but drifted apart when they both left for college.

"I've been fine, Marty. You look good. I don't think that you've changed a bit. I recognized you the minute I saw you."

"It took me a minute to realize who you were, Teresa."

"Well, I have put on a few pounds."

"Who hasn't?" Marty said, patting his stomach. "Say, what are you doing here? Do you know some of these people?"

"Yeah, I know most of them," Teresa replied. "We lost touch after we both went to college, but I ended up going to law school after I finished my under graduate degree. I've been practicing law for several years now."

"Oh really," Marty was intrigued. "I would have never pictured you as a lawyer. I ended up going to medical school and then doing a residency in ob/gyn."

"I knew that. I've kept up with you Marty."

Marty was surprised that Teresa had made that comment. He hadn't thought about her in years. He was finally up to the front of the line at the bar.

He asked her. "Can I get you anything?"

"Sure, a glass of white wine would be great."

Marty placed his order with the bartender for a white wine and a Diet Coke. After getting their drinks, Marty and Teresa walked out to the patio at the rear of the house. As they stood there under the cloudy night sky, they continued their conversation.

Marty was curious. "What did you mean when you said that you had kept up with me?"

"Well, I just kept up with where you were. For instance, I knew that after you graduated from college at Ole Miss, you went to medical school at the University. From there, you did your residency in ob-gyn, also at the University. I was surprised when you took the job at the Women's Health Inc. clinic. I didn't know that you were into that issue, but I was impressed."

"You shouldn't be impressed," he said. "It wasn't the issue that attracted me. It was the job. I'm in it for the money."

"It doesn't really matter. I'm just glad you're providing the service. It can be really hard for a woman to get the procedure in a safe, secure environment."

Marty gave Teresa a questioning look. "I never knew that you had an interest in the pro-choice issue. You never seemed the type."

Teresa tilted her head back with laughter. "And what type is that, Marty?"

"Uh, uh, uh, y…y…you know, one of those radical types," Marty stammered.

"I wouldn't exactly label myself a radical," Teresa said still smiling at Marty's awkwardness. "I'm just interested in the proper access to the procedures that women need for their health. It's important that women have a choice if they end up with an unwanted pregnancy."

"When did you become so interested in this?"

"Do you remember the last time that we saw each other, Marty?"

"Sort of. I think that it was after we had both gone off to college," he said, obviously struggling to remember.

"It was spring break of our freshman year. I came over to see you," she explained.

"Yeah, I remember now. You said that you had a doctor's appointment for some kind of an exam. I remember that you caught me a little off guard. You seemed to be searching for something. I couldn't tell exactly what it was."

"You're right, I was searching for something," she said turning serious. "I was trying to find out if there was anything left between us. It had been so long since we had talked, I wasn't sure how to ask."

"Ask me what?"

"I was pregnant, and I was looking for advice."

"You're kidding! I didn't know." He wasn't sure what to say. "You should have told me."

"I just couldn't bring myself to tell you. It wasn't your baby and I didn't know how to talk to you about it. After we had been so close, I knew that you would be disappointed that I had gotten pregnant. When I saw you that day, I felt that whatever closeness we had experienced before was gone. In just a few minutes, I knew that we had nothing left together. So after I left you, I went straight to the clinic and terminated my pregnancy."

"That's why you were going to the clinic," Marty exclaimed, suddenly understanding. "Why didn't you tell me? I wish we could've talked about it."

"Well, Marty, when I stopped by to see you that day, it was very clear that we were done. I just didn't think that you cared enough for me to share that kind of problem with you. I didn't want to burden you with it."

"Wow. I'm stunned. Did you have anybody else you could talk to?"

"Not really. You were my last hope. I had already broken up with the guy who had gotten me pregnant. He and I both had considered it just a little fling. In fact I've never seen him since then, and he never knew that I was pregnant." Teresa replayed the details with no emotion. "No, Marty, you were the only one I thought that I might be able to talk to."

Marty's mind was reeling. He had flashed back to the many good times that he and Teresa had together. The conversation that she had described to him had now rushed back into his mind. He now remembered every detail of that conversation. It dawned on him that he had been very selfish that day. He had still carried a grudge against Teresa about the way that they had ended their relationship at the beginning of the school year. In fact, he remembered that he was anxious to end their conversation in his parent's driveway, so that he could go meet the guys for a game of basketball. How could he have been so selfish? Why didn't he pay more attention that day? Maybe he could have helped her.

"Did the procedure go okay?" As lame as it sounded, it was all Marty could think to say.

"Yeah, the procedure went fine," she said. "It was the mental stuff that I had to deal with afterwards. I got depressed and started gaining weight. And as you can see, it hasn't come off since then." Teresa held her arms straight out from her body and looked down at herself as she said this. "But, I've gotten over it. Now I take every chance I get to work for the cause."

Marty was a little puzzled. "What do you mean, work for the cause?"

"By the time that I was finishing my undergraduate degree, I had decided that I wanted to go to law school and do as much as I could legally to make sure that women always had a choice regarding their bodies. Now that I'm out of law school, I take every case I can that relates to the support of the pro-choice movement. I even represent the clinic you work in, when they are involved in legal matters in our local courts."

"What kind of legal matters do they get involved in?"

"Oh, you know, every time some protester chains themselves to the front door. Or when they harass the patients as they enter the clinic by preaching to them. I file the suits on all of those kinds of cases. Then, I defend the clinic when the anti-choice guys start filing frivolous lawsuits, and they do that a lot. In fact, I've sort of made a cause out of taking these guys to court every chance I get."

"Teresa, this is a lot of information for me to process all at once. I'm just totally blown away that you came to talk to me about terminating a pregnancy and I wasn't listening. I am so sorry that I let you down. Can you forgive me for that?"

"Listen, Marty, I've been let down by a bunch of people over the years. It's been that way almost all my life. And to be honest, it probably wasn't fair for me to even think that I could talk to you about it. I wouldn't have even mentioned it to you now, if you weren't working at the clinic."

"But can you forgive me, Teresa?"

"Sure. Don't think another thing about it. By the way, it's been good talking to you, Marty. I've got to leave now. I see the people that I came with heading for the door. Please don't think any more about all of this, because it's in the past. I'm just glad that you and I are working toward the same goal now. I've gotta go. See ya, Marty."

With that, Teresa gave him a quick hug and was hurrying across the room. She was weaving in and out of the throngs of talking people, as she made her way to the front door.

Marty was totally absorbed with the information that he had just received. It was almost too much for his mind to process. He began to sift through the data just like he would if a patient had presented him with the facts of a complex case.

He was engrossed in his own thoughts as he moved down the hallway to the bathroom. How would he have reacted eleven years ago, if Teresa had confided in him? Would he have encouraged her to terminate the pregnancy? Would he have encouraged her to pursue the other available options?

Marty was pondering these questions, when he almost ran over a man coming out of the bathroom.

"Excuse me, sir. My mind was wandering and I wasn't paying any attention to where I was going."

"Don't worry about it, son, just be careful that you don't hurt yourself. By the way, I don't think that we've had the pleasure of being introduced. My name is Richard Stanley." The Judge extended his hand toward Marty.

Marty grabbed his hand and shook it. "Judge Stanley, it is certainly a pleasure to meet you. My name is Marty Smith."

Judge Stanley was a very elegant man. He was tall, slender and impeccably groomed. The top of his head was bald and tanned. It was ringed with snow-white hair. You could tell by the way that he carried himself that he was from the old school, where manners and graciousness meant everything.

"Your name sounds familiar. Oh yes, you're Allison's friend. Aren't you an obstetrician working at one of the clinics in town?"

"Yes sir, I am. I work at Women's Health Inc. I just got out of residency last summer."

"I remember that Allison told me that you were working there. How do you like working at the clinic? Is it meeting your professional goals?"

Marty was a little startled that the Judge would ask him a question so personal after just meeting him. "Actually, it's not exactly what I was hoping for long term. However, it's a job and I've got to pay the bills."

Judge Stanley looked around to make sure that no one was listening. "Look, Marty, I know we've just met, but I'd like to give you a little advice. I've heard you're a good kid and an excellent doctor, so I wanted to give you a heads-up regarding the people you're working for. In case you don't know it yet, the people you're working for are very serious about their business. I don't know them personally, but I have enough connections around this town to know of them. I would advise you to find something else as soon as possible. You really shouldn't get involved with them."

"I'm afraid I don't understand, Judge Stanley. Do you mean that they are serious about the procedure we offer and the choices we provide to women?"

"No, son, that's not what I mean at all. The people you work for could care less about offering abortions or the pro-choice movement. It's just a convenient mechanism to achieve their other goals."

"I still don't understand, Judge. What are their other goals?"

"Listen, Marty, I'm not going into it right now and I've probably already said too much. Let me just warn you to be careful. Don't rock the boat too much and be looking for a way to get out. Make sure that you pay attention to what's going on around you and stay clean."

The Judge glanced up and down the hall again. Making sure that they were still alone, he turned to Marty again. "Look, Marty, you seem like a nice guy. The people you're working for are involved with some things that could ruin your career, as well as your life. Just be careful."

With that, the Judge clapped him on the shoulder and moved off down the hallway. He turned his head and called out, "It was great meeting you, Marty. Hope you enjoy the party."

"It was a pleasure meeting you, Judge Stanley. Thank you for having me."

As Marty watched Judge Richard Stanley walk away, he realized that he had just completed the second of two of the most bizarre conversations that he had ever had. And he was still struggling to understand exactly what it all meant. The confusion that he felt from these conversations was clouding his ability to deal with the information logically. t was as if a fog had rolled in and he couldn't see through it.

Chapter 11

Kevin looked up from his work on the computer in his living room and noticed that it was almost 11:00. For the second night in a row, he had been totally engrossed trying to find out the business details of the abortion clinic.

He had spent the evening following the trail of the money through the clinic. He had gone back to the first of the year and the pattern was very consistent. Every day more cash was put into the clinic's account at the bank than was collected in the office. It didn't appear that the money was moved into the account electronically. As far as he could tell from the account entries, the money physically was brought into the bank.

Kevin sat back in his chair and wondered how that could happen. Each day, the clinic prepared three separate deposits. He knew that an armored car picked up the deposit and took it to the bank on the same schedule every day. They made pickups at 10:00 a.m., 2:00 p.m. and 5:00 p.m. It seemed simple enough. What could be happening? Was someone showing up at the bank with a sack of cash and putting it into the clinic account? None of this made any sense.

Kevin was staring out of his window at the lake when a chime sounded on his computer, indicating the arrival of a new email. He clicked on his email and saw that the email was from Wheels. He opened it and began reading.

From:	Wheels
Sent:	Friday, December 3, 1999, 11:16 p.m.
To:	KayMac
Subject:	Heads-up

We've started to make a little headway. Before I get started on the details we know so far, let me give you a warning first. It looks like the people involved with this company are a rough crowd, so be very careful.

The initials "GFE" that you found on the server are an abbreviation of the company name. "GFE" stands for Giovanni Family Enterprises. I traced the company's origins to Chicago and ran into some dead ends. I then got in touch with an old friend in the Chicago area, to see if I could find out anything else about GFE.

Well, my friend got real schizoid when I mentioned GFE. I didn't think that he was going to talk to me at all. He finally agreed to talk, if I would promise him total and permanent anonymity. He says that the Giovanni's are the leading Mob family in Chicago. They have grown so big that they have begun to branch out into nontraditional lines of business. They are also moving into many new communities. Many times these moves are into legitimate businesses. However, even when the surface appears legitimate, they usually resort to their typical business practices over time.

KayMac, it looks like your guys are real "wise guys." I've done my own research about the Mafia's use of e-business. Overall, they began to start using it in the mid-nineties. Your guys have only recently begun to use electronics in any significant way in their business. Although they have some of the best equipment available, it appears that their usage and techniques are still in the neophyte stage. Their security measures are pretty basic.

I've included a hyperlink at the end of the email that will help you pursue some additional information, if you're interested. You'll see that the Giovanni's are into a lot of business ventures. Let me give you a word of caution, if you pursue this. Don't forget some of our old tricks for avoiding detection. Don't leave any cybertracks for someone to follow. Remember, KayMac, always leave yourself a way out.

I'll still be looking for anything else I can find. I'll let you know if I see anything. Remember – don't use the chat rooms for this!

Catch you later.

⊗

Kevin immediately responded.

From: KayMac
Sent: Friday, December 3, 1999, 11:28 p.m.
To: Wheels
Subject: Re: Heads-up

Thanks for the information. I'll be watching my step and covering my tracks. If you get any more ideas, keep me posted. If I make any progress, I'll let you know. Thanks again.

KM

Kevin minimized his email and got up from the desk. He walked into the kitchen and began to make himself a cup of tea. As he busied himself around the kitchen, he was thinking about all of the new information that he had received over the last two days. It was a little unsettling to find out that the Mafia was involved in the Women's Health Inc. clinic. Of all of the possible scenarios that he could have imagined, this one didn't even get on the radar. Why would the Mob be interested in an abortion clinic in Little Rock, Arkansas?

The water in the kettle on the gas stove began to boil. Kevin poured the water over a tea bag he had placed in a large ceramic mug., picked up the mug and walked through the living room and out the back door of the cabin. He had to have some time to think this through and the night air would be good for him. He walked across the small backyard and went out on the stone patio by the lake.

As he looked around, he was reminded again why he had been so excited about renting this place. When the owners had remodeled the home, they had also redone all the landscaping. They had even replaced the old seawall with a wooden plank and beam wall. They had also built a new dock that formed the boundary of one side of the swimming area. The dock was constructed of two-by-twelve cypress planks and huge poles, which were the diameter of telephone poles. The poles supported the dock and rose above the dock a good five feet. It reminded him of an old Louisiana plantation down on the bayou. This had been the perfect place for him to plan his mission. The house was on a wooded island that was connected to the shoreline by a narrow causeway. The driveway to the house went across the causeway and the house was very secluded from all the neighbors.

Kevin walked to the end of the dock, a good thirty feet from the shore. He sat down at the end of the dock and lifted the mug of tea to his mouth. The aroma of the Earl Grey tea was warm and soothing. He had gotten into the habit of relaxing this way almost every evening. At this time of year, there were never any boats on the lake. The only sounds were the wind whistling through the trees and the waves lapping against the shore. The rain had paused temporarily, but you could look up at the sky and tell that it wouldn't be long before it started again. The wind felt as if it were carrying a cold front into the city on its strong shoulders. He zipped his coat tighter around his neck to keep the chill away.

He sipped his tea and thought about the events of the day. The details of his plan were coming together. Before he left the office today, Kevin had turned in his resignation. He told his supervisor that he would work at least two more weeks, but possibly he might work until the end of the month. His supervisor had left the door open for him to come back to work. His performance had always been outstanding and they would love to have him come back to work, his boss said. Kevin was appreciative of the compliment, but he knew that he would not be back. In fact, he anticipated that before the end of the month, he would need to be far, far away from this place.

When he had rented this place, he had signed a lease for one year. The lease was up at the end of the month. After the expiration of the lease, he had arranged to continue renting on a month-to-month basis. He had already paid to stay in the house through January. That should give him plenty of time to get lost before anyone would be looking in this house for him.

The rest of the pieces were beginning to fall into place. He had contacted Mike Hanks earlier in the week with the specific requirements that he had in a vehicle. He had asked for an older model four-wheel drive SUV. He didn't want anything that was new enough to draw attention. It also needed to have a large cargo space. He had to make sure that he would be able to carry all of the materials necessary to carry out his mission. He had decided that an older Ford Bronco would fit the bill perfectly. In addition to the four-wheel drive capabilities, it also had a higher ground clearance than most of the newer model SUVs. When Kevin contacted Mike with the request, he was told he could pick it up early Friday morning at a downtown parking lot. He had brought it back to his house and had it in the garage before sunrise. He wanted to make sure that if any of the neighbors happened over to his place that they would not associate this vehicle with him.

The countdown for "mission go" had begun. The transportation was in place. It shouldn't be more than two weeks before the mission was executed.

He had a list of items that he needed from the hardware store. He had done his research online and found out everything he would need for the project. He would make those purchases tomorrow. He would use cash, of course. When he picked up the Bronco earlier in the day, an envelope filled with cash had been hidden under the driver's side floor mat. It contained $20,000 in bills of small denominations. All of his purchases for anything related to this project would be paid for in cash. The money in the envelope should cover all of his expenses. No one would be able to trace any of the materials used on this project back to him.

The envelope had also contained everything he needed for a new identity, as well as a new debit card. As per his instructions, Mike had opened an offshore bank account for him. The debit card would allow him to access money from that account without being traceable to him. The account was supposed to contain a $50,000 balance. He didn't really perceive the money as a payoff, because that would make it appear as if the mission were a criminal activity. Kevin knew that the mission was not a crime, but a fulfillment of his calling. The money was only there to help with any costs that he may have when he disappeared after the completion of the mission.

Kevin stood up and shivered in the cold December air. He pulled his coat up tighter around his neck and walked briskly back to the house. His mug was empty and he moved to the kitchen to get a refill of tea. As he was waiting for the water to boil, he saw the door leading to the basement from the laundry room. He was planning to use the basement as a workshop to get all the pieces assembled for his project. It would be the perfect location. The basement had no other entrances or windows, other than the door from the laundry room. No one could accidentally stumble upon his work. It would be very secure.

He poured another mug of tea and moved over to his computer. It was time to follow the trail of money out of the clinic's account. Through the clinic's server, he was able to move into the bank's record of the checking account activity. It was apparent that the money that was deposited into the account did not stay there for very long. It looked like very few checks were actually written on this account. However, the average daily balance was really small for so much money to be passing through the account. Almost all of the money was being transferred out of the account electronically. It looked like it was going to two different accounts.

Kevin clicked on the specific transfers to get the details of the transactions. The first one he looked at was one of the smaller transfers. This transfer was made to First Midwest Bank in Chicago and the amount was $31,590.34. It appeared that this transfer had been made to cover checks presented for operating costs. This was not too surprising based on the information he had received from Wheels earlier in the evening. It looked like all the expenses for the clinic were paid out of Chicago. The next transfer that he looked at was $105,800. He clicked on this transaction and brought up the details. This transfer had been made to a bank in Panama. There was a transfer similar to this in the account every week.

With every step he took in unraveling the details of this business, it became harder and harder for his mind to hold on to the direction this was heading. As he delved deeper into this clinic, the banking trail was becoming more complicated than he had expected. It was going to take some time to find the end of the trail. He had tried several times to get into the account at the Panamanian bank, but had been unsuccessful. He had several other tricks that he could try, but they required more information than he currently had. He had not yet looked at the link that Wheels had included in his email. That might give him a lead that he could use to find a way into the account.

Kevin minimized the bank program and opened the email from Wheels to review it and scrolled down to the link, clicking the cursor on it. The link took him directly into the GFE server. As he maneuvered through the GFE network, he was able to see the list of related companies that the Giovanni's included in their control. It was amazing. Most of the companies appeared to be legitimate businesses. The list included restaurants, hotels and courier services. He found the Women's Health Inc. clinic on the list. The list also contained several other clinics. He assumed that these were other abortion clinics. Ten other clinics were scattered throughout Middle America. In addition to the clinic in Little Rock, several were in the Chicago area, two were located in Memphis, one in Jackson, Mississippi, and one located in Gulf Shores, Alabama.

As he scrolled through the remainder of the list, one of the companies caught his attention and stopped him cold in the midst of his search. Lucas Armored Transport was listed as one of the GFE companies. He could see the company's blue and white logo in his mind. This was the same service that picked up the deposits from the clinic.

It seemed a little too convenient that the clinic and the transport service were interconnected. The deposit discrepancies must be tied up in this business relationship. What else could he find out that would add complications to his mission? He needed to find the answers to some of these questions before he would be able to complete his mission.

He looked over at the corner of the desk. The key had been lying there all evening. The finish on the key was perfect. It reflected the light from his computer screen and you could almost read the words on the screen from the reflection in the key. In just a few short days, he would use this key to enter the clinic. No one else would be around. He would make the final preparation and complete the mission.

As he stared at the key, he was almost in a trance. He began to think about the reasons that he had started this mission in the first place. He knew how important it was. Every day that they were allowed to go on in that clinic meant more death. With all the people in this country that wanted to adopt babies, he couldn't believe that people allowed this destruction to continue. He was amazed that America would send troops all over the world to keep different ethnic groups from killing each other, but would allow women to walk down to the corner clinic in the United States and kill their babies. None of it made any sense. He had watched this issue for years. He had been watching ever since his own mother had told him about the effect that it had had on his family. At first, it didn't mean much to him, but then he started his research. When he began to see the real truth behind abortion, he knew that he had to do something. The further that he had dug, the darker the truth had become.

He reached over and touched the key. He picked it up and turned it over in his hand. The look and feel of this key was mesmerizing to him. Not because of anything special about the key itself, it was what the key represented. The mission enthralled him. He was still overwhelmed that he had been chosen to complete this mission. He had been called and he knew it.

The clock on the bookcase chimed one o'clock and brought him back to reality. He had big plans for Saturday morning. He needed to get to bed, so that he would be ready for an early start. Several of the places that he would be purchasing supplies from in the morning would be closed by noon.

Kevin stood up and placed the key back on the corner of the desk. He went to the back door and opened it. He stepped out on the deck and looked up into the sky. It had begun to rain again. It would be good for the rain to continue. It would help him cover his tracks, just like darkness covers evil. His mission would uncover a great evil. He was going to shine a great light in this big evil hole.

Chapter 12

Carla pulled into the empty clinic parking lot at 9:30 on Saturday morning. She parked her car in the space closest to the back door of the clinic, grabbed her briefcase and ran through the rain to the staff entrance. She opened the door and quickly punched her code to disarm the security system. The stairs leading to the administrative area and her office were right around the corner from the security keypad. She took the stairs to her office, as was her habit. The hours that were necessary for her to keep up with all of the aspects of her job had gradually crowded most other things out of her life. She barely had time for her son Thomas, much less some form of exercise. Climbing the stairs at the office had become her one feeble attempt at fitness.

She put down her briefcase, turned on her computer and went to the staff kitchen to brew some coffee. Sounds from downstairs told her that someone had entered the building. Very quickly she knew that Marty Smith was in the building. You usually heard him long before you actually saw him. This morning his jaunty steps and slightly off-key whistling signaled his pleasant mood. He bounced into the kitchen and tossed an empty Diet Coke can through the air towards the trashcan, like a basketball shot. The can slammed against the back of the trashcan and fell straight to the bottom.

"It's good!" Marty yelled. "Good morning, Carla. I hope you had a good evening."

"It was fine. Just a quiet night at home with my son. I really don't get to do enough of that these days."

"Well, I had to spend the evening at a party with a bunch of lawyers. A quiet night at home sounds like a great alternative."

Marty reached into the refrigerator and pulled out a cold Diet Coke. Carla poured herself a cup of coffee and they both headed for her office.

"What do we need to accomplish today?" Marty asked.

"It seems that we have two major items that we need to accomplish this morning. First, we need to review some of the charts that you have questions about. The second item is looking at the details of the financial questions that we were asking yesterday. I hope that we can get to the bottom of both of these today." Carla was quite skilled at organizing projects.

Marty had slumped into a chair across the desk from Carla. He propped his feet up on the corner of her desk and set his Diet Coke on the floor by the chair.

"Marty, why would someone be tampering with the documentation in the charts?" Carla asked. "I mean, what are they going to accomplish? Very rarely do we ever bill insurance for these procedures. It would seem to eliminate insurance fraud as an alternative. Altering the chart documentation after the fact would not allow the clinic to collect more money from the patients, especially since the charge is established prior to the procedure and we collect so much on the front end. I'm not sure where this would be leading."

"I'm not sure where it's leading either," Marty said.

"Do you have any idea which patient charts might be affected by the changes that you think have been made?"

"Yeah, I've got some ideas to get us started." He reached into his back pocket and pulled out a folded piece of paper. "I've been working on this since we talked yesterday. I created a file and printed it. This should get us started. I've been keeping a private list for quite some time. The list represents the patients that were far enough along in their pregnancy that an ultrasound could have been fudged to indicate a higher level of service."

The clinic used ultrasounds in many cases to determine the gestational age of the fetus. If it could be determined that a patient was at least fourteen weeks into her pregnancy, the more complicated Dilation and Evacuation procedure, or D&E as it is commonly called, could be performed. A D&E procedure involves dilating the patient's cervix and evacuating the fetus using sharp techniques, suction and other instruments including forceps. Due to the increased complexity of this procedure, the cost was higher than the simpler early term procedures.

Carla looked down the list that Marty had assembled. There were several hundred names. In addition to the patient name, the list included the date of the procedure.

"I'm sure that there are other possibilities, but that is all that I could account for with the notes that I had kept," Marty replied. "How do you think that they get more money from the patients? It would seem that you would have heard from patients that were being charged more after the fact."

"I've wondered about that." Carla was still absorbed with the list. "I've never heard any complaint like that from a patient. We don't send out many bills and when we do make a mistake on one of them, I almost always hear about it. I wonder how many of these patients received a bill from us. We'll check that when we pull the charts."

"Why don't we get started? We don't want to be here all day." Marty grabbed his Diet Coke and moved to the door.

He and Carla went downstairs to the medical record files and began to pull the charts. Twenty minutes later, they had hauled them all back to Carla's office to review. They had stopped pulling charts after they had located the first one hundred charts on Marty's list.

They organized the charts into piles alphabetically. Marty would grab a chart and begin to review the clinical notes that he had dictated at the time the procedure was performed. He would then compare that with the notes that he had made for himself and kept at home. After Marty finished with the chart, Carla would take the chart and review the financial information that had been entered into the clinic's computer system. After a dozen charts, Marty was the first to notice a pattern.

"Some of these charts have been altered from the original, but it hasn't been done in every case. In the charts that have been tampered with, it is always those cases that are right at fourteen weeks. In each chart, an ultrasound has been added to the record and my dictation has been slightly altered to make the case look like it was a D & E procedure performed."

"How could you possibly know that type of details about cases you did six months ago? And why are you keeping that kind of details about those cases? Are you just obsessive, compulsive or what?"

"Well first of all, in case you've forgotten, to become Board certified in Obstetrics and Gynecology, you must first sit for a written examination after you've completed your residency program. I did that last month. The next step is to keep track of all procedures that you perform for a twelve-month period and report them to the American College of Obstetrics and Gynecology. Then you get to take an oral examination. That event allows you the opportunity to have an intense discussion with three wise old physicians. For several hours, they get to grill you unmercifully about your cases, or anything else they please."

"Man, that doesn't sound like much fun."

"You're right, it's not much fun. However, it is necessary to maintain a high standard in our specialty. Most physician specialties have a similar requirement to maintain Board certification."

Marty sifted through another stack of charts and moved them in front of Carla.

"That's the reason that I have so much information about these patients. I have to submit detailed information about each case that I've performed. I've been keeping this information on my computer at home. Each night I make entries for the cases that I performed during the day. If I don't do it that way, I lose track of the cases."

"Marty, can you be certain that these records have been altered?"

"Sure I can. Take this case for example." Marty spread the chart he had been reviewing on the desk in front of Carla. "I had entered into my file at home that this patient, Amber Henley, had a D & C procedure performed on 9/15/99. I also noted that she was approximately eleven weeks into her pregnancy and she experienced no complications. If you look at the clinic chart, you will see that she had a D & E procedure performed on 9/15/99. This chart states that she was approximately seventeen weeks into her pregnancy. This chart even has an ultrasound in it. I never ordered, nor did I see an ultrasound on this patient, until this very minute!"

Carla took the chart and turned to her computer. She began a search for Amber Henley's financial records. Within a few seconds, the details of her account appeared on the screen. Carla scanned the information briefly, using her mouse to move back and forth between screens.

"Come and look at this."

She turned slightly and motioned for Marty to move behind the desk, so that he could view the screen himself. Marty moved around the desk and bent down to look over her shoulder.

"You can see by looking at this screen that this patient was originally charged for a D & C, but it was later changed to a D & E." Carla was pointing to the information on the screen, so that Marty could follow her. "The patient paid cash for the D & C procedure on 9/15/99, the day of the procedure. If you follow this account all the way through, you can also see that an additional cash payment was made on the account several days later. The total payments equal the charge amount for the D & E procedure."

"It seems weird that the patient would come back in and make an additional payment on a procedure that she never had," Marty said. "Don't most of these patients make complete payment by the day of surgery and then leave, never to be heard from again?"

Carla was already reviewing the next chart in her stack.

"Yeah, most of these girls are not interested in coming back to the clinic, or for that matter, they usually don't want to ever hear from us again. You can see that Amber was eighteen years old at the time that she had this procedure, whatever kind of procedure that she had."

"I told you what kind of procedure she had," Marty said with an expression of hurt on his face. "Don't you believe me?"

"Sure I believe you. I was just kidding. Can't you take a little humor?"

"Sorry, I guess I'm getting a little intense about this whole thing." A sheepish look had crept onto Marty's face.

"As I was saying." Carla looked up at Marty with a smile on her face, as she proceeded with her explanation. Marty was leaning across the arm of her executive chair with his hands resting on his knees. "Amber is an eighteen-year-old white female. She is probably a senior in high school, or a college freshman. She is exactly the kind of patient that comes into this clinic expecting complete anonymity. She doesn't really care what it costs her. She just never wants to hear from us again. She doesn't want to file this on her daddy's insurance plan. She doesn't want to get a bill for an unpaid balance at home for her mom to see. She doesn't want a collector calling her house at night. She just wants the whole thing to go away."

"I kind of remember her from my notes," Marty said. "It seems like she was probably from an upper middle class family. That appears to be a fairly common profile for my patients; late teens to middle twenties, white, middle to upper middle class. Is that kind of patient demographic typical in this business?"

"It's surprising, but it's true," Carla said. "Very seldom do we ever get patients from the lower economic classes at this clinic. The thing that throws most people off when they stereotype the patients who use a clinic like this, is the argument from the pro-choice movement. Most of their publicity centers on the right of equal access, regardless of race or economic status. They lead you to believe that wealthy white females obtain these procedures at their private physician's office, while the poor minorities do without. I can tell you from my experience here, that we definitely do not discriminate based on race. We do, however, freely discriminate on the ability to pay."

Marty's face showed surprise at Carla's comment. "Is that company policy?"

"I was surprised too. I've been involved with other types of clinics, but this was the first time that I had ever seen a focus on money like this. When I first started working here, I was told by some of the staff that the unofficial motto of the clinic was, 'If you can't pay, you can't stay.' It really caught me off guard when I heard that."

"Well surely other clinics have to pay attention to money."

"Of course they do. It's just that most other clinics at least put a good face on being more concerned about the patient than the money."

Marty had moved back to the other side of the desk and sat down again. He was shuffling through more charts as Carla turned around and watched him. He was attractive in a boyish kind of way. He had an intensity about him, as he dug into the charts, that was really appealing to her. Carla began to wonder about his personal life. She thought that she had heard the nurses talk about his girlfriend in the past, but that was a long time ago. She would find a way to quiz him about last night before they finished their work this morning.

Thirty minutes later, Marty stood up to stretch. They had both been busy going through the details of the charts. The communication between them had dwindled to only the necessary, as they were engrossed in their work. The charts were being organized into stacks on Carla's desk. On top of each stack was a handwritten list that itemized the names of the patients involved and the details of their case.

Marty surveyed the work that they had done, as he ran his fingers through his hair. Carla was still going through the last of the charts. She had been going back and forth from her computer to her calculator. She had streams of adding machine tape clipped to the top of each stack of charts.

Marty spoke for the first time in several minutes. "I've checked a hundred charts and only eight of them have not been changed."

Carla looked up. "I assume that's the stack on the corner of the desk. I separated those out also. Those eight patients all had private insurance. The other ninety-two paid in cash. There were some other similarities that I found, but that was certainly the most striking."

Marty moved over to the corner of the desk and flipped through the stack that Carla indicated.

"Yeah, these are the ones," he said.

"Did you find anything else?" Carla asked.

"Not much more than what I knew before I started. Most of these patients I had recorded as being between eleven and fourteen weeks of pregnancy. With the added information, the charts now reflect gestational ages between sixteen and eighteen weeks. There were even a couple at twenty-one weeks."

"Were they all documented in the chart the same way?"

"Yes and no. They all have similar transcription that has been dictated almost exactly like I would have done it. They all have ultrasounds in the chart. However, the ultrasounds are not all the same. I could identify at least three separate pictures. I'm not exactly sure how the computer on the ultrasound equipment works. I'd like to look at it and see if you can use pictures that are on file and change the names and dates."

Carla was thinking through the details that Marty had pointed out about the charts. "Have you ever done a procedure at twenty-one weeks or more?" she asked him.

"Just once, it was during my residency. When the pregnancy gets to that stage, you can't use suction anymore. At that point, you have to use the D & E method to get the fetus out of the uterus. It nearly made me sick to perform the procedure."

"Why did it make you sick?"

"Well, it's a pretty gruesome procedure. The fetus is too large to come out unless you trim it up a little bit. When you pull out the parts, they are easy to identify. You don't have to know anything about medicine to know those parts came from a human body.

There's just something about counting body parts to know if you're done with a procedure, that doesn't sit well on my stomach."

"That's gross, Marty. I think you've already told me more than I wanted to know."

Marty looked at Carla with a sense of amazement. "What do you think goes on in the OR here? You can talk about 'procedures' as much as you want to, but in the end all we're doing is abortions."

"I know that we do abortions here. But, we also provide a service for women that they can't get just anywhere. The work that we do here is very important. I'd like to think that we are helping to provide these women with a choice that the Supreme Court has guaranteed them."

"Yeah, right, right, right." Marty sighed with exasperation. "You know as well as I do that somebody around here is making a ton of money. I'm not sure, but I doubt very seriously that if the owners of this place, whoever they are, weren't making money hand over fist, they would have very little interest in the activities of the Supreme Court, as it relates to the rights of women."

"You're probably right," Carla admitted.

"Yeah, it kind of surprised me that you would take that perspective on it. For some reason, I thought that you were in it for the money, like me."

"The money is certainly a very convincing reason to be in this business," Carla said. "The only problem is now I feel trapped by it. I don't think that I could go anywhere else and make this kind of money."

"Me either. In a way, that kind of scares me. I mean I know performing these types of procedures each and every day is not the most glamorous job in the world. Because of the kind of work that we do here, I would expect some additional compensation. But, even I have been amazed at the kind of money these people are willing to spend on staffing these clinics. It would be hard for me to find this kind of financial opportunity anyplace else."

"I get the feeling from listening to you that money is not the only thing you're after. It sounds like you're focused on getting out of here sooner or later."

"You've got that right," Marty exclaimed. "I've got a plan to get rid of my debt, start a nest egg and get out of here. I want to find a real OB practice where I can focus on prenatal care, normal deliveries and C-sections. Those are the fun things that I dreamed about when I first started my training. Maybe one day soon, I'll get that opportunity."

Marty had his head in his hands and was rubbing his temples.

"Carla, what is it in your life that gives you the feeling of being trapped by the money of this job? You seem to be way too experienced to be in that position."

"I've been involved in clinic management for fifteen years and this is the first time that I've worked in a clinic like this," she explained. "Several years ago, my husband left my son and me. We haven't heard from him since. It gets a little scary trying to raise a kid by yourself and I was struggling financially. I had all of the right experience, but I had hit the proverbial glass ceiling and still wasn't making ends meet. It was about that time, when I was at my wits' end, that Brad Giovanni called."

"How did he get your name?"

"I had done some consulting work for their clinics. When the work was complete, Brad asked me to stay on."

"So he made you a pretty good offer?"

"Good? I could have worked twenty more years in the direction I was going and not been making what he offered me to start here. It was unbelievable. Now I've got the potential to make even more."

"Don't you think that it's a little odd that most of the key people around here have some personal need that keeps them tied to this place? Do you think the people working here really know what these procedures are all about?"

Carla looked at him with incredulity. "You mean do the employees know that we do abortions here?"

"Of course they know that we do abortions here, that's not what I mean. I'm talking about the way that we sanitize our conversations about 'The Procedure.'" Marty used his hands to emphasize the quotation marks around the procedure. "We never talk about abortion in the clinic. We just talk about the procedure. We never talk about the babies. We just talk about 'Products of Conception.' I'm not sure that the employees know the gory details of what we're doing here."

Marty got up from the chair and walked to the door.

"Come with me. I want to show you something downstairs."

Carla followed Marty down the stairs and through the sterile area surrounding the operating rooms. He led the way to the back of the clinic. They came to a door marked "Clean-up Room."

Marty turned to Carla. "Have you ever been in here?"

"No, but I've heard about it," Carla said with a nervous twinge in her voice.

"It's hard to fully appreciate until you've seen it for yourself. I've only been back here once before."

Marty turned the knob and pushed the door open. Carla gasped and put her hand up to cover her mouth. She was afraid that she might scream. The room had gray metal shelving all around the walls. There were also some freestanding units in the middle of the room. On each shelf were stacks of clear plastic containers with red tops. Each container had varying amounts of dark red fluid and pieces of solid tissue. Carla knew exactly what these were. These buckets contained the POC, or products of conception. This is where the fetuses came after they had been aborted. They stayed in this room until the waste management company came for them.

Carla was stunned to see how many containers there were. Every shelf was full and stacked as high as they could possibly go. Of course she knew how many procedures they performed each day, but seeing them like this put a whole new light on it. Each bucket had a hazardous waste sticker on it. On each sticker, someone had written the patient's last name and the date of the procedure. Very quickly, you could tell that the size of the container was directly related to the length of the pregnancy. The larger containers tended to have more fluid in them. They also had more pieces of tissue floating around.

Carla began to feel herself get nauseated. She rushed out of the Clean-up Room to the restroom. Marty could hear her retching from the hallway.

After several minutes, Carla came out of the restroom. She and Marty silently made their way back upstairs. As they walked by the break room, Marty went in and got them both a Diet Coke. They sat down in Carla's office and neither of them said anything for quite some time.

Finally, Carla spoke up. "When we put together the work schedule, staffing the shift in the Clean-up Room is always the hardest one to fill. I only have a couple of employees who will work in there. Everyone else refuses. Now I understand why."

Marty thought the sight of the POC would overwhelm her. He was pleased that she had reacted that way. He knew that he couldn't become involved with someone too calloused to be affected by that sight. He surprised himself when that thought had entered his mind. He had not planned to begin a new relationship so soon. The more he was around Carla, the more he felt himself being attracted to her. Maybe this job would finally have some aspect of it that would bring him a little happiness. The money was certainly not doing it.

"Carla, I think that we've done enough for one day. Let's finish up and get out of here. Maybe we could meet later for dinner."

Carla looked at him with a surprised look on her face. "I'd like that a lot," she said, as a smile came across her face. She would save the rest of her questions for later.

Chapter 13

Kevin pulled his rental car to a stop in front of his rented lake cabin, just after noon. He had been gone all morning and had made purchases at four different hardware stores. Kevin had split his purchases up between several stores in different towns. He had been to hardware and building supply stores in Hot Springs, Benton, Malvern and Sheridan.

The police, and other authorities, would soon be investigating his mission. He, of course, planned to be long gone. Once the federal authorities got involved in the investigation, it would just be a matter of time before they began to put a trail together that included the location of all of his purchases. He had researched the mistakes that others had made in the past. Most often someone had remembered that the suspect had made an unusually large purchase of materials, and the investigators followed the trail from the site of the crime. He made his purchases from multiple locations to eliminate the suspicion of any one clerk. He didn't plan on being caught on a fluke chance.

He also made what he thought would be his last pickup from Mike Hanks. The package was very special and very dangerous. It had been the one item that would be the most critical to making the first phase of his mission a success. For the remainder of the mission to be successful, he just needed to escape.

Kevin spent the next 20 minutes moving all of his purchases from the back of his SUV into the house. He took his time because of the sensitivity of a number of his purchases. In some cases, the sensitivity was related to the delicate nature of the equipment. In other cases, it was related to the dangerous nature of the material. He had spread his inventory out across the kitchen counters. He was using this as a staging area before moving the supplies downstairs to the basement. He couldn't afford to leave anything in plain view in the main living area of the house. You never knew when someone might come to the door unexpectedly, or peek in the windows to see if he was home. The materials would be stored out of sight.

He went through the laundry room and opened the door to the basement. He flipped on the light switch at the top of the stairs. A light went on down in the basement and cast a faint glow on the stairs. As he went down the stairs, each step creaked, straining from years of inactivity. It was like exercising muscles that had lain dormant for years, moaning from the sudden activity, but never breaking. The spiders had made themselves at home on the staircase and had packed their webs in like the condominiums around the south end of the lake. Before Kevin made it halfway down, he was stopping to wipe the spider webs out of his face and hair. In the dim light, he could not tell where the next spider condo would be. He was moving even slower now, with his hands grasping in the darkness before him, looking to avoid a face to face confrontation with a spider.

At the bottom of the stairs, he was standing on a dirty concrete floor. Oil stains dotted the floor, as reminders of past projects, undertaken by previous occupants. The basement had a stale, musty smell. As the scent permeated his nostrils, Kevin became aware of the dampness in the air. In the middle of the room, there were two workbenches made of wood. Each bench was four feet wide by eight feet long. The benches had been placed end to end to create a long continuous workspace. They were covered in dust and dirt. It was obvious that no one had been using them for quite some time. Against the far wall was a row of old rickety metal shelving. The damp air in the room had been a ready invitation for rust to set in on the shelving. The shelves contained several boxes of old tools and one box of papers left by a previous owner. The remaining details of the room were impossible to see in the dim light. A flashlight would be necessary to complete the inspection.

Kevin stood in the middle of the room surveying the accommodations. He had made a cursory examination of the basement when he first moved into the house. It would work perfectly for the preparation that lay ahead of him. He would have plenty of space to spread out and assemble the next phase of the mission. The basement was situated totally below ground and that eliminated the possibility of any type of accidental discovery.

He spent the next hour cleaning the basement in preparation for the time that he would spend there over the next several days. He cleaned the cobwebs off the stairway, swept the floor of the basement and cleaned off the workbenches. Once again he stood back and surveyed the room, ready to set up the items that he had purchased earlier in the morning.

He carefully brought the sacks and boxes that contained his purchases down the stairs. He unloaded everything and spread it out on the workbenches. Kevin arranged the materials in the order they would be needed in the assembly process. He left space at the end of the workbench, closest to the stairs, for his assembly area. During his earlier inspection of the room, he had found an old metal stool with an aging wooden seat.

He had purchased several flashlights earlier in the day, and he now took one out and put batteries in it. He shined the light around the portions of the room that had been left in the dark by the single dim light bulb that hung overhead. He started to explore the rest of the basement by sifting through the boxes that had been left under the stairs. There he found more boxes of paper that appeared to chronicle the history of the house. One box contained receipts from past purchases. Another box held correspondence received by an occupant of the house fifty years ago.

As Kevin was flipping through the different boxes, he happened to look up and notice a shelf that had been built under the top step of the stairs. Tucked away under the step, so that it was more like a cubbyhole, and it was very difficult to see. He moved one of the boxes around, so that he could stand on it and look into the shelf. He saw three mailing tubes, each one about three feet long. Pulling the tubes out, he stepped down off the box and moved over to the workbench. Kevin emptied the contents of the tubes and spread them out on the surface of the workbench.

Each tube contained the blueprint of a building. One blueprint was of a commercial building of some type. The other two blueprints were of homes. As he examined the blueprints more closely, he realized that one of the homes was the cabin that he was renting. He looked around and spotted several old paint cans on the metal shelving. Grabbing four quart-sized cans, he placed them on the corners of the blueprint to prevent it from curling up. He sat down and began to study the floor plan of the cabin.

The original house, as shown on the blueprint, was no more than a twenty-foot by thirty-foot box. It was designed as a small cabin with screened-in sleeping porches around three sides. By positioning the porches in this manner, it not only gave optimal views of the lake, but it also provided the opportunity for cross breezes to keep the owners and guests cool on hot summer nights.

The date on the original blueprint was in 1931. As the needs of the owners changed, it was obvious from the documentation Kevin was looking at that at least two remodeling projects had taken place over the years.

On a separate, smaller piece of drafting paper, a drawing of the basement was detailed. The date at the bottom of the paper indicated that it had been drawn at the same time as the rest of the original cabin. It appeared that while the basement was built with the original house, it was never included as part of the official drawings of the house. Kevin was puzzling over this bit of information as he spread the drawing of the basement out on the workbench.

He was poring over the drawings when he realized that they contained specifications for an underground tunnel from the basement of the cabin to the lake. Kevin had been in the basement a couple of times and had never seen anything that resembled a tunnel. He looked back at the drawing to find the exact location of the tunnel. After he got his bearings on the drawing, he realized that the tunnel was located just beyond the metal shelving in the corner of the room.

Kevin picked up a flashlight and walked back into the darkness of the corner. Several old yard tools were piled in the corner, along with two empty five-gallon buckets. He shined the flashlight at the wall behind the tools and saw the outline of a door. He moved the tools and buckets away from the wall. Kevin grabbed the broom and swept the cobwebs away from the door. He set the broom down, stood back and illuminated an old, rusty metal door with the flashlight. He reached out and tugged at the handle of the door. It would not budge. The door was stuck from years of non-use. He found a crowbar on a shelf and wedged it between the door and the doorjamb. He tried it at several different points; wiggling the crowbar in as far as he could force it, attempting to loosen the door. He then tried once again to open the door. It gave a little this time. By now, he was drenched with sweat. After working with it for several more minutes, he finally got it open.

He put the crowbar down and picked up the flashlight. Kevin shined the light all around the inside of the tunnel. He could see cobwebs hanging everywhere. It looked like the far end of the tunnel was only about thirty feet away. He grabbed the broom with his free hand and began to ease down the tunnel. He used the broom to clear the cobwebs out of his way. The tunnel was about four feet wide. The walls and floor were lined with bricks. The roof of the tunnel had been formed with heavy four-by-four beams that supported a metal ceiling, by resting crossways across the bricks on each wall. It was not quite tall enough for him to stand upright, so he had to crouch slightly as he made his way to the end of the tunnel. When he came to the door at the lake end of the tunnel, he noticed that the floor of the tunnel was slightly wider. It was five feet from wall to wall at this point. The tunnel floor was slightly damp and it was obvious that water frequently made its way up the passageway. The mustiness of years of exposure to the water hung heavy in the air. He had almost made it to the end of the tunnel when he hit his shin on something solid and tumbled to the ground. The flashlight flew out of his hands as he reached out to catch himself. Kevin crawled over to retrieve the flashlight and then turned and shined it towards the object that had caused him to fall.

Lying on the ground at the end of the tunnel was an old aluminum canoe. The canoe had settled into the mud that had accumulated over the years on the floor of the tunnel. Two wooden paddles were resting on the bottom of the canoe. Like everything else in the basement, the canoe had not been used in quite some time. He stood up and brushed himself off. He moved over to the canoe and walked from one end to the other, about six feet in all, shining the flashlight over every inch of the canoe. Aside from the thick layer of dirt over the small craft, the boat appeared to be in excellent shape.

Kevin peered through the darkness, looking for the way that the canoe had entered the tunnel. The glow from his flashlight cast a dim yellow circle of light on the far wall of the tunnel. He had reached the end. In the middle of the wall was a metal door. By his calculation, the door must lead to the lake. The door was locked with a heavy-duty deadbolt lock that Kevin could turn from the inside of the tunnel. t was designed to keep unwanted visitors from entering the house from the lake. He unlocked the door and gave a hard tug to pull the door open. The door did not move and he again found himself in front of a rusty old door that had become comfortable in its closed state after years of inactivity. Kevin went back to the basement and returned with the tools that he needed to encourage the door to open. After several minutes of straining with all his might, his shirt was soaked with sweat and the door was once again functional.

With the door standing open, it revealed an opening that was overgrown with weeds and vines. He could barely see the lake through the space between the growth. He walked up the tunnel to the basement and picked up a weed eater, pruning shears and a shovel. He went through the house and the back door, to the shoreline. He had not seen a door along the shore when he had been back here in the past. However, he had certainly never been looking for a door. Kevin stopped and looked back at the house. He went over the layout of the basement in his mind and calculated the angle of the tunnel to the lake. He went down to the shore and jumped from the seawall to the dry bed of the lake. The water level of the lake was always down at this time of the year. The Corps of Engineers used the dams on the lake to draw down the level of the lake to allow for maintenance work to be done around the shoreline. He walked about fifteen feet from the dock and swimming area, poking into the underbrush as he went, before he found the opening of the tunnel. He used the tools that he had brought to remove the brush and give clear access to the tunnel.

Kevin stooped through the opening of the tunnel and turned to look back at the lake. It suddenly dawned on him. This was one of those places on the lake that had an escape route from the house to the boat dock. Ever since he was a boy, he remembered hearing stories about the gambling, prostitution and bootlegging that had gone on in this town. Stories were told that the local authorities allowed these activities at locations around the lake, for a fee. The local folklore held that several of these homes and restaurants provided a route of escape to the lake, just in case any uninvited guests came calling. This cabin would have been perfect for this.

Closing the door behind him, he moved up the passageway to the basement. He put the tools back in their place and sat down at the workbench. The materials for the project were laid out before him like an assembly line for any common household appliance. Although many of the components were similar, the appliance that he would build over the next week was far from common.

Kevin rolled the blueprints up and placed them back in their appropriate tubes. He replaced the tubes on the shelf under the stairs and then climbed the stairs back up into the house, turning off the light as he went. He hurried to the bathroom to take a quick shower and get cleaned up. As he quickly went through the motions of his shower routine, he continually thought of his mission. It never left his mind now. Everything he did made him think of the mission. He hated to admit it, but he had become obsessed with it.

He came back dressed in a sweatshirt and a pair of jeans. He put his coat on and went out on the back deck. The back of the house faced a northwesterly direction. Dusk was just settling in over the lake. He had been working on the project all day. The sun had just dropped behind the treetops on the far shore of the lake. The sunset had painted the sky with bright oranges, reds and pinks. The rain had finally let up and it appeared as if the sun and sky were celebrating together on this joyous occasion.

Kevin walked to the end of the dock and sat down. The rainbow of colors in the sky was a shimmering reflection in the lake. He was pleased with his progress today. The completion of the mission was getting really close now. All the necessary pieces had been gathered. The assembly would happen this week. He would spend time on it every night after work and the end of the mission could occur by the end of the week. It was that close. Just the thoughts of finally being that close sent a shiver down his spine.

The sun was now shooting streaks of violet and purple through the sky. He glanced toward the shore as the shadows crept slowly over the seawall. The door to the tunnel was recessed into the seawall. The height of the bank at that point gave a perfect cover for the door. It was practically invisible.

The discovery of the tunnel had been an unexpected, but pleasant surprise. He wondered how many of the guests at the house had ever used the tunnel for an escape. Had the house been used for illegal activities during prohibition? Had the local authorities come knocking on the door? Had the mob used this house in the past? Had a rival gang ever come knocking on the door, sending the guests home through the escape route?

Finding the tunnel had been a stroke of good luck. He had no plans to leave from this house after the mission. He had planned to have everything packed and ready to go before he left for the final stage of the mission. But, you never knew. Wheels had warned him to leave himself an escape route. He had certainly been trained that way. You could never be too cautious. He would have to think that one through.

Darkness had settled over the lake. The winter wind had picked up and the temperature was dropping again. He loved being able to look out over the lake with the quietness all around. It was so peaceful. Over the last several months, Kevin had grown accustomed to the solitude of his existence. He had thought it necessary given the nature of what he was about to do. No one would believe that he would be capable of doing something like this and they would be surprised. In the end, Kevin would be surprised too.

Chapter 14

Carla arrived at the restaurant right on time. Marty was late, as usual. They had agreed to meet at Cheers, a local hangout that was located just off Kavanaugh Street in the Heights. Marty had suggested they meet here for dinner. She waited for him in the entryway to the restaurant.

She couldn't believe how nervous she had gotten while getting ready tonight. It had been a long time since she had been nervous about having dinner with a man. Not that she had dated a lot in recent years. What few dinners she had been out on were business related. Her usual dinner partner was her son Thomas, and for the most part, that was fine with her. For some reason, tonight had struck her as different. Nothing obvious had happened or been said that made her feel this way. But still, there was something that she could not quite put her finger on. Getting together tonight had been so informal that she had not had time to get nervous earlier.

Over the years, dealing with physicians and the pressures of running a business had left her pretty calloused. Though she hated to admit it, her divorce from Thomas' father had also contributed greatly to her increasing lack of sympathy for others. Nervousness about relationships was something she hadn't felt for a long, long time. It kind of surprised her. She didn't expect that with Marty.

His Mazda came quickly around the corner from Kavanaugh Street. He maneuvered the car skillfully into a parking place in front of the restaurant, and hurried inside.

"Hey Carla, sorry I'm late. It seems that I'm chronically trying to cram too much stuff into too little time. How are you doing?"

"Fine and I've only been here for a few minutes so it's no big deal."

"Have you given them our name yet?" Marty was looking around to find the hostess.

"No, I was waiting until you arrived before I did that. I didn't want to get stuck waiting at a table by myself if you decided not to show."

Marty looked at her with surprise on his face. "You didn't think that I would stand you up, did you?"

"Well, not really. I just wanted to be sure," Carla said sheepishly. "Since we hadn't seen each other outside of the office before, I was a little uncertain what to expect from you. I hope that doesn't disappoint you."

Marty gave her a sad look like a whipped puppy. "Yeah I'm just heartbroken. I don't know if I'll ever be the same again." He ducked his head and slumped his shoulders. "I don't know what I'm gonna do."

Carla poked him in the arm. "Oh stop that. You're just making fun of me now."

"I never miss a chance to give someone a good-natured, old-fashioned ribbing."

The hostess finally appeared back at her station. "Two for dinner tonight?"

"Yes ma'am." Marty was giving her his best aw-shucks demeanor. It was coming out as thick as molasses.

She smiled sweetly at him. "Just follow me please."

They were led to a table towards the back of the restaurant. A waiter appeared almost instantly and took their orders for drinks, iced tea for her and a Diet Coke for him. They settled into their table and started soaking up the atmosphere of their surroundings. On the other side of the room from them, a band was playing a pleasing mix of Southern rock and modern country music. The music was loud but they could comfortably hear each other in almost normal conversational tones. Within minutes they were both tapping their feet to the music.

The drinks they had ordered arrived quickly. Marty thanked the waiter as he left them.

"I'll be back in a few minutes to take your order," the waiter said with a slight nod of his head.

"Have you been here before?" Marty asked looking at her.

"No, I haven't. In fact, this is not a part of town that I've spent much time in at all. How about you, I guess you've been here before?"

"Yeah, this is a pretty popular hangout with a lot of the residents and students from the Med Center, cheap food, loud music, close by, what more could you ask for?"

"I haven't spent a lot of time getting out and seeing the sights of Little Rock. Most of my time away from work is spent running Thomas around. The places that we frequent for dinner usually don't make the best restaurants in Little Rock list. Our main requirements are quick, easy and basic. Thomas doesn't like to try a lot of new things."

The waiter stopped at their table, ready to take their order. Carla ordered grilled mahi-mahi with spicy rice and Marty ordered grilled chicken with sweet potato chips. They also ordered cheese dip and chips for an appetizer.

Carla wrinkled her face. "Sweet potato chips? What's that?"

"You're obviously not from around here. Little Rock has a sweet potato thing. We make pies out of 'em. We make fries out of 'em. And we make chips out of 'em. They're great."

"If you say so." Her face conveyed her doubt.

"No really, they really are good. You'll have to try one of mine." Marty was giving her his best sincere look.

"Well you're right about one thing. I'm not from around here."

"Where are you from then? When did you move here? Tell me all about yourself." He put his elbows on the table and leaned forward towards her.

"Thomas and I are from Memphis. In Memphis, we don't do anything with sweet potatoes except let our grandmothers cut them into small chunks and bake them with marshmallows over the top at Thanksgiving and Christmas. We do barbecue in Memphis."

"We do barbecue in Little Rock too." Marty gave her a look that showed he took great offense in being excluded from any barbecue recognition.

"You can be offended if you want to, but you don't do barbecue like we do. Memphis does the best barbecue in the world."

"Now that we've gotten your competitive juices flowing, when was it that you and Thomas moved from the land of barbecue?" His eyes were twinkling with mischief as he made fun of her a little more.

Carla stuck her nose into the air, batted her eyelids and did everything she could to ignore his tackiness. "It was in January of this year, so we've been here almost a year. It's not quite home yet, but we like it."

"Do you have family in Memphis?"

"Most of my family still lives in Memphis. I've got a brother who moved to Atlanta, but otherwise everyone else is there, even my grandmother."

"How old is Thomas?" Marty watched the gleam in Carla's eyes as she talked about her son.

"He's twelve and he's become quite the man of the house. He loves basketball and is always out in the driveway shootin' hoops, as he says. I guess he would play around the clock if I let him."

"Where is he tonight? You should have brought him with you."

"Oh, I wouldn't do that to you. He would have worn you out with his endless questions. He's at the neighbor's house down the street. His best buddy lives there and I'm sure they are outside playing basketball as we speak. I'll pick him up on my way home tonight."

The waiter came back through and refilled their drinks. Carla and Marty had settled into a rhythm of conversation. They had both leaned in closer to better hear one another over the music and the din of conversation and activity in the restaurant. Marty was using his skills developed as a physician to learn all about Carla. It was just like gathering information for a history and physical on one of his patients. He had learned her family and her professional history by the time that they were through with their appetizer. When dinner arrived, he was well on his way to learning her entire personal history as well. Finally, Carla changed the direction of the conversation.

"You've managed to steer this conversation for the better part of an hour and all we've done is hear my life story. With all the questions you've been asking, it reminds me of dinner with my son."

"I'm so sorry. I didn't mean to grill you." Marty folded his hands in front of his chest and bowed his head in a mock show of penance. "I promise that I'll never do it again. Now please ask me anything you want to know."

Carla's face creased with a smile. "That's more like it. Okay, let's start with your family. Where are you from and where is your family living now?"

Marty took a bite of chicken and chewed very slowly and deliberately. He was keeping all expressions off his face. Carla folded her arms across her chest and gave him a scolding look that she usually saved for Thomas.

"Okay, okay, I give up. I'll tell everything, but please don't torture me with that look." He broke out into a big smile. "Let me start at the beginning. I grew up in North Little Rock and lived there until I went to college at Ole Miss. After college, I came to Little Rock for medical school and I've been here ever since."

"That's more like it," Carla said. "What about your family? Where do they live?"

"My father passed away while I was in college. My relationship with my mother was never the same after that. She still lives in North Little Rock and I don't talk to her very much anymore." Marty said this very matter-of-factly.

"I'm sorry to hear about your mother. Did she ever remarry?"

"Yeah, she's remarried about three times now. I think that was the downfall of our relationship. She could never find anyone as good as my father. I think she's still looking and I wish she would never have started."

They both sat quietly eating their dinner for a few minutes. The conversation had taken a somber turn that neither of them had expected.

"Well enough of that kind of talk. What else can I tell you about the life of Marty Smith?"

"What about brothers or sisters, any of those?" Carla was happy to move on to something else.

"I've got one brother. He got a scholarship to go to UCLA and he never came back. He moved to Northern California and got involved in the computer industry. We talk on the phone about once a month and I've been out there once to visit him."

They finished dinner and ordered dessert. Carla had coffee with her dessert and Marty had a refill on his Diet Coke.

"I guess I've never seen you drink anything other than a Diet Coke," Carla said looking at his latest refill. "Do you ever drink anything else?"

"Not very often. Every once in a while I'll drink iced tea, but that's about it. I guess I've just developed a taste for it."

The conversation went on through dessert. It was obvious that they were enjoying each other's company. As the evening was winding down, they had become totally relaxed together. Carla had still not asked him about his dating life and he had not volunteered anything to this point. She was certainly not going to let the moment pass without finding out about any girlfriends that he might have.

"Marty, have you been dating anyone recently?" She looked down at her coffee as she asked him.

"Well now, we're finally getting down to the nitty gritty, aren't we? What took so long to get around to this? I thought you had the reputation for being direct and to the point." Marty was rubbing it in because Carla was known for being so tough at the office.

"Look, can you just answer the question without any sidebar comments? If you had heard all the rumors at the office about your girlfriends, you wouldn't act so surprised." Carla feigned annoyance at him.

"Girlfriends? What girlfriends? What rumors? How come I don't know anything about this?"

"What do you expect, it's no fun to spread rumors if you have to actually talk to the person involved. So, what about it?"

"Okay, I'll tell. I haven't really dated anyone in quite some time. In fact it has been almost a year. I do currently have a female roommate, but we're not dating."

"Oh right, that really looks good." Carla said in disbelief. "I'm convinced." Her sarcasm was dripping onto the table.

"No really, we dated a little right before we moved in together and then it faded as fast as an alcoholic at a Baptist picnic. It's never been anything physical for us and to be honest, I'm not sure why we ever shared a condo in the first place. I guess it was economics or something real noble like that. She's totally focused on becoming a lawyer and I doubt that she will ever focus on anything else. The only reason she asked me to go with her last night was because she was expected to come with a date. I saw her on the way in and on the way out, that's it."

They were quiet for a few minutes. The music from the band had gotten a little louder during the evening. They sat listening to the band, while they both mulled over the turn of the conversation.

Marty was the first one to break the silence.

"You know, I really enjoy being around you and I don't want to do anything that might jeopardize the possibility of starting a relationship with you. I know that this is kind of sudden, but I wanted to tell you that before this night got too far off track. I hope I'm not jumping the gun by saying this."

Carla seemed a little surprised. "I don't think you're jumping the gun. I wasn't really expecting you to say something like that, but I'm glad that you did."

Marty reached over and took Carla's hand. They sat hand in hand for a long time listening to the music and staring at each other.

"I'd like to meet Thomas sometime." Marty was smiling at Carla as he spoke. "I'd like to learn as much about you as I can."

Carla almost blushed. She did not expect him to be so direct. "I want you to meet him. He'll like you."

She was using her fork to play with the remains of her dessert, more out of nervousness than anything else. She couldn't believe that this situation was making her nervous. She was accustomed to dealing with tough situations. Why was she getting so nervous around Marty? she thought to herself. He was very easygoing and he certainly didn't intimidate her, but she still couldn't totally relax yet. Maybe it was just the general thought of dating again. It had been a while for her. Maybe she was afraid that she really wanted it to be a serious relationship.

He startled her out of her private thoughts. "I'm sorry that I put such a damper on our conversation. I have a tendency to blurt things out and sometimes I can be inappropriate."

"Oh, it's okay, you weren't inappropriate. I'm glad that we got that out of the way."

"If it's okay with you, I'd like to take you out to dinner again."

Carla smiled. "I'd like that very much."

The conversation was warming up again.

"You know, dating could make work a little complicated. I've never dated anyone that I've worked with, then again, this is my first real job."

She agreed with him. "Well, after our time in the office this morning, it sounds like it wouldn't take very much for either of us to be persuaded to leave the clinic."

"You've got that right," Marty exclaimed.

Carla was watching Marty closely. "Were you serious about changing jobs?"

"You bet I was. Doing abortions full-time is not at all what I had in mind when I trained. I wish that the money had not been such a big deal to me when I was getting out of residency, but it was. I was really worried after the first several interviews when I didn't get an offer."

"Where do you think that you might be able to go? Are there any other good opportunities out there?"

"Sooner or later something will open up. At some point in time, female obstetricians will become commonplace and not so much of a novelty. Everybody will have one, so it won't be a big deal anymore. People will get back to a focus on finding the best person for the job regardless of gender. Hopefully that won't take too long."

The waiter brought their check and Marty put cash down on the table to cover it.

"Are you ready to go?"

"Sure," she said sliding her chair back.

Marty quickly jumped up and helped her as she rose out of the chair. They moved out of the restaurant and stopped in the small courtyard in front of the building. They turned toward each other to say goodbye.

Marty was holding her hand and looked into her eyes. "I really enjoyed this tonight."

"Me too," Carla said holding his gaze. "I hope that the conversation didn't get too heavy for a first date."

"I think it was fine." Marty reached for her other hand and took it in his, as they stood facing each other. "I'll call you and we'll do this again. Maybe Thomas can come with us the next time."

"That would be nice." Carla liked him even more for including Thomas. "I bet we can find a time that will work."

Marty leaned over and kissed her lightly on the cheek.

"Good night, Carla. You drive safely going home."

"Good night, Marty."

They turned and headed to their respective cars both smiling over the pleasant surprise that the evening had brought and both hoping that it would be the start of something long-term.

Chapter 15

The day was bright and beautiful. The sky was a brilliant blue with white cumulus clouds moving slowly high above the ground. It was a welcome relief from the incessant rain of the past few weeks. A cool December breeze made it the perfect morning and reminded everyone that winter was still lurking around the corner.

The crowd coming into the First Fellowship Church seemed to be arriving earlier than usual. When Kevin McLaughlin took his seat towards the rear of the sanctuary just under the edge of the balcony, he noticed that an excited buzz seemed to fill the air. The congregation had a sense of anticipation about them.

The service began in the usual way. The choruses of praise were sung. Prayers were offered. The crowd this morning was more excited than normal. Kevin noticed that everyone appeared to be participating in the singing and prayer time. He knew that this day would be special for him. He came to the service this morning with the expectation that something different was going to happen.

As the singing continued, the songs became more emotional. The worship leader was really on a roll now. He had worked the crowd into a worship frenzy. Many were waving their hands in the air as they sang loud and strong with the worship leader. Between each song, he had words of encouragement to further inspire the crowd.

Although Kevin was not one to show strong public displays of worship, he felt himself being caught up in the emotion of the moment. He was swaying with the music now and his hands were raised. Something very special was going to happen today, he could feel it.

One of the church leaders, the chairman of the deacons George Ferguson, climbed the steps to the stage and took a position behind the pulpit. He led the church in prayer in preparation for the message that the pastor was about to bring.

As he finished the prayer and moved off the stage, a quiet stillness filled the auditorium. With almost twelve hundred people in the service, it was amazing that it could remain that quiet. It was so quiet that Kevin was concerned that the people sitting in the pew with him could hear his heart beating. He was so excited about this moment that it felt like his chest would split open from the pounding of his heart. He was ready for this. For months now, he had the sense that his time would come soon. He thought that he knew his calling, but he really wanted some other confirmation. Somehow, the time seemed right for him this morning. Maybe there would be something in the sermon that would help him. He had not doubted his mission before, but with the time for completing the mission nearing, he really wanted some assurances that he was on the right track.

* * * * *

Pastor Bill Roberts took the stage. The suit he wore was of the latest fashion. It was a three-button jacket and it was made of the finest Italian silk. The material was black in color and so fine and pure that it glistened under the harsh lights of the stage that illuminated the area so brilliantly for the television cameras. Brother Bill, as his congregation knew him, had almost quit wearing neckties. This morning he was wearing a rounded-collar shirt that he had buttoned to the neck. The shirt was a deep charcoal gray color that gave just the right contrast to his suit. He wore an oversized Rolex watch that inevitably peeked out from the end of his left shirtsleeve as he reached or stretched his arms out to the congregation.

Brother Bill moved to the pulpit and a hush came over the crowd. He placed his Bible and his notes on the podium. With a deliberate gaze, he slowly took in the entire auditorium, looking from right to left.

* * * * *

Bill Roberts was looking over the crowd. They were waiting expectantly. The setting was perfect and his staff performed according to his plan, of course, as they always did. They had the congregation primed and ready for him. He had laid the groundwork in previous sermons and today would be the big day. Today would launch him to new heights of visibility. After the sermon today, he would be known far and wide. He would become the new spokesperson for the unborn.

Bill adjusted his notes on the podium and then he moved to the side and leaned against the podium. He looked directly into their eyes all around the auditorium. He had a special way of connecting to his audience and he knew it. He knew that each one of them would feel as if he was speaking to them personally.

He began quietly and solemnly.

"I have something to share with you this morning that has been weighing heavy on my heart for some time. You have heard me speak of it before, but it has become critical that we deal with this issue head on. Many times in our culture today we have a tendency to sidestep the hard issues. Many times in our culture today we do not want to deal directly with our brothers and sisters in their sin. Many times in our culture today we are unwilling to confront sin in our community. But today, my friends," Brother Bill's voice had risen in volume and he paused for effect, "today, my friends, that has to change."

He paced to the other side of the stage and looked directly into the camera. His hands were together, fingertip to fingertip, in front of him.

With a calm steady voice, he began again. "Today we are going to talk about a crisis that has invaded our country. This crisis is eroding the moral fabric of our nation. This crisis is destroying the future of our country. Today I want to talk to you about abortion."

As he was speaking, he paced back and forth across the stage. He moved slowly, turning to face the congregation every couple of paces. The sound crew had equipped him with a wireless microphone. It gave him unrestricted movement while he was speaking. He used every square foot of space that was available on the stage. The choir was seated behind him. He made a great effort to get them involved in the sermon. With the constant movement on the stage and the dramatic way in which he gestured with his arms and hands, the audience could not help but stay riveted on him. And he knew it.

From a very early age, he had possessed amazing oratorical skills. His time in college and the seminary had honed these skills into a tool that he could use with surgical precision. With these skills, he could motivate people to actions that they would have never considered before, and he knew it. If everything went according to plan, he would accomplish that today.

"In 1973, we, in America, legalized abortion. We legalized the killing of innocent children. Legalized murder." Bill stopped and looked into the crowd. He spoke again with a little more authority and volume in his voice. "Well that is what we are doing. Is it not? You know, my friends, that abortion has killed over thirty-seven million children in our country alone. You know, my friends, that we now allow abortions to be performed through the ninth month of pregnancy. Do you know that with today's technology, babies born as early as the sixth month of pregnancy have a chance for survival?" He was looking right into the camera again. "Actually, babies have been known to survive after birth as early as twenty weeks into pregnancy. Can you imagine that? In one room of a hospital, you can have a medical team doing everything they can to save the life of a premature baby, born at twenty weeks. In another room, you can have a team working to kill a baby at twenty weeks. I don't get it. What are we thinking? How could this make sense to any civilized nation?"

He stopped at the front of the stage and folded his arms across his chest. He raised his left hand, with his index finger extended, to his chin, in a pose of reflection. He was shaking his head as he began to speak again.

"Thirty-seven million. How do we explain that? Do we try to convince ourselves that they are not really people? I really don't think we can do that. We've looked at those Scriptures before. We know what the Word of God says about it. If you read the same Book that I do, it is very plain God knows us before we are formed in our mother's womb."

He was pacing again. He had yet to look at his notes since he had started his sermon and he had not missed a beat yet. He had this one down. It would be delivered unlike any sermon he had ever preached before. He was ready.

"Thirty-seven million people. Many people today say that it is all about choice. A woman should have the right to choose. Have we sacrificed thirty-seven million babies on the altar of choice? Are we not taking away the choice of life from those who cannot speak for themselves? Are we allowing the commission of murder to give more choices to people who have already proven that they are not very good at making choices anyway?"

He had clasped his hands behind his back as he paced. He stopped and turned to the congregation. With a loud voice he bellowed.

"Thirty-seven million people. Thirty-seven million human beings. Thirty-seven million living, breathing beings created by God Almighty. My friends, when Nazi Germany was responsible for the deaths of six million Jewish people, we were horrified. We called it war crimes. The world put the people responsible for those crimes on trial for murder. My friends, we have sat back and watched while more than six times that many people have been killed. In 1945, the world looked on these atrocities as a holocaust. Today we look at the atrocity of abortion as freedom of choice. Are we so enlightened that we cannot distinguish between right and wrong anymore? Have we focused on ourselves so much that we have forgotten that Jesus has called us to be a light to the world? How can we say that we are light when we stand by and watch the slaughter of thirty-seven million people? Are we any different from those who allowed the slaughter of six million Jews during World War II?"

He was standing in front of them now at the front of the stage. His arms were stretched to the ceiling and his gaze was fixed on heaven. The entire auditorium was bathed in silence. The audience was holding its collective breath, waiting for him to start again. He slowly dropped his arms to his side. He looked out into the audience and began to speak directly to them as he pointed the index finger on his right hand at them.

"Do you know what it says in the Bible about the sacrifice of children?" He paused and it was deathly quiet throughout the entire sanctuary. "Well, do you?" He was shouting now. "I'll tell you what the Scripture says. In Deuteronomy, the Scripture tells us that it is an abomination to the Lord for innocent blood to be shed. In fact, the Lord specifically warns against the sacrifice of children. In the Book of Joel, the prophet tells us that, 'Egypt will become a waste, and Edom will become a desolate wilderness, because of the violence done to the sons of Judah, in whose land they have shed innocent blood.' Did you hear that?"

He was leaning forward from the front of the stage with his hand cupped around his ear. His voice was booming so loudly that it virtually echoed off the walls.

"Well did you?" He dropped his hand from his ear and put both of his hands on his hips. "Well if you know anything about Egypt, you know that it is pretty much a wasteland. And does anybody know anything about Edom? No, of course not, because it has been wiped off of the face of the earth! All of this because of the shedding of innocent blood."

He was pacing again, scratching his chin, and gesturing with his arms. He was in constant motion.

"In Psalms chapter one hundred and six, verse thirty-seven and thirty-eight, it says, 'They sacrificed their sons and daughters to the demons, and shed innocent blood, the blood of their sons and their daughters, whom they sacrificed to the idols of Canaan; and the land was polluted with the blood.' Then it says in verse forty and forty-one, 'The anger of the Lord was kindled against His people and He abhorred His inheritance. Then He gave them into the hand of the nation and those who hated them ruled over them.' The Scriptures are full of examples that demonstrate how God punishes those who shed the blood of innocent people. God does not have a history of dealing in a merciful way with these people. He has been harsh in His judgment of them."

He had stopped at the pulpit and grabbed both sides with his hands. He sternly looked into the eyes of his congregation.

"The verses that I have just shared with you demonstrate God's response when His people are disobedient. In these verses, the people were disobedient and followed the ways of the world. Many of us today are following the ways of the world, instead of following God's ways. As Christians, we are commanded to change the world. Instead we are allowing the world to change us. The voting record of Christians is the same as non-Christians; the divorce rate in the church is the same as in the world. Instead of reforming the heathen world, we have commingled with them and become just like them. Just as the Israelites turned to the gods of the Canaanites, as we just heard, so too are Christians today turning to the idols of the world. Many Christians today are serving the same idols: materialism, money, education, career and selfishness. We are putting ourselves in the same position that the people of Israel did many years ago. We are doing those things that God hates. We are doing those things that cause God to turn His people over to the enemy."

He moved to the front of the platform and paused momentarily before taking two of the four steps down to the floor of the auditorium. He stood there talking to them as you would to an old friend.

"Maybe you agree with everything that I have said this morning. Maybe you hate the shedding of innocent blood just like God does. Maybe you hate abortion just like God does. But you have not participated in this horrible sin. You haven't had an abortion. You haven't been involved in the promotion of legalized abortions. You say, 'I don't have anything to be guilty of, do I?' Maybe you need to think about that again. In the twentieth chapter of Leviticus, the Scriptures tell us of God's attitude towards pacifism on this issue. God says that if we, as a community, ignore a man who sacrifices his children to idols, then He will turn His face from us. Did you hear that?"

He stepped back up to the top of the platform, pausing between each step. He never missed a beat with his sermon. He was speaking as he went. The crowd was mesmerized by his performance.

"Are we called to a higher level of accountability? Although it is legal to kill unborn children in our country, are we held to a higher moral code? Does the Scripture that we have talked about this morning indicate to us that we should look beyond the laws of our country and rest solely on the laws that God has given us? I think so."

He voice was becoming louder. The scowl on his face was becoming darker. His gestures were much more intense.

"If you remember the story of the birth of Moses, the great leader of the Jewish people, you have an example of one of the great acts of civil disobedience. When Moses was born, Pharaoh had given a decree in the land. The decree stated that any male child born to the Jewish people should be drowned in the Nile. Moses' mother decided that she would not obey the law of the land. She made a conscious decision to engage in civil disobedience. So instead of drowning in the Nile River, Moses floated on it and God used him for a great purpose. Because of one woman's disobedience to the laws of the nation that she was living in, God was able to use her son for a mighty work."

He paused and waited. He wanted them to squirm in their seats. He wanted them to be uncomfortable with the silence. He stood there waiting, looking out over the crowd.

"We have allowed the politicians of our day to determine the morals of our country. Our politicians are compromising their pro-life position in the hope that it will gain them a political advantage. And we have let them do it. We have convinced ourselves that we can compromise on abortion, as long as the economy is going well. We have convinced ourselves that we can compromise on abortion, as long as Social Security is safe. We have convinced ourselves that we can compromise on abortion, as long as our candidate meets most of our other measurements."

His voice was rising and he was rocking back and forth on the balls of his feet. His hands were grasped firmly in front of him.

"I am here to tell you that God is not happy with our conduct in this matter. Are we to stand for compromise or for conviction? Are we to stand for compromise or for righteousness? Are we to stand for compromise or for justice?"

He was at the critical point in his message. He was going to set the hook. He could tell by the look in their eyes that he had them.

"Our nation is at a crossroads today. The days of fence sitting are over. We must not let our politicians get away with it. We must make them commit. And if they are against the Word of God, then we must get them out of office. In 1964 after receiving the Republican nomination for President, Barry Goldwater made the following statement in his acceptance speech. He said, 'I would remind you that extremism in the defense of liberty is no vice. And let me remind you also that moderation in the pursuit of justice is no virtue.'"

"Have we become so passive in our Christianity that we are unwilling to be extreme in our defense of liberty? Have we developed such moderation in the pursuit of justice that the shedding of innocent blood does not bother us? Are we prepared to sit by and do nothing and accept God's judgment?"

He was standing at the podium. He had leaned over the podium and grabbed the front edge. He was beginning to reel them in. He began loudly.

"Our approach has been passive. We should be ashamed of our efforts. Each year over a million unborn children are put to death at the hands of abortionists that hide behind the medical and legal communities. While this innocent blood is being shed, we sit idly by. We think we are clean and guiltless. But, our hands are stained with blood. Our shoes are splattered with the blood of these innocent children as if we were in the operating rooms ourselves. What have you personally done to stop this tragedy? Are you willing to be extreme in your defense of liberty and your pursuit of justice? We have to change our response to this sin in our nation. We have to be willing to do whatever is necessary to rid our nation of the stain of innocent blood."

His voice had reached a crescendo.

"Yes, my friends, it has to change now. Let me tell you a story that I found in the Bible in the book of Joshua. Joshua had taken over as leader of the people of Israel after the death of Moses. God was directing Joshua on the conquest of the land of Canaan, the Promised Land. The Israelites had won a battle at Jericho. It was after this that they came to the city of Ai. After being defeated by the people of Ai in their first attempt, they attacked again. Remember that the people of Ai were Canaanites. They were evil people. They engaged in the practice of child sacrifice. They were old hands at the shedding of innocent blood. God commanded Joshua to utterly destroy the city and its inhabitants. And that is exactly what Joshua did.

"Yes my friends, the time has come for change. We must change and take our responsibility for the innocent seriously. We must be willing to utterly destroy the sin of abortion in our country. God instructed Joshua to burn the city to the ground and destroy all the inhabitants of Ai. What is He calling you to do to eradicate the sin of abortion from our nation?"

He moved down the steps in front of the stage. He was standing on the auditorium floor, speaking to them in a prayerful tone.

"Are you willing to respond to the call of God today? Are you willing to take His fight against sin into our community? Can you be bold? Can you be extreme? Don't wait another day. Innocent lives will depend on you every day. Come now and respond to this message."

His face was full of emotion. He was gesturing to them, motioning them to come to the front of the auditorium, beckoning them to respond. And they were moving to the front from all over the auditorium. hey were responding.

* * * * *

Kevin couldn't believe it. The message was made for him. God must be speaking directly to him. A chill was running up and down his back. It had to be for him. He was overwhelmed. He had never before been spoken to so directly in a sermon. Wow! It was unbelievable. He had to complete his mission. He knew that it was his destiny to strike out against this horrible sin. It was his calling. He had the skills to do it and he wouldn't let God down. He had a plan and he knew it would work. Now, he had the public blessing of his pastor.

As all these thoughts were swirling through Kevin's mind, he was looking around the auditorium. He wondered if anyone else had heard this message like he did. Across the auditorium, he caught the eye of Mike Hanks. Mike was watching him. As Kevin stared, Mike nodded his head. It was all Kevin needed for a final confirmation. He decided right then that he would finish the mission before the end of the week.

* * * * *

Bob and Barbara Jones walked out of the sanctuary after the service and crossed the parking lot to their car. Bob slid in behind the steering wheel and sat there too stunned to move. Both of his hands were gripping the steering wheel with such force that his knuckles were turning white.

"What was that?" he asked his wife. "Did I really hear him say we need to take things into our own hands? Did he say for us to get extreme? Is that what he said? What do you think he meant by that?"

"Surely we must have misunderstood him, Bob. I know that God dealt with the people in the Old Testament days differently than He did after Christ came."

"Yeah, that's what I thought. God had to deal with the children of Israel differently. God always manages to deal with us where we are in our life. I guess I always thought that the wiping out of cities was God's way of dealing with sin in the Old Testament. I mean I'm not a biblical scholar or anything, but I've been around here long enough to know that he's taking the Scripture out of context. He's twisting it around to fit his needs, whatever they are. I think that God has other ways for us to deal with sin today. I thought that God was supposed to judge man. With a sermon like that, it sounds like we've already taken care of the judging part and now Brother Bill wants us to carry out the sentence."

"Now Bob, we're overreacting. I'm sure no one else felt that way. Besides, I don't think that anyone would ever do what you're insinuating."

Bob just sat there in shock, unable to bring himself to start the car.

* * * * *

John Baker was stretched out on his couch in the living room of his home. He had sat down over an hour ago with the Sunday newspaper. He had just started reading the paper, when the broadcast of the morning services of the First Fellowship Church came on. It was broadcast over one of the local access cable channels that are picked up over all of central Arkansas.

John's ears perked up immediately when Bill Roberts' message began. John was the news director for one of the local network affiliates. He was always interested in a good story. By the time the service was over, John found that he had become so engrossed with the message that he had put everything else down. He had not even finished the front page of the paper. He couldn't believe what he had heard. They had to get on this right away. He called his best reporter.

"Darren, this is John. I just heard the most amazing thing on the local cable channel this morning. There's a preacher down in Hot Springs that is calling for the eradication of abortion from our country."

"What's so amazing about that? Some fanatic is always pushing the abortion button."

"Yeah, I know that, but this was different. He was calling his congregation to extreme measures."

"What kind of extreme measures?"

"He didn't come right out and say. That's where you come in. I want you to go down there tomorrow and find out exactly what he means. You might want to watch a tape of the sermon in the studio before you go. It's pretty good entertainment."

"Alright, I'll get on it first thing tomorrow."

"You'll probably have fun with this, Darren. I think this guy is crazy."

With that, John went back to reading the Sunday paper.

Chapter 16

Courtney Ferguson was sitting in her junior English class looking at the calendar that she kept in her purse. The nausea had started last Friday. It was Monday morning and she was still nauseated. Over the weekend, she thought that she might have the flu. There was a lot of that going around her school.

Her period was late. Courtney kept hoping that the nausea was just the flu, but she was beginning to panic. She and her boyfriend Shaun had let things go a little too far one Friday night after a football game. They had never done that before. They had never had sex until that night. In fact, she had been a virgin. She was worried now. Surely she couldn't be pregnant. She had only had sex once in her entire life. It must be the flu.

While her English teacher was droning on about some boring dead poet, she was counting the days since her last period. It came to exactly six weeks. She had never been this late before. It could be the flu. She knew two other kids in her first period class who came down with the flu last week. She could have caught it from them. She was around them in Chemistry lab.

What if she was pregnant? It would be terrible. Her parents would freak. Shaun would freak too. He had been asking her if she was all right ever since that night. How would he react? Would he still love her? How would she tell her friends? Maybe she wouldn't have to tell them.

Another wave of nausea swept over her and she almost threw up. She needed to get out of there and get something in her stomach. She needed a cracker or something. Just a little something to settle the queasy feeling that she was having. Maybe it was just the flu.

The bell rang, ending the class and Courtney bolted out the door and ran to the cafeteria. She grabbed a package of crackers from the salad bar stand and put her money in the machine to get a 7-Up. She sat down by herself in the cafeteria to eat the crackers. As she washed the crackers down with the 7-Up, the queasiness in her stomach began to subside. She was feeling better, but maybe she should try one of those home pregnancy tests just to be sure. She would stop on the way home and get one from the drugstore. Taking the test would help ease her mind. She was certain that it was a touch of the flu.

* * * * *

The telephone had been ringing off the wall all morning at the First Fellowship Church. Everyone was calling about the message that Brother Bill had given at the morning service the day before. The receptionist had been fielding most of the calls. The callers had a variety of responses to the sermon. Almost 80 percent of the calls were expressing some degree of support for the way that Brother Bill had interpreted this issue. Out of the 80 percent, almost a fourth of those indicated a willingness to become radical for the cause. The remaining 20 percent of the calls ranged from crank calls to callers expressing indignation over the fanatical tone of the message.

Betty was keeping a list of all the calls she received and the callers' level of interest. Brother Bill had given her several key groupings that he was interested in tracking. One of the groupings was the people who expressed a desire to become physically involved in the new movement for the unborn. A second group was those who were more radical in their approach. A third grouping represented individuals interested in donating money for the effort. The last category was for the media.

Midway through Monday morning, Betty received the first media call. The light flashed on her phone indicating a transfer from the receptionist. When she picked it up, she heard the voice of the receptionist.

"Betty, line one is a guy from the media in Little Rock. I think that he's with one of the television stations. His name is Darren something. I didn't catch the end of it."

Betty rolled her eyes. "Please try to get complete information next time. It's hard enough trying to keep up with all these phone calls, please don't make it any harder."

"Yes ma'am, I'll do my best." The receptionist responded with a tinge of sarcasm in her voice.

Betty punched the button for line one on her phone and picked up the receiver. "This is Dr. Bill Roberts' office, Betty speaking, may I help you?"

Darren Cooke was on the other end of the line. "Betty, this is Darren Cooke with KBTE-TV in Little Rock. I am a reporter for the station. I saw a tape of Dr. Roberts' sermon that he gave yesterday morning and I was wondering if I might be able to speak with him about his message."

"Well Mr. Cooke, Dr. Roberts spends each morning in his office studying. He cannot be disturbed. Could I take a message and have him call you back?"

"Yes ma'am, you could do that, but on second thought, do you handle his scheduling?"

"I sure do."

"Do you think that it might be possible for me to schedule a time to meet with him for an interview?"

"It is possible, but I would need to confirm it with him before we could finalize it. What would you like to speak with him about specifically?"

"I would like to get his thoughts on the pro-life movement and its resurgence in Arkansas and around the country. He seems to have some definite ideas on the direction the movement should take and I would like to speak with him about it."

"Mr. Cooke, I think that he would be interested in visiting with you about those issues. I'll still need to confirm it with him. How about tomorrow afternoon, around 2:00?"

"That would be great, Betty. I'll be there."

"Let me get your phone number and if there is any problem with this time I'll call you after I've spoken with Dr. Roberts. Let me also give you directions to our church."

They shared information and ended their conversation. The lines were flashing again on Betty's phone, but she ignored them for the moment. She pressed the intercom button on her phone and rang into Brother Bill's office.

"I'm studying, Betty. You know I don't like to be interrupted." It was the first thing he said when he picked up the phone.

"I know, Brother Bill, but you said you wanted to know as soon as the media contacted us. I just got off of the phone with a reporter from one of the network affiliates in Little Rock. He wants to interview you."

"What did you tell him?"

"I set up an appointment for tomorrow at 2:00 p.m., just like you said."

A smile came across Bill Roberts' face. It was working just like he thought it would.

"Thanks, Betty, good job. Let me know if you get any more."

He released the intercom button and he was alone with his thoughts once again. Now he had something interesting to study. He would approach this interview just like he did everything else. His preparation for the interview would far exceed that of the reporter. He would have all of the facts and figures at his fingertips. He would be ready. The world would soon know about a new champion for the unborn. His rocket of fame was about to launch, and he was ready for the ride.

* * * * *

Oh no, I can't be pregnant. Courtney was sitting in her bathroom staring at the home pregnancy test in her hands. The plus sign was blue, indicating a positive result. She was pregnant and didn't know what to do. Her parents would go ballistic, especially her dad. They were extremely conservative, and not very tolerant about things like pregnant teenagers.

What was she going to do about this? She had always been able to talk to her parents about everything. This was going to be different. She knew what she had done was wrong. Her parents had taught her better than to get herself in this type of situation. She had messed up and now she was going to have to pay the consequences.

Maybe she could take care of this without her parents finding out. She could get one of her friends to take her to see a doctor and get an abortion. Her mind was full of questions. How long does it take to get an abortion? How long do you hurt afterwards? Do they put you to sleep? What does it feel like when it's over? After you're pregnant, when does it really become a baby? She knew from Biology class that during the first part of pregnancy it's called a fetus. But what is a fetus? Is a fetus a baby? She couldn't remember enough about the human reproduction part of her Biology class to answer all these questions.

She couldn't really have an abortion, could she? Just yesterday in church Brother Bill talked about how evil abortion was. He called it murder. Is it really murder? Would I be murdering my baby?

Who could she turn to for advice? She knew that expecting anything from Shaun was wishful thinking. He really wasn't much help with the big things. Her friends at school wouldn't be of any help either. They were much more into money, clothes and cars than knowing what to do about something like pregnancy.

The tears began to well up in her eyes. She had been pretty strong about this problem so far, but it was beginning to be more than she could bear. As the tears rolled down her cheeks, she began to feel hopeless. She didn't really have a place that she could turn for answers. Courtney had never felt more alone than she did at this very moment.

Within a few moments, she was sobbing uncontrollably. She fell unto her bed and buried her face in her pillow. How could she have ever let herself get into a position like this? She knew better. Who would have ever thought that having sex one time would lead to this? Why did this have to happen to her? She knew of plenty of girls in her school that talked about having sex all the time. Why did she have to get pregnant? Those other girls deserved it much more than she did. She was the good one. Everybody always looked at her as being one of the best kids at school. She was never in any trouble. She studied hard and made good grades. She went to church all the time and was active at school in all the important clubs. Why was she the one who got pregnant?

Her tears stopped for a moment. She rolled over on her bed at looked at the ceiling.

"God, why did you let this happen to me?" She said it audibly. She lay there as if waiting for an audible response. The tears came again and soon she was sobbing. Courtney could see her future going down the drain. Everything she had worked for would be wiped out if she had a baby.

She would have to tell her parents. There was no way to get around it. How would they react? They wouldn't be very excited about becoming grandparents. She would tell them tonight after dinner. That would give her a few hours to get her thoughts together and try to make it go as well as possible.

* * * * *

Marty Smith had finished another long day at the clinic. His enthusiasm was fading fast for this kind of work. He had performed twenty-six procedures today. Not a single patient was over the age of eighteen. It was depressing to think that so many people looked at their pregnancy as unwanted.

His patients today came from all over Arkansas and every surrounding state. It was amazing how many wanted to escape from their local environment to have an abortion. They didn't want their neighbors to know. They were willing to travel to another state to keep anyone from finding out. If the choice of abortion was such a wonderful thing for women, why did they all go to so much trouble to keep it a secret?

He walked out of the OR and threw the latex gloves and the paper surgical mask into the trashcan in the hallway. He went over to the phone by the nurses' station and dialed a number in administration. Patsy answered the phone on the second ring and transferred his call to Carla.

The phone rang and Carla picked it up.

"Hello, this is Carla Sharkley, may I help you?"

"Hey Carla, this is Marty. Are we still on for tonight?"

"Of course, dinner at my house at seven o'clock. Thomas is really looking forward to meeting you."

"Well I'm anxious to meet him also. Do you need me to bring anything? I can stop on the way."

"No, I think I've got everything covered. f I think of anything else, I'll call you."

"Okay, I'll see you at seven."

* * * * *

Dinner was very routine that night. The weather had begun to turn colder and the skies were clouding up again. The conversation around the table was low-key and steady. Courtney tried to participate as usual, but it was hard for her to stay focused. Her mind felt that it had heavy weights tied to it. Every time she tried to think of something else, the weights brought her back down to the pregnancy. She could think of nothing else.

Her mother had just poured coffee for her dad and herself. As she was sitting down, she said, "Courtney, you seem a little distracted tonight, is there something wrong?"

Courtney was using her fork to move the food around on her plate. "Yes ma'am, there is. I've got a problem I need to talk to you and Dad about."

Her dad set his coffee cup down and said, "What is it, Court? Is it something we can help you with?"

"Well I hope so. I tried to think of some other way around this, but it just seems impossible. I really don't have any place else to turn."

Her dad gave a little chuckle and said, "I hope that you don't always think of me and your mother as the choice of last resort."

"Now George, Courtney seems to be very upset by something. Let's not make a joke about it." Her mother was always very intuitive about these kinds of things.

"I'm sorry, Courtney. Tell us what's bothering you. We'll try to help if we can." Her dad took the mild scolding from her mother to heart.

"This is really going to be hard. I'm not sure that I know where to start." She paused. She was still playing with her food. It was obvious that she was extremely nervous. The butterflies in her stomach were flying at a rapid speed with no apparent pattern.

She put her fork down and looked directly at her mother. "Mom and Dad, I think that I'm pregnant." She glanced over at her dad and then back to her mom.

"What do you mean?" her dad blurted out.

"I mean that my period is late and I took a home pregnancy test this afternoon. It was positive."

The silence was so thick in the room that you could barely breathe. Her dad put his coffee cup down. His face was beginning to flush red.

"How could this happen? What's been going on that your mother and I didn't know about?"

Her mother interrupted. "Are you sure? You know that those home pregnancy tests can sometimes give false readings," her mother said.

"Who's responsible for this? Do you know who the father is?" Her father's blood pressure was rising. You could always tell with her dad.

The tears were coming to her eyes again.

"Of course I know who the father is. I've only had sex once and it was with Shaun. Daddy, I'm responsible too. He didn't make me do it."

"Why did you do this, Courtney? What are people going to think?" Her dad had buried his head in his hands.

Her mother spoke up. "George, we have more important things to think about than what other people think. Our daughter is having a major crisis in her life. We can't be worried about other people."

"Mom, I'm so sorry. I can't believe this is happening to me. I make one mistake and now I've ruined my life."

The tears were streaming down her face now. So far this conversation wasn't helping her sense of hopelessness.

"Courtney, you can't have a baby right now. This would be terribly embarrassing to our family. We are a well-respected family in the community. We are leaders in our church. How would it look for us to have an illegitimate grandchild? How would we ever live that down? Plus the fact that pregnancy would ruin your chance to go to West Point and that's something that you've always dreamed of doing."

"What do you mean, Daddy?" Courtney was beginning to sob again.

"I mean that you can't be pregnant right now, much less have a baby. It would be disastrous for you and for our family. I don't think that you should have that baby."

"What do you mean, George?" Her mother was bristling at the end of the table.

"Yeah, Daddy, I'm not sure I understand?"

"I mean that she should terminate this pregnancy. She is too young to have a baby. It will ruin her life and our family."

"You can't be serious, George! You're talking about Courtney getting an abortion. It would be wrong for us to even consider that option."

"It was also wrong for Courtney to have sex without being married. Because of that one wrong decision, her entire life is going to change. Our life is going to change." He was looking at his wife when he said this.

"Daddy, isn't abortion wrong? Isn't that what we heard in church yesterday?"

"Of course it's wrong, Courtney, but you've left us with no other choice. You've put us in a situation that's impossible to fix any other way."

"But Daddy, what if I don't want to get an abortion? Couldn't I put the baby up for adoption?"

Her dad was pacing in the kitchen now.

"I'm sorry, Daddy. I...I...I didn't mean to upset you." She was sputtering to talk now between the gasps for breath from crying so hard.

"You're sorry? Now is a fine time to think of being sorry."

"George, don't you think that we should take our time and think through this? This is a big problem. Maybe we should think about it before we jump to any immediate solutions. Getting an abortion is a major event. It can leave scars for a lifetime."

"Of course getting an abortion is a major event, almost as major as getting pregnant. Can you imagine what this will do to our marriage?" He was looking at his wife now, with his hands on his hips.

He stopped right beside Courtney's chair and knelt down to look at her eye to eye.

"Courtney, I know this is a major decision to make," her father said. "But, I am dead serious about ending this pregnancy. I think that it will be the right thing for you to do in the long run. I am so serious about this that I am willing to do whatever it takes for you to make the right decision. If that means that I have to take your car away from you to get your attention, then I'll do it. If that means that I have to make you quit your job, then I'll do it. If that means that I have to restrict you to this house, then I'll do it. Whatever it takes, I'll do it. Do you understand what I'm saying? For years, you've had a goal to attend West Point. Well guess what – they don't allow cadets with babies at West Point. Even if you gave the baby up for adoption, it would sidetrack your preparation to get into the Academy. You need to take care of this pregnancy and never look back."

She nodded at him with tears dripping off her chin. He stood and turned towards her mother who was still seated at the end of the table.

"Your mother may not agree with me on this decision right now, but in the end, she'll see that it was the best decision to make, given the cards that we've been dealt. I'm sorry that I have to be so harsh, but you've really left me with no other choice."

He moved to his place at the table and sat down. He slumped in his chair, with the burden of the decision obviously weighing heavy on his mind.

"I'll make some calls tomorrow to find out whom you can see about getting this resolved," her father said. "Does anyone else know about this?"

"No, Daddy, you and mom are the only ones I've told," she said as she wiped the tears from her face.

"I think that it would be best if we kept it that way. The fewer people who know about this problem, the better." He had his head in his hands again, running his fingers through his hair.

"Why don't you go on upstairs to your bedroom, Courtney? I think that your mother and I need to talk about this alone."

"Yes, Daddy." Courtney left the table and noticed as she passed her mother that her mother was crying. They embraced quickly and Courtney hurried up the stairs.

As she fell into her bed, she realized that once again the hopelessness of the situation had swept over her. She wondered if life could ever be any worse. It was a terrible thing for a seventeen-year-old to feel, but she couldn't help it. It was as if she was having a terrible nightmare and she couldn't wake up. Why did she and Shaun have to do this? Why did she have to get pregnant? She still couldn't believe this was happening to her.

Chapter 17

Kevin McLaughlin stood in front of the door to his house juggling his laptop and the armload of stuff he had brought home from the office. He had worked out a deal with his boss to get all of his projects for the next two weeks and work on them from home. He would get these started and probably work straight through for a couple of nights and be done with it and then his obligation to the office would be complete. It would give him uninterrupted time to work on deciphering the financial details of the clinic and the Giovanni family.

Kevin loved this kind of work. By working from home, the morons at the office would not distract him. He could work at his own pace, just like he used to do in college. It was so much more productive when the shackles of corporate bureaucracy didn't bog you down. Not only would he get two weeks of work done in a couple of days, including the all-nighters that would accompany them, but he would also be putting the finishing touches on the mission. It was beginning to look like the mission would wrap up at the end of the week. The timing was perfect and he should have everything in place and ready by then.

It was a little after 5:00 in the afternoon and it was already dark. The glow from the halogen nightlight that the owners of Kevin's rented house had installed over the basketball goal in front of the garage cast an eerie light into the rooms along the front of the house. This allowed him to enter the house with his hands full and move around the kitchen without the need of turning on lights. Kevin dropped everything in his arms down on the kitchen counter. He reached back and closed the door. He had also brought in a sack of takeout Chinese food for dinner. He busied himself around the kitchen getting dinner ready. Kevin set a kettle of water on the stove and turned on the gas flames to boil water for tea.

As he was waiting for the water to boil, Kevin set his laptop up and connected to his wireless network to access his office. He spread the other materials from the office over his desk and began to organize them for his work during the evening. The teakettle whistled and he went to the kitchen to get dinner.

Kevin brought his plate of Chinese food and the tea over to the desk and sat down to work. He was working on a new product that was in development. The product was a new technology and Kevin was part of the programming team responsible for the communications function of the software. Once he finished his portion of the programming, he would be able to download his work to the server at the office. The team leader would then be able to tie his work into the rest of the project.

The clock on the bookshelf indicated that it was 6:00. By this time on Wednesday morning, he should be through with his programming project and his work responsibilities would be complete. He downloaded his file from the server at the office and began to work.

* * * * *

Carla was standing at the kitchen sink doing the dishes from dinner with a smile on her face. She could hear Marty and Thomas in the next room playing video games. They were having a blast.

Marty had come over after work to meet Thomas and have dinner with them. Marty had grilled hamburgers with Thomas' help. She had sliced potatoes, seasoned them and roasted them in the oven. She had also prepared baked beans. It was nothing fancy, but it was easy and everyone enjoyed it.

Carla had been so worried that Marty and Thomas would not hit it off. She and Thomas had grown accustomed to being on their own. She wasn't sure how Thomas would react to someone new in her life, but Marty made it easy. He had Thomas with him every step of the way. They grilled the burgers together. They set the table together with Thomas showing Marty where everything was located. They were playing video games together. And they were already planning to watch a college basketball game on television at 8:00.

Carla had been thinking a lot about Marty since Saturday night. It had been a long time since she had felt this comfortable around a man, especially a doctor. Carla had been working for doctors for many years and it had been a long time since she had seen one as down to earth as Marty. It made her feel especially good to see Thomas having a good time. Since her divorce, she had focused almost exclusively on providing for Thomas. She worried about him all the time. She worried about his future if something happened to her. She worried about providing for his education. She worried about making sure that he had the same opportunities as his friends did. In fact, providing for Thomas had consumed her. His security was the main reason that she had taken the job at the clinic. She thought that she would be able to stop worrying about the future, if she knew that her finances were secure. But the worry continued. She was making more money than she had ever imagined and she was still worried. Now she worried about losing this new income and lifestyle that she and Thomas had become accustomed to. She knew how fickle it could be working for doctors. She knew of good managers that were fired just because a doctor was having a bad day.

Maybe it was time for her to focus on relationships for a while. Developing a relationship with Marty might really help alleviate her fears of the future. Carla knew that she needed something else in her life. Maybe this new relationship was just the thing.

Carla finished the dishes and went into the den. She called out, "Guys, it's almost 8:00. Are you ready to watch the ball game?"

Thomas' eyes never left the screen. "Just a minute, Mom, we're almost done with this game."

Marty was just as engrossed. His fingers were flying rapidly over the game controller that he held in his hands. "Yeah, we'll be done in a minute," he shouted in Carla's general direction.

Carla sat down on the couch. The guys were sitting on the floor in front of the television. She watched them silently for a few minutes. They were both bobbing and weaving with the action on the screen. Within a minute, a squeal of delight erupted from Thomas and a groan of disappointment came from Marty.

"Ha! I beat you again, Marty." Thomas raised his clenched fists into the air in a sign of victory. "You have to admit it now, Marty. I'm better than you." His face was beaming with a huge smile.

"Okay, okay. I'll admit it now, even though I still think that you got lucky," Marty said sheepishly.

"Lucky? How can you say that? I beat you three times in a row." Thomas was very proud and it showed.

Marty looked wounded. "Well maybe so, but I demand a rematch."

Carla was enjoying the banter between them. "Wait a minute, guys, it's time for the basketball game. You guys can have a rematch another time. I'm ready to watch the game."

Thomas put up the video game and turned the television to the ball game. "It's a good thing that you came along, Mom. I was beating him real bad and I think it was just going to get worse." Thomas had a gleam in his eye, as if he was trying to get Marty stirred up.

"That's okay, Thomas, I can be a good loser for now, but I can promise you that it won't last for long."

"You mean you're going to turn into a sore loser?" Thomas was struggling to keep a straight face.

"Yeah right. You know what I mean. You won't be winning like this the next time we play."

They were settling in to watch the game and Marty asked, "Would anyone like something to drink?" He was getting up and moving to the kitchen. He had such ease about taking care of other people.

Thomas was the first to place his order. "I want a Dr. Pepper, Marty."

"Now Thomas, don't you think that you should call him Dr. Smith instead of Marty? That's not a very respectful way to address an adult." Carla was acting as if she were offended by the informal reference. The scowl on her face showed it.

"It's okay, Mom, Marty asked me to call him that."

"That's right, Carla. I told him to call me Marty. I prefer it that way."

"I guess it's okay. I think you guys outnumber me anyway. I'm not sure I stand a chance."

"Of course you stand a chance, Carla, you're the boss around here, right, Thomas?" Marty was winking at Thomas like he had something stuck in his eye.

Thomas gave Marty an exaggerated wink back. "Sure she is, Marty. You better ask the boss what she wants to drink."

Carla ordered an iced tea and called after Marty, "Do you need any help with the drinks? I feel bad that you're serving everyone."

Marty was rummaging around in the kitchen. "I know where everything is. Thomas is a good teacher. He showed me where everything is kept earlier and I don't mind at all."

After a few minutes, Marty brought the drinks back into the den. They settled in and became absorbed in the basketball game.

Carla looked around the room and realized that this was what most of America dreamed of, quality time spent with those that you care about. She realized then, that she was beginning to care about Marty Smith a great deal.

* * * * *

The clock on his bookshelf showed 10:30, as Kevin stood up from his desk. He stretched and rubbed his neck, which had a crick in it that made it feel as if he had slept on it all night in a terribly unfortunate position. He had been hunched over his laptop all evening and had made significant progress with his work assignment. By Wednesday morning he should be done and he could focus entirely on finishing his mission. He was almost there and it felt good.

He went to the kitchen and got a refill on his caffeine fix. The break from the programming that he was doing gave him an opportunity to think through his next step in following the Women's Health Inc. money. Like most things in this world, the key to putting the final touch on his mission would be the money. A plan was already formulating in his head. Kevin wanted to find the trail of the money and divert some of it away from the clinic. Maybe his attack on the clinic could have a two-pronged strike. Maybe he could inflict financial damage, as well as physical damage.

Kevin wandered back over to the desk and turned on his laptop. As the machine was booting up, he was doodling on the legal pad that he had on the desk. Kevin was attempting to diagram the information that he had so far regarding the flow of money. He knew that money was picked up from the clinic at least three times a day by an armored car service that was owned by Giovanni Family Enterprises. He knew from looking at the transactions in the clinic's account that more money was being deposited in the account than was being collected in the office. The only explanation that was plausible was that the drivers of the armored car were making extra deposits on the clinic's behalf. If that were true, it would beg the question, "Where were they getting the money?" He knew from examining the transaction records that the majority of the money in question was cash.

As he wrote the different variables out on his legal pad, Kevin had a thought. He got online and initiated a search for the phrase "money laundering." The list of related sites and information was quite long. Kevin settled in and began to scroll through the list. He glanced at the clock on the bookcase and made a mental note to spend no more than 45 minutes working on this. He would need to get back to work on his programming and he knew that searching the Internet was like smoking cigarettes, once you started it was hard to stop.

* * * * *

Carla had finally gotten Thomas to go to bed. By the time that the basketball game was over, his adrenaline was pumping so much that his mouth was racing to keep up. At first, Marty had been no help at all in getting Thomas quiet. In fact, he was egging him on. Carla had to resort to giving him the look. Although Marty had never been married, he must have remembered getting the look from his mother during his childhood. He recognized it right away and quietly slipped into the background.

It was 11:00 and Carla came back into the den from checking on Thomas to find Marty seated on the couch. He looked at her with a hint of embarrassment.

"I'm sorry that I kept Thomas too hyper tonight. I should have backed off sooner," he said to her.

"Oh, don't worry about it. He loved having you here. It's been a long time since I've seen him have so much fun." Carla was looking at Marty, wondering just how serious this might become.

"Carla, you ought to be proud. Thomas is a good kid. He is so good-natured, it makes him very easy to be around."

"It makes me feel good to hear you say that. I've tried so hard to make it good for Thomas. He's been such a joy for me."

The room was quiet except for some soft jazz music that Carla had put in the stereo system after the ballgame. They were sitting at opposite ends of the couch.

Marty's facial expression showed that he was deep in thought. "You know, I've been thinking about our work at the clinic. I think that I am rapidly approaching the point of no return in working there. Every day I have to talk myself into getting back into the

OR and doing these procedures. It's beginning to weigh heavy on my mind. I'm really not sure how much longer I can do it."

Carla's brow furrowed slightly as she considered Marty's words. "Are you talking about making an immediate change?"

"I'm not sure. I don't have a plan yet, nor do I have another job lined up, but I've been thinking about it almost non-stop. It was hard to operate today because the thoughts of leaving were cluttering my mind."

"I know what you mean, Marty. I've been thinking about it since Saturday morning when we toured the Clean-up Room. I was astounded by the horror of seeing all those containers. It embarrassed me that I got sick to my stomach, but I'll never forget that sight. It will be ingrained in my mind forever."

Marty reached over and took her hand. "It's really nothing to be embarrassed about. It has that effect on most people. The average person has no concept of what an abortion is all about. The aftereffects are not very pretty and you've just seen the products of conception. The mental anguish that some of these women and girls go through is unbelievable."

Carla looked up at Marty's face. "Have you dealt with the mental side of this?"

"Not really," Marty said, shaking his head. "I saw the staff physicians deal with it a few times during my training, but I never dealt with it personally."

"What about at the clinic?"

"Are you kidding? Our clinical process is so structured that Janet Rawls handles any follow-up like that with a patient and I never see it. I never hear of any problems, but I know that they are out there."

"What kind of problems do patients have after having an abortion?"

Marty shifted into his clinical discussion voice. "The most common problems are usually grouped into a disorder called Post-Abortion Syndrome, or PAS. PAS occurs when a woman is unable to work through her emotional responses due to the trauma of an abortion. Some of the common symptoms are anxiety, guilt, nightmares, suicidal impulses and drug and alcohol abuse. In the long run, most of these women become unable to sustain an intimate relationship."

Carla looked surprised. "Wow, I didn't have any idea that there was so much baggage associated with an abortion. Why don't these women receive counseling about this?"

"I suspect it's the money. You know, if Brad Giovanni can afford the kind of salaries he's paying to the doctors and management, he must be making a fortune on this place. I'm sure that the payback for effective abortion counseling is not quite as lucrative."

They sat still for a few minutes listening to the music. The wind was howling outside and you could tell that it was getting colder.

It was Marty's turn to ask a question. "Carla, what are your plans? I mean you seem to be struggling with some issues on this one too."

Carla's countenance was troubled. "I am struggling with it because it doesn't feel right. My biggest problem is the security of this job."

Marty scooted a little closer to her. "Is it the money? Is that what is keeping you from pursuing something else?"

"I guess it is. I told you before that this is the best opportunity that I have ever had. It's hard to turn away from that because you never know if you'll have another opportunity like this, that is so financially rewarding."

"Well now that I've met Thomas, I understand your dilemma. Being able to provide for him must really put the pressure on you."

"I guess that it does. I need to put some additional thought into this. I certainly have a new understanding of what we are doing. I guess that I need to come to grips with my role in all of this."

They became quiet again. After a few minutes, Marty looked at his watch.

"I guess I should be going. It's a quarter to twelve and we both have to work tomorrow."

"You're right. I'm so glad that you came over tonight. I think that Thomas has a new best friend."

Marty smiled. "I thoroughly enjoyed it. The food was good and the company was even better."

As they walked to the door to say goodnight, Marty noticed that Carla's face was the reflection of troubled thoughts. "Look, Carla, don't worry about the things that we were talking about tonight. We all have to do things in the short run that we may not like. It happens to everybody, so don't get so down about it."

They were at the front door and he took her face in his hands. He held her close and looked into her eyes. "Okay, I don't want you to worry about it."

She looked up and he noticed that her eyes were moist. "I don't want anything to come between us. I'm worried that these issues at the clinic may push us apart."

"Look, don't worry about it. I feel like something is going to change and we won't have to worry about the clinic anymore."

"I hope you're right."

"Sure I'm right. Don't worry about it."

They kissed and Marty went home.

* * * * *

Kevin had been through most of the Internet sites that looked interesting. He had learned a great deal about the intricacies of laundering money. He realized very quickly that someone was using smurfs to get extra cash into the accounts. Kevin discovered that smurfs was the slang term for couriers who scurry from bank to bank to conduct multiple cash transactions under the $10,000 reporting limit. The name "smurf" is from the hyperactive blue cartoon characters that seemed to be everywhere at once. He needed to do a little more investigation in the bank transactions of the clinic. He wondered if there were other accounts at their main bank and if there were other banks. He would check that later, when he got into the bank records.

There was an additional piece of information that he found interesting related to the other end of the money trail. Historically, a money launderer would use the smurfs to deposit the dirty cash and then eventually have the money moved out of the country. Once it was out of the country, the money could then be transferred into other assets and eventually brought back to the United States.

However, the world of e-commerce was beginning to change all that. Even the business of money laundering was undergoing a transformation. In some of the more sophisticated laundering schemes, the hard currency was being changed into anonymous digital cash. This not only gave the owner of the now clean money many more spending options, it also made the money almost impossible to trace.

Kevin was beginning to understand the potential for a business like the clinic as a part of Giovanni Family Enterprises. He could also understand the possibilities for him to meddle. He would enjoy this. This project would be the most challenging he had tackled in a long time.

He got a fresh cup of tea and went back to work on his project for the office. He was just a few hours from completing his last assignment. He would work through the night and maybe finish sometime Tuesday afternoon. He would get done earlier than he had projected. This was perfect. He would be able to get to work full-time on his mission. He had the momentum now. The plan was going to work perfectly and he would even get an added bonus. He was going to disrupt them financially too.

As he was moving around to get back in front of his laptop, the light from his desk lamp reflected off the key that was lying on the corner of the desk. Kevin reached over and picked it up.

He turned it over several times in his hand. He spoke out loud to himself.

"This is going to be good." A smile came across his face. "This is going to be really good."

Chapter 18

Carla was running a little later than usual on Tuesday morning. It had been a challenge to get out of bed. After Marty had left just before midnight, she was too excited to go right to bed. She stayed up another hour getting some work done around the house. Marty was becoming one of the best things that had happened to her in a long time.

As she pulled into the clinic parking lot, she saw right away that Brad Giovanni's car was already there.

"Oh great!" she said out loud to herself. "What's he doing here? Of all mornings for me to be running late, this is really poor timing."

Carla parked her car and hurried up the back stairs to her office. She quietly slipped into the administrative area and caught the eye of her secretary Patsy.

"Is he here?" She mouthed the words for Patsy to see.

Patsy motioned over her shoulder towards Carla's office door and spoke softly. "He's in your office. He's been in there for about 15 minutes."

"This is just perfect. I guess I'll have to barge on in and face the music. Any idea why he's here?"

"No, he hasn't given me any idea why he's here," Patsy said. "He just asked when you usually got in and then he went in and made himself at home. I could hear him rummaging around, but I've not checked on him. He scares me."

"Yeah, he scares me too. Well, here I go. Wish me luck," Carla said as she straightened her business suit.

"Do you need me to get you anything?" Patsy asked helpfully.

"Why don't you come in with some coffee in about five minutes," Carla replied.

"I'll be there," Patsy said with a smile. "Good luck!"

Carla strolled into her office with as much confidence as she could muster. Brad was sitting in one of the side chairs across from her desk. He had some papers in his hand that he was apparently studying.

Carla spoke first. "Good morning, Brad. I wasn't expecting you this morning. What brings you to our fair city?"

Brad looked up from his reading. He smiled at Carla as she settled in behind her desk. She turned on her computer on the credenza behind her and spun to face Brad as the machine came to life.

"Good morning, Carla," he said. "I haven't been to see you in quite some time, so I thought that I should drop in and see how things are going." Brad sat there with the smile on his face unchanging.

Carla was always a bit unsettled when Brad smiled at her. The way the corners of his lips curled upwards always gave the impression that he knew something that you didn't. It gave his smile a perpetually sly appearance.

"I hope that I didn't keep you waiting too long," she said. "I'm usually at the office earlier than this, but I was running behind this morning."

"Oh, that's all right. It's given me some time to get caught up on a few things. I hope that I haven't barged in at an inconvenient time."

Brad had not taken his eyes off her since she entered the room. And the sly little grin was still on his face. It made her terribly uncomfortable, when he stared at her like this.

Carla responded to him. "Oh no, it's a perfectly fine time for you to stop by. I'm always happy to see you." It was a lie and Brad probably knew it. She couldn't imagine anyone being happy to see him coming, maybe not even his own mother, if he had one.

Brad Giovanni was an interesting case study as a person. He was a fairly attractive man. He wore his jet-black hair slicked straight back on his scalp. He was about six feet tall with a medium build. He wore expensive suits and shoes that had the look of being imported from Europe. But what made his attire so noticeable were his ties. He always wore ties that were pure silk and handmade in Italy. Every tie that Brad had worn when they met was of the most striking and vibrant colors that Carla had ever seen in a man's wardrobe.

Brad was not smart in an academic sort of way, but he always seemed to be a step ahead of you. He was street smart in his business dealings. Maybe that was the thing that made Carla so uncomfortable around him. He just seemed a little too slick.

The smile on Brad's face remained unchanged. "So how has business been?"

That's an odd question for him to ask, Carla thought to herself. She knew that Brad was a fanatic for keeping up with all of the details of the clinic's business. Although she had not seen him in person for several months, she spoke to him over the telephone frequently. He kept his laptop with him at all times and he would regularly check the activity at the clinic while he was on the road. His laptop was even equipped to dial in to the network through his cell phone. On one occasion, he had called her within ten minutes, when a deposit was not ready for one of the regular pickups. They both knew that he was aware of exactly how the business was going.

She answered him with a note of caution. "Business has been great. Our procedure volume has been up. Our cash collections have been excellent. We are even slightly below budget for operating expenses on a year to date basis. Overall, our business has been exceeding all of our projections."

"Yeah, I know it is." Brad was watching her reaction to this conversation and she could tell it.

"Why is he doing this?" she thought to herself. "What's he looking for?"

With the pause in conversation, Patsy came into Carla's office carrying a tray with two cups of coffee and an assortment of additives. She stopped by Brad first and placed a cup of coffee in front of him on the desk.

"Mr. Giovanni, this cup of coffee is black. As I recall, you prefer it that way. But, in case your preferences have changed, I've brought a variety of sweeteners and some cream."

"You have an excellent memory, Patsy, and my preferences have not changed a bit." Brad gratefully accepted the coffee.

Patsy turned and set a cup of coffee in front of Carla. As she moved towards the door, she spoke to them again.

"Please let me know if I can get you anything else. I'll be right outside."

Brad continued with his train of thought without missing a beat. "How have you been doing, Carla? Do you like your work here?"

Carla gave him a puzzled look. "I think that I have been doing quite well. You just have to look at the numbers to see the improvement since I've been here."

The smile on Brad's face was replaced with a terse look. "I'm not talking about the numbers. I know that the numbers indicate this is one of the best clinics that we have. What I want to know is how Carla Sharkley is doing personally?"

Carla was still bewildered. "I guess that I'm confused, Brad. Every time that we've spoken in the past it's been about the numbers. I just assumed that your focus this morning was on that area again."

Brad's eyes remained locked on hers. "I understand your confusion," he said. "I just want to make sure that I'm not confused."

Carla sat back in her chair mystified at the direction of this conversation. She responded cautiously to Brad's comments. "I am doing very well from a personal standpoint. I appreciate your concern, Brad."

Brad stood and walked to the windows on the wall next to Carla's desk. The windows looked out over the parking lot and the rolling hills of West Little Rock beyond. As he gazed out the windows with his back to Carla, he spoke again.

"How do you like Little Rock, Carla?"

"It's a nice city, Brad. I've enjoyed it very much so far."

Brad was still facing the window. "How does your son like Little Rock?"

"He likes Little Rock. He has made some good friends and has gotten involved in sports and all the other activities that interest twelve-year-old boys."

"He's going to a private school, isn't he? How does he like his school?" As Brad asked this last question, he turned and faced Carla.

Carla's mind was racing. How did Brad know that Thomas went to a private school? Did she mention that to him at some point? She couldn't imagine that she would have talked to Brad about Thomas' school. For that matter, she could not ever remember having a conversation with Brad that was not business oriented.

All of her senses were on alert, as she answered Brad's question. "He loves his school. He has fit in well with the other kids in his class."

"That's good. I'm sure that the well-being of your son is a high priority for you." The sly smile eased back on to his face as he said this. "Has this job been rewarding for you?"

Carla knew that he was going somewhere with this line of questioning, but the destination was not clear to her yet. "Of course it has. You know what my compensation package was before I came here. It's been a tremendous change for me."

Brad was pacing in front of the desk now. "Has it been enough of a change?"

Carla was perplexed. "What do you mean?"

"Has the money been enough for you?"

"This conversation is just too weird," Carla thought to herself.

She spoke to Brad. "Well, it's certainly provided for a lot of nice things and that has been a change of pace. But, I wonder if any of us ever really get enough money."

Brad stopped and looked at her. "It's interesting that you would say that." He sat down in the chair again, silent for a few moments. When he started speaking again, it caught Carla completely off guard.

"Carla, tell me what you know about my family."

The surprise in Carla's face was visible. "I don't really know anything about your family," she said. "I suppose the only detail that I am aware of is that your family is in Chicago. I know that only because it is our company headquarters."

His smile was back. "Have you heard any rumors from the staff?"

"Brad, I've been in this business long enough to know that you don't pay a lot of attention to staff rumors. If you did, you would never get any work done." Carla delivered this line with enough firmness that she hoped would end this part of the conversation.

"Oh come on, Carla. Surely you've heard some rumors that have piqued your curiosity. Rumors that are outside of the normal office gossip." The smile on his face was now so intense that it looked like he would break into uncontrollable laughter at any minute.

Carla decided to let him hear it. "I've heard a few rumors suggesting that your family may have ties to organized crime."

Brad seemed amused by her comment. "Why do people say that?"

Carla shrugged her shoulders. "I don't know. Maybe it's because your family name ends in a vowel. Maybe it's because you're from Chicago. How should I know? It's just gossip as far as I'm concerned." She was feeling very uncomfortable about this conversation.

Brad leaned forward slightly in his chair and stared intently into her eyes. "What would you say if I told you the rumor was true?"

Carla was too stunned to speak.

"My family has one of the largest business organizations in Chicago, or in the Midwest for that matter. We control a number of illegal activities in Chicago and other cities in the Midwest. In addition, we have a number of legal businesses that we own. The clinic you work for falls into that category. The involvement in a business like this clinic helps us establish a sense of legitimacy in the community. It assists us in a variety of ways when we make a connection like this."

Brad was thoroughly enjoying Carla's response to his revelation. He went on with the disclosure that had left Carla speechless.

"With the hundreds of businesses that we are involved with, many of our employees never realize that they work for one of the largest crime families in America. For most of them, it doesn't make any difference who their employer is. Most of these employees are just grateful to have a job with good pay and benefits. You'd be amazed at the things that people will overlook to keep a good job. If you check with your staff, you would find that most of them could not even begin to afford the health insurance that we provide for them. These people don't care that we engage in criminal activities, because they are more concerned about their pocketbooks, than their conscience."

Brad was practically gloating now.

"Do you know that it was harder to get my family involved in these abortion clinics than it was almost any other activity that we are involved with, both legal and illegal? Imagine that. Because of our Catholic background, many of our family members wanted to shy away from a business like this because of the open conflicts with the Church. Of course, when we showed them the money involved, they quickly forgot any conflict with the Church." Brad laughed out loud at his last statement, obviously enjoying the irony of the situation. "You see, we're just like everybody else. Money rules everything."

Carla sat staring at the top of her desk. She was struggling to digest the information that Brad had just dumped on her. Brad sat across the desk from her watching her facial expressions as she tried to assimilate the conversation.

The silence was deafening. Brad let his news to Carla hang heavy in the air. He got up from his chair again and began to pace back and forth across the room.

Finally he spoke again. "Do you know why I'm telling you this, Carla?"

Carla looked up from her desk in shock. Her expression was that of a deer caught in the headlights of an oncoming car. She stammered, "I…uh, I…I don't have any idea." Her voice trailed off, as if her thoughts had already moved on and taken up residence elsewhere.

The sly smile was back on Brad's face. He was totally in control of this situation and he knew it. He stopped his pacing and stood behind the chair that he had been sitting in and placed his arms on the back of the chair. He leaned forward and in the most menacing look that Carla had ever seen, he stared deep into her eyes.

"Carla, someone has been poking around in our corporate computer network. The techies at corporate have not been able to track down the perpetrator yet, but it's just a matter of time. The hacker, whoever he or she is, has been using your password to get into the system."

"That's impossible. I've never been into any part of the system that I was not authorized to access and I've never given my password to anyone else. There must be some mistake!" Carla was getting flustered with this turn of events.

"Oh, it's no mistake. There have been several instances in the last week. Someone has logged on with your system password and proceeded to get into the inner workings of our network. It is causing some people to get very nervous. These nervous people wanted me to talk to you right away. Carla, I hope that you understand that these are not the type of people that you want to make nervous."

Brad paused for effect. It was obvious that Carla was out of her league.

He continued. "Carla, your success at this clinic has not gone unnoticed. Personally, I am very grateful for the work that you have done. You have taken a marginal business for us and turned it into a shining star. I don't want to see that change. Your work here has been very rewarding for the company and me and I want it to continue. I want you to keep your nose clean and stay out of trouble."

"But Brad, I don't have any idea how or why someone might be using my password. I don't have any intention of causing trouble. I hope that you believe me."

"I do believe you, Carla," he said. "You said exactly what I expected you to say and you didn't lie. I can always tell when someone is lying to me. I can see it in their face. You've got an honest face, Carla. Don't do anything to mess it up. And don't worry about the people that are using your password, we'll find them. We always do."

Brad got up and moved to the window again. He spoke to her as he gazed out across the parking lot. "You know, Carla, sometimes shining stars shoot quickly across the sky and then burn out, never to be seen again. Don't let that happen to you."

Brad turned and looked at her with eyes so cold that she felt as if she had just walked into a freezer. As he leaned against the windowsill, he uttered the most haunting words that she had ever heard.

"Carla, I'm very concerned for the safety of yourself and your son Thomas. Please don't disappoint me and endanger that safety unnecessarily."

Carla felt a chill go down her spine that caused her to shiver uncontrollably. She was frightened by the callousness that she had seen in this man. It was beyond her wildest imagination that her employer had just threatened her.

Brad walked over and leaned across her desk, placing his hands in the middle of the work surface of the desk. After he leaned forward, his face was less than twelve inches from hers. He was so close that she could smell the coffee on his breath.

"Carla, I like you and I want you to continue working in this clinic. Let's not do anything to screw that up. Okay?"

He stayed in that position for what seemed like an eternity, his eyes never leaving hers. The stare was so penetrating that it made her feel as if he had taken a piece of her soul.

He suddenly leaned back and headed for the door. He stopped before he left her office and turned back.

He smiled slyly. "Have a good day, Carla. I'll check with you later in the week. By the way, it would be a good idea for you to keep this little conversation to yourself. We certainly don't want any other complications."

With that, he was gone.

Carla released a long slow sigh and leaned her head back in her chair. She realized that she was perspiring profusely and her head was throbbing like a big bass drum. She closed her eyes and began to rub her temples to ease the pain. Carla had to catch her breath because her breathing had been so shallow.

What was she going to do? She had no idea how this had happened to her. And now Thomas was involved. Brad had made the implication very clear that he would not hesitate to use Thomas as a pawn to keep her in line. This was crazy. How did someone get her password? Why would someone want it? Why would they be hacking into the network?

The questions were making her dizzy. Her world was changing before her eyes and she didn't understand it and she couldn't stop it. Of course she had heard the staff talk about the Giovannis' crime connection, but she thought it was idle office gossip. Carla would have never expected the Mob to be involved in an abortion clinic. Now she was working for the Mob.

It was unbelievable. No wonder the money was so lucrative. She had often thought that the money was too good to be true. Now she knew that was the case.

Carla tried to think through the developments of the last hour. The thoughts were racing through her mind like a freight train. She needed to talk to Marty. He could help her think through this crisis. She could count on Marty. He would help her find a way out.

Chapter 19

Marty's morning had been a whirlwind. He had arrived at the clinic later than normal. He was not accustomed to staying out as late as he did last night. He had really enjoyed spending time with Carla and Thomas last night. It amazed him how quickly he was becoming attached to those two. He and Carla had not talked about a steady relationship, but he knew that discussion would happen soon and he was looking forward to it.

Marty had just finished his fifth case of the morning. So far every case had been on patients between eleven and fourteen weeks gestation. They had been easy cases and he had almost caught up from his late start.

He came out of the OR and discarded his latex surgical gloves in the trash receptacle. He reached into the under the counter refrigerator that held soft drinks for the patients who experienced nausea or a dry mouth during their postoperative stay in the recovery room. Both of these reactions from patients were the side effects of the anesthesia used in some of the procedures. He opened a Diet Coke and took a huge gulp. He stood in the hall between the two operating rooms waiting for the staff to prep his next patient. Since the clinic was a freestanding ambulatory surgery center with a focus on only one type of procedure, the turnaround time for his next case would be minimal. He would barely have time to finish his Diet Coke.

Tammy Hawkins, his favorite nurse in the OR, waved at him from the nurses' desk. "Dr. Smith, I've got a message for you."

Marty walked over and retrieved the message. He opened the note and saw that it was from Carla. As he walked back to the OR, he read the note.

Marty,

Something has come up. It's urgent that I see you. Please come to my office as soon as you can.

Carla

Marty was puzzled by Carla's message. He knew that it must be something important because she had never before contacted him while he was working in the operating room.

"Dr. Smith? We have your next case ready."

It was Janet Rawls, the OR supervisor. She had stuck her head out of operating room one. Her announcement interrupted his train of thought.

"I'll be right there, Janet."

He paused in the hallway for a moment outside of the door to operating room one. He turned to face the nurses' station as he was holding the message from Carla in his hand.

"Hey, Tammy! Can you call Ms. Sharkley's office and let her know I'll stop by after I'm done with this next case? It should be about 15 minutes."

"Sure, Dr. Smith, I'll call right now."

Tammy immediately got on the phone and began dialing. Marty turned back toward the operating room, looking at the note one last time. He shrugged his shoulders, crumpled the note in his hand and tossed it into the same receptacle that he had tossed his surgical gloves into a few minutes earlier.

Marty entered the operating room as he put on a new pair of surgical gloves and grabbed the chart of his next patient. Her name was Cathy Weintraub. She was eighteen years old and twelve weeks pregnant. Cathy would be his sixth procedure of the day. It would be another day full of choice.

* * * * *

In exactly 13 minutes, Marty had completed his sixth case. Just outside of the operating room, a desk was built into the wall. It allowed the physicians to complete their chart work as they stood in the hallway. Marty walked over and dictated an op note for Cathy's chart accessing the dictation system through the telephone on the desk. After completing the dictation, he initialed and signed all of the appropriate paperwork then placed the completed chart in the out-box on the desk.

Marty headed for the back stairway that led upstairs to administration. He called back over his shoulder to Tammy, who was still manning the nurses' station.

"Tammy, I'll be back in a few minutes. I'm going upstairs to Ms. Sharkley's office. Have the OR crew get the next patient ready and I'll be right back."

"Sure thing, Dr. Smith," Tammy responded as the door to the stairwell closed shut.

Marty hurried up the stairs and burst out into the second-floor hallway. He crossed the hall and entered into the administrative offices. Patsy greeted him with a smile that was a little less inspired than was normal for her.

"Hey Patsy, is Carla in her office?" Marty was obviously in a hurry, but he noticed that Patsy was distracted. "What's wrong, Patsy? You seem to be upset."

"Ms. Sharkley is on the phone, but I know she really wants to talk to you. Something's going on, but I don't know what it is. Mr. Giovanni was here first thing this morning and I think that it has something to do with his visit."

Marty looked surprised. "Brad was here this morning? Carla didn't say anything about him coming to the clinic today."

"Oh, no one was expecting him, he just arrived unannounced. Ms. Sharkley was very surprised to see him." Patsy kept glancing back at the door to Carla's office.

"Do you know what he wanted?" Marty asked.

"No idea and I haven't had a chance to talk to Ms. Sharkley about it. She's been on the phone since he left. Just from overhearing her voice, she appears to be upset."

Patsy got up from behind her desk and moved towards Carla's office door.

"I'll let her know that you're here."

Patsy stepped partially through Carla's office door and got her attention. A moment later she came back into the outer office where Marty was waiting.

"I told her that you were here and she asked that you come on into her office," Patsy said as she motioned to the door behind her.

"Thanks, Patsy. Maybe I can find out what's happening."

Marty went into Carla's office and saw that she was seated behind her desk and still on the phone. She looked up and waved for him to take a seat in front of her desk. He sat down and noticed that Carla looked tense. It was obvious from her expression that she was not enjoying the telephone conversation that she was having.

"What's going on around here?" Marty thought to himself. "Patsy was right, something is wrong."

After a few more moments, Carla hung up the phone. She leaned forward over her desk and spoke in a hushed voice to Marty.

"Marty, you won't believe what happened to me this morning."

"Well, according to Patsy, something weird is happening and she doesn't have a clue what it is," Marty said in a whispered tone that matched Carla's.

"Oh, I forgot to tell Patsy! This morning has been a blur. Remind me to fill her in when we're done."

Marty's voice showed his concern for Carla as he spoke. "You seem to be shaken. What happened and why are we whispering?"

"To answer your last question first, I'm afraid this office might be bugged." Carla said this as she looked around the room.

"You're what?" Marty interrupted her in astonishment. "Why in the world would you think that?"

"Keep your voice down, Marty. I don't want anyone to know that you are here. If you will settle down for a moment, I'll tell you what happened to me this morning and you can come to your own conclusions. It all started when Brad Giovanni was waiting in my office as I arrived this morning." With that, Carla began to tell the events of the morning.

After she completed her story, Marty sat staring in stunned silence.

Carla watched him as he mentally digested the details of what he had just heard. "That's exactly how I felt when Brad left this morning," she whispered. "I was speechless also."

Marty finally came out of his daze. "I can't believe this place is owned by the Mob." His disbelief was evidenced by the look on his face. "Brad actually threatened you and Thomas? That's unbelievable!"

Carla answered him. Oh, he was very smooth in how he did it. He never really came out and directly threatened us. You had to be paying attention to catch it at first, but after he repeated it several times, you would have to be stupid not to get it. He left no doubt in my mind that both of us would be in danger, if things did not turn out as he planned."

"What do you think the deal was about your access to the computer? Do you think it was the stuff we were doing last Saturday?"

"I can't imagine that would have gotten his attention. The only programs that I was accessing were those that I had been given permission to access," Carla replied with a sense of puzzlement in her voice. "It has to be something else, but I don't know what it could be."

Marty was looking around the room. "Do you really think this office could be bugged?" He was whispering again.

"I really don't know what to think, Marty. All of this is very confusing, but given whom we're dealing with, we at least have to consider it. I don't know anything about the Mafia, other than what I've seen on television. It always appears that they will do anything to get their way." Carla leaned a little more over the desk in order for Marty to hear her as she spoke in low tones. "Maybe we should finish this discussion later, outside of the office."

"That's a good idea. Let's meet in the parking lot after work and we'll decide where to go from there." Marty glanced at his watch to check the time. "If I hurry and get back downstairs, I should be ready to go by five thirty this afternoon."

Carla stood up and moved around to the side of the desk where Marty was. "Thanks for coming up to see me so soon, I really appreciate it. I needed someone to talk to and I didn't know where else to turn."

Marty reached out and took her hand briefly in his. "I'm glad that you thought to call me. Don't worry about this. We'll work something out."

They both turned and moved towards the door.

Carla said, "I'll meet you at five thirty in the parking lot. If anything comes up, let me know."

"I will. See you later."

With that, Marty was out of her office and Carla was left alone with her thoughts and her work.
Marty stopped and leaned over Patsy's desk. "I'm sure that Carla will fill you in on the details soon. In the meantime, promise me that if anything weird happens up here, you will call me. I'm worried and I don't want to see anything bad happen to her."

Patsy looked startled. "What do you mean? What's going on?"

"I can't tell you right now, Patsy, but Carla said she would be talking with you soon and I don't think that I should interrupt the flow of information up here."

"As much as I hate to do it without knowing all of the details, I'll promise to let you know of any strange events that happen. I don't want anything to happen to her either." Patsy was extremely concerned with the cryptic information that Marty had given her. "Dr. Smith?"

Marty had turned to leave the administrative office suite, when Patsy called his name. He turned backed to her.

"Yes, Patsy?"

"Will you return the favor and promise me one thing?"

"Sure, what do you need?"

"I want you to promise me that you'll take care of her."

Marty smiled. "I'll do everything humanly possible to protect her."

Marty left the offices in a hurry and headed back to the surgical suite. He was getting further behind and his seventh case was waiting.

Chapter 20

Darren Cooke pulled his car into the parking lot at the First Fellowship Church in Hot Springs. He was supposed to meet his cameraman here. Darren had elected to travel to Hot Springs in his own vehicle in case he needed to hang around after the interview to do some background follow-up. He looked at his watch and saw that he was about five minutes early. He pulled his notes for the interview from his beat-up leather backpack and began to review them one more time.

Darren had been working as a reporter for KBTE-TV for three years. Prior to his current job, he had worked in radio and newspaper as a reporter. He had been doing this kind of work for a long time and he was good at it. He had developed an expertise in interviewing difficult subjects. He was the best there was at KBTE and maybe the best there was in Little Rock, which also meant the best in the state. His boss, John Baker, acknowledged his skill by assigning him the best stories. And usually, the best stories had some of the toughest interviews.

After John had called Sunday afternoon, Darren had spent a considerable amount of time researching the First Fellowship Church and its pastor. Even after searching the Internet, he had been able to find very little on the church itself. Apparently, it had once been a part of one of the mainstream denominations. There had been a "falling from grace," so to speak, from the main theological thought of the national denominational organization. He could not find any details about the specific reasons for the separation. He had made a note to ask Dr. William Roberts about that event.

Dr. William Roberts was truly a study in modern evangelical leadership. Darren had watched the video from the previous Sunday's service several times. He was amazed each time that he had viewed it. As a journalist, he felt a certain obligation to go through life with a liberal viewpoint on all issues of importance and he did this well. It was with this viewpoint that he had mentally stepped back and analyzed the message that Dr. Roberts had delivered on Sunday. The analysis had appalled him. He could not believe that this man was saying these things in a public forum. He had all but incited the people in that auditorium to riot against abortion.

It was when Darren switched off his journalistic mentality late last night and sat back to watch the video one last time that he began to realize the power that this man had as a speaker and a leader. Darren had become mesmerized by the performance that Bill Roberts had given. He found himself caught up in the fervor that the crowd in the church had experienced. He could not believe that it had happened to him. He thought himself far too sophisticated to fall for that type of performance.

Darren sat in the parking lot, realizing that he would have to be careful as he conducted this interview. Clearly, Dr. Roberts was a persuasive force to be reckoned with. He would have to be at his best to complete this interview successfully. He would also have to guard against falling under his mesmerizing spell.

This interview would be one of his most challenging in quite some time, but it could also be one of those that define the future of a career. Just the thought of matching skills with Bill Roberts gave him a charge. He had prepared for the interview as much as he possibly could on such short notice, but that's the way it was with television. It was necessary to move on the hot stories while they were still hot. The viewing public didn't want to see a story on last week's news. Sometimes you had to move with the story before you were really ready with all of your research.

He had just finished going through his notes for the second time, when his cameraman drove into the parking lot. Darren looked at his watch. As usual, Jerry, his cameraman, was barely on time. Darren, of course, would complain about this. It was the acknowledged duty for the people in front of the camera to complain about those behind it. Darren willingly accepted the assignment.

They both got out of their respective vehicles at the same time. Darren spoke first.

"Well it's about time you got here. I've been waiting for you. I thought that I was going to have to start this interview without you."

Jerry was not intimidated in the least by any reporter on staff at the station. "Who are you trying to kid? You know that you're nothing without me. Without this camera around, you probably couldn't breathe more than just a few hours. It's your lifeline."

Jerry knew that every reporter lived to have a story on prime time news. The more face time they got in front of the camera, the happier they were. He knew there was no way in the world that Darren would have gone in without him and he wanted Darren to know that he knew it. Now that he had established his position of importance in this relationship, he was ready to get down to business.

* * * * *

The crew from KBTE-TV went into First Fellowship Church. They were directed to the reception area and from there, they were directed to the pastor's office on the second floor. The pastor's secretary greeted them at the door of the office suite and she directed them to a small conference room.

"Brother Bill asked that I have you set your equipment up in this room. Will this space be adequate?" She seemed very interested in accommodating them.

Jerry set his equipment down and began to move around the room checking the light. Darren took a quick look around and immediately spoke.

"I think that this room will be fine. We'll set up our equipment and be ready in a few minutes. Will Dr. Roberts be joining us soon?" Darren was always striving to move things forward as quickly as possible.

"Oh yes, he will be here momentarily. He is just finishing his previous appointment. May I get you anything to drink? A soft drink or a cup of coffee?"

Darren responded before Jerry could even open his mouth. "We're fine. We don't need a thing, but thank you anyway."

"Let me know if you change your mind," she said as she backed out of the door.

"Gee thanks, Darren. Maybe I wanted something to drink." Jerry seemed a little peeved at Darren's willingness to speak for him.

"Oh get over it, Jerry. You're going to be too busy to be juggling a cup in your hands. You need to focus on getting this segment done. If you're thirsty, you can get a drink afterwards." Darren was not about to cut a cameraman any slack. Nobody cared who ran the camera. t was the person in front of the camera that captured everyone's attention. Darren would make sure that Jerry realized that.

Jerry moved around the room grumbling under his breath as he set up the equipment. Darren took great pains to ignore him as he positioned the chairs around the end of the small conference table to suit him. He had a very controlling personality and it came through loud and clear in times like these. He would make sure that there were no variables to get the interview off track. Usually dealing with the subject created enough unknowns by itself. He certainly did not need a cameraman or the layout of the room to distract anyone.

The door at the far end of the room swung open and Dr. William Roberts walked into the conference room. He immediately moved to greet the two men.

"Hello gentlemen, my name is Bill Roberts. I'm glad that you were able to make it over to Hot Springs today." As he spoke, he stuck his hand out to Darren.

"It's good to meet you, Dr. Roberts. My name is Darren Cooke. I am a news reporter from KBTE-TV." As he let go of Roberts' hand, he motioned to his cameraman. "This is Jerry Wright. He is one of the cameramen at the station."

Roberts moved over to shake hands with Jerry. "It is very nice to meet you, Jerry. Thank you for coming over today."

"You're welcome, Dr. Roberts. It's a pleasure to meet you." As usual, Jerry did not have much to say.

Bill Roberts surveyed the room and looked to Darren as he spoke. "Well fellows, how do we want to do this today?"

Darren gestured toward the seat closest to the door through which Roberts had entered the room. "Why don't you sit there at the head of the table and I'll sit over here. Jerry has his equipment set up. Are the lights okay, Jerry?"

"Fine," Jerry mumbled.

"Great!" Darren was on a roll now. "I would like to ask you about your thoughts and beliefs regarding abortion. I have seen a tape of your sermon this past Sunday and I would like to follow up on some of your comments from that sermon."

"That's fine with me. How long will the interview be?" Roberts had taken the seat that Darren had pointed him toward.

"We'll probably need about 30 minutes. In addition to the questions about your sermon, I'll be asking you some background questions as well. Jerry will be rolling the camera the entire time. It usually takes quite a bit of film to produce a segment for the news." Darren was in complete control now. The interview was setting up just as he had anticipated.

Bill Roberts had settled into his seat. He was leaning forward slightly with his hands clasped lightly together on the table in front of him.

"That sounds good, Darren. I've been looking forward to this interview. Let's get going." Bill Roberts was looking quite confident as he sat, waiting for the camera to roll.

Jerry had his eye to the camera and brought his hand up to signal that he was ready to begin.

"Ready to roll in three, two, one and…" Jerry's hand came down and he pointed to Darren as the red light on top of his camera came on.

"Good afternoon, Dr. Roberts." Darren was starting slowly. He wanted to get Roberts very comfortable.

"Good afternoon, Darren. I want to thank you for coming over to my church today. I am honored to have you as my guest." Roberts had his eyes locked on Darren's.

"Dr. Roberts, how long have you been pastor at First Fellowship Church?" Darren was going to cover the basics first.

"Well Darren, I came to Hot Springs five years ago to take on the senior pastor duties at this church. I have enjoyed these people immensely and my family and I love the community of Hot Springs."

"Now Dr. Roberts, I understand that you have just recently received your doctoral degree of divinity. Is that correct?"

"Yes that's correct, Darren. I just received my degree in July of this year. It was the culmination of many years of work and study. I am thankful that the churches in which I have pastored have allowed me the opportunity to achieve this accomplishment."

"Dr. Roberts, I understand that your church is one of the largest in Hot Springs. How many members do you have in your church?"

"Darren, we have over three thousand members in our church and we are one of the largest churches in the community."

"In what ways does your church get involved in the community, Dr. Roberts?"

"I am really glad that you asked that, Darren. Our church has many programs that allow us to reach into the community to meet the needs of those that are less fortunate than we are. The programs that we have in place meet needs that are physical in nature. For example, we participate with other area churches in staffing a soup kitchen for the homeless. We also have programs that meet financial needs. This is an area where we have been able to assist people who need a little help to get back on their feet. We have made utility payments for people who have fallen behind and we have also provided groceries to families who had a short-term need."

Roberts was beginning to gesture with his hands as he spoke. It reminded Darren of the video that he had seen.

"And of course, we meet the spiritual needs that people have. Reaching out to the community and sharing our faith with them, is one of the most important things that we do as a church."

"What about the political needs of the community, Dr. Roberts? Does your church attempt to guide this community in their political thought?" Darren began the process of bringing the questions to the issue at hand.

"Oh, I don't think that we do that at all, Darren. Our stance as a church is politically neutral. As the pastor of this congregation, it is my duty to preach the scriptural truths and allow the people to follow their hearts as God directs them."

"Dr. Roberts, I reviewed a videotape of your sermon this past Sunday. In that sermon, you encouraged your congregation to rise up against abortion. Would you not consider that giving your people political direction?" Darren was moving in now.

"Not really, Darren." Roberts' jaw began to set in a determined look, but the smile that he had worn, like a comfortable suit, from the beginning of the interview was still there.

"I do not consider abortion a political issue, but a moral issue. It is in that context that I spoke to my congregation on Sunday. I think that it is very important for the people of God to be prepared for the moral attacks that they face in the community. My sermon was designed to give them the tools they need to deal with an issue like abortion that eats at the moral fiber of this country. If they are unprepared to make a moral stand on an issue as dramatic as this, I feel that I have failed them as their spiritual leader."

There was a pause in the interview. Darren was beginning to realize why this guy was so good. His powers of persuasion were extraordinary.

Darren followed up. "Dr. Roberts, I understand the rationale that would lead you to the conclusion that abortion is a moral issue as opposed to a political one, but in your sermon you asked your congregation to be extreme in the fight against abortion. What exactly were you referring to with that statement?"

"Too many times in the America that we live in, we have lost our passion to pursue liberty. The citizens have become complacent and are perfectly willing for someone else to deal with the problems our nation faces. I am simply pointing out to my congregation that as Christians they have a duty to right the moral wrongs in our community and abortion is one of those wrongs."

"But Dr. Roberts, the highest court in our land has determined that abortion is legal. Are you suggesting that your congregation should take extreme measures against the laws of this country?"

"Darren, sometimes the degree of extremism is in the eye of the beholder. Do you think that if you were a white law enforcement officer in Montgomery, Alabama, in the mid-fifties, that you would have considered the refusal, by a lone black woman, to follow the segregation laws of the day extremism? I would venture to say that most people would have considered it a form of civil disobedience. In fact, the majority of the white citizens in Montgomery would have thought the protests downright illegal. But you know what, Darren? The legal system at that time did not offer any relief for African Americans involved in civil disobedience. It took extremism to force a change. t took the efforts of many people working in extreme ways to move that community and the nation toward a change for justice. Did that justice require a change in the thought process of our nation? Of course it did. Did that justice require a change in laws? Sure. Did that justice require a change in the passionate extremism in which our nation pursued liberty for all people? Absolutely!"

Roberts paused momentarily for effect. Darren was spellbound by his argument.

"In order for our country to move out of the shackles of slavery and into the true pursuit of liberty and justice for all, it took extremism. It is my contention that the pursuit of liberty and justice for all includes the unborn. If it takes extreme action to bring this issue to a resolution, then we must passionately pursue it."

It was a good thing that Jerry had the camera trained on Roberts, because Darren would not have wanted the look on his face to be preserved for future use. He realized that his jaw had dropped and his mouth was open. He had never interviewed someone so persuasive. He had interviewed countless numbers of politicians and other public personalities, but no one had possessed these skills. He understood the influence that a man like this could have over a group of people. In fact, Darren felt himself being drawn into the man's circle of influence. Darren had never been a hardcore proponent of abortion, but he did feel that it made sense for a woman to have the right to choose. Darren considered himself a progressive thinker and progressive thinkers believed in the pro-choice viewpoint.

But Darren was struggling with the comparison that Roberts had made with the civil rights movement. There were people in the fifties and sixties with the mindset that African Americans did not have the same rights as other people. Could that same thought process apply to the unborn? This whole line of reasoning was becoming very confusing for him.

With so many thoughts going through his head, it was difficult for Darren to get his focus back on track. He shook his head slightly and realized that he had taken his eyes off Roberts. As he re-established eye contact with Roberts, he saw the smile on the man's face. Darren had to recover this interview and Roberts knew that he had made an impact. Darren could feel the wheels turning inside his head and he was not sure that they could get any traction until he resolved the questions that Roberts had raised.

Darren composed himself and muddled through the remaining questions.

"Dr. Roberts, do you advocate the use of violent measures to resolve moral issues such as this?"

"Darren, how could I ever presume to know how God speaks to each and every member of my congregation? But, I will tell you my personal thoughts on the issue. I know from reading Scripture that God has used men and women through the ages to do His work. At times, this work has been violent. It is also quite clear in Scripture that God does not like 'lukewarm people.' In fact, God said that he would spit the lukewarm from His mouth."

Roberts leaned forward and stared deep into Darren's eyes. "It is obvious that God views the killing of innocent children as a big issue. How He chooses to deal with this, I do not know. The only thing that I know for sure is this. God's people need to be ready to respond to His call, whenever it comes and whatever it entails."

With a few more follow-up questions, Darren Cooke concluded one of the most remarkable interviews that he had ever conducted. He was certain that this would not be his last encounter with Dr. William Roberts.

Chapter 21

Courtney Ferguson pulled her car into the only available space in the Women's Health Inc. parking lot. She exhaled very slowly and closed her eyes as she extinguished the car's motor. After several seconds, she opened her eyes and looked into the mirror. It would be obvious to anyone that she had been crying. In fact, she had been crying during the entire trip from Hot Springs. Her eyes were red and puffy. The tissue she had been using to wipe her eyes was soaked.

Her appointment was at four thirty. She had made it with five minutes to spare. This was going to be agonizing, but it did not seem that she had a choice. Courtney took a deep breath and exhaled very slowly. She mustered as much courage as possible and opened the car door.

It was a dreary, drizzling day. As she walked across the parking lot to the front door of the clinic, Courtney pulled the collar of her coat up tight around her neck. The wind had picked up and the temperature was dropping. It was beginning to feel like winter.

Courtney went through the front door of the clinic and signed in on the clipboard at the reception desk. She hated to even put her name on the list or anything else at this place. The guilt that she was feeling desperately wanted anonymity.

She had been sitting in the waiting room less than a minute, when one of the clinic employees stepped through a door and called her name. Courtney got up out of her seat and followed her to a small conference room. Courtney could see by the woman's nametag that she was the clinic receptionist. The nametag identified her as Wanda, but her most identifying characteristic was the way that she smacked her chewing gum continually. Wanda motioned for her to take one of the seats around the small table in the room.

"One of the counselors will be with you in a few minutes." Wanda said this between smacks on her gum. "They are running a little behind on the schedule today. Just make yourself comfortable."

With that, Courtney was alone with her thoughts once again. Even though she had been around her friends all day at school, Courtney had never felt so alone. She ached inside from the loneliness. She wondered if the heaviness in her heart would lighten after the abortion. Would the technical procedure of removing her baby give her any comfort? While she was at school today, Courtney had begun to refer to it as her baby. The turmoil had consumed her all day. It was a baby, wasn't it? If it was a baby, did that make what she was about to do murder? If it was murder, then why had her father been so insistent on her having an abortion? It was a wonder she had been able to function at school at all. She had dreaded this moment and now she was facing it – alone.

The receptionist had ushered her into a room just large enough for two people to move around the table and sit in the chairs. The conference room that she was in was rather drab. There were no pictures on the walls and there were no windows. The room had a real claustrophobic feeling. Courtney was beginning to feel a little uneasy, when the door opened and someone in a surgical scrub suit walked into the room.

"Hello, my name is Janet Rawls. I am the OR Supervisor for the clinic. You must be Courtney Ferguson?" Janet had finished her nursing duties and was working the last two counseling sessions of the day.

"Yes ma'am, my name is Courtney Ferguson."

"Well Courtney, I need to go over a few things with you. First of all, I assume that the reason you are here is to terminate a pregnancy. Is that correct?" Janet was all business when she counseled patients.

"I…I…I guess so. I found your clinic online. The information on your website gave me the impression that I could come here and find out about my options."

"I can certainly go over the options that you have, but first we need to establish the certainty of your pregnancy." Janet was writing in a chart and looked up at Courtney over the top of her reading glasses. "How did you determine that you are pregnant?"

Courtney was having a hard time looking Nurse Rawls in the eyes as she was answering these questions. It was bringing the shame of her situation front and center once again.

"My period was late and I thought that I might be pregnant. So I used a test kit that I bought at the drugstore."

Janet gave her a condescending look that made Courtney feel totally inadequate to be in the same room with her.

"Of course, we don't accept those type of results. Results from those types of test kits are not always accurate. We must have a blood test performed at a certified laboratory to give us a positive determination that you are pregnant. After we are finished here, you can have your blood drawn at our lab and we'll get the results while you wait."

Courtney continued to feel overwhelmed. "Yes m…m…ma'am," she stammered.

Janet slowly took her gaze from Courtney and looked back down at the chart that she held in her hand.

"Courtney, how old are you?"

"I'm seventeen."

"Do your parents know that you're here today?"

"Yes ma'am."

"Do you know who the other party involved in this pregnancy is?"

"Yes ma'am."

Janet looked back over the top of her glasses. "Are you sure?"

Courtney blushed. "Yes ma'am. I've only had sex once."

"I'm sorry that I have to ask these questions. You would be surprised at how many times the people that come through here aren't sure." Janet was emotionless as she said this. It was just business.

"Does your partner know that you're here?"

Courtney was staring at the floor now. "No ma'am. He doesn't even know that I'm pregnant."

Janet continued gathering information. "What was the date of your last menstrual period?"

"My last menstrual period was October twenty-fifth."

"Have you ever had a problem with your period being late before?" Janet still had her eyes focused on the chart in her hand.

"No ma'am."

"Now Courtney, tell me why you're here today."

"I think that I need an abortion, but I guess that I ought to check out my other options first."

Janet looked up from the chart in her hands and settled her gaze on Courtney. She studied Courtney's face for a few moments before she spoke.

"Courtney, I assume from your comments that you are not married. Is that correct?"

Courtney's face blushed again. "Yes ma'am."

"Do you have a job?"

"Yes ma'am, I have a part-time job."

"Are you still going to school?"

"Yes ma'am, I'm in the twelfth grade."

"Do you intend to go to college?"

"Yes ma'am. I've been planning to go to West Point and study Chemistry."

Janet raised her eyebrow at this. "So you already have career plans?"

"Yes ma'am. I would like to either be a doctor or teach Chemistry."

Janet shook her head slowly for Courtney's benefit. "Well, obviously you will not be able to follow through with those plans, if you choose to allow your pregnancy to go through to delivery."

Courtney's face had a pained expression. "Yes, ma'am, I'm aware of that."

Janet moved in for the kill. "Do you know that most teenage girls that get pregnant never finish high school? How could you possibly expect to get through college and then medical school, while taking care of a baby? It would be next to impossible."

Courtney sank even lower into the uncomfortable chair. She had not even begun to think of those kinds of consequences. Not only would she have to give up her dream of going to West Point, she would probably struggle to complete college at all. Her world was changing.

"How do you think that you would support yourself and this baby? Do you have any idea of the cost of supporting a baby?"

Janet reached into a folder she had brought with her into the room. She pulled out a sheet of paper.

"Look at this, Courtney." Janet slid the paper over for Courtney to see. "This is some information that we have compiled on the cost of supporting a baby from the newborn stage to age five. Take a few minutes to look at this. I think that you'll be surprised."

Courtney was surprised. The costs were astounding. The list of expenses seemed to go on forever. Diapers, baby food, clothes, day care, medical care. It was overwhelming. Once again, Courtney began to feel the hopelessness of her situation. She knew that it was all her fault, but that didn't seem to make any difference now. Her life was crumbling like a stale piece of cake, right before her eyes.

Janet saw that Courtney's eyes were beginning to mist over. She knew that it would be just a matter of minutes before the tears were rolling down her cheeks. There had been many girls before Courtney that had sat in front of her and gone through the same emotions. Janet was always able to get them to the point that the decision was already made for them. She was very good at this part of her job. In fact, she considered it more than a job. She considered it a crusade. In the beginning, Janet's crusade was to make sure that women in America maintain the right of choice for their bodies. She was a real fanatic in her feminism. The cause was everything and it was worth any sacrifice that needed to be made. If corners needed to be cut to keep the clinic open, she was willing to cut them for the cause. Over time her priorities changed. Her new cause became greed. At first, it was just a bonus here and there for good performance. Eventually, it became an integral part of her compensation. Now her compensation at the clinic was based on the number of procedures that were performed each year. She was financially motivated to convince every girl that came through the doors of the clinic to have her pregnancy terminated. And Janet was very convincing.

Janet had been working in this clinic long enough that the people who walked through the doors were no longer patients in her eyes. They had become numbers and those numbers had dollar signs in front of them. She knew within just a few minutes of any counseling session with one of the patients how much money would be generated by the services performed on her. Occasionally, Janet could twist the facts around until she could squeeze a few more dollars out of the case.

Janet had let reality settle into Courtney's life long enough. The tears were trickling down her cheeks. She spoke gently to Courtney.

"Do you have any questions, Courtney?"

Courtney looked at Janet. Janet could see that her eyes were swimming not only in tears, but also in the realization of what her life had become.

Courtney spoke softly. "I guess I don't have much choice, do I?"

"Sure you do, Courtney. By making a decision to terminate this pregnancy, you're making a choice for yourself. It's the best kind of decision you could make. You're making a choice for your future. If you give up a chance to go to the college of your dreams, you'll never forgive yourself. If you brought a child into this world and did not have the means to support it, what kind of choice would that be? Would it be fair to forever burden a child with that?"

Janet used this tactic frequently when she was counseling. It always planted a seed of justification for the patient. And every girl that came through the clinic needed that seed. If they did not need it today, they would need it before this was over.

Courtney was confused and it showed in her face.

"Maybe it is the best decision." Courtney was sounding less than convinced. "I don't know what else I could do."

Janet reached over and patted Courtney on the shoulder. "It's the best decision for you, Courtney. I think that when you consider all the responsibilities and expenses that come with a baby, you'll understand that this is the best choice you can make."

Courtney was defeated. She had no other defenses against Janet's arguments. Janet had been at it for years. Courtney was just a rookie.

"Yes ma'am, I guess you're right."

"Courtney, these papers that I have are consent forms for the procedure." Janet slid the papers in front of Courtney. "If you will sign at the bottom of the second sheet, we can go ahead and get started with the process."

Janet was holding a pen out for Courtney to use. Courtney took the pen and without another word, signed the consent form.

"Come on, Courtney, let's go down the hall and confirm your pregnancy with a blood test." Janet grabbed her gently by the arm and led her to the door of the room. Courtney was still in a daze. As they walked down the hall, Janet tried to reassure her.

"It will be alright, Courtney. This will turn out to be the best decision for you right now." Janet guided her down the hall to the laboratory. "After they are done with your lab work, they will take you to the scheduler to make an appointment for your procedure. We should be able to get to it before the end of the week. If you have any questions, please let us know."

Janet left her in the lab and the remainder of Courtney's appointment went by like a hazy dream. She could see it happening to her, but she couldn't feel anything. It was as if she had already checked out mentally, but her body was still going through the motions.

* * * * *

Marty came out of the OR and looked at the clock. It was 5:15. He had just finished his twenty-sixth procedure. He had barely taken a break all day. In fact, the only time that he had been out of the OR for any length of time was the time that he had spent in Carla's office early this morning.

It had been difficult to concentrate on his surgical cases after learning of Carla's visit with Brad. It had been unsettling to think of the threats Brad had made to Carla. Marty was playing his time working at the clinic back through his mind looking for anything that would confirm or refute the claims that Brad had made. There was nothing definitive that came to the forefront of his mind, but the entire process was a distraction during the day.

Marty went to the dictation station and began the documentation of his last case. He first scribbled a few of the pertinent facts into the "Op Notes" section of the chart. This part of the chart contained the highlights of the operation. In a few minutes, Marty would dictate the complete operative report, to be transcribed and placed into the chart.

"Dr. Smith, do you need anything else before I leave for the night?" It was Tammy Hawkins. She was consistently the one nurse who went above and beyond the call of duty to make sure that all of the work was done and every patient was accommodated. Marty had to smile at her dedication.

"I'm fine, Tammy," Marty replied. "I'm finishing my last chart and I'll be out of here right behind you."

"Just checking. I'm the last one out of here, except for Janet of course. I'll see you tomorrow morning."

Janet Rawls was almost always the last person to leave the clinical area of the building every day.

"See you tomorrow, Tammy. Have a good evening."

"You too, Dr. Smith," Tammy called out to him as she headed down the hallway to the back door.

Marty yelled after her. "How many times do I have to tell you? Don't call me Dr. Smith! My name is Marty!"

"Okay, okay, okay Dr. Marty. Anything you want." Tammy looked over her shoulder with a big smile as she pushed her way through the door.

Marty laughed as he turned back to his chart work. It was the first smile that had crossed his face since this morning after he had talked to Carla. He was almost done. He finished the dictation of the Operative Report and returned the microphone to its cradle. He placed the chart in the tray for completed charts.

Marty looked at his watch. It was 5:25 and he had just a few minutes before he was to meet Carla in the parking lot. He would not have time to go by his condo to change his clothes. He walked to the changing room for the surgical area and grabbed his car keys and wallet from his locker. He quickly pulled on some clothes that he kept in the locker and went out through the back door.

He shivered as he walked across the parking lot to his car. The temperature had dropped significantly since he had entered the building this morning. Like most days, he had not left the building all day, not even to eat lunch.

As Marty was heading for his car, he noticed someone in a car in the row of parking spaces that were closest to the street. From where he was, it looked like a girl with her head leaning on the steering wheel of the car.

Marty walked over to the car, wanting to make sure that she was all right. The car was a newer model BMW. He approached the door of the car and tapped lightly on the driver's side window.

Obviously startled, the girl in the car jerked her head up and turned quickly to look at Marty. Marty could tell that she was in her late teens. She had long blond hair and was very pretty. Her mascara was streaked down her face by the tears streaming from the corner of her eyes.

Marty called out loudly enough to be heard through the window. "Are you okay?"

The girl nodded her head affirmatively.

Marty tried again. "My name is Marty Smith. I'm a doctor and I work in this clinic. Is there anything I can do to help?"

She opened the window of her BMW about three inches and spoke to him. "I'm okay. I've just had a really bad day."

Marty knelt down beside the car and leaned his elbows against the door. "Were you a patient in the clinic today?"

The tears welled up in her eyes again. "Yes I was."

"You know, I see a lot of patients who come through the clinic that are upset or have some anxiety about their situation," Marty said with a calming voice. "Maybe I can help you through this process. Let's start with your name. Do you mind letting me know who you are?"

"My name is Courtney Ferguson," she said.

"Great!" Marty said. "It's good to meet you, Courtney."

Courtney reached down to the center console in her car and pulled out a tissue. She dabbed her eyes with it.

"It's good to meet you, Dr. Smith," Courtney said. "I appreciate your concern."

"Was this your first time in the clinic?" Marty inquired.

"Yes sir," Courtney said, still dabbing tears from her eyes.

"Do you know for sure that you're pregnant?"

"Yes," she said. "They did a blood test and it was positive."

"Do you know how far along you are?" Marty was going through his routine list of questions for new patients.

"Yes I do," Courtney said, a sad resolve in her voice. "I'm exactly six weeks pregnant."

Marty raised an eyebrow. "You sound pretty sure of yourself."

"I am," Courtney said. "There's only one time that it could have possibly happened. I don't have any doubt at all."

"I see," Marty said as he pursed his lips in thought. He was thinking of the ramifications of Courtney's predicament. She was a pretty girl with a bright future ahead of her and now everything had changed. She had to make a decision that would change her life forever, one way or the other.

Marty looked at Courtney who was obviously deep in the thoughts of her situation. He decided that he would try to help her through this. He had seen the struggles of many young women as they had wrestled with this choice. Courtney looked like she needed a little extra support. "So you've decided to terminate your pregnancy." He made it a statement to see her reaction.

"Yes, I have," Courtney said with an air of determination. "She scheduled me for this Friday."

Marty was curious. "Who did you talk to about the options for your pregnancy?"

Courtney thought for a moment. "I spoke with Ms. Rawls. I'm pretty sure that she is a nurse."

"Yeah, she's a nurse," Marty said with a hint of disgust in his voice. "She's a convincing counselor. I'm not surprised that you felt that you had no other option."

Courtney was staring straight ahead now. Marty noticed again that the temperature had dropped. The cold wind was blowing through the light jacket he was wearing. It was obvious to Marty that Courtney was really struggling with her choice.

"Courtney, do you really want to terminate your pregnancy? Are you comfortable with that choice?"

"I'm comfortable that this is the only choice that will allow me to reach my goals," Courtney said visibly irritated.

Courtney was becoming angry, as evidenced by the tone of her voice.

"I'm just mad at myself for screwing up. I knew better than to let this happen, now I'm suffering the consequences," Courtney said with anger in her voice.

Marty saw that Courtney's eyes had traded fire for tears once again.

"Courtney, do you have any family that you can talk to about this? This is a pretty big decision to make on your own."

"Yes, we talked last night," Courtney replied, her eyes full of tears. "My dad told me that I didn't have any other choice. He told me that I would never be able to reach my goals, if I had this baby. He's right."

Marty's brow furrowed in deep thought. "Have you ever been in trouble before, Courtney?"

"No, I haven't," she said as she tried to sniffle back the tears. "I've been too focused on my goals to get into trouble – I've been too busy."

"You sound like you're pretty determined about your goals," Marty observed.

"I am," she said with her jaw firmly set. "I've been planning on going to the U.S. Military Academy at West Point, since I was a little girl. Everything I've done in high school has been done to get me there. I've taken the right classes. I've made the grades. I've been in the right clubs. I got a nomination. And last month, I got my acceptance letter. I've done everything right until this!"

Marty now understood her dilemma.

He too knew what it was like to struggle to reach your dreams. Nothing had been easy for him. To keep his grades up in high school, he had to study twice as much as anyone else in his class. In sports, he was not a natural athlete and he practiced twice as hard as anyone else. Looking at Courtney Ferguson, Marty knew the struggle of making it on your own.

"You see, Dr. Smith, one mistake and everything's gone," Courtney said looking at Marty. "It was never in my plans to be pregnant. I had not planned on having to make this choice. I don't really want to have an abortion, but I can't have a baby."

"Courtney, I'm sorry that you have to go through this," Marty said. "I know that it's a difficult situation for you. I don't think that there is anything that I can say that will make your decision any easier, but I can promise you that we will take good care of you on Friday."

"Thanks, Dr. Smith. I appreciate your concern."

Marty saw Carla come out of the clinic. He stood and stretched his legs.

"Listen, Courtney, it's been good talking to you. If you have any other questions, just call the office and they'll get the message to me."

Marty glanced over his shoulder and saw Carla looking his way. He waved to her and turned back to Courtney.

"Thank you so much for your help," Courtney said. "Thanks for taking the time."

"Best of luck, Courtney."

He walked over to Carla's car and stood there with her for a moment as they watched the little BMW pull out of the parking lot and speed off.

"Who was that?" Carla asked, as she saw the taillights disappear down the street.

Marty turned back to Carla. "It was a patient who was in the clinic today and has a procedure scheduled for Friday. She's struggling with her decision and she looked like she needed a little help."

"Well let me know if you talk her out of it. I want to be ready for the fireworks when J.P. hears about it," Carla said with a smile on her face. "I don't know how much more excitement I can take in one week."

"Oh, you should give me more credit than that," Marty said with a twinkle in his eye. "I'll be much more discreet next time I turn away business."

Marty helped Carla get in her car. Before shutting the door, he asked about their plans.

"Let's go someplace where we can talk," Carla said.

Marty responded, "I know a quiet place close by where we can talk. Why don't you just follow me?"

"Lead the way, I'll be right behind you."

Marty closed the door to Carla's car and went to his old Mazda. He slid behind the steering wheel and started the engine. They quickly left the parking lot and headed away from the clinic.

Chapter 22

The last line of code had been written and the testing was complete. The file containing the program was attached to an email and with a press of the Enter key was sent to the office. Kevin McLaughlin was through with his part of the project. The project leader would incorporate this portion of the program into the remaining pieces of the project. By the end of the month, the client would receive the complete software package for implementation into his business.

As many as ten different programmers would end up working on this project and several of them would be working on it from their homes, just as Kevin had. Kevin's piece of the package was not the first that was submitted to the project leader, and several of the programmers would not be done until the last minute of the last day.

Kevin checked his email account for the last time. He wanted to make sure that he had nothing else outstanding with his employer. He logged off the company server, with no plans to check back again. He had completed his employment obligations. The desktop computer that he was using would sit idle for now. The time had come to turn his undivided attention to the mission to which he was called.

In biblical times, it was well documented that many people were called by God to do a task. Kevin knew from his years of sitting in a church pew that God still called people to serve and he certainly knew his calling.

The pieces had been falling into place steadily over the past few weeks. Kevin knew that the time had come for him to complete his mission. It was as plain and real to him as the nose on his face. He knew his purpose was to create an event big enough to change the way that people thought about abortion. He knew that it was his responsibility to get the ball rolling. And he was prepared. The mission would be completed this week.

He had all the tools that he needed. Now he only needed to assemble the final pieces and get them in place.

Kevin pushed back from the desk in his living room and looked out the window at the lake. The weather was getting colder outside. Kevin could tell by the color of the water. The lake always turned a grayish green as the weather turned cold. The wind had also picked up, turning the channel outside of the cabin into a rolling wave of whitecaps.

The laptop that he used for all of his personal projects was sitting on the desk. It had been on all day, but he had not spent any time reviewing his email or any other activity. As he stood in front of the desk stretching, he tapped a few keys to check for any news.

A schedule of events began to formulate in his head. If he were going to make this happen before the end of the week, he would need to organize his activities to ensure the success of the mission. He looked at his watch. It was Tuesday, 5:35 in the afternoon. He was now considering that Friday would be the day that he would complete this mission.

Kevin's plan would include an event with as much impact as possible. He wanted the public to focus on abortion and see its entire ugly underside. He knew from his research and his firsthand observation that most of what the public understood about abortion was spoon-fed to them by the media. The media had a way of taking an issue and glamorizing it. He wanted people to see that there was nothing glamorous about abortion. And he wanted to make his point with a bang.

He laughed out loud when he thought about the irony of that comparison.

He opened the door to the basement and went down the stairs. He had some work to do on his project, and the basement was not heated from the central gas system upstairs. The basement was equipped with two electric space heaters that took several minutes to heat up. With the heaters plugged in and turned on, he spread out the materials he needed for the device he would build to use on Friday. The opportunity to craft something with his hands was a welcome break from the many hours he had spent hunched over the keyboard of his computer. Kevin had more computer work to be done prior to Friday, but he needed some time to stand up and move around.

It was amazing what you could find online these days. Even as familiar as Kevin was with using the Internet, he was still surprised with the information available to anyone with some deductive skills and a little time.

The printout that he spread on the table was the narrative detail to build a bomb. The boxes on the table contained all of the parts necessary to assemble the bomb. As was his habit, some would say obsession, the appropriate type of explosive device was researched extensively. Dynamite would be used to create the blast for the bomb. Kevin did not realize how hard it was to find dynamite these days. It had been one of the items that he had requested from Mike Hanks. It had been in the package that was included with the Bronco. He was not sure where Mike had obtained the dynamite, but he had assumed that it was probably stolen. They used dynamite at construction sites and farms all over Arkansas. It was probably easy to find if you knew where to look. The four sticks of dynamite that he now held in his hands would be more than sufficient to do some serious damage to the Women's Health Inc. clinic.

The rest of the materials on the table were the electronic parts that would be used to trigger the device. Kevin sat down at the table and began to review the blueprint for the bomb. He had checked his parts list several times and he knew he had everything he needed. He put a pair of latex surgical gloves on and checked it once more. He had exhibited extreme caution each time that he had handled the parts for this bomb. He would not make the kind of stupid mistakes that had caused others who had tried similar feats to be captured by the police. His goal tonight was to put the firing mechanism together and test it. He would make sure that it worked before connecting it to the dynamite on Friday. Everything would be perfect Friday night.

The media attention that would focus on the clinic after the bombing would be intense and Kevin had a plan to make sure the focus would include the gory details of the activities in the clinic prior to the bombing. The plan was ingenious, even if he must say so himself. He would begin to set the media portion of his plan in action later this evening from his computer.

Everything was beginning to fall into place. The rush that came over him was exhilarating. It would be an unbelievable feeling to complete this mission. He had never before felt so at peace about anything in his life. He knew that it was his destiny. His calling. It was so obvious to him when he had heard Brother Bill's sermon on Sunday. It was the final confirmation that he needed to know without a doubt that he was on the right track.

When the idea of bombing an abortion clinic first came to his mind, he dismissed it out of hand. He could never do that. He was taught better than to destroy other people's property and maybe even put lives in danger. The calling had changed his perspective. It was no longer the destruction of private property, but the furtherance of God's cause. It was no longer the disruption of a private business, but the rescue of hundreds, maybe thousands of lives.

He now understood the importance of his mission and its importance in the bigger picture. If he could ignite a new movement against abortion with this bomb, then it was worth it. What were a few broken laws, with the lives of all these unborn children at stake? In reality, was it even a crime at all?

The justification of his mission had become easier and easier. He had long since stopped asking himself the questions normally associated with an overactive conscience. He no longer felt it necessary to make any justification for this mission. He knew that this was what he was supposed to do. He could feel it down into his very soul.

When he had finally come to that realization, he marveled at how his life and this mission fit together like a hand and glove. Growing up in Hot Springs, he had been raised as an only child. His parents were in their late forties when he was born. His father passed away before Kevin entered high school. His father had been involved in law enforcement for a number of years. He had even been County Sheriff for a few years.

Most of what Kevin knew about his father, he learned from his mother after his father's death. The only actual memories that he had of his father were memories of a bitter man, who was old before his time. It was the summer after his senior year in high school that he began to learn the real past of his family.

Kevin was getting everything in order to leave for college in August of that year. He was prowling around in the basement of his home, when he stumbled across an old scrapbook that he had never before seen. In the scrapbook were pictures of his father in a police uniform. He had taken the scrapbook upstairs to ask his mother about it. When his mother saw the scrapbook, she had become hysterical. She sobbed for several days before she was able to gain her composure and talk to Kevin about the pictures in the book.

Kevin spent the remaining days before he left for school discovering the secrets that his family had hidden for almost twenty years. The truth behind the secrets came out of his mother slowly and painfully. It was hard for her to relive the events that tore her family apart and changed the course of their lives forever.

That summer, Kevin learned that he was not the only child to be born to his parents. He learned about the sister that died before he was born. It was unbelievable that he had never heard this before he was eighteen years old. His parents had been very diligent about keeping the family secret.

The cause for the secrecy was the information that would change Kevin's life. Even at the young age of eighteen, he realized the depth of despair that his family had been through. It was the revelation that was responsible for the course his life had taken, since the day he heard it. His mother told him the story of how his sister had died.

The story began with his mother describing his sister. Kevin loved to hear his mother talk about her. It was obvious from the pain that his mother was going through to tell the story that she had had a very special relationship with her daughter. She had been everything parents could hope for in a daughter. She was going to be the first one in the family to go to college. She had been the apple of her daddy's eye. Until she came home pregnant.

When his mother came to that part of the story, she broke down again. It was two days before she could talk about it. His mother told him about the argument, about the yelling and the screaming. She told about his father, the Sheriff, trying to fix it for his sister. She said that his father would not even talk to her about their daughter's pregnancy. Kevin would never forget the rest of that conversation as long as he lived.

Her husband had come home one night and told her that he had made arrangements for their daughter's pregnancy. When she pressed him for more details, he told her that he had scheduled an appointment with a doctor downtown. He would take her tomorrow night and the doctor would abort the pregnancy. His mother said that she didn't understand at first. In that day and age, good people didn't know much at all about abortion. When she realized what her husband was proposing to do, she lost it. She said that they screamed at each other into the night and most of the next day. She begged him not to do it, but he didn't listen. He made arrangements with the one doctor in the area who would perform an abortion. The next night, father and daughter drove off together.

Kevin's mother got really quiet. "That's the last time that I saw her alive. The next time that I heard from your father was early the following morning. He drove up the driveway, alone."

His mother continued with the story. The relationship with her husband was never the same after that. Oh, they tried to make it work and that's where Kevin came into the picture. They thought that maybe having another child might ease their pain and patch up their marriage. They loved Kevin and they enjoyed having a baby in the house again, but it never filled the void. His father was heartbroken over the loss of his daughter. He blamed himself completely for her death. Seeing a baby crawling around on the floor of their home just reminded him of the sacrifice he had made to keep his grandchild from doing the very same thing.

"He would sit for hours watching you with tears streaming down his face," his mother had said with tears streaming down hers. "You could almost see his heart breaking a little more each day."

"Your father," his mother continued, "was never the same after that night. He tried, but he never got over it. Years later, he would talk about that night in such detail, you would think that it had happened the night before. He never forgave himself. I still think that he died from a broken heart. The doctors gave some technical sounding cause of death, but I lived with him, I knew what killed him. He died slowly, a day at a time for fourteen years. The pain of waking up each day without his baby girl took something out of him. It just took fourteen years before there was nothing left to take."

When the story was over, Kevin was overwhelmed with emotion. He found out more about his family in those few days than he could have ever imagined. Nothing was ever the same again for him. His mother died before he graduated from college and for all practical purposes, he was alone in the world. But, given the cards that he had been dealt in life, that was okay. It just gave him more time to plan. It left fewer distractions.

Everything that he had done since that conversation with his mother was in preparation for this week. Even when he was unsure of how it would all fit together, he continued to plan for this day. The courses he took in college, the hobbies he pursued, the friends he made, it was all a part of getting him to the position he was in today. From the very first time that he heard the story about the sister he never met, he knew that one day he would have a chance to right past wrongs. He knew that one day he would be able to strike back at the evil that had taken his sister and destroyed his family. In fact, you could say that he was left alone in this world because of abortion.

And Kevin McLaughlin was ready to settle some old debts.

The desire to resolve his battle with these old demons had dominated his life since the family secrets had been revealed to him. His time had come and he was prepared.

The sudden chill in the air surprised Kevin and snapped him out of his thoughts of days past. The temperature must be dropping outside. He looked at his watch and realized that he had been in the basement for almost two hours. While he was lost in his thoughts, he had been assembling and disassembling the trigger mechanism for the bomb. Over the past two hours he had become quite adept at putting the pieces together in working order. The amazing thing was the simplicity of the parts. The trigger mechanism for this bomb would be made entirely of parts that could be found at the local hardware store.

It frightened Kevin that it was so easy to find the parts and the information to build a bomb. Here he was just a regular guy and he was able to pull this off. Imagine how easy it must be for a terrorist, a crazy person, to do something like this.

He stood up from the table and stretched. He carefully placed all the pieces that he had been working on back into the box on the table. Kevin turned off the space heaters and headed upstairs. This part of the project was ready. There was nothing more for him to do with the mechanical part of the project, until it was time to set the bomb in place.

Upstairs in the house, Kevin turned up the heat to take the chill out of the air and began to quickly fix himself some dinner. He still had a lot of work to be done before Friday. As he left the food warming on the stove, he walked over to his computer to check for any new messages. When he brought the screen to life, he saw that he had an unopened email from Wheels and he opened it.

The message had been sent just minutes ago. Kevin had barely missed it in real time. The message caught Kevin off guard.

> From: Wheels
> Sent: Tuesday, December 7, 1999, 7:40 p.m.
> To: KayMac
> Subject: Caution
>
> Hey KayMac,
>
> You might want to be extra careful on your project. I've seen someone working to track down my inquiries. As always, I used multiple paths to access the information and I covered my tracks out very well. You need to be careful if you hit the server we discussed earlier.
>
> These people may be a little more sophisticated than I had thought at first. The tracking program they are using is pretty good. Of course, I'm better! I don't think that anyone is good enough to find me.
>
> Have you been able to get everything that you were looking for? Let me know if you need any more help. Be careful.
>
>

Wheels was concerned, Kevin could tell by the tone of the message. Not many computer issues concerned Wheels; these guys must be pretty good. They must be tracking the hits on their system through the IP addresses. If he remembered from their college days, Wheels had a habit of using multiple IP addresses. He always had a way of using them sequentially, leaving several layers for someone to wade through to find the real address, and thus the origination point of the message. Wheels was right. He was good and he had never been caught. Kevin would have to make sure that he was good enough to avoid being caught. He could not afford to slip up now.

He sent a response to Wheels' message.

From:	KayMac
Sent:	Tuesday, December 7, 1999, 7:51 p.m.
To:	Wheels
Subject:	Update

Wheels,

Thanks for the heads-up. I'll be watching the back door. I've found almost everything I've been looking for. I'll be putting all of the pieces into play over the next two days.

I may call you, when I get down to the final details. I'm working on a couple of financial angles that might get a little tricky. I'm still trying to penetrate some security on a couple of systems. Once I do, I should be able to bring it all together.

I'll keep you posted.

KM

A few seconds later, Kevin received a notification that Wheels had received and read his email. It always made Kevin feel better knowing that Wheels was working with him. Wheels was so good that it added an extra sense of security to anything with which he had an association.

Wheels' response came quickly.

From:	Wheels
Sent:	Tuesday, December 7, 1999, 7:54 p.m.
To:	KayMac

Subject: Help

KayMac,

You know I can break that kind of security in my sleep. Don't stress yourself too bad before you call for help. Hate to think about you struggling there all by yourself, when it would be a piece of cake for me.

Remember some of the projects that we worked on at school. They were similar to what you're thinking about now.

Let me know.

⊗

The confidence that Wheels had always made Kevin chuckle. Those who knew him never interpreted his attitude as cockiness because they knew that he could deliver.

Kevin sent his reply.

From:	KayMac
Sent:	Tuesday, December 7, 1999, 7:59 p.m.
To:	Wheels
Subject:	Feedback

Wheels,

Thanks for the offer. I'll keep you updated.

KM

With that, Kevin went to the kitchen to get his dinner. As he sat eating at the dining room table, he began to prioritize the tasks yet to be completed before Friday. Most of the remaining pieces required his skills on the computer.

He would spend the rest of the night working out the details. Tomorrow morning he would begin the implementation. By Friday, all the pieces would fit together like a jigsaw puzzle.

Chapter 23

Their food arrived during a lull in the conversation. It was the first break in their discussion since they had arrived at the restaurant. Carla had followed Marty to a small Mexican restaurant in the Heights. Marty had suggested the restaurant for its out of the way location. The interior of the restaurant was dark and the noise level was low enough that you could carry on a regular conversation without screaming at one another. Marty had discovered this place during medical school. It was a popular hangout for medical students because of the large quantity of food and cheap prices.

They had been huddled over the table for the last 20 minutes rehashing and analyzing the conversation that Carla had with Brad. After the waiter set their food in front of them and left, they started on their food and resumed the conversation.

"Marty, I'm not sure where to start with what I heard from Brad today. It left me with so many questions that I can't even begin to piece it all together," Carla said, obviously flustered.

"I know what you mean, Carla. It's overwhelming," Marty said understating the obvious. "I've always found the best way to handle these types of situations is to make a list and systematically go through and resolve each item. I always did that in my training when we had a particularly tough case."

"I guess that probably makes sense," Carla said. She had never realized how analytical he was.

Marty fished a pen out of his pocket and grabbed an unused napkin, which he spread out on the table beside his plate.

"Good, let's get started," Marty said. "Sometimes organizing the problem can be half the battle. Okay, what was the first thing that Brad brought up?"

Marty put a big forkful of enchilada in his mouth, as Carla was thinking it over.

"The first thing that he mentioned was Thomas and his school." Carla said this with a thoughtful look on her face. "I think he was trying to get my attention and it worked."

Marty was scribbling on the napkin while he was munching on his food. "That's good," he said between bites, "what's next?"

"Then he mentioned money. He asked me if I was making enough money." Carla put a bite of burrito in her mouth and began to chew slowly as she thought. "I'm still not sure why he asked about that."

Marty had his head down writing notes on the napkin with his right hand, while his left hand was absently stuffing chips into his mouth. "Okay, that's good. What did he say after that?" Marty asked with his mouth full, never looking up.

"He then went into the spiel about his family. That totally shocked me." Carla was playing with the food on her plate, pushing it around with her fork. "I don't know if I was more shocked to find out that the rumors were true, or that he actually admitted it."

"What did he tell you after that?" Marty was focused on solving the problem at hand. He did not want any tangential discussions right now and was trying to keep Carla focused.

"I guess that's when he told me that someone was using my password to access restricted areas of the corporate computer system. How could someone do that, Marty?"

"I'm not sure, Carla. I don't know enough of the technical details to answer that question. Let's not get bogged down with that yet," he said hurriedly. "We need to finish our list and then we'll come back and try to make sense of it all."

He was still scribbling as he spoke. "Now, was there anything else?"

"Yeah, only the little thing about the threat he made to Thomas and me," Carla said with a trace of sarcasm.

"Oh yeah, I almost forgot about that," he said apparently lost in his thoughts.

Marty finished writing and spun the napkin around for Carla to see. As she read down the list, he began the next step of his process.

"Okay, we need to go through each item on this list and try to make some sense out of it," he explained. "Is there anything on the list that jumps out at you right away?"

Carla pondered that thought for a few moments and then spoke. "I guess the first thing that really jumps out is the organized crime connection. It makes me wonder if we are engaged unknowingly in any illegal activities. Certainly the stated business of the clinic is legal enough, but what might be going on that we don't know about?" She paused and then continued speaking. "Being a Mob employee was not exactly part of my career plan."

Marty was listening intently as she spoke. "Why do you think he told you all of the things he did? Why wouldn't he just talk to you about the password to the system? You know, give you some standard corporate lecture about proper system security. Maybe give you a reprimand for allowing someone else to get your password. I don't know, it just seems a little excessive to spill his guts about his family without a more significant reason."

Carla responded thoughtfully to Marty's points. "I think that he was testing me."

"What do you mean?" Marty said with surprise.

"He wasn't sure if I had actually been in those restricted areas or not. He was fishing. He was waiting to see my reaction. I'll never forget the way he was staring into my eyes. It was really spooky. I'm afraid of the way he would have responded if I had reacted differently. If I would have been lying to him, I have no doubt that he would have known immediately. That man frightens me."

"Okay," Marty said slowly, "where do you think Brad will go from here with this information? Are you free and clear now?"

"I don't think so, Marty," Carla said cautiously. "If he was testing me, I have a feeling that there was more to it than what I heard this morning."

"Why do you think that?" Marty was curious.

"It was the way he kept weaving Thomas into the conversation. He obviously wanted me to know how familiar he was with my family. I think he did that to make sure that I didn't make any sudden moves. He wanted me to know that he had leverage over me."

"So where do we go from here?" Marty asked.

The conversation stopped. They had both finished their meal and the waiter appeared to take away their plates. The remains on the plates indicated that neither of them had much of an appetite. Carla ordered a cup of coffee and Marty ordered one more Diet Coke. They sat silently for several minutes, each of them thinking through the details of their discussion about the day's events.

Marty spoke again. "What will Brad do next?"

"I was just thinking about that," Carla said. "I'm sure that I've not heard the last of this. I think that he will use this to get me involved in some of the illegal aspects of the operation, whatever that might be. Once I'm involved, he's got me hooked."

"What would happen if you refused to get involved?"

"I'm afraid to even think about that," Carla said with a shudder. "I think that he would make me an offer I couldn't refuse."

Marty kept the conversation moving. "What are we going to do? Are we going to continue working at the clinic under these circumstances?"

"Listen, Marty, you don't have to be involved in this," Carla said. "You weren't brought into the discussion at all this morning. This is really between Brad and me. I don't want you to lose your job over my issue."

"I'm offended that you would even think that," Marty said. "I thought that we had begun to develop a personal relationship that was beyond what happened at work. I care about you and I don't want to see anything bad happen to you."

"I know that, Marty," Carla said, "but I don't want to jeopardize your job over this."

"Carla, I think that this is becoming bigger than a job. I could care less about this job. I am more concerned for your safety. And what about Thomas? Now that slimeball Brad has dragged Thomas into this, that's not fair." Marty's voice had risen in volume as he spoke. "As far as I'm concerned, when he threatens you and Thomas, he threatens me."

"I have a sneaking suspicion that these people are not very concerned with playing fair," Carla said, noticing Marty's willingness to become involved with her life.

"So, back to the original question." Marty wanted to move towards a resolution. "Where do we go from here?"

Carla sat for a moment staring into her coffee, pondering the answer to that question. "I think that we need to formulate a plan to get out. This job has been a wonderful opportunity for me. It has provided for Thomas and me in a way that we were unaccustomed to. It's going to be hard to give that up, but today changes everything. I won't be able to work with these people knowing what they are all about. I can't live day to day worried about Thomas' safety."

She paused momentarily. "What about you, Marty? You've not been very happy working at the clinic anyway. What do you think?"

Marty slumped in his seat and rubbed his temples with his hands. Carla had seen him do this enough to know that it meant he was feeling some stress.

"I think you're right," he began. "We do need a plan and I want us both to be a part of it. At this point in time, it will be easy for me to leave. With the kind of money that the clinic pays physicians, they'll have no problem filling my position. I'm ready to be in a real ob-gyn practice."

He sat up now and leaned forward across the table toward Carla.

"You know," he started, "the money I'm making at the clinic has become intoxicating. I've never had money before, and it's almost unreal to finally have some purchasing power. I'm paying off my school loans way ahead of schedule and also putting a little in the bank. I guess that I've been blinded by the money."

"It sounds like we were both a little blinded by the money," Carla said, more than a little embarrassed.

"Yeah," he said looking down at the table, "I'm really embarrassed. Money is not the reason I went into medicine, but it's turned out to be the guiding force in some of the decisions that I've made. I've let dollar signs cloud my judgment. I always despised those physicians who paid more attention to money than to patient needs. I never thought that it would happen to me. Now I'm just like them and maybe a little worse. I'm working for the Mob!"

"Don't be so hard on yourself," Carla sympathized. "We had no idea that this clinic was connected to the Mob. I'm not sure that there was any way for us to know. I see the books every day and I couldn't see it."

"It just came to me," Marty exclaimed.

"What just came to you?" Carla asked.

"I bet this is what Judge Stanley was talking about at the party the other night." Marty quickly relayed to Carla the conversation that he had with Judge Stanley about the owners of the clinic.

"I was puzzled at the time, but it all makes sense now," Marty said. "I would imagine a guy like the Judge would be well connected enough to know who's doing business in town, especially when it's the Mob."

"How do you get out of a business relationship with the Mob?" Carla asked.

"Very carefully," Marty replied. "In the movies most unsuccessful business ventures with the Mob are ended by leaving in a coffin."

Marty's last statement brought a sense of apprehension to their planning. The reality of their circumstances was staring them in the face and they were frightened. Neither one of them was prepared or equipped for the challenge of dealing with the Mob.

"We've got to come up with something that will let us get out without the fear of retaliation," Carla stated. "How can we do that?"

"Could we just walk away?" Marty asked.

"Maybe you could," Carla said. "After the little revelation from Brad this morning, I don't think that I can just walk away."

"Humm." Marty sighed. "You're probably right. Now that Brad has given you inside information, he can't afford for you to leave. How do you think they're using the clinic in their other business interests?"

"I've been wondering about that," Carla said. "Could it have anything to do with the discrepancies we found last weekend? I originally thought those might be routine clerical errors or maybe even a little paranoia on your part. Now I'm beginning to have second thoughts. There has to be more to it than what we've figured out so far."

"Thanks a lot for the paranoia comment," he said sarcastically. "Don't you realize that all physicians are trained to be paranoid?"

"I didn't mean it in a bad way," Carla said, recovering quickly. "I just thought you were being a little over-reactive when we started. Now it seems that maybe you were on to something after all."

"Do you think that Brad could be using the clinic for money laundering?" Marty asked.

"I've heard stories about that," Carla said. "How does it work?"

"Usually, they take money earned from illegal sources, like prostitution, drugs or extortion, and run it through a legitimate business," Marty explained. "In this case, they could use the clinic to deposit dirty money and when it comes out on the other side, it's clean!"

Carla was thinking through the details of the process that Marty had just described. She was trying to fill in the blanks with the information that they knew.

"If Brad was laundering money, then those extra deposits we found weren't mistakes," Carla mused. "They were deposits of dirty money from other sources. It would seem that the armored car company would have to be involved for this to work. How else would the money get to the bank?"

"Doesn't the armored car company just pick up a deposit bag and give you some kind of receipt?" Marty quizzed.

"Yeah, that's right," Carla conceded. "What are you getting at?"

"Only that it doesn't necessarily mean they are involved," Marty said. "They could pick up bags of money at other locations, with no knowledge of the contents or the source of those contents. Then they leave the bags at the bank and the bank processes the contents according to the instructions in the bag. The deposits could come from anywhere, even outside of Little Rock or Arkansas, for that matter."

"Why do you think that they picked the clinic to launder their money?" Carla asked.

"First of all, this is a high-volume cash business," Marty explained. "Second, most of the people that come through our doors would rather not have anyone know that they've been here. It leads to the perfect opportunity for no questions to be asked. Didn't you tell me the other day that the clinic actually does very little billing?"

"That's true," she said, "I hadn't thought about it quite that way. It really is perfect for what you're describing. No one wants to get a bill. No one wants their insurance to get billed. They generally don't want any paperwork generated. They don't want any trace of their visit to the clinic to exist."

"See, it's perfect," Marty said. "And if someone at the clinic is altering the charts to generate higher charges, who would know. Since no bills go out, no one ever realizes that the procedure performed is not the same as the procedure in the chart. It would allow the clinic to show more business on the books. Then if anyone ever checks the books against the deposits, they would find supporting documentation."

"Wow, it's starting to fit together," Carla exclaimed.

"You know," Marty said, "if they do this at all of their clinics, they could wash a lot of dirty money."

Carla thought about that for a moment. "Our clinic probably does the highest volume of all the clinics. If I understand what you're describing, it would probably be easier for this to work with higher volume. The more transactions that flow through the bank account during the normal course of business, the more your chances for success with money laundering activities."

"I'll have to look back through the computer tomorrow with this new perspective and see exactly what kind of money we're talking about," she said. If I remember correctly, the sum is quite large."

"Now that we've made some progress and know what we're up against, how do we get out?" Marty was still concerned about their chances for success.

"Do you have any thoughts?" Carla asked.

"We've got to assume that Brad will not want you to leave." Marty was shifting back into his scientific, physician mode. "You need to start looking for a way to exit gracefully. Otherwise, I'm afraid of the consequences."

"I agree with you," Carla said. "I will think it over the next two days. Surely by Friday, I can come up with something that will work."

"Good," Marty said, "I'll plan on giving my notice on Friday. I'll check my contract and see how much notice I'm required to give."

"The sooner that we can get out of here," Carla said, "the better I will feel. I'm afraid of what they might do to Thomas, if I do something to upset their plans. How long do you think it will take for us to get out?"

"I don't know. Maybe we can be out of here within a couple of months," Marty speculated. "We just need to make sure that we remain as low-key as possible until we're out."

Marty started again. "Do you have any place that you could send Thomas until this gets settled?"

"I hadn't thought about that," Carla said. "Maybe I could send him to stay with some relatives in Memphis. His Christmas break is scheduled to start at the end of next week. He could go then."

"I don't know, Carla," Marty hesitated. "I think you should go ahead and send him now. It will be easier to pull this together if we know that he's safe."

"You're right, Marty." Carla was nodding her head. "I could send him over Friday. That way, he'll just miss a few days of school, until we can figure out a longer term plan."

"It looks like this plan is coming together," Marty said. "I feel better now – like we have a little more control over the situation."

They both sat back from the table with a sense of relief. The problems from earlier in the day seemed somewhat smaller now.

"I'm glad we were able to work this out together," Carla said with a smile. "Thanks for caring about us. Thomas and I have been on our own for a while. We've not been used to people helping out."

"I know that it has been a fairly short period of time, but you and Thomas have become very special people in my life," Marty said. "I want to make sure that we have a chance to develop a long-term relationship, if that's what works out."

Carla reached across the table and Marty stretched out his arms to hold her hands. They sat gazing into each other's eyes. Their friendship was growing closer, more rapidly than either one of them had anticipated. The intensity of their circumstances had made them more vulnerable and receptive to a serious relationship. They were both surprised and pleased that they were moving quickly beyond friendship.

"We better go," Marty said, still staring into her eyes. "We're going to have a busy week."

"You're right," Carla said. "Let's go. I need to get Thomas prepared for this little interruption."

They stood to leave. Marty left money on the table to take care of the bill and the waiter. As they left the restaurant, Marty had his arm around Carla. She had her head resting on his shoulder. They were happy with the change that life had brought them. Their lives and circumstances had changed dramatically since they had started seeing each other. Things were about to change again and neither of them realized how permanent the changes would be.

* * * * *

Courtney arrived home after dinner. With the rush hour traffic leaving Little Rock, it took longer than usual to get back to Hot Springs.

Her mother had saved her a plate of food that she took to her room to eat. She finished the food quickly and had been locked in her room ever since.

Courtney had all of her materials for West Point in one folder that was now two inches thick. She was sitting on her bed with the contents of the folder spread out before her. The process of being accepted at West Point had taken her two years. She flipped through the pieces of paper – each piece representing a commitment that she had made to be the best.

She had wanted to go to West Point since she entered the ninth grade. Her desire was to be something out of the ordinary – something different. She had never been happy as part of the crowd. Courtney sat down that year and mapped out her course to get to West Point. Acceptance at West Point had been her entire focus during high school.

And she did it. She was in!

Now this – pregnant! It was her worst nightmare. Courtney kept hoping that she would wake up and discover that it was all a bad dream. But she didn't and it wasn't.

Chapter 24

Carla was at her desk much earlier than usual Wednesday morning. Her car was the first one in the parking lot. She had not slept well during the night. The mental weight of the previous day's events had burdened her mind way beyond the capacity for sleep. Being wide awake anyway, Carla decided to go to the office and get some work done. She had left her house at four thirty after checking on Thomas. He of course was sound asleep. She would swing back by the house in time to get him off to school.

The unanswered questions were bouncing around in her head like marbles in a pinball machine. Carla's life was extremely organized and orderly. She planned everything. She was unaccustomed to this many unresolved issues. As she tossed and turned during the night, Carla realized that she could not begin to make plans to leave before she knew exactly what was going on at the clinic.

The discrepancies that Marty and she had found on Saturday were still troubling her. She had a gut feeling that it all tied together somehow, but she couldn't make the pieces fit – not yet anyway.

Carla knew, from the research they had already done, that the discrepancies tended to focus in two areas: cash flow and chart documentation. Her first task this morning was to check out the chart documentation before anyone else arrived at the clinic. She wanted to follow up on something that Marty had discovered in the charts on Saturday. He had found copies of ultrasound reports that he had never ordered or seen. Carla was going to find the answer to that question this morning.

The record room was locked, but Carla had a master key that gave her access to the entire building. She unlocked the door and let herself into the room. She took the folded piece of paper that Marty had left her out of her pocket and checked the patient names once again. She quickly pulled the charts and soon had a stack of twenty-five patient records. Carla sat down and methodically went through each chart in detail looking for the piece that would lead her to understand the pattern of the changes that Marty thought had been made to these charts.

After a few minutes, Carla realized that in every chart the ultrasound that was documented represented a pregnancy of either seventeen or twenty weeks. These dates represented the break points for pricing. At seventeen weeks, the price jumped from $500 to $850. At twenty weeks, the price jumped again to $1,850. According to Marty's notes, all of the patients represented by these charts were between eleven and fifteen weeks pregnant.

Carla sat back and was absently shuffling through the charts looking at the ultrasound prints. She was trying to organize the facts in her head, when a thought came to her. She sat up and sorted through the charts to group them by length of pregnancy. The end result was two piles of charts – the pile for seventeen weeks and the pile for twenty weeks.

She began to sift through the seventeen-week charts comparing the ultrasound prints. Carla knew very little about ultrasounds, but the images looked strikingly similar. She picked one up and began to examine the information that the computer had printed on the ultrasound images. The information included the patient's name, the identification number of the person performing the ultrasound and the estimated gestation period of the pregnancy. The sonographer took measurements of different parts of the fetus. The measurements used for dating the pregnancy were a head circumference, a biparietal diameter, femur length and abdominal circumference. The computer used these measurements to calculate the age of the baby and give the estimated date of delivery.

The first thing that Carla noticed was that the Gestational Age, or GA as the computer referred to it, on each print was exactly the same. Every chart in the stack indicated that the patient was exactly seventeen weeks and two days into her pregnancy. As Carla studied the information on the ultrasounds, she quickly realized that each measurement was exactly the same on every patient.

She sat back in the chair and spoke out loud. "That's impossible. Those measurements are down to a hundredth of a centimeter. There's no way that the measurements could be exactly the same for eight different patients."

Her mind was racing, thinking through the possibilities. She stood up and started looking through the charts in the twenty-week stack. She knew exactly what she was looking for now.

Within minutes, she had confirmed her suspicions. She found exactly the same pattern in these charts. Each patient was twenty weeks and four days into her pregnancy and just as in the other stack of charts. All seventeen charts had precisely the same measurements of the baby.

The next detail that she wanted to check was the ultrasound machine itself. Carla did not understand how the machine could be manipulated to get the results that she had seen in the charts that were spread before her.

She filed the charts back in their appropriate places in the shelves. She then walked the short distance down the hallway to the clinical area where the ultrasound machine was located. The machine was in a room that was just slightly larger than an exam room. The room contained a bed for the patient to lie down on and a stool for the sonographer that was positioned between the bed and the ultrasound machine itself.

Carla sat down on the stool and examined the machine. The machine had two transducers that were passed over the abdomen of the patient to record the status of the pregnancy. The ultrasonographer viewed the progress of the exam on a monitor. Below the monitor was a keyboard that was used to control the different functions of the machine. Carla noticed that the keyboard had a function that was labeled "Archive." If the results of the testing were being altered in any way, this would be the logical path to accomplish it. She pulled out the manual for the machine and quickly found the description for the archiving process. Underneath the keyboard was the main processing unit for the machine. It was there that the drive for a rewritable optical disk was located. On the cart that held the machine sat a small plastic container that held several of the rewritable optical disks. Carla opened the container and flipped through the disks. Most of the disks appeared to be system back-ups, but the last two disks in the container were different. She pulled these out and examined them more carefully. The label on one of the disks read seventeen-week ultrasound. The label on the other disk read twenty-week ultrasound. Both of the disks contained the initials "JR" in the lower right-hand corner.

Now it was beginning to make sense. Janet Rawls was not only the OR Director of the clinic, but she was also trained as an ultrasound technician. Janet was the one employee in the clinic who did not report directly to Carla. Because of her clinical responsibilities, she reported to Dr. Straun, the Medical Director. Janet would almost have to be in on any scheme that involved an alteration of ultrasound documentation. She knew the operations of the ultrasound equipment better than anyone else in the clinic.

Carla was thinking through this new information. "If Janet was involved in the deception, who else might be involved?" she thought to herself. It would almost require that Dr. Straun be involved. Janet spent a lot of time with J.P. and they worked very closely together.

Carla paused for a moment. "Does that mean that they are working for Brad at a different level than the rest of the clinic employees? Who else might be in on this?" If there were many other employees involved, Carla would have surely heard of this before now. She and Marty had concluded that the purpose of the discrepancies was to pass extra money through the bank account of the clinic. What benefit would Janet Rawls receive from this? Did she have a separate financial arrangement that Carla did not know about?

The questions were flying through her head in a rapid-fire mode and it was causing her mind to spin. She wanted to sit down with Marty and go through all the variables. He was so good at that process. It must have been his training in medical school and residency. It would take a logical evaluation to put these pieces together.

Carla looked down at her watch and realized that she needed to hurry to get back home and get Thomas off to school. She quickly put everything back in place and hurried out to her car. Within minutes she was wheeling out of the parking lot and heading west.

* * * * *

Janet Rawls was driving into the clinic a little earlier than usual. Ahead of her, Carla Sharkley was pulling out onto the street and heading west. "That's odd," Janet thought to herself. Carla had been working at the clinic for almost a year and had never arrived at the office before 8:00 a.m. Something must be going on.

Janet used her cell phone to call J.P. Straun. "Dr. Straun," she said when he answered his phone, "this is Janet Rawls. I just saw something unusual and I thought that I should report it to you. As I was driving to the office this morning, I saw Carla Sharkley leaving the office."

"What time does she usually get into the office?" he asked her.

"It's usually around 8:30 before she comes in," Janet responded.

"Is there any reason that you know of for her to be at the clinic this early?" Dr. Straun asked.

"None," she replied.

There was a moment of silence on the phone. Dr. Straun was thinking. "Look around when you get there and let me know if anything is out of place. I'll get back with you later if we need to do anything else."

With that, the connection ended.

Janet smiled to herself as she put her phone down. It was going to be a good day. She loved this kind of work.

* * * * *

Marty was midway through another day. Every day was now a major struggle for him to complete. He was in the middle of his twelfth procedure of the day and the joy was certainly gone. Technically, his work was perfect. He had no complications with his patients. His surgical technique was textbook. It was the mental boredom that he was wrestling with. The money was great, but the repetition of doing the same thing over and over, day after day, was killing him. The training that he had received during his residency certainly considered an abortion appropriate medical care, but it was different when it filled his day, with no end in sight. It was different when you looked into their faces day after day. The training he received didn't prepare him for that. They didn't tell you about the empty stares and the despair that was reflected in their eyes. They didn't tell you about the girls who would show up for their abortion clutching their favorite stuffed animal. They didn't tell you about the girls who would sob through the entire procedure. Marty needed to see a little happiness from his patients from time to time. He thrived on the positive feedback…

"Are you okay, Dr. Smith?"

The nudge on his shoulder startled him from his thoughts. The question and the nudge were from Tammy Hawkins, the nurse who was helping him on his current case.

"I'm fine, Tammy," Marty said. "I was just thinking about something else."

"I was worried for a minute there," Tammy replied. "You hesitated longer than I had expected, and I was afraid that I had missed something."

"Everything's fine," Marty said glancing at the head of the table to see the patient's face. "Who talked to this patient before she came into the OR? She's an emotional wreck!"

Tammy looked at the chart. "It was Janet. She doesn't waste a lot of time with emotions. I didn't think that we would ever get this one quieted down."

195

The patient had been almost hysterical when she had first come into the OR. She had a death grip on a stuffed teddy bear that she had brought with her. She had not been scheduled for any additional medication for the procedure, but it had become necessary to give her twenty-five milligrams of Valium to calm her down.

"After she settled down some, I tried to talk her out of going through with this procedure until she was emotionally stable, but she wouldn't hear of it," Marty commented. "She was going to have an abortion no matter what. I don't think that anyone could have talked her out of it."

"Janet certainly does a good job of scaring them to death," Tammy replied with disgust. "She hardly ever loses one. She would have been really mad at you if you had talked this one out of a procedure. You're already in her doghouse over the one last week. If you had done it again, she would have had Dr. Straun jumping all over you with both feet."

"Yeah, like he didn't already do that," Marty said with a hint of embarrassment. "I thought he was going to fire me on the spot last week."

The patient shifted slightly as Marty repositioned the suction curette inside her uterus. She appeared to be getting a little uncomfortable, that was just part of the process. The patient always became uncomfortable and restless toward the end of the procedure. He could see by the decreasing flow into the POC container that the procedure was almost complete.

"How's she doing, Tammy?" Marty asked as shifted up briefly to look at the head of the table.

"She's fine," Tammy replied. "Hopefully, the medication that you gave her will allow her to wake up calmly."

Tammy looked thoughtfully at the patient lying on the OR table in front of them and then she spoke up. "Why do you think she was so upset about having this procedure done?"

Marty was busy finishing the procedure and did not look up as he spoke. "Maybe she wasn't sure that she really wanted it in the first place. You know it's a pretty big decision for a woman to make."

"Of course it is," Tammy said forcefully. "Thank goodness she had the opportunity to make the decision."

Marty was surprised by her determined response. "Tammy, what do you think about the work that we do here?"

"It's great," she replied. "I think it's a tremendous community service. This clinic is the only one in Little Rock and we serve women from all over the state. If we didn't provide this service, what would these women do?"

"How do the other employees feel about this place?" Marty inquired.

"A couple of people are here for the cause, but for most of them it's a job that pays well," Tammy summarized. "It's hard for most people to get committed to any cause these days – everybody's so busy with their lives."

They worked on in silence for a few moments with the noise of the suction machine the only sound in the room, before Marty spoke up again.

"What about Janet Rawls? Where do you think she stands in all of this?"

"I'm not sure," Tammy pondered. "At times, I've thought that she was committed to the pro-choice effort. On other occasions I just thought that she just needed to be committed."

Marty laughed. "What do you mean by that?"

"I mean that she is so intense that she almost seems crazy at times. I've seen her go into a rage and cuss out an employee over the smallest thing. But, the scariest thing is to watch her deal with the patients that come here. She seems like she's possessed," Tammy said. "You ought to watch her eyes sometime while she's counseling a patient. It's like she's in another zone."

They completed the procedure. Marty reached over and turned the suction machine off. Tammy was busy cleaning up the OR. Marty checked on the patient. She was coming out from under the sedation still clutching her teddy bear.

"Why do you think that Janet is so intense about the patients here?" Marty asked.

"All the other employees seem to think that she is tied in financially with Brad and Dr. Straun in some way," Tammy commented. "Nobody knows what the connection is, but she is way too intense for a regular employee." After a moment's thought, she spoke again. "Maybe she's part of the Family."

Marty looked up with a start. "You mean the Mafia connection? I thought that was just a rumor."

"Who knows," Tammy said with a smile. "It would make more sense than anything else that we've dreamed up. It would certainly explain her intensity."

Marty was pondering that thought, when a new voice spoke up.

"Is it over with yet?"

His patient was awake.

Chapter 25

Kevin stood and stretched. He had been pounding away at the keyboard of his computer since the previous night. It was now noon on Wednesday and he was pleased with his progress. His muscles ached from the constant hunching over the keyboard for all those hours.

But it was worth it. He had finally broken through the passwords early this morning. After that, it had been complicated and time consuming to follow the money. His suspicions had been correct. The Giovanni family was using their abortion clinics to launder money from their other various illegal operations. The money had passed through numerous accounts, mostly in offshore banks, before arriving eventually in an account in a well-respected Chicago bank. The complication was in the number of accounts that were used to filter the money. Many of the trails seemed to lead to a dead end. In each instance though, Kevin knew to keep looking until something else came up. After the first couple of times that the trail vanished, he wrote a short program that automatically began to look through the routing records of the bank. The program would search for any number of common or similar factors. It would search for transfers of dollar amounts that matched the balance of funds that he had traced into the account. He even had the program sort totals from multiple transfers, just in case the transfer did not go out in a single transaction. Whenever he encountered a new hurdle that had been thrown up in front of his search by the security of the Giovanni system, he would initiate his program and within minutes he was back on track.

Finding the trail and discovering their modus operandi had been the first big breakthrough. The second came as he realized how efficiently the Giovanni's were moving and hiding their money. The activity in and out of the various accounts was fast and furious. As he saw the overwhelming number of transactions in the accounts and how rapidly they occurred, it clicked with him how he was going to hurt them and their abortion clinic completely. He decided that he would reroute some of their money for other uses.

This morning Kevin had set up the accounts that he would need for the transfers. He had a string of ten different accounts that he would use to hide the trail and disguise the final location of the money. The money would eventually end up in a brokerage account with a small regional firm and there he would convert the money to equities and bonds. By the time those investments were made, the trail would be so cold that no one would be able to find anything.

This final angle of the mission that he had developed was perfect. What better way to drive the final nail into the coffin of the Women's Health Inc. clinic? He would not only shut them down, they could not see patients in a clinic that had been damaged by a bomb, but he would also redirect their profits.

Kevin was pleased. He had almost felt guilty about this part of the plan. Blowing up the clinic was one thing; he had already been through the justification process on that one. Stealing money was something entirely different, or that's what he thought at first. He had never stolen anything in his entire life, so this had been hard. He had spent a great deal of time working through the moral aspects of stealing from the clinic. Then the realization came to him that stopping this horrible sin was far more important than some minor detail about the ownership of the money. He reminded himself that the mission was more important than anything. Although the mission had begun as the bombing of the clinic, he now believed that the destruction of the financial structure of the clinic was just as important. With that, the justification process was complete. The theft of the once dirty money was now an integral part of the mission.

Kevin looked at the clock. It was noon. He had been working at his computer for over twelve hours without a break. He needed to get up and move around before rigor mortis set in and he was stuck permanently in this hunched position. His mind was cluttered with the thousands of details that made up his mission. He got something to drink in the kitchen and walked out on the deck. The water in the lake was as smooth as glass across the bay behind his house. The air was crisp and cold with a little bite to it, as it crept down the back of his neck under the denim shirt that he was wearing. He took a deep breath and the cold, fresh air cleared the cobwebs in his head and filled his lungs with a sense of rejuvenation.

Maybe he needed to stay outside and get some exercise. The next two and a half days were going to be intense and it would require him to be very sharp. A little sweat and exercise would do him some good. The heavy workload had caused him to get out of his regular exercise routine. Normally, he was diligent about exercising at a high level of intensity.

Then a thought occurred to him. What about the canoe down in the basement? It would be an ideal day to get out on the lake. The motion of paddling would stretch out those muscles that had become cramped while sitting at the computer. While it had been a couple of years since he had been in a canoe, he used to do it all the time. It would great to get back in a boat.

Kevin turned and went into the house. He set his glass down on the kitchen counter as he passed through on the way to the basement stairs. He started down the stairs and flicked on the light in the basement. He grabbed a flashlight off the table and went down the tunnel to the lake. He tugged and struggled to get the door open.

The light coming into the tunnel from the open door eliminated his need for a flashlight. The canoe was at the end of the tunnel and Kevin bent down to grab the edge of the boat. He lifted the canoe over the threshold of the doorway and began to drag it down to the water. He was halfway down the ten feet to the water's edge and dropped the canoe to look inside.

Under the dust that covered it, the canoe looked to be in excellent shape. There were no visible holes in the hull and all of the seams fit tightly together. On the floor of the boat, Kevin found two wooden paddles and two life jackets. This would be perfect, he thought to himself, and he pushed the canoe into the water. He grabbed the edge to steady it, as he jumped to get in the boat.

The canoe wobbled from side to side as he settled down and reached for a paddle. Kevin waited for a moment until the canoe quit rocking. He used the paddle to push the canoe away from the shore. He looked up and down the bay and decided to paddle out to the mouth of the bay. It took him several minutes for the rhythm of paddling to come back. By the time he was several hundred yards from the shoreline, he was making good time and doing it in a straight line.

The bay was not much more than half a mile wide at this point. Kevin was studying the homes that lined the lake. The homes along this part of the shore were a mixture of huge new homes and old summer cabins. It had become very popular to buy a piece of lakefront property and tear down the small cottages that were the typical construction from the fifties and sixties and build a new home. Along the main channel of the lake, it had become quite common to purchase two or three lots, demolish all of the old structures and build what could only be called a mansion by Hot Springs' standards. Along the bay in which he lived, the mega building had yet to completely take over. This bay was known as the Little Mazarn. It was named for the small creek that ran into Lake Hamilton at this point.

Kevin had reached the mouth of the bay and was looking across the main channel of the lake. It was almost two miles across to the other shore from here. A map of the lake indicated that this was the midpoint of the lake. It was halfway between Carpenter Dam, which formed Lake Hamilton, and Blakely Dam, which formed Lake Ouachita to the northwest.

He turned the canoe around and headed back into the bay at a much slower pace. It was then that he noticed the weather had changed. It was definitely getting colder and the wind was picking up a little. Clouds continued to cover the sky.

Kevin noticed that the view was dramatically different from the lake. Now he understood why some real estate agents showed lake property by boat. The houses were much more impressive from this perspective. As he approached his house, he was struck by how isolated it was. Even with all of the homes along both sides of the small bay, the house was more obviously secluded than it appeared from the road. The small island that it sat on gave it a unique atmosphere that separated it from all of the other homes along the shores of the Little Mazarn.

He had paddled back to the dock that was behind his house. Instead of going directly back to the shore, he circled the property to give his muscles one last workout. The island was connected to the shoreline by a short one-lane bridge, which served as the driveway to the house. He paddled under the bridge and came around the north end of the island and back into the bay. He completed the circle as he steered the canoe back onto the bank by the door to the tunnel. It felt good for him to exercise something other than his mind for a change. As he sat on the shore, the wind picked up and he realized that he would need additional gear to keep warm if he was going to get the canoe back out tomorrow.

Kevin raised himself from the shore and stretched again. He was feeling better already.

* * * * *

Whitney Simpson walked through the door of the Women's Health Inc. clinic. She signed in at the reception desk and took a seat. Although Whitney had never been in this clinic before, she knew the drill. This was her third pregnancy and she had yet to become a mother. It was her intention to delay that accomplishment as long as possible. The easy availability of abortions fit her lifestyle perfectly and as far as she was concerned, a change in lifestyle was not in the cards.

"Whitney Simpson." A clinic employee in a surgical scrub suit called her name from the door beside the reception desk.

Whitney rose from her seat and crossed the room to the open door.

"Hi Whitney!" the employee said with a smile. "Please follow me."

As they walked down the hallway, the employee was making small talk. "My name is Bobbie! It's very nice to meet you, Whitney. Is this your first time at our clinic?"

Whitney cringed. Bobbie was so perky it was about to make her nauseated. Luckily, she had a strong stomach.

"Yes, this is my first time at your clinic," Whitney said with a forced smile. She decided that Bobbie was not the person to talk to in the clinic. She was certain someone else would be coming to "counsel" her. Bobbie did not appear bright enough to handle anything too important.

They came to a small conference room and Bobbie motioned for her to take a seat.

"One of our counselors will be with you in just a moment," Bobbie said, her smile never wavering. "If you need anything, I'll be right down the hall."

With that, she turned and left Whitney alone. Whitney was already bored with the whole thing. How come they put you through all of this for a lousy old abortion? She never understood why they made such a big deal about it. She had done it twice before and didn't consider it to be much more trouble than getting a cavity filled. To her, it was just bad luck, like getting in an automobile accident. You knew it was going to happen from time to time, but you hoped it didn't happen to you.

The room that she was waiting in was certainly not a candidate for inclusion in *Architectural Digest* and neither was any other part of the clinic that she had seen so far. This was the third abortion clinic that she had been in as a patient. She found that they were all pretty much the same when it came to décor – drab. Each clinic had been very functional and that was about it. You didn't come to a place like this for comfort and warm, fuzzy feel-goods. You came for one purpose and one purpose only. You came to end an unwanted pregnancy.

A new person breezed into the small conference room and Whitney could tell right away that this one was in control.

"Hi, my name is Janet Rawls," the nurse in the scrub suit said. "I am the Nursing Supervisor of the clinic. I need to discuss your visit to the clinic today."

She paused and looked down at the chart in her hands. "Whitney, I see from the information sheet that you filled out that this is your first visit to our clinic." Her eyes shifted up from the chart to look at Whitney.

"Yes, that's correct," Whitney, said.

Janet looked back down at the chart. "And why are you here today, Whitney?"

"I'm pregnant and I need an abortion," Whitney said matter-of-factly.

Janet looked up with her eyebrows arched in surprise. "Oh really. Are you certain that you're pregnant?"

"Oh no, I'm not certain," Whitney said sarcastically. "I came here for the wonderful ambience of this place. I can't imagine why any woman would want to spend an afternoon anywhere else."

Janet was staring at her with a look that would turn steel into molten liquid. Whitney just flashed a drop-dead look back at her and continued.

"I know I'm pregnant because I've done this before." Whitney paused. "In fact, this will be the third time that I've been pregnant and I aborted the first two. If it's okay with you, I'd like to abort this one too."

Janet was fuming. She set the chart down on the conference table and calmly began to fill out an encounter form to order a pregnancy test from the lab. Janet was not used to anyone talking to her like this. She was about to lose her cool and she didn't want it to happen in front of a patient, even someone as obnoxious as Whitney Simpson. Janet patiently finished the paperwork, much slower than usual to regain her composure before speaking again.

"Since you have been through this before, you know that we must confirm your pregnancy with a blood test before we can schedule you for a procedure," Janet began in a methodical fashion. "Typically, we like to schedule your procedure within three to five days after we have confirmed your pregnancy."

"I would like to schedule the abortion for this Friday, pending a positive pregnancy test," Whitney said, interrupting Janet. "I would like to have Dr. Straun do the abortion on Friday."

Janet was surprised. It was very rare that a patient came into a counseling session requesting a specific physician.

"Okay," Janet responded. "Let me check the schedule and see if Dr. Straun will be here on Friday."

Janet flipped through the stack of information that she had with her and found the schedule for the week.

"It looks like you're in luck," Janet said. "Dr. Straun will be in the clinic on Friday. It looks like it won't be a problem for him to do the procedure. Can you be here at one o'clock on Friday afternoon?"

"One o'clock will be fine," Whitney said.

Janet wrote the information down. "I'll have the receptionist put this into the computer and you can get an appointment card on your way out of the clinic today. There is one other thing for us to discuss and that is the cost of the procedure."

"Don't worry about it," Whitney said. "I talked to the girl about the fees over the phone. I'll be paying cash in advance as I leave today."

Janet stood and motioned for Whitney to follow her. "Well then, I guess that's all we need today. I'll take you to the lab to have your blood drawn. If there are any problems, we'll call you, otherwise, we'll see you Friday afternoon."

After Janet dropped her off at the lab, she took the remaining paperwork to the front desk. As she turned to walk to the OR, Janet thought to herself, this one is going to be trouble. Janet did not like this one at all. Whitney Simpson had a little too much attitude for her own good. They would have to watch her closely. This one had the potential to be disruptive. That was okay though. Janet could handle difficult people. She could handle them very well.

Chapter 26

Brother Bill Roberts was wrapping up a very busy day. It was five o'clock and he was just getting done. On a normal day, he was out of the office by four thirty, but nothing was normal now. Since his sermon this past Sunday, the phone had been ringing off the hook. The calls had been an interesting mix of unflagging support and questions about his mental stability. However, the tide of support was beginning to swell in his favor. He had to smile when he thought about it. Who would have ever thought that he would be in this position now? He was on the verge of greatness. He was going to be the next leader of the pro-life movement. The very nature of the issue would propel him into politics, where he was destined to be.

Those who doubted would be sorry. Those who failed to support him would receive their just rewards. In fact, he was already preparing the campaign to discredit them and turn people against them. He would use his pulpit, like he had done before. Not many people could withstand the power of the pulpit.

The television in the bookcase across the room from his desk caught his attention. He had turned it on, with muted sound, waiting for the five o'clock news to begin. He saw that it was just beginning and used the remote to turn on the sound. The anchorwoman was introducing the lead story for the evening.

"Good evening, I'm Anne Hansen," she began. "Thank you for joining us tonight. The issue of abortion brings out a variety of emotions that touch people emotionally, spiritually and politically. We have seen this play out in situations across the United States."

She paused and shifted her gaze into a different camera. "Arkansans have dealt with the abortion dilemma in the typical low-key ways. They have participated in organized marches, both for and against abortion. They have pursued state legislation, both for and against. They have supported political candidates based on their views on abortion."

She shifted cameras again. "This week, these emotions have been intensified in our state. This past Sunday the pastor of a church in Hot Springs declared war on abortion. Our KBTE reporter, Darren Cooke, has the story."

Brother Bill smiled as the screen filled with a camera shot of Darren.

"Thanks, Anne," Darren began. "This past Sunday Dr. William Roberts, pastor of the First Fellowship Church in Hot Springs, attacked abortion as an evil blight on our society. I have an excerpt of that sermon to show you."

For the next forty-five seconds, KBTE rolled a clip from the sermon. Brother Bill's smile grew even wider. It was some of his best material.

They switched back to the live shot of Darren.

Darren continued with his narrative. "I had the opportunity for an exclusive interview with Dr. Roberts. You can see by the clip of this interview, that Dr. Roberts makes a very persuasive and passionate argument."

KBTE showed the people of Arkansas approximately thirty seconds of the interview. Brother Bill thought it was prime-time stuff. The entire state would now know that William Roberts was a man who could lead people. They would know him and be ready to follow him when the time came.

Darren was back on the screen. "As you heard, Dr. Roberts has issued a challenge for people to stand up and oppose abortion in any way that is necessary. In Dr. Roberts' words, it is worth the risk to protect the unborn. He further compared abortion to the Holocaust during World War II. Dr. Roberts has laid a bold challenge of action in front of those in our state who have pro-life beliefs. This is Darren Cooke reporting for KBTE-TV, now back to you, Anne."

Brother Bill muted the sound once again. He leaned back in his chair and put his hands behind his head. This was working quite well, he thought to himself. The media was playing this exactly as he had hoped. They were giving it enough exposure to guarantee name recognition. They were also giving him the type of coverage that would lead to interviews by some of the national media outlets. They were giving him legitimacy.

This was perfect. It could not have gone better, if he had planned it himself. He smiled and thought, but of course he had.

* * * * *

Kevin had been out most of the afternoon, returning to the house just in time to catch the evening news. Brother Bill's interview was wonderful. The media was going to be primed for the events of the week. He would begin to release his "public relations" material later tonight. Over the past year, he had collected reams of information that told the real truth about abortion. Most of the information came from the Internet, although some of his best materials were pictures that he took when he was working on the cleaning crew at the clinic. He had taken the pictures with a digital camera and downloaded them on his computer. He had sifted through a tremendous amount of information to pare it down to something the media could use. Over the next two days, he would be providing them background information, as well as sound bites that they could use on their broadcasts. He had already presorted the information to catch their attention and keep them pushing the story. Tonight he would trigger the email program that would send them new information every four hours. The photos and video had been scanned into his program and would be the hook that would keep them on this story. The most gripping photos were those of the storage room at the Women's Health Inc. clinic. Seeing row after row of plastic containers filled with body parts floating in bloody liquid would get their attention. The television newsies could not resist putting that kind of stuff on their broadcast. It was too gory and shocking to pass up.

And now this. The segment that KBTE did on Brother Bill was the perfect lead-in to his plan. It was all coming together so well, just like the pieces of a puzzle. The piece that the media put on the board tonight was unexpected, but welcome. It was almost spooky how well it was going. To Kevin, this could only be the will of God directing him to complete this mission. Every step that he took seemed to fit perfectly. With the final piece that he would put into place on Friday night, the mission would be finalized. It made Kevin feel good to know that he was right where he was supposed to be, doing the will of God.

He took the purchases from the afternoon down into the basement and laid them on the table. He was most excited about the wet suit that he had purchased at a local sporting goods store. It would be perfect for him to wear canoeing. Wearing the wet suit would keep him warm and dry and he would be able to get some exercise in regardless of the weather.

Kevin went back upstairs and logged into his computer. It was time to get busy and make his next move. He had everything set and ready to go. Tonight he would initiate the start sequence of the financial attack and the public relations blitz.

Kevin saw that he had new email. He began to scroll through each of them looking for anything important. Right away he saw that he had a new message from Wheels.

From:	Wheels
Sent:	Wednesday, December 8, 1999, 4:14 p.m.
To:	KayMac
Subject:	Trace

KayMac,

Your friends in Chicago are doing their best to trace the hits to their system. I left a long trail that led nowhere and I've been watching it. They are about to track it to the end. I just wanted to remind you to be very careful. These guys are pretty good. Do not underestimate them!! I repeat – Do not underestimate them. Do you need any help?

⊗

Kevin quickly tapped out a response on his keyboard.

From:	KayMac
Sent:	Wednesday, December 8, 1999, 5:21 p.m.
To:	Wheels
Subject:	Re: Trace

Wheels,

Thanks for the warning. I have everything planned. It will go into motion tonight. It might be good for you to keep an eye on my back to make sure that no one follows too closely. I'll be pulling an all-nighter, so let me know if you see anything. Thanks again.

KayMac

Good old Wheels. He was always watching out for his friends. With Wheels on the back door, it should be safe. Kevin made a mental note to be extra careful anyway.

Kevin settled down in front of his computer and began to work. It was going to be a long night, but his adrenaline was pumping. The last stages of programming on a big project were always exciting for him. The importance of the project made it even more exciting. And this one had more significance than anything else he had ever done. He had never before been involved with something that was so obviously from God. It was an experience that he would never forget.

* * * * *

The ten o'clock news had a replay of the abortion story from the five o'clock program. Carla and Marty saw the segment come on just as Marty was about to leave for the evening. They had spent a quiet evening at Carla's preparing and eating dinner. Thomas only had one more night at home until he left for Memphis during the Christmas holidays. Carla was already beginning to miss him. She wanted to stay at home in order to spend more time with Thomas. Marty was happy to have dinner at Carla's tonight. He enjoyed being around the two of them.

They had watched the story in silence. Thomas was already in bed.

"Wow, that was pretty powerful," Marty said, still staring at the screen.

"Yeah, that guy is very persuasive," Carla, commented. "He has a charismatic personality. I'll bet he has a strong following in Hot Springs."

"If he keeps getting this kind of press," Marty exclaimed, "he'll have a following way beyond Hot Springs."

"You know," Carla said, "the more I think through this whole abortion thing, the more troubling it is. I've still not made a decision how I feel about the pro-choice versus pro-life debate, but I know for sure that I don't want to be involved with the process, especially with the Mob involved."

She turned on the couch and faced Marty.

"Do you think we'll be able to walk out without any problems following us?" she asked. "I'm real worried that Brad will not let go very easily."

"I'm worried about that myself," Marty said. "I've been thinking of a plan. What if this Friday, I give my notice of resignation? I'll give them thirty days' notice and we'll see how it goes. If all goes well, then you can follow in a couple of weeks with your resignation. If a problem comes up, we can bail out together on short notice."

"How do you think Brad will react to that?" Carla asked. "He's not known for accepting a change in plans very well."

"I'm not sure," Marty said. "He's not been very visible in the clinic lately. Maybe he has more important things on his plate right now. This might be a good time to slip out, if he's preoccupied."

They were silent for a moment, as they thought about the few options that were available to them. The reality of the work they were doing in the clinic was finally settling over them like an ominous cloud. It was not something that either one of them wanted to be doing for the rest of their life. The fact of working for the Mob was just downright scary. They were still unsure what that would mean over time, but they both felt that it could not be good.

"I'm so glad that you're here to help with this," Carla said as she curled up next to Marty on the couch. "I don't know how I could have dealt with this alone."

Marty put his arm around her. He turned off the television with the remote in his other hand. They sat quietly for a few moments.

"I know we've only been seeing each other for a short time, but it feels like I've known you forever," Marty said seriously. "I hope we can work through this, because I want to be together with you for a long time. I don't want anything, or anybody to mess it up."

"I know what you mean, Marty," Carla said. "I'm a little surprised myself that things have moved along so quickly. I'm looking forward to our time together without the complications of the clinic hanging over our heads."

"I'm ready too," Marty agreed.

"Do you think we'll get there soon?" Carla was anxious.

"I think that things will change quickly at the clinic," Marty speculated. "I have a hunch that we'll be free of that place very soon."

Carla snuggled in tighter to the crook of Marty's arm at his comforting words. He had a way of making her feel secure.

"Do you think that I'm doing the right thing with Thomas?" Carla was still fretting over her decision to send Thomas to Memphis.

"Of course you are," Marty replied. "We've been over that a dozen times and you know that it's the best option for him. If things start happening quickly, we don't want Thomas' safety at risk. Even though I'm going to miss him, just like you are, I don't want him getting hurt in any way just to make us feel good having him around. He'll be okay for a couple of weeks. It'll be an adventure for him. He'll love it."

Carla looked up at Marty and smiled. "You really care about him, don't you?"

"Yeah, I do," Marty admitted. "I want to make sure that nothing happens to either of you. You have become very important to me."

"Maybe we can get this thing resolved," Carla said hopefully.

"I hope so," Marty said. "I am ready for a change and I'm ready for it to happen soon."

* * * * *

Courtney had spent another long day at school. Keeping her pregnancy quiet was causing her a great deal of anxiety. Although she was not looking forward to the procedure, Courtney was ready to have the pregnancy behind her. The constant fear of discovery was stressing her out. She just knew that someone was going to find out.

Dinner with her parents had been very quiet. The pregnancy was straining their relationship and Courtney hated it. She had always enjoyed a closeness that most teenagers did not experience with their parents.

The West Point file was in her hands. She couldn't quit thinking about it. The dream of attending West Point was playing over and over again in her mind like a broken record. Looking down, she realized she was holding her acceptance letter in her hands. A tear started down her cheek. There had been a lot of tears shed since she discovered that she was pregnant.

She was in her room crying, when she saw the ten o'clock news. Brother Bill, her pastor, was being interviewed. The entire interview was about abortion, just like his sermon on Sunday. Brother Bill left no doubt about his stance on abortion. Apparently, it was God's stance also. Brother Bill had outlined it very clearly for the reporter.

Opposing abortion was much easier, when it wasn't personal. Having her West Point letter in one hand and a report for a positive pregnancy test in the other had changed her perspective. She no longer cared about the politics of abortion. She didn't even care what her pastor thought about abortion. He didn't have to worry about getting pregnant. Abortion was a choice for her now – a choice that would allow her to keep her dreams.

Courtney put all of the papers back in the file and laid it on her nightstand. She fell back unto to her bed and curled up in a fetal position. Burying her head in her pillow, she cried herself to sleep.

Chapter 27

Carla was at her desk Thursday morning, when the phone rang. It was the intercom line that let her know that her secretary was trying to get her.

Carla picked up the phone. "Yes, Patsy."

"Ms. Sharkley, Mr. Giovanni is on line two. Do you want me to ring it in?" Patsy asked.

"Sure," Carla said, "I'll take the call."

Carla had not heard from Brad since the day that he had threatened her. She wondered if this would just be a follow-up to the previous harassment. She took a deep breath to prepare herself, before she picked up the ringing line.

"Good morning, Brad," she greeted him. "How are you today?"

"Good morning, Carla," Brad replied. "I'm just fine, thank you. I think that maybe I should be the one asking you that question."

He made the comment with just enough sarcasm to let her know the issues they talked about earlier were still on his mind.

"I'm fine, Brad," she said. "What can I do for you?"

"I'm sending someone by today to see you," he said. "She represents a company that provides supplies to companies and universities for medical research."

"I'll be happy to talk to her, Brad," Carla said.

"I want you to do more than just talk to her," Brad said. "I want you to cooperate with her. If we can work with her, the clinic stands to make a lot of money."

"I'll work with her any way I can," Carla said, not appreciating Brad's tone. "When can I expect to hear from her?"

"I told her to come by the clinic later this afternoon," Brad explained. "You'll need to meet with her and get the specifics of her company's requirements. She will also want a tour of the clinic."

"I'll be happy to help." Carla sighed. "Is there anything else you need?"

"Yeah," Brad responded, "don't mess this up, if you know what I mean. This is a big deal. I'll check back later to see how things went."

With that, the line went dead and Carla was left sitting with the phone to her ear, listening to a dial tone.

* * * * *

The phone in Dr. J.P. Straun's Porsche rang as he was driving to a lunch meeting. He was working at the clinic in Jackson, Mississippi, today. This clinic was part of the Giovanni's chain of abortion clinics. It bore the same name, Women's Health Inc., as the clinic in Little Rock. The only designation between the clinics in the corporate files was the city name.

J.P. picked up the phone and noted the identity of the caller. He sighed and debated whether or not to answer the call, but he knew that he had to talk to her at least until she went through with her promise.

"Hello," he answered.

"Hi J.P.," she said. "Why didn't you call me last night? I tried all night to get you."

"I told you that I would be in a meeting most of the night," he snapped. "I told you that we would talk today." She was driving him crazy.

"Did you go to the clinic?" he asked anxiously.

"Yes," she replied, "I went by there yesterday afternoon. The counselor I spoke to was really rude. She treated me like I was an idiot."

J.P. couldn't imagine why. He thought that was pretty perceptive of the counselor.

"But I stopped her," she said. "I gave her a piece of my mind and made her listen to me."

J.P. thought that it was dangerous for her to be giving away even a small piece of her mind. If she did that too often, pretty soon she would be the girl with no brain.

"She acted like I had no idea if I was pregnant or not," she continued. "I told her that of course I knew what it felt like to be pregnant and certainly I can count. I know when I'm late."

J.P. couldn't believe how she was rambling. What did he ever see in this girl? He must have been crazy to get involved with her.

"She was just doing her job," J.P. interrupted. "Did they give you an appointment for a procedure?"

"Of course they did," she said a little surprised. "You told me not to leave without one. I know how this works. This is not my first time."

"When did they schedule it?" he asked impatiently.

"My appointment is one o'clock Friday afternoon," she responded. "I'm scheduled to see you, just like you said."

"Good," J.P. said with a smile, "we'll get it taken care of tomorrow."

"Will you be back in Little Rock tonight?" she asked.

"No," he said, "I won't make it in until early tomorrow morning. I'll see you right before we do the procedure."

"If I'm feeling okay, maybe we can see each other tomorrow night," she said.

"Sure," J.P. replied, "we can talk about it tomorrow. Listen, I've got to go. I've made it to my lunch appointment and I don't want to be late."

"Okay, J.P.," she responded, "I'll see you tomorrow."

J.P. hit the disconnect button on his cell phone and terminated the call. He let out a long sigh of relief. Tomorrow afternoon, this little adventure would be over. He still couldn't believe that he had gotten her pregnant. How could he let himself get involved with a girl like this? He must be losing his touch. Usually, he had much more discretion than that. He should have known better, but he would learn from this mistake. The next time he would be much more careful, so the pregnancy thing wouldn't become an issue. When the girl gets pregnant, they expect so much more than dating.

Well, tomorrow he would perform an abortion on her and it would all be over. Once the procedure was over, that would be the last time he would see Whitney Simpson.

*****

"Ms. Sharkley?" It was Patsy, her secretary.

"Yes, Patsy," Carla responded, pressing the button on her phone to use the speakerphone.

"There is a lady here to see you," Patsy said. "She is with Custom Research Inc. She said that Mr. Giovanni sent her."

"Oh yes," Carla replied, "he said that someone would be coming over this afternoon. Please send her in."

"Yes ma'am," Patsy said as she hung up the phone.

Carla moved around her desk to the door of her office to greet her guest. A tall blond woman approached her door.

"Hi, my name is Carla Sharkley," Carla said sticking out her hand in greeting.

"Hi, Carla. My name is Maggie Craig," said the attractive woman. "I'm the area representative for Custom Research Inc. Brad Giovanni suggested that I speak to you about the services that my company offers."

"Please come in and have a seat, Maggie," Carla said. "Brad mentioned that you would be by today. What can I do for you?"

Carla moved around behind the desk and took her seat. Maggie took a seat in front of the desk.

"Let me give you one of my business cards, Carla," Maggie said. "Do you have a card?"

"Sure," Carla said fishing around in her desk drawer for a business card, "I've got one in here somewhere." She found the card and reached across the desk to exchange cards with Maggie. "Brad seemed interested in the services of your company, but he didn't mention what those services were."

"Yes," Maggie said, "I would say that he was very interested. You see, my company is involved in providing the necessary materials required by organizations that engage in medical research. Of course, one of the primary needs that these companies have is fetal tissue."

"Fetal tissue?" Carla was puzzled.

"Sure," Maggie said, "fetal tissue is one of the key components of many research programs throughout the world. We sell tissue to researchers, pharmaceutical companies and universities. It is a struggle to find enough tissue supply to meet the demand of the marketplace."

"Does your company perform abortions?" Carla asked, still confused.

"Oh no." Maggie smiled. "We just handle the tissue. We don't do the abortion procedures. We act as a broker for the products."

"So what exactly does this have to do with our clinic?" It wasn't clicking for Carla yet.

"Brad really didn't tell you much about us, did he?" Maggie seemed surprised by the lack of communication.

"No, I'm sorry, but he didn't," Carla said. "I guess that I need to listen to your sales pitch."

"Well, Carla," Maggie said a little amused. "It's a little more than a sales pitch. You see, Brad signed a contract to do business with our company. I'm here to give you and your staff an orientation to our process. This clinic will be our newest supplier of fresh fetal tissue."

Carla was shocked. "I can't believe that Brad would make a decision like this without telling me. What is involved? Is it labor intensive? I don't think I can spare any staff to deal with this."

"Don't worry about it, Carla," Maggie said. "My company does all the work, that's the beauty of it. We will provide staff in your clinic to harvest the tissue and prepare it for shipping. Our clients are very specific about their research needs. We specialize in fulfilling customized requests, hence our name, Custom Research Inc. Because of the custom nature of the requests we receive, we will begin to review your patient charts prior to the procedures to ensure that we can deliver the freshest tissue in the industry. We custom harvest most of our tissue. This allows us to maximize the reimbursement for our services and therefore provide a higher rate of return for your clinic."

"I thought the sale of body parts was illegal," Carla quizzed.

"It is," Maggie replied. "However, since we will be on-site, our attorneys have found a loophole in the law for us. We don't technically purchase the fetal tissue from you. We lease space from you at a very favorable rate. Favorable for you that is. We also help you cover other items of your overhead. The amount and quality of tissue that you can provide will determine the total amount of support that you receive. Our clients are only interested in normal tissue. This is usually not a problem though, since only 2 percent of aborted tissue is typically abnormal."

"So, let me get this straight. You provide the staff," Carla said quizzically.

"Right," Maggie said.

"You harvest the tissue and ship it to your clients," Carla said.

"Right," Maggie said.

"What does my staff have to do?" Carla asked.

"You need to provide my people space to perform the harvesting process," Maggie replied. "You also need to provide us with a list of the patients that are scheduled for procedures. Occasionally, we may make a suggestion to the physician regarding the specific technique used in performing the procedure. This, of course, is based on the type of requests that we have pending from our clients."

"What does that mean?" Carla asked. "Will you be telling the physicians how to practice medicine?"

"Oh no," Maggie exclaimed, "we would never do that. Our goal is to help you maximize your revenue based on these procedures. Our suggestions are nothing more than information regarding the monetary potential of each case. The physicians are always free to make their own decisions based on the appropriate information."

"Are we talking about a lot of money?" Carla asked.

Maggie reached into her briefcase and pulled out a folder. She slid it across the desk to Carla.

"I think you can see by the prices on the top sheet in the folder that this could add up to a lot of money in a hurry." Maggie was speaking with great confidence now. This part of the presentation always reeled them in. "These numbers are why Brad was so interested in our services."

Carla looked down the list. She was stunned. The list contained a catalog of fetal body parts and each one had a price beside it. Eyes and ears. Brains. An intact trunk. A wave of nausea came over her. Carla thought that she might get sick right on top of her desk. It was the second time in less than a week that her job brought her to the point of nausea. The thought of buying the body parts of aborted babies off a shopping list was disgusting. How much lower could this place sink, she thought to herself.

"I can see how these numbers would get your attention," Carla muttered, breathing deeply to keep the bile from coming completely up her throat.

"Oh yes," Maggie explained. "A clinic with this type of volume can easily generate close to an additional $1 million on an annual basis."

The silence hung in the air briefly as Carla continued to stare down at the price list in her hand.

"Since Brad has already made the decision, I guess we need to show you around," Carla said. "When did you want to get started?"

"Actually, we were thinking about starting tomorrow," Maggie said. "We have some clients in this area and we would like to meet their needs locally. I know it's short notice and I hope that it won't be too much trouble."

"No, I g…g…guess that will be fine," Carla stammered. "I need to introduce you to Janet Rawls. She is our OR Director. She can show you around and help you get settled."

Carla pushed the button on her phone to activate the intercom. "Patsy?"

"Yes, Ms. Sharkley," Patsy replied.

"Would you please contact Janet Rawls and have her come to my office?" Carla said. "I need her to show Ms. Craig around."

"Sure, Ms. Sharkley," Patsy said. "I'll contact her right away."

"Thanks, Patsy," Carla said as she hung up the call.

"Janet will be right up to show you around," Carla said to a smiling Maggie Craig.

Chapter 28

Lying in the middle of the desk was a pile of pink message slips from news organizations all over the country. His secretary had been frantically fielding phone calls all day long. Bill Roberts sat back at his desk, a smile creeping across his face. A feeling of exuberance permeated his entire body.

Since the interview had aired last night, the attention had been fabulous, much more than he could have hoped. He had in the pile of messages over twenty requests for interviews from television, radio and magazines. They were already focusing on him as the new leader for the pro-life movement. They were asking for his opinion on everything from Supreme Court candidates to new medical technologies related to abortion. Overnight, he had become the expert on all abortion issues.

His preparation for this moment had been extensive. He had spent many hours locked away in his study at the church researching the many facets of abortion. He was prepared to deal with any aspect of this abomination to society. He had studied the mistakes of others who had tried and failed to become the leader of this movement. He would not make their mistakes. He would not give the media an opportunity to destroy him as others had done. The seeds of conspiracy that he had planted were too deep for him to be tainted by their actions, when it was time for them to sprout. The plan was perfect.

He had done almost everything that he could in his current position to leverage himself up to the next level. He had worked every possible angle in his pastorate to gain this status. It would not be long before he left this church and moved on to his next role. He intended to parlay this into a very public position that would make his name and face known throughout the country. Ultimately, he might even use this to get into politics as a candidate for public office. There had been other men with much less going for them to make it in that arena. If he played this out right, the opportunities would be endless and they would all be very public and very rewarding.

The phone on his desk rang. He could see from the flashing light that it was his secretary. He pushed the button and spoke to her.

"Yes, Betty?"

"Brother Bill," she started, "Mike Hanks is out here to see you. Are you ready for him?"

"Sure, Betty," he replied. "Send him in."

There was a knock on the door and Mike Hanks let himself in the office.

"Good afternoon, Brother Bill," Mike said as he extended his hand across the desk to his pastor.

"Hello Mike," Bill said as he stood to shake Mike's hand. "I'm glad that you could come over. We have a lot to talk about this afternoon. Please sit down."

They both took a seat and Bill began the discussion.

"Have you seen the interview?"

"I saw it last night," Mike said. "It was great! I don't think that we could have hoped for anything better."

"I agree," Bill said. "The local channels were very kind to us. We now need to move on to our next step and raise the stakes in this battle."

Bill motioned to the pile of messages on his desk. "There is a lot of interest in this from the national news media. The next step is to hold a press conference and begin to push our agenda on a broader scale."

"How soon do you plan on doing the press conference?" Mike asked.

"I want to do it tomorrow afternoon," Bill replied. "By the indications on these messages, the national press is not waiting for my response before they fly into the state. It looks like most of these people will be in Little Rock by noon tomorrow. If our press conference is at two o'clock, they should have plenty of time to work it into their schedule."

"What do you need me to do?" Mike asked. "Do I need to get the press conference organized?"

"No, I've got Betty working on that." Bill noted the disappointment on Mike's face. He smiled to himself. It's what he liked so much about Mike. He was always so eager to please. "But, I do have something that you could help with." Mike lit up at the suggestion.

"I want to have protesters at the press conference," Bill continued. "I want some hard-core radicals marching and yelling in the background."

"I can make that happen," Mike said with confidence. "Where are you going to have the press conference?"

Bill sat back in his chair and clasped his hands behind his head. "The press conference is scheduled to be held in front of the Women's Health Inc. clinic," he said with a wicked smile on his face.

Mike's jaw dropped. "Why are you going to have it there?" Mike was astonished. "Don't you know that our friend is supposed to be there tomorrow? That's crazy to have the media there!"

Mike was getting a frantic look in his eyes. Bill loved it. Mike got up and began to pace around the office. He was mumbling nervously as he paced.

"Won't the media put a crimp in the rest of our plans? I don't think I can get to him to delay the bomb. I gave the go-ahead earlier this week. I don't think that I can even get in touch with him now." Mike was babbling. "The plan was for no additional contact to occur after the go-ahead signal was given. It's going to happen now. That bomb is going to explode right in the middle of the press conference."

Mike was sweating profusely now. Brother Bill just sat back and let him go. Finally, Mike stopped and turned to him.

"Why aren't you worried about this?" Mike asked. "It looks like a disaster waiting to happen."

"Just stop and think about it for a minute," Brother Bill said. "Our guy is only trying to disrupt the business of the clinic. He is not trying to kill the mothers and babies that we are trying so hard to protect, that would be counterproductive."

Mike was considering Brother Bill's comments.

"I think our man will choose to set off his bomb sometime during the night while the clinic is closed." Bill paused to let the thoughts sink in. "He has obviously spent a lot of time putting this plan into action. I don't think that he will make a mistake of that magnitude."

Mike sat back down and smiled. "You're always a step ahead on all of this."

Roberts stared at Hanks and said, "That's the only way to make it to the top and I don't plan on allowing a detail like that to trip me up. I've been planning for this for a long time and I know exactly what it will take to make this work. Now, I need you to focus on these next few days and make these pieces come together for me. The timing of all these events is critical to the ultimate success of our mission. God has put this plan in my heart and I don't need you to question the direction we're going anymore. I just need you to make the details work. I will not tolerate a lack of faith about my vision."

Mike Hanks was looking at his pastor like a whipped puppy. He was embarrassed that his questions had come across as doubt. He believed in this mission and his pastor more than anything else. He would not let Brother Bill down again.

"I'll make sure that the protesters are there early," Mike said.

"Good," Brother Bill said, "It will give the cameras something for background footage."

The room grew quiet as Mike stared at his hands that he held folded in his lap and Bill pondered the remainder of the plan.

"After the press conference," Brother Bill began, "I will give a series of one-on-one interviews. Betty has rented a room at a hotel just around the corner from the clinic. We are in the process of scheduling those interviews now. Before the weekend is over, the entire country will know about William Roberts and the cause that he represents."

Brother Bill leaned forward across the desk and stared deep into Mike's eyes.

"This is going to be the most important time of my life," Brother Bill said slowly. "I don't want you, or anyone else to screw it up. This is a time for strong faith, not doubt. This is a time for decisive action, not second-guessing. I need your support, or I don't need you at all. What will it be, Mike? Do you have enough faith?"

"I'm with you, Brother Bill," Mike said. "I'm sorry my questions came across that way. I really didn't mean it to appear that I doubted you. I'm with you 110 percent."

"Good," Bill smiled as he spoke, "I'm glad that you're with me. We still have a lot of work to do before this all fits together and we need to get focused. I'm sure that this pile of messages will grow even bigger after tomorrow night. Everyone will be calling for my opinion and I do not want to disappoint them."

Bill Roberts turned in his chair and gazed out the windows of his office. Dusk was settling in on Hot Springs. They had a lot of ground to cover and he was determined to leave nothing to chance. Mike and Brother Bill spent the next two hours finalizing the details for the next few days. The plan came together and they left ready for the developments that the new day would bring.

* * * * *

"Marty, this has become completely unbearable," Carla said as she and Marty sat on the couch in her den. She had just told Marty the about the encounter that she had had with Maggie Craig earlier in the day. "Can you believe they broker baby parts? It's pathetic that a company can make so much money buying and selling body parts. I checked them out online today and could not believe how successful they have been."

Marty was listening patiently. It was not the first time he had heard this story tonight. Carla was curled up under his arm on the couch. As Carla went through the story again, he thought about how close they had become in such a short period of time. He knew that it was ridiculous for him to be thinking this way, but he couldn't help it. He was beginning to think that this was going to turn into something serious. They had spent almost all of their free time together during the last week. After they had finished dinner, they had come into the living room to relax. Carla had turned on some music and it was playing softly in the background. They were becoming very comfortable with each other.

It was late and Thomas was already in bed. He was leaving early the next morning for Memphis.

As the story wound down again, Marty spoke up. "You know, this whole thing has made me think real hard about my career. I wonder if you ever reach a point where you just walk away from it all, regardless of the consequences. My whole life, I've thought about nothing else except dedication to a career. Now, I'm beginning to have second thoughts about that mindset."

"I know this stuff at the clinic has been a real negative for you," Carla said, "but don't you think you can find something more traditional that would put you back on the right career track?"

"It's not just the clinic." Marty hesitated slightly. "It's also you and Thomas."

Carla looked up at him with surprise.

Marty looked down at her and started again. "I know that this is going to sound a little corny, but getting to know the two of you has changed my perspective a lot. The focus on my career, as everything in my life, has changed. Since we have spent so much time together this past week, being with you has become much more important to me than a career that might separate us somehow. This job at the clinic has made me realize that the difference between a respectable career and a marginal existence hinges on factors that I cannot control. I'm ready to identify those things that are important to me, and change my priorities."

Carla was sitting up now, looking Marty in the eye. "Wow, I didn't realize that you felt that way."

"Well, I didn't either until the last few days," Marty said. "I've been doing a lot of soul searching and frankly I found quite a hole. I know it has just been a few weeks that we've been seeing each other, but as far as I'm concerned, I'm ready for this to become a serious relationship."

"Marty, I don't know what to say," Carla said. "I'm surprised that you feel that way. I'm glad you do, because I feel the same way. I was already stressing out over sending Thomas to Memphis, and then I began to worry about losing you through these changes at the clinic. I'm not sure that I could stand losing either one of you."

Marty wrapped his arms around Carla and hugged her. They stayed in each other's embrace, neither one of them wanting to let go. Finally, Marty turned his head to whisper in Carla's ear.

"I love you," he said.

Carla pulled back, so that she could see his eyes.

"I love you too," she responded.

Their eyes locked together for what seemed like an eternity, both of them thinking about the future. Both of them wondering how they would get free from the clinic and live a life together away from the grief they were now feeling every day that they walked into that building.

Chapter 29

The computer had been running all day long. The programs that had been initiated the previous evening were automatically transferring money to a number of predetermined accounts. The trail of the money from the Women's Health Inc. accounts and those accounts of various related companies was growing cold.

Kevin had monitored the progress of the programs from time to time during the day. Everything was working beautifully. He looked at his watch. It was eleven o'clock. By the time the sun rose tomorrow morning, the money that the Giovanni family had laundered so well would be unrecognizable even to them. From Kevin's perspective, it was important that it be unrecognizable especially to them. His life depended on it.

Between the progress checks he made, Kevin spent the rest of the day outside. The weather had become progressively worse during the day. In spite of this, Kevin was determined to get some exercise. He had spent so many hours over the last week totally engrossed in his programming that he was afraid that he would lose his edge. After tomorrow night, he was uncertain what the future weeks would bring and he needed to be as sharp as possible, mentally as well as physically. He was prepared to disappear for an extended period of time, if it was necessary. He thought that he had covered every track, but you never knew when the cops would get lucky.

It galled him to think that as soon as they identified him as a suspect in the bombing, he would become a hunted man. While at the same time, at locations all over the country, clinics like this would keep on operating and killing babies. They could kill hundreds of thousands of babies each year and the government would actually encourage it. He had discovered that many of the public school systems distributed information from these clinics to their students. It was sickening to him that the killing of innocent children was allowed to continue and there was nothing that could be done legally to protect them. He hoped that his mission would be the catalyst to change that mindset.

Kevin had spent most of the afternoon paddling around the lake in the canoe. He had worn the wet suit that he had purchased the previous day. It had made a tremendous difference protecting him from the wind and cold water. He was actually becoming quite good at moving across the lake in the canoe. He had experimented with his paddling until he had developed an efficient stroke that allowed him to quickly cover a great distance with minimum effort.

The aching that it had left in his muscles had been very rewarding. With his schedule during the last few months, it had been impossible for him to maintain any type of exercise routine. It felt good to get out again.

He focused again on his computer. With the access he was able to get through the clinic's system, he had been able to gain entrance into most of the key functions of the Giovannis' corporate network. It was through this access that he had found the bank accounts in the Cayman Islands. The program the computer was running had used over a hundred accounts at fifty different banks in five different countries. In most cases, the money remained in the account only a matter of minutes before new commands were sent to move the funds to the next location. The concept of digital cash had made this process infinitely less complex.

The final resting place for the money had been a source of amusement for Kevin. It appeared that he would have almost $10 million to work with by the time that the program had fully executed. He decided first of all that he should set aside some money for his personal use in case he became a fugitive during the mission. The program had transferred $3 million split into five different accounts that he had access to through the false identification that had been provided to him. The program had also been designed to transfer money into the accounts of several of the staff members of the clinic. Kevin had made these transactions easy to trace. He was using this to divert attention away from any trail that he might leave. He hoped that this would be the first direction that the Giovanni's pursued after they discovered the missing money. It would be natural for them to suspect insiders first.

He had also decided to have a little fun with some of the transfers. He had chosen several appropriate charities to receive donations. Both the Giovanni's and the charities themselves would be surprised.

In order to pull this off, Kevin had used a great deal of information that Wheels had provided to him. Wheels had always been a wealth of information when it came to the details necessary to execute a top-notch hack into a system. Wheels had provided access to account numbers and passwords to access the various systems on Kevin's list.

In addition to the attack on the finances of the clinic, he wanted to initiate a public relations attack. He used his laptop to begin a random distribution of technical and statistical information on abortion to the media. Kevin had performed an amazing amount of research on abortion over the years. He would now put that information into the hands of reporters. He had programmed his computer to send this information out anonymously. He wanted to make sure that the reporters would have everything that they needed to expose the ugly truth behind abortion. By Saturday morning, every media organization in the state would be doing stories on abortion. Kevin wanted them to get it right.

Kevin pushed away from the computer and left it as it cranked through the remaining portion of the program. He wanted to check the equipment one more time before tomorrow.

He went down the stairs to the basement. The table in the middle of the room was now piled high with the equipment and materials he would need for tomorrow and the supplies that he might need beyond Friday.

The preassembled components of the bomb were in boxes at the far end of the table. Kevin slipped a pair of latex gloves on and grabbed a duffel bag off the shelf and began to carefully place the parts of the bomb into the bag. He had already wiped down these parts to eliminate any fingerprints and hopefully any stray DNA. The duffel bag would make transporting all of the pieces of the bomb into the clinic much easier. He organized the components in the bag to make the assembly of the bomb in the clinic much simpler and quicker. Although the bomb would not technically be capable of exploding until he had completely assembled it, he was taking no chances.

The entire inventory of the bomb parts, including the dynamite, fit into the small duffel bag. Kevin placed the bag at the bottom of the stairs. The excitement had been building all week. Seeing the duffel bag packed and ready reminded him that he had been preparing for this event for a long time. He could hardly believe that the time was almost here.

Kevin took off the gloves and threw them in the trashcan. All the trash would leave with him tomorrow. He then began to organize the remaining supplies and equipment that were left on the table.

He had been preparing for the possibility that he might end up on the run from the authorities. Kevin had planned an escape route that would lead him out of heavily traveled areas and reduce his chance of capture. Arkansas had many hiking trails and back roads that would allow him to travel with minimum human contact. He had been accumulating hiking and camping equipment and supplies for several weeks. Just as he had with his purchases of the parts for the bomb, he had paid for all of these purchases with cash.

Kevin had purchased a large expedition-size backpack and he began to fill it with the supplies that he would need for three weeks, if it became necessary. He loaded the pack with cooking utensils and food. He also packed matches, a flashlight, two changes of clothes and water. One of the most important items that he purchased was a GPS. The handheld GPS would allow him to keep on course at all times. The unit also contained an electronic compass, altimeter and barometer in a waterproof case. He placed the GPS in one of the small wing pockets on the pack. It would need to be within reach if he had to move quickly.

After he had finished loading the pack, he strapped a new tent and sleeping bag to it. Both the tent and sleeping bag were high quality and lightweight. With the adjustable suspension harness and load control system, the pack would ride well on his back. He should not have any problem with the amount of gear that he had. The gear would allow him to endure for at least three weeks without the need to replenish any of his supplies.

Kevin placed the loaded pack on the end of the table closest to the bottom of the stairs. He stood back and looked around the basement. All of the items that he had spent weeks accumulating were now packed and ready to go.

He looked at his watch. He had been down in the basement for over an hour. It was after midnight.

Satisfied that everything was in order, he went upstairs and walked out on the back deck. The chill in the air surprised him. Kevin pulled the collar of his jacket tighter around his neck. As he stood there looking out over the lake, he realized that the wind had changed since earlier in the day. The wind was blowing from the northwest and it was much colder. He reminded himself that he should check the forecast for the next couple of days.

It was now Friday. A chill went down Kevin's back that had nothing to do with the weather. He was anxious and excited, all rolled up together. He had been waiting a long time for this day – even before he knew exactly what the day would bring. Since he had discovered the toll that abortion had taken on his family, he had been waiting for this.

He stuck his hands into his jacket pockets to protect it from the cold. As he did, his fingers struck the lone key in his pocket. His face transformed into a smile.

The key to the clinic was his reminder that patience is sometimes required to bring closure. He turned the key over in his hand within the confines of the pocket. He loved the touch of that key.

He loved the touch of that key because he knew what it meant. It meant that the completion of the mission was close at hand. It meant that he would be striking back.

Turning the key over in his hand reminded Kevin of all the hours that he had spent planning for this day. And now it was here.

It reminded him of the pain that his family had suffered because of this great abomination called abortion. It reminded him of the great debt that was owed to his family because of abortion. And now it was time to collect that debt.

The turning key reminded Kevin of the sweet taste of revenge. Vengeance is mine sayeth the Lord.

Kevin was ready to be used to complete this mission. He was called to this mission. And now it was time to answer the call.

Chapter 30

The chirping of the phone irritatingly awoke him from the deepest sleep that he had had in a long time. He looked at the clock on the nightstand. The illuminated digital face of the clock told him that it was 2:07 in the morning.

Ronaldo Giovanni struggled to lift his large frame up on his elbow in order to reach the phone. It just reminded him of the grief that he had recently taken about his weight from the doctor his wife made him see.

He finally picked up the receiver to the phone and the annoying chirping sound ceased.

"Hello," he growled into the phone.

"Mr. Giovanni, I'm sorry to disturb you so late, but I thought that it was important."

"Who is this?" Giovanni demanded, still growling.

"This is Andy Costello down at the office. One of the guys in the IT called me about a problem and I thought that I should relay it on to you."

"Well, are you going to tell me what the problem is, or am I going to have to guess?" Giovanni was growing impatient with this minion who had the nerve to wake him in the middle of the night.

"Sir, the night shift crew monitors our computer system to make sure that everything is running without any problems." Andy was nervous about waking Mr. Giovanni and it was causing him to speak quickly. "About 20 minutes ago they found a little problem in some of our bank accounts."

"What kind of problems did they find, Andy?" Giovanni was growing weary of this conversation. The computer nerds were always finding problems that no else cared about.

"Well sir, it appears that some money is missing from our accounts." Andy was really getting nervous now. He had heard about Giovanni's legendary temper and sometimes it didn't matter if you were just the messenger.

"What do you mean some money is missing?" Giovanni was sitting up in bed now, paying very close attention.

"We were running some routine screens and the system flagged some unusual activity. When we checked into it, we found numerous transactions that moved some large sums of money out of our accounts in the Cayman Islands." Andy was trying to talk through his nervousness and communicate very clearly with Mr. Giovanni.

"How much money are we talking about?" Giovanni asked.

"We're not exactly sure yet, but it looks like it was around $10 million in the process of being transferred." Andy had barely gotten the words out of his mouth before Giovanni screamed out.

"Ten million dollars!" Giovanni jumped to his feet. He had not moved that fast in years. "How could someone transfer $10 million out of our accounts and we not know about it? Somebody's head will roll because of this. Have we got total idiots working for us? Is anybody paying any attention? What do we pay these people for?"

Giovanni was pacing the floor by his bed, screaming into the phone. His wife had risen up in the bed to see what was happening.

Andy waited for a break in the screaming before he tried to answer some of the questions and to give Mr. Giovanni more information.

When Giovanni finally paused to catch his breath, Andy spoke up.

"Mr. Giovanni, we did catch the problem and it looks like we are going to be able to recover some of the money," Andy said.

"How much?" Giovanni asked still pacing.

"We've already tracked down three million and we're in the process of transferring the money back to our accounts," Andy replied. "It looks like there is at least another two million that we should be able to get to pretty easily and we're working on that."

"So there's at least five million that is still missing?" Giovanni was not happy.

"Yes sir," Andy responded. "That's right."

The silence over the phone was deafening.

Finally, Giovanni spoke. "How did this happen?"

"Well sir, it appears that someone at one of our businesses in Little Rock, Arkansas, has used their password to access our network here in Chicago. Going through the network, they were able to access information that allowed them to track our cash flow and find the accounts where we send our money for scrubbing." Andy paused for a moment to make sure that Mr. Giovanni was still with him.

"Go ahead," Giovanni said evenly.

"Whoever did this was a pretty good programmer, or maybe I should say a pretty good hacker," Andy continued. "A program was used to automatically transfer money from our accounts to accounts that she apparently controls. Some of the transfers were easily traced; they went straight into an account and stayed. The rest of the funds have been transferred to multiple accounts and then right away were transferred again. We are still trying to track down that money. It's already hit several different accounts since the first transfer and we're having a hard time keeping up with it."

"You said she," Giovanni said.

"Pardon me," Andy replied.

"When you were talking about the person in Little Rock that is involved in this, you said she."

"That's right," Andy said. "We cross-referenced the password in our system and found out where this activity originated."

"Have you got a name?" Giovanni asked.

"Yes sir, we do," Andy replied. "The name is Carla Sharkley."

"Yes, Uncle Ronaldo, what can I do for you?" Brad was wiping sleep out of his eyes with his free hand.

"Brad, I have some very disturbing news," Ronaldo said. "It appears that you have some security problems with your operation there."

"What is it, Uncle?" Brad asked.

"It seems that our computer people here have found some irregularities in our bank accounts," Ronaldo explained. "Someone has breached the security of our computer system and made some unauthorized transfers of funds."

"How much money are we talking about?" Brad asked.

"The computer people tell me that almost $10 million was involved," Ronaldo said. "It appears they have already recovered a portion of it."

"Ten million dollars!" Brad was shocked. "Uncle Ronaldo, how could they have stolen $10 million from the accounts of the clinic? We never have that kind of money in our accounts. The money that we deposit is transferred almost immediately to the corporate accounts in the Cayman Islands."

"That's where the problem lies," Ronaldo explained. "The hacker entered our system by using a password issued at your clinic and then made his way through the computer to our other bank accounts. This person was very good and knew what they were doing."

"Do you have any information on who did this?" Brad knew that this was a major deal and his uncle would expect to see some decisive action taken.

"The information that I was given indicates that the password was issued to Carla Sharkley," Ronaldo said. "Who is she, Brad?"

"She is the clinic administrator at our Little Rock clinic," Brad replied. "Uncle, I don't think that she has the technical skills to accomplish what you have described to me. She has been a good manager at the clinic, but I don't see her as being a hacker."

"Maybe so," Ronaldo said thoughtfully, "but I think that it's time to find out and take care of things. We have to fix this before it ruins us. We cannot let any word of this get out."

"Don't worry, Uncle," Brad said. "I know what I have to do. Ms. Sharkley will receive a visit from some very persuasive people. She will be given an opportunity to talk about this and then we'll take care of her permanently."

"Excellent, Brad," Ronaldo said. "I knew I could count on you. Please don't let any time pass on this one. We need to make sure that we get this back under control as soon as possible. This could be disastrous to the family."

"I'll take care of Ms. Sharkley, Uncle, but don't stop looking," Brad warned. "I have a suspicion that there is more to this than Ms. Sharkley. Tell the systems guys to keep digging."

"I will, Brad," his Uncle Ronaldo Giovanni, said. "I will."

With that, the phone line went dead. As Brad held the receiver in his hand staring at it, he knew that he should not disappoint his uncle. Blood kin or not, his uncle would not allow something like this to go unpunished. You don't mess with the boss of one of the major crime families in Chicago and get away with it.

Brad would have to come down hard and he knew just how to do it. In just a few hours, he would have a plan underway and this would be over very quickly.

Chapter 31

"Mom, I don't want to leave," Thomas said with his lip quivering. It was very uncool for twelve-year-old guys to cry. It was for that reason that he was biting the inside of his lip.

"I know you don't, Thomas," Carla responded, "but we've been over this. It's just for a few extra days. We were planning to go to Memphis anyway over the holidays. You'll just be getting a head start on me. I'll be there in a couple of weeks and we'll celebrate Christmas just like we planned."

"I'll be lonely without you, Mom," he whimpered. "It'll be the first time that we've been apart since…" Thomas could not finish the sentence.

"I know, honey," Carla said as she placed her hands on Thomas' shoulders. "We've not been apart since your father left, but everything will be alright. I promise."

They were standing in front of the Delta gate that was currently boarding for a flight to Memphis. Marty was standing off to the side to give them a few moments alone. The clock on the wall indicated that it was ten minutes after six.

The agent on duty had just made the last boarding call for the flight. Carla had booked Thomas on the first flight out of Little Rock that morning.

He had finished the first semester of school the previous day. He would be visiting his cousins in Memphis until Carla arrived a few days before Christmas.

Thomas turned to Marty. "Will you take care of my mom while I'm gone?"

"Sure I will, Thomas," Marty said as he walked over to them. "I'll take very good care of her. We'll all be back together in no time."

"Thanks, Marty," Thomas said with tears in his eyes. "I love you, Marty."

"I love you too, Thomas," Marty replied.

They all stood for a moment locked in embrace.

Finally, Carla spoke.

"Thomas, it's time to get on the plane," she said. "They are ready to close the gate."

"I know, Mom," he replied.

They all turned and headed for the gate. Thomas hugged his mother one last time and then walked down the jetway.

"I love you, Mom," he said over his shoulder.

"I love you too, sweetie," she said. "I'll see you in a couple of weeks.

Carla and Marty stood and watched until the plane rolled away from the gate. When they could no longer see the plane, Marty spoke.

"I guess we should leave now."

"I hope that I'm doing the right thing," Carla said, as she stared out at the empty runway. "I just want to do what's best for Thomas."

"It's the right thing, Carla," Marty assured her. "We have too many unknowns that we're dealing with right now. We still don't know how they are going to react to our resignations. Brad is far too scary to let Thomas get in the way. With the comments that he has already made, I'm almost certain that Brad would use Thomas to get to you."

Carla continued to stare through the window.

"I know," she said. "You're right. We've been over this a hundred times. I know that it's best for Thomas." She paused for a moment, obviously deep in thought. "I just can't shake a feeling of permanence about him leaving. It's got me a little spooked."

Marty put his arm around her and pulled her away from the window.

"Come on, let's go," Marty said. "Thomas will be fine."

* * * * *

The day was dawning on a cold, cloudy morning in Jackson, Mississippi. Brad Giovanni hated this weather in the South. At least in Chicago, you would get a good snow out of weather like this. He had spent most of the week in Jackson working with one of his family's clinics. The call early this morning from his uncle had been disturbing. The clinic in Little Rock had been the star of the system. In fact, his time in Jackson had mostly been spent trying to get this clinic to be as productive and efficient as the one in Little Rock.

Now he had a crisis. Although Giovanni Family Enterprises was run by his Uncle Ronaldo, whom he had always had a good relationship with, this kind of problem could end his career and his life. Uncle Ronaldo was tolerant of a lot of things, but the loss of $10 million was not one of them. Many times he had heard Uncle Ronaldo use the phrase, "nothing personal, just business," when delivering bad news. He was concerned that he would soon be hearing those words.

Brad dialed the phone number that he retrieved from the contact list in his Blackberry. It was the number for a local strongman that he had used in the past.

The phone rang and a gruff voice answered.

"Yeah."

"Charlie, this is Brad Giovanni. I've got a job for you."

"Okay, let's hear it," Charlie said. Charlie was used to dealing with thugs and he didn't consider Brad any different from them, even though he was part of the Mafia.

"I've got an employee in Little Rock that I need you to visit," Brad said. "I need some information from her."

"What's wrong, Brad, is the state labor board keeping you from talking to your own employee?" Charlie chuckled at his own joke.

Brad hated dealing with people like Charlie. He had to tolerate this behavior in the South, but if he were back in Chicago, he would have some of Uncle Ronaldo's boys take care of a guy like Charlie.

"Yeah, that's real funny, Charlie," Brad replied. "Look, this is a big deal and I need some help. I don't have time for jokes. I need you to find out what this woman knows and I can't be associated with anything that happens to her."

"After I find out what she knows, what do I do with her?" Charlie asked.

"If you find out what I expect you to, I'll probably want her shut up permanently," Brad said.

"How soon do you need this done?" Charlie asked.

"Right away," Brad replied. "I want you in Little Rock today. I'm getting pressure from Chicago to fix it soon and I don't want to have to answer their questions about why I let another day go by."

Brad knew that Charlie would respond better if he knew that Chicago was interested. Charlie might jerk him around, but he wouldn't dare do that to the boys in Chicago.

"Okay, I'll get on it right away, but it'll cost you extra. I've got several big jobs I'm working on and I'll lose money if I have to put them off," Charlie lied. He hadn't had a decent paying job in months.

"Right, right, right," Brad said with exasperation. He didn't want to quibble with Charlie over a few thousand dollars, when millions were at stake. "I'll give you a $10,000 bonus if you will take care of it today."

"Ten thousand dollars!" Charlie was impressed. Usually Brad was a cheapskate, when it came to things like this. "Will I need any help, or can I do it myself?"

"I think that you can get it done by yourself," Brad responded. "Let me give you a few details."

Brad spent the next ten minutes filling Charlie in on details about Carla.

After Brad had finished, Charlie took a moment to think through the specifics of the job.

"So after I am done getting information from her, you want me to call you," Charlie repeated from Brad's instructions.

"That's right, Charlie," Brad said. "Call me on my cell phone and I'll decide what to do next."

"Now, if I have to whack her, it's going to cost you more. You know that, don't you?" Charlie asked.

"Of course I do, Charlie," Brad said. "We always pay more for permanent solutions."

* * * * *

He picked up the ringing phone.

"Hello?"

"Mr. Giovanni, this is Andy Costello again." Andy was still nervous, but not as bad as the first time. He was beginning to feel like he was getting some control over the situation.

"Hello, Andy," Ronaldo said. "I hope you have some better news for me this time."

"I do, Mr. Giovanni," Andy replied. "We've done quite a bit of work since I first spoke to you earlier this morning. I think that we have a pretty good handle on the situation."

"Tell me about it, Andy," Giovanni responded. He had learned long ago not to get too excited about solutions until they started bearing fruit. A man didn't get to a position like his by believing everything he heard. He always waited for the action to occur.

"Well, Mr. Giovanni," Andy started, "by tracking the registration of IP addresses, we have been able to track down the hacker that has been in our system."

"I don't understand all of what you just said, but go ahead," Giovanni said patiently.

"By using a tracking mechanism in our system," Andy continued, "we were able to track down the actual computer that was hacking into the system. This gave us some information that we did not previously have. It told us that the computer that was used to hack into our system was not in one of our buildings."

"I guess that I'm a little confused, Andy," Giovanni said. "I thought that we knew that the password used to enter the system belonged to one of our employees, a...Carla Sharkley." Giovanni had to consult his notes for the name.

"Yes sir, that's true," Andy replied, "Ms. Sharkley's password was used to enter the system. Now we also know that it was not used on her computer. In fact, we have traced the computer to a location in Hot Springs, Arkansas."

"We don't have any businesses in Hot Springs," Giovanni said.

"Yes sir, I know that," Andy said. "That's why we did a little more work to find out something about the computer. We were able to trace it to an engineering company in Hot Springs."

"Will you be able to find any more information about this?" Giovanni asked hopefully.

"We hope to have a name and an address before the end of the day," Andy said.

Giovanni was considering this new information.

"How is this connected to Ms. Sharkley?" Giovanni's mind was spinning with the possibilities.

"We don't really know, sir," Andy said. "She could be an accomplice in this or she might not know anything about it. It's possible that this person, whoever they are, could have stolen her password and used it to access our system without her knowledge."

"Is there any way to know for sure who was involved and how?" Giovanni asked.

"We are currently scanning the company's database to pinpoint the name and location of the hacker," Andy said. "I'm certain that we will have the information that we're looking for, today. However, without talking to Ms. Sharkley, I'm not sure we'll be able to verify any connection between her and the hacker."

Silence filled the air as Giovanni thought about this new information.

"What about the money?" Giovanni asked.

"The good news is that it looks like we found it in time to recover over $5 million," Andy said. "The bad news is that the remaining $4.5 million seems to be gone without a trace. We tracked it through several transfers before we lost it."

"What about Ms. Sharkley? Did you find any of the money in her account?" Giovanni asked.

"Yes sir, we did," Andy replied. "It was pretty easy to find. The money that ended up in her account was transferred only once and then it stayed there."

"Was that the only transfer that ended in that manner?" Giovanni asked.

"Yes it was," Andy said.

"Why do you think that this one transfer was so easy to find?" Giovanni was thinking out loud.

"I'm not sure, sir," Andy said. "Either we stopped the program before it could finish the instructions to complete the transfers, or someone didn't care if we found this money."

"I was thinking the very same thing, Andy," Giovanni said thoughtfully. "Thank you for the information. Let me know when you find something else."

Giovanni terminated the connection and sat puzzling over his options. This problem seemed even bigger than he had previously thought. If someone from outside of the organization was getting into his business records, he could be in big trouble. The possibilities were endless.

He picked up the phone and called a number that he had not used in a long time. Things had been peaceful in the city. He had not ordered a hit in several years. The various Families around Chicago had learned to be content with their own turf.

The phone was answered on the second ring.

"Hello?" It was a calm, professional voice.

"This is Ronaldo. I've got a job for you."

"Mr. Giovanni! I haven't heard from you lately. I hope things are going well for you," the voice said.

"They were going well, until recently," Giovanni replied. "That's why I'm calling you."

"Oh yes," the voice said knowingly. "It's always in times of crisis that the call comes. How can I help you?"

"I need you to go south," Giovanni said. "It's an odd request, but I need you to get there soon and wait for a name."

"That is odd," the voice mused.

"Let me explain," Giovanni said.

Giovanni spent the next 15 minutes explaining the situation, including the urgency. When he hung up, Giovanni had an arrangement in place and a cell phone number to call with the final information.

Chapter 32

Kevin was up early. The anticipation for this day had generated nervousness in his stomach. Although he had planned to sleep later in the morning, he had been up for over an hour and it was now just five minutes until seven.

All of his gear was ready. He had checked it one last time. There was nothing left to do until he left for Little Rock later in the afternoon.

He decided the best way to kill some time until he had to leave was to get out and exercise. He grabbed a flashlight and went down the passageway to the lake. Kevin turned the deadbolt lock on the door and pushed it outward. He stepped out on the shoreline of Lake Hamilton. Standing there, he breathed deeply to fill his lungs with the cold morning air. The darkness of the night was slowly giving way to morning. As he gazed at the horizon across the lake, clouds filled the sky. It promised to be another dreary day.

Kevin dragged the canoe out of the passageway onto the shore. He pulled a life jacket from the canoe and put it on, zipping it securely up his chest. He made sure that the paddles were in the canoe and then pushed it into the water, hopping in at the last minute. He smoothly paddled away from the shore. His canoeing skills had improved dramatically over the past few days and he had the boat moving quickly out towards the main channel.

In addition to the exercise that he got from paddling the canoe, he was able to totally clear his mind. As he moved the canoe across the water, he did not think about the mission. The quietness of the water was very relaxing. It was the only time that he had been able to give his obsession a break in quite some time. It was during these trips that he had begun to learn his way around the lake. He was now able to navigate around the many nooks and crannies that made up the shoreline.

He also had learned to pay attention to the weather when he was out on the lake. He had been out one afternoon when the wind shifted and blew hard out of the southwest. The wind churned up the lake and made for a rough ride back to the dock. It became obvious to him very quickly that this canoe was not built for rough water on the open lake.

Today, Kevin noticed something different about the sky. The clouds were a shade of gray that he had not seen. The wind was also different this morning. It seemed to be bringing a new kind of chill to the lake air. He wondered how this would affect the weather for the rest of the day. He was still too much of a novice to understand all the nuances of the weather signals. He made a mental note to check the forecast before he left for Little Rock this afternoon.

The cold air was invigorating, whipping around his head, as he labored from the exertion of paddling across the lake. He was going out for a long ride today. His muscles would really be aching by the time he got back.

* * * * *

Marty was at the clinic earlier than usual, since he rode directly there with Carla. He had spent the extra time this morning catching up on the stacks of charts that were waiting for his review.

Looking at the schedule for today had really depressed him. The schedule was completely full. He would be working at full speed today. Although Fridays were usually pretty busy, the staff tended to be more upbeat in anticipation of the weekend. But, today would be different – J.P. was scheduled to work.

J.P. always seemed to leave a trail of depression wherever he went. The staff would be on edge all day. The only good aspect of this would be the opportunity for Marty to talk to J.P. face to face about his resignation.

As Marty continued to examine the schedule, he saw a name that seemed familiar. Courtney Ferguson. Why was that name familiar to him? Then it dawned on him. She was the girl that he had spoken to in the parking lot.

His mind shifted gears and he thought about his pending conversation with J.P. Talking to J.P. would be difficult. J.P. didn't take rejection very well. He thrived on being in control and this would upset his world. It also occurred to Marty that he would have to speak to Brad at some point in time. He was really not looking forward to that encounter.

Yes, he thought, this would be a very long day indeed.

* * * * *

Carla was in her office trying to get some work done. It was hard to concentrate. Her mind was wandering to the events of the past week.

So much had happened in such a short period of time. It was mind-blowing. She had gone from a peaceful, content life to having her whole world turned upside down. She looked at her watch. It was only 9:00 in the morning. This day was already dragging.

Carla was missing Thomas. He had called her when he got to his cousin's house to let her know that he was all right. They made plans to speak again later that night. She reminded Thomas that she and Marty were going out to dinner and it would be after 10:00 p.m. when she called.

The noise outside her window startled her. She stood up to see the cause of the commotion. The protesters were back. When she had first begun work at the clinic, the protesters were a daily occurrence. Over the last six months, they had been very sporadic. In fact, it had been almost three weeks since they had been on the sidewalk in front of the clinic.

In the past, Carla had despised the protesters. She had viewed them as a disruption to the business that she was hired to run. Now she was beginning to see them in a different light. After spending time with Marty during the past few weeks and learning some of the darker side of this business, she was finding it difficult to hate the protesters this morning. She was amazed that she actually felt some sympathy towards them and their cause. Sympathy aside, Carla wished that they had chosen a different day to start their protests again.

Patsy, her secretary, knocked on the door and came into her office.

"I guess you heard the protesters," Patsy said.

"Yes, I heard them," Carla said staring out of the window. "I wonder why they chose today to come back?"

"Didn't you hear about the news conference?" Patsy asked.

"What news conference?" Carla turned from the window to face Patsy.

"There is a minister from Hot Springs that has scheduled a news conference on the sidewalk in front of the clinic at 2:00 this afternoon," Patsy explained. "I'm sure they have timed this to get exposure from the media."

"Is it the guy that was interviewed on TV earlier in the week?"

"Yes, it is," Patsy replied. "I saw the segment on the news. I also watched the replay of his sermon last Sunday. It was the sermon that got him the airtime for the interview."

"What did you think of his perspective on abortion, Patsy?" Carla was curious. "You go to church, don't you? You must have an opinion."

"I do have an opinion, but it is not determined by my church attendance," Patsy responded. "My opinion on abortion is based on my Christianity. While I agree with most of the points that he made about abortion being wrong, I do not agree with his extremist approach. He seemed to be proposing that we take things into our own hands and that is wrong. Only God can deliver judgment."

Carla was watching Patsy. Carla found it amazing that Patsy could work in a place like this. Carla was struggling with it and did not have near the moral convictions about abortion that Patsy did.

"Patsy, why do you work here?" Carla asked.

"I decided a long time ago that the only way that I could ever be happy was to let God direct my life," Patsy said. "This is where he wants me to be right now. It may not be forever, but for now, this is the place."

"Why would God want you here?" Carla was struggling to understand it.

"I think that God wants me here to help people," Patsy said. "This is such a unique place that I'm sure that He has something special in mind."

"What kind of help are you supposed to provide for people?" Carla asked.

"I don't know, Carla," Patsy replied. "Maybe I'm here to reach out to just one person. Who knows, I could be here for you. I could be here to show you how faith works."

"Are you talking about Christianity?" Carla was a little uneasy. "I'm not sure that I could handle something like that right now. I've got too many other things going on."

"Sometimes, it's when you're going through things like this that you need it the most," Patsy said. "Anyway, you'll know when it's time."

Chapter 33

It was a few minutes before two o'clock. The pro-life protesters had been marching in front of the Women's Health Inc. clinic all day. Based on previous encounters with the police, the marchers knew to stay on the sidewalk and give anyone entering the clinic a clearance of thirty feet. The protesters had begun with just a handful of marchers that morning, but now the group had swollen to over a hundred people.

A crowd was also gathering to watch the press conference. The various media representatives had been busy over the past 20 minutes preparing their technical equipment. Eleven news organizations were present to document the proceedings.

A small podium had been set up on the sidewalk. With all of the participants and onlookers, the sidewalk had become crowded to the point of people spilling over into the street. The protesters were carrying signs and chanting as they marched back and forth in front of the clinic. The hand-scrawled messages on the signs proclaimed various pro-life slogans. Several police officers were watching closely from just beyond the edge of the crowd.

The stage was set and everyone was waiting for the man to appear.

* * * * *

Bill Roberts had been in a suite at a nearby hotel in West Little Rock for most of the morning. He had arrived from Hot Springs early to make sure that everything was in order.

Mike Hanks had been with him all morning. For the last hour, Mike had been on the phone coordinating the logistics for the day. With the cell phones that he carried with him, he sometimes had three calls in progress at once.

Brother Bill was anxiously moving around the suite. He was already focused on the press conference, so much so that he didn't even notice Mike on the sofa making his calls. Bill was moving into his "zone." It was the mental state he slipped into when speaking in front of a crowd. A crowd of people sent his adrenaline soaring. The bigger the crowd, the more important the event, the deeper he moved into the zone. He was in deep now.

"Brother Bill?" Mike interrupted.

Bill stopped and turned to see what was so important that it required an interruption.

Mike continued. "Everything is in place. The media has completed their setup, the protesters have been marching since this morning and your podium is wired and ready." He paused for a moment and then continued. "It's time for us to go. I have a car waiting downstairs. When the press conference is over, the car will be waiting to bring us back to the hotel. All the details are in order."

Bill was impressed. Since he had scolded Mike yesterday, Mike had been like a new man. He was so focused and committed that it was scary, even to someone like Bill.

"Thank you for all of your help, Mike," Bill said quietly. "Your part in this has been invaluable. When I move on from here, I will remember all that you have done. There will be a place for you."

"Thanks, Brother Bill," Mike replied, "I'm just happy to be of service. Now we really do need to leave. Are you ready?"

"Let's go," Brother Bill responded. "I've been waiting for this moment all my life."

* * * * *

The atmosphere outside of the clinic was emotionally charged. Pro-choice demonstrators were now on the scene to counterbalance their philosophical opposites. The television crews had set up their lights that were blazing through the cold gray sky. The roar of the protesters was drowning out the sound checks that the crews were conducting with the reporters.

The police had set up a barricade in the street to keep out any new onlookers. A secondary crowd was forming just beyond the barricades. The police had separated the two groups of protesters to eliminate any chance for physical conflict between them. The verbal conflict was almost deafening. It was two minutes until two o'clock.

Carla and Marty were watching the proceedings from the window of Carla's second-floor office.

"It's turned into a real circus out there," Marty observed, leaning with both hands on the windowsill.

"Yeah, it has," Carla, agreed.

They quietly watched the different participants jockeying for position in front of the clinic. Carla had turned on a television in her office to one of the local stations, anticipating the live coverage of the event unfolding below them.

"Do you want to watch and listen from up here, or do you want to go down there and be part of it?" Marty asked.

"I think it would be better to stay up here, Marty," Carla said, her eyes never leaving the action on the sidewalk. "I would prefer not to be interviewed as part of this show."

"What do you think the preacher will have to say?" Marty posed the question to Carla. "What more could he add to his comments on TV the other night? He made his viewpoint on the issue very clear."

"I don't know," Carla replied, "but the media must think that it's going to be good. Look at them swarming around down there!"

* * * * *

The crowd on the other side of the barricade slowly parted. A new Lincoln Continental crept through the crowd to the barricade. One of the police officers manning the barricade moved around to the driver's window and leaned down to speak to the driver. He looked into the back seat and then stood up to wave to his colleagues to move the barricade and allow the car to pass.

The car slowly made its way past the television vans and stopped adjacent to the podium that was set up on the sidewalk. The rear door of the car opened and a man stepped out of the car. He scanned the crowd, their faces reflected in his mirror sunglasses.

Satisfied that everything was in order, Mike Hanks leaned back in the car and spoke. "Brother Bill, everything is ready."

Roberts then slid across the back seat and exited the car just as Mike Hanks had. A murmur went through the crowd. Although this was the first time that anyone outside of his congregation had seen him in a public venue like this, Brother Bill's reputation had preceded him. The television exposure earlier in the week had made his face familiar to the crowd gathered in front of the clinic. The pro-life protesters began cheering immediately, just as they had been instructed to do by their leaders. A chorus of boos from the pro-choice crowd quickly countered the cheers. Being outnumbered by Brother Bill's supporters, the sounds of disapproval were instantaneously overwhelmed by the renewed enthusiasm of the cheers. The crowd was already emotionally tied to the event and it had yet to truly begin.

A path was cleared to the podium and Brother Bill made his way there, shaking hands with those who reached out in support. He moved behind the podium and motioned for the crowd to quiet down. Of course, the pro-lifers responded as if on cue and the rest of the crowd followed their lead. Everyone was intrigued by this new spokesperson for the pro-life movement and they were waiting for his comments, each with their own expected response.

The crowd was quiet and Roberts was ready.

"Thank you for coming today," Bill began. "I have called this press conference today to address a problem that has created a blight on our country. I am going to make a statement and then I will be available to answer any questions that you may have."

The television crews had their cameras focused on a close-up of Roberts. Brother Bill grabbed the podium with both hands and looked across the crowd gathered in front of him. His gaze was not a quick cursory glance, but a deep penetrating look. The kind that made you feel uncomfortable when he made eye contact with you – and he was making eye contact with many. t was the kind of look that made you feel guilty and you never knew why.

"Ladies and gentlemen, I am here today to talk to you about an issue that is haunting the future of America." Roberts was as steady as a rock, leaning into the podium, his strong jaw struck in a forceful pose towards the crowd and the camera. "I am here to talk to you about an issue that is clouding the future of each and every American. I am here to talk about abortion."

Bill paused briefly. He had no notes with him at the podium. His statement this afternoon would be delivered extemporaneously.

"Thousands of innocent children are killed each and every day at abortion factories, like this one, all over America." Bill turned and gestured to the clinic. "Women walk into clinics like this with a new life inside of them and walk out a short time later alone. They never realize until it is too late that this experience will not only murder the child inside of their body, but it will leave them hollow, physically, mentally and emotionally. They will never be the same again."

Brother Bill's face was clouded with anguish as he spoke.

"Since 1973, our nation has stood by watching as a generation of women have endured the heartache of abortion. We have kept silent, as those with an abortion agenda have convinced the women of America that in order to be completely fulfilled as a woman, you must have reproductive freedom. They have convinced the women of America that the choice of abortion is necessary to be complete."

Roberts' voice was rising now.

"But I am here to tell you, ladies and gentlemen, that this choice has not given the women of America freedom. This choice has enslaved the women of America to the horrors of mental and emotional torture. This choice has enslaved the women of America to the physical complications that the plague of abortion leaves on their bodies. This choice has enslaved the women of America to the guilt of murder."

He paused to gauge the reaction of the crowd so far. He spoke again with a calm, soothing voice.

"Recently, in our nation's capital, we dedicated a museum to the Holocaust that the Jews suffered during World War II. During the dedication ceremonies for that museum, many of the speakers told us that this museum was a reminder to never let something like this happen again in our world. Well, my friends, I am here today to tell you that this clinic behind me represents just the sort of abomination that we are supposed to prevent. This clinic represents what is wrong with America. This clinic represents the tragedy of pacifism. Just as the world stood by and failed to intercede in the tragedy that fell upon the Jewish people, America is on the sidelines watching the next holocaust."

His voice had risen to a fever pitch. Roberts was rocking on the balls of his feet, towering over the podium in front of him.

"How can we let this happen?" Brother Bill paused and stared into faces all across the crowd. "Why have we made excuses for our convenience? Have we not learned from history?"

He had grabbed the edges of the podium again. He looked as if he might just pick it up and throw it into the crowd.

"My friends, it is time for the people of this country to stand up for the innocent. It is time for us to stand up for those who are too weak to stand up for themselves. It is time for us to stand up against the laws of this country that are wrong. It is time for the people of America to shut down clinics like this one behind me that specialize in death."

Bill Roberts reached into his suit pocket and pulled out a handful of pink pieces of paper. He held them up for everyone to see. The crowd was watching him without a sound.

"These are messages that I have received over the last few days encouraging me to continue with my mission to eliminate the acceptance of abortion from our national policy. It is my intention to take the advice of these good people and do everything in my power to eradicate abortion from our moral landscape."

He paused and put the messages back into his pocket.

"Now, I'll be happy to answer any questions that you may have."

Roberts reached inside the podium and pulled out a bottle of water. He took a long swig out of the bottle, as the reporters in the crowd began to shout questions to him. He finally pointed to one of the local television reporters for a question.

"Dr. Roberts, my name is Jason Greene and I'm with KCAR-TV here in Little Rock." Jason was the stereotypical young reporter trying hard to work up the ladder. He needed to provoke with his question. He might not get another chance. "I would like to ask you about your comment regarding shutting these clinics down. Exactly what do you mean by that? Are you advocating violence in dealing with those that support abortion? And if you are how, do you reconcile that stance with the Bible that you preach?"

"Well Jason," Brother Bill chuckled softly, "that was quite a mouthful. I'm not sure that I can even remember all of your questions."

Soft laughter rippled through the crowd.

"But I'll do my best to respond to each of your questions," Roberts continued, "and I'm sure that you will jog my memory if I miss anything. First of all, throughout the history of our country, there are many examples of the public protesting against a business and causing that business to change its practices. Product boycotts are a prime example of this. The second issue that you raised is a question that I'm glad that I will get the opportunity to answer today. I would never advocate violence against another person. That is exactly what we are trying to stop at these clinics, violence against the unborn. As far as reconciling our activities with God's Word, the Bible is very clear that we are to obey the laws of man, as long as they are not in conflict with the laws of God. A law that allows the murder of a human being is not one we are required to support."

The questions went on for another ten minutes. The last five minutes of that time was filled with questions that had already been answered. They were being asked in a slightly different format, by the reporters who were not lucky enough to be recognized during the first half of the press conference.

* * * * *

Carla and Marty were still watching from the window of the clinic. They had the television turned up behind them to hear the audio portion of the press conference.

"Wow," Marty exclaimed, "that guy is good."

"He sure is," Carla replied. "He is a worthy opponent for the abortion industry."

"I'm glad we're going to be out of it soon," Marty said

Chapter 34

Marty left Carla's office and headed back down the stairs to the OR. He anticipated that he would be behind and he was not disappointed. A chart was in the holder outside of OR 1. He had been working in OR 1 all morning. J.P. had been in OR 2.

Tammy was pacing nervously in front of the door to OR 1. "Dr. Smith!" she said anxiously. "Where have you been? Everything is going crazy around here."

She grabbed his elbow and led him toward one of the consultation rooms.

"We're having problems with one of the patients," Tammy explained. "We were getting her ready for surgery and she decided that she wasn't going to go. Janet has been in there already to talk to her and make her do it, but Janet came out screaming at her. Can you please talk to her? She asked for you."

"Sure, I can talk to her," Marty said. "Where is she?"

"Right here," Tammy said, moving to one of the consultation rooms.

Tammy held the door to the consultation room open and Marty walked in. Marty was looking down at the chart that Tammy had handed him.

"What seems to be the problem here?" Marty said trying to find the name on the chart in his hands.

Marty looked up to see a young girl sitting on the exam table with her arms around her knees pulling them to her chest. Her chin was resting on her knees.

"I...I...I'm not sure I'm ready for this," the patient said with an unsteady voice. "I'm scared."

Marty sat down on a stool at the end of the table. "Listen, if you're not positive that you're ready for this, you don't have to do it today. The procedure is perfectly safe, but it's not for everybody. You should take your time making your decision. When you're ready, you can call us back."

He stood and patted the girl on the shoulder. "I'll have a nurse come in and check on you in a few minutes. If you're still not sure, the nurse will help you get your things so that you can leave."

As Marty was moving to the door, to leave the room, the patient looked up. "Are you a doctor?" she asked softly.

"Yes, I am. I'm Dr. Smith."

"Thanks for talking to me," she said with a tear rolling down her cheek.

"Sure," Marty said as he left the room. "Take your time."

He handed the chart to Tammy as he walked to the nurses' station. "Please check on that patient in a few minutes. I doubt that she will be having a procedure today. Where do I go next?"

"You have a patient waiting in OR 3."

Marty turned and headed towards OR 3. "How far behind am I?"

"About 45 minutes," Tammy yelled as Marty disappeared into the OR.

As he entered the OR, he saw the patient on the operating table and realized that it was the girl that he had spoken with earlier in the week in the clinic parking lot. He picked up the chart to jog his memory for her name.

"Hi, Courtney. It's good to see you again. Are you ready for your procedure?"

"Yes sir. I'm ready to get this behind me."

"I'll go ahead and get started." Marty sat on the stool at the end of the table and started the procedure. Ten minutes later the procedure was complete and Courtney's dreams for West Point were intact.

Marty walked out of the OR and immediately Tammy grabbed his arm.

"You need to go to OR 1, Dr. Smith. They're having some problems and they need your help right away."

Marty hurried over to OR 1 and noticed that the chart was no longer in the rack outside the door. He pulled his surgical mask on and went into the OR.

"Okay, what's going on in here?" Marty asked with authority. "I was told there was a problem in here."

Two nurses were working around a patient on the OR table. Marty could see that Janet Rawls was one of them. The other nurse turned and Marty could see a frantic look in her eyes.

"What's wrong, Janet?" Marty asked as he moved quickly to the patient's side.

"It seems that this patient waited a little too long to come and see us," Janet responded, busy with the equipment set up to monitor the patient. "She's in labor and her cervix is dilated to nine. This baby will be here in a few minutes."

The patient was crying.

"It's okay, we're going to take good care of you," Marty said patting her shoulder.

"It wasn't supposed to be like this," the patient said through her sobs. "It wasn't supposed to be like this."

"Doctor, the baby is almost here," Janet said. She was sitting on a stool at the foot of the table.

"Do you mind if I step in for this?" Marty sat down on the stool as Janet got up and stepped aside.

Marty could see right away that the delivery was about to occur. He could see the crown of the baby's head.

"Ahhhhh..." the patient screamed. The pains of the contractions were sweeping over her.

"Has this patient had any pain medication of any type?" Marty asked the nurses.

"No, Doctor," Janet responded. "We were in the process of prepping her for her procedure when we realized that she was in labor. We didn't get to the pain medication. Do you want us to go ahead and give her something now?"

Marty thought for a moment. It had been months since he had delivered a baby. The last one was the week he left his residency program. The delivery would be easy for this patient, she had already done most of the work herself, but he would have to think about the appropriateness of administering pain medication at this stage of delivery.

"I don't think that we should give her anything," he said. "We need her to push and medications might slow her down at this point. Janet, you stay down here with me."

He looked at the other nurse and motioned for her to move to the head of the table. "Why don't you stand at that end of the table and coach her through this?"

Marty had taken charge of the room. "Do we have instruments ready to deliver this baby?"

"Yes, Doctor," Janet, replied, moving the instrument tray around so that Marty could reach it.

"The way this is going," Marty commented, "we may not need anything. This one is coming out fine without any help."

The patient moaned loudly one last time and the baby's head appeared. Marty reached down and gently held the baby's head.

"Can you push one more time?" he asked the patient, looking up at the head of the table.

The patient pushed and the baby landed in Marty's hands. Marty grabbed a suction bulb to clean the mucus out of the baby's mouth and nose. Having clear airways, the baby began screaming. Marty took a pair of scissors off the instrument table and cut the umbilical cord. He turned and handed the baby to Janet.

"Janet, take this baby into one of the pre-op rooms and check him out," Marty instructed. "We probably need to send this baby to the hospital, since he's a little premature. I'll be out in a minute to check on things."

Marty turned to the new mother. "You had a baby boy," he told her. "He seems to be fine, but I would like to send him to the hospital to be examined by a pediatrician. We'll try to get you ready so that you can go with him."

Marty spent a few minutes finishing with the patient and then he left the OR.

He walked out of the OR door just as a scream came from the nurses' work area. Marty hurried over to see what the problem was. As he arrived just outside the pre-op rooms, Tammy was coming out of one of the rooms. Her face was ashen and she was shaking uncontrollably.

"She killed it! She killed it!" Tammy was hysterical.

Marty rushed into the pre-op room to see Janet fluffing a pillow and placing it back at the head of the bed. The lifeless body of the newborn that he had just delivered was lying in the middle of the hospital bed.

"You didn't," he asked staring at Janet.

"Of course I did," she said returning his stare.

"How could you do that?" Marty gasped. "How could you kill that baby?"

"Oh, don't get so high and mighty with me," Janet said with a smirk on her face. "You do it every day. It's just a matter of timing. I did this one a little later than you do yours, but the result is still the same."

"I can't believe you did it," Marty said with a moan as he put his hands up to his head in disbelief. "That baby was healthy. He had every reason to live."

"Don't be so naïve, Dr. Smith," Janet said with disgust. "This baby had no reason to live." She pointed to the dead baby boy on the bed. "In case you've forgotten, his mother was in here to have an abortion. He was dead either way you look at it. She didn't come here to have a baby." Janet paused as she thought. "You might say that I just gave her what she wanted."

Marty was stunned. He thought it impossible for someone to commit an act so heinous. What should he do? He needed to contact the police and turn Janet in.

"You have no proof, you know," she said with a smug look. "You can accuse me all you want to, but it can't be proven. I'm certain that this baby died of respiratory complications as a result of delivery."

Marty couldn't believe that this was happening. The first time that he had been able to bring life into this world in months and this monster had snuffed it out. She had to be punished.

"Don't even think about contacting the authorities, Dr. Smith," Janet said. "You don't realize who you're dealing with here. This operation is way out of your league. It would be best for you to walk out of here and forget that this ever happened. You don't need to cross the people who own this clinic. This clinic has connections with the authorities that you couldn't begin to imagine. It's amazing the kind of cooperation we've been able to get with the authorities, after we've performed abortions on their girlfriends. In fact, your friend Judge Stanley has sent us some business."

Marty jerked his gaze from the body lying on the bed to Janet's eyes. "What are you talking about? Are you talking about the Chief Justice of the State Supreme Court?"

"Of course I am," Janet said with an evil grin.

"How did you know that I know him? What's he got to do with this?"

"We know a lot more than you would ever imagine, Dr. Smith. And Judge Stanley has sent a young lady over here that no one knew about – shall we say, a little indiscretion that the Judge was involved with. If you called the police, all it would take was one phone call and this little event would disappear forever."

Marty was speechless. He couldn't believe what he was hearing.

Janet grabbed the body off the bed, wrapped it in a towel and headed for the Clean-up Room. Marty was leaning against the wall of the Pre-op Room, his mind numb from the encounter with Janet.

He wandered out to the nurses' station, not really focused on where he was going or what he was going to do next.

"Dr. Smith?" It was one of the nurses monitoring the patient flow in the OR's. "Your next patient is ready in OR 1."

Marty staggered into the OR and went to work without a word. He trudged through his next two cases in a mindless routine. He had no interaction with the patients and barely spoke to the nurse assisting him. The emotion of the moment was overwhelming. He was shell-shocked. His body was going through the motions, but his mind was wrestling with one more moral quandary that this place had given him. He was just finishing a procedure, when the door to the OR burst open and a nurse screamed into the room.

"Dr. Smith, come quick!" The nurse was frenzied. "Dr. Straun needs you. We have a patient coding in OR 2."

The news snapped Marty back into reality. He jumped up from his stool and left the nurse to finish his routine case. He ran to OR 2 to find J.P. frenetically working on a patient that was on the OR table. Sweat was soaking through his surgical cap.

"What's wrong, J.P.?" Marty asked.

"I had some problems," J.P. replied. "We had a perforated uterus during the procedure. While I was working to repair it, she coded."

J.P. and one of the nurses were administering CPR to the patient. J.P. was doing chest compressions and the nurse was using an Ambu bag to attempt to restart the patient's breathing.

"I think that she must have had an anesthesia complication," J.P. continued while he was working. "She was doing fine and then suddenly she crashed."

A nurse moved the crash cart into place at the side of the table. Marty opened one of the drawers of the Craftsman tool chest and grabbed a needle and syringe.

"Have you given any drugs yet?" Marty asked.

"I gave her .1 milligrams of epinephrine," J.P. muttered. Marty could tell that his jaw was clenched under the surgical mask. "It didn't help so we started the chest compressions."

Marty drew .4 milligrams of atropine into the syringe. He injected the drug into the IV that was hanging on the pole at the head of the bed. They all watched the monitor, waiting for a change in the tracings that would indicate the drug was having an impact on the patient's condition. The wait seemed like an eternity.

Nothing. No change. The patient was not responding.

"Are you ready for the defibrillator, J.P.?" Marty was deferring to J.P.'s judgment as lead physician on the case.

"I think we have to. She's not responding to anything else."

Marty turned and a nurse was waiting with the paddles to the defibrillator. Marty took the paddles and rubbed them together briefly. He turned back to the patient, holding the paddles over her chest.

"Okay, everybody ready?" Marty was poised to go.

"Ready!"

"Clear!" Marty shouted.

He then placed the paddles on each side of the patient's chest. The jolt of electricity from the defibrillator lifted the patient off the table.

Everyone in the room stopped and stared at the monitor.

Nothing. This patient was gone and not coming back.

They worked for several more minutes before J.P. finally called out the time of death. Everyone in the room was exhausted. J.P. slumped on the stool that had been pushed aside to the corner of the room.

Marty ripped off his surgical mask and pushed through the door of the OR. He sat down at the nurses' station and ran his hands through his hair, his thoughts consumed with emotion. The room was filled with gloom. It was as if everyone was moving in slow motion. The gravity of the events of the afternoon was bringing the entire staff down. Usually the nurses' station was the center for activity in the surgical suite. The silence that had enveloped the room was oppressive. This place would be changed forever. Marty would be changed forever.

The two deaths that he had witnessed this afternoon were so unnecessary. How could things like this happen in a medical facility?   A place like this should help people, not…his train of thought stopped. What was he thinking? For six months, he had been a part of the taking of life. Janet Rawls' words were ringing in his ears. "It's just a matter of timing." She was right. He was just as guilty as she was. If that patient had been in the clinic just a few hours earlier, he would have been the one that killed her baby, not Janet. It was just a matter of timing.

J.P. came shuffling out of the OR. He was dazed.

"J.P., I've got to talk to you," Marty said. He couldn't stand it anymore.

"Huh," J.P. grunted with a faraway look in his eyes.

"I can't do this anymore," Marty started. "This is not what I was trained to do. I have got to get out of this place. The emotional baggage that I'm picking up here is too heavy for me to carry. I have got to find a place where I can get out of the death business and back in the regular practice of medicine. I don't think that I can take it for another day. I want you to accept my resignation effective immediately."

J.P. just stared at him. Marty wasn't even sure that J.P. had heard him.

"Did you hear me, J.P.?" Marty was waiting for J.P.'s reaction.

"Yeah, I heard you," J.P. finally replied. "Whatever you want to do, Marty. You have to do what's best for you."

With no other reaction, J.P. turned and slowly went down the hall towards the physician dressing room.

Marty watched him go. It was not at all what he had expected from J.P.

"That was weird," he said to no one in particular. "I've never seen him react that way about anything."

Tammy was back at the nurses' station and heard Marty's comments.

"Don't you know who that patient was that ya'll were working on?" She had tears in her eyes as she waited for Marty's reply.

"I don't have any idea," Marty responded.

"That was J.P.'s girlfriend," Tammy said.

Chapter 35

Marty had changed out of his scrubs and into the clothes that he had worn to the airport that morning. This day had been unbelievably long.

The patient, whose name he later learned was Whitney Simpson, was transported to the morgue by ambulance. The arrival of the ambulance had pretty much put an end to their procedures for the remainder of the day. By the time that he and J.P. had finished the paperwork required for an expired patient, it was almost 6:30.

Marty was worn out. He went out to the parking lot to wait for Carla. The night air had turned bitterly cold. He got inside of Carla's car and turned it on to keep warm. He turned on the radio and slumped down in the seat, trying to cleanse his mind of the horrors of the day.

He had just dozed off when Carla opened the door and slid into the car.

"What a day," she exclaimed. "I keep thinking that they can't get any worse, but they keep surprising me."

"I know what you mean," Marty said, "and you don't even know the half of it."

"Let's go get something to eat and you can tell me about it," Carla said.

They pulled out of the parking lot, never noticing the dark sedan that was following them. When they came to a stop in front of a restaurant on Kavanaugh Boulevard, the sedan stopped a block away and waited patiently. The driver was in no hurry. For the kind of money that he was making on this job, he could wait all night if it was necessary. Brad Giovanni was paying him well and he would make sure that the job was done right.

* * * * *

Kevin was driving to Little Rock. The duffel bag with the materials for the bomb was in the back of the Ford Bronco that he was driving. A tarp was draped over the duffel bag to shield it from any wandering eyes.

Kevin was careful to drive within the speed limit. He was careful to follow all other traffic laws. He wanted no chance encounter with the police that might require a search of his vehicle. It was just that type of foolish mistake that could ruin his mission.

He smiled at the thought of the mission. He could feel the hair on the back of his neck stand up in anticipation of the completion of the night's work. He had been waiting for this day for a long time.

As Kevin drove down Interstate 30 to Little Rock, his mind wandered back to the time when he first learned of the destruction that abortion had brought to his family. He remembered the sorrow in his mother's eyes as she told him the story for the first time.

You might say that abortion had robbed him of a normal family life. Instead of the joy of childhood, he had only experienced the agony of heartbreak. Instead of the sweet taste of the perfect family, his mouth had only tasted the bitterness of despair.

He jerked when he realized that his focus had drifted away from his driving. He looked down at the speedometer and saw that he had crept over the seventy mile an hour speed limit. He looked in his rearview mirror for the blue lights of a state trooper's car. Seeing none, Kevin breathed a sigh of relief and immediately brought the Bronco back within the speed limit.

He could not get careless now. He had come too far to fail.

He drove carefully through the communities of Benton and Bryant. He soon came to the exit for Interstate 430. This highway was a major corridor through West Little Rock, which Kevin turned onto and headed north.

Within a few minutes, he took the exit for Shackleford Road. He was now heading into the heart of West Little Rock. As he was driving, Kevin noticed snowflakes falling on his windshield.

After a short stint on Shackleford Road, he made a left turn onto Kanis Road. He drove about two blocks and pulled into a parking lot for a business that had been closed for several hours. This parking lot was adjacent to a wooded area that separated Kanis Road from the street that ran in front of the clinic. Kevin would park the Bronco here and take a short walk through the woods to the clinic.

He got out of the Bronco and went to the rear of the vehicle to retrieve the duffel bag. He swung the bag over his shoulder and closed the rear door. He glanced carefully around to make sure that no one was watching. He had to be careful now. He was too close to his objective to make a mistake.

Satisfied that he had not been seen, Kevin began the short walk through the woods to the clinic. His senses were fully alert. He could not believe he was this close after so long.

The snow was coming down harder. It was not sticking to the ground yet.

Kevin stopped as he reached the edge of the woods. He could see the clinic from here. He stood watching, looking for any signs that would cause him to abort his mission. The clinic was completely dark. There was only one car in the parking lot. It was the Porsche that belonged to one of the doctors that worked at the clinic.

He waited. The rest of the clinics and businesses on the street were also dark. It appeared that everyone had left for the weekend, just as he planned. He knew that if he scheduled this part of the mission for Friday night, it would be his best chance for finding the place empty. The maintenance crew would not be in until tomorrow afternoon. It was pretty typical that they would plan for a big night out on the town and Saturday morning to sleep it off. Their car was not in the parking lot. Kevin knew that they had stayed true to form.

The doctor's car in the parking lot had him concerned. He had not expected that. He could only see two sides of the building from his current position. Kevin quickly decided that he would circle around the building so that he could see the remainder of the clinic. He had to make sure that no one was inside.

He had been standing at the edge of the woods for about 15 minutes. The snow was beginning to accumulate on his jacket. He left the woods and circled around behind the clinic, walking through the parking lot of the adjacent business, a psychiatric clinic.

Kevin circled around and came to the staff entrance of the clinic. There were no lights on in the entire building. He knew from the time that he had spent in the building working on the maintenance crew that, with the exception of the OR area, all of the work areas and offices had windows. If someone was working late, they were working in the dark.

He looked again at the car in the parking lot. Kevin knew about Dr. Straun's reputation as a ladies' man. He probably left the clinic with another one of his conquests.

Kevin didn't know much about Porsches, but he did know that they were expensive. Well Dr. Straun, he thought, after tonight, you will have to make your big dollars someplace else to pay for your expensive habits.

Kevin looked up and down the street one more time. He slipped his hands into a pair of gloves and slid the key into the door. With a wave of excitement and a sense of fulfillment, he entered the clinic.

The building was dark, the only light coming from the green glow of the emergency exit signs. Kevin looked at the security system keypad by the door. As usual, it was not armed. He knew from experience that the alarm was very seldom set when the last person left for the day. The alarm was set by the monitoring company to come on automatically at midnight. Like most companies with alarms, the clinic had had too many false alarms and did not bother to set it manually.

Kevin reached into the side pocket of his duffel bag and pulled out a small, powerful flashlight. He stood still as he shined the light around the dark hallway. He would not be inside the clinic very long, so he wanted to make sure that he was not inadvertently discovered. The stillness of the clinic gave it an eerie feel, but Kevin knew the work that was done here. It was more than the stillness that made it eerie. The work of the Devil was done in this place. It was an evil place.

Satisfied that he was alone, Kevin went to work. He walked down the hall a short distance to the closet that was used to store dirty linens and the mops and buckets that the maintenance crew used. Propped up in the corner was a ladder. Kevin set the ladder up in the middle of the small closet. He hauled the duffel bag to the top of the ladder and set it down. He reached up to the ceiling and pushed the two-by-two tile up into the crawl space above. He opened the duffel bag and pulled out the timing device. He placed the timing device in the crawl space next to one of the support beams for the second floor. Next, he brought out the dynamite. Kevin placed the dynamite next to the timing device and attached the wires from the timer to the blasting cap that was connected to the explosives.

The timer was set for ten o'clock. Kevin turned it on. The bomb was ready.

Kevin replaced the ceiling tile and stepped down off the ladder. He grabbed the duffel bag and slung it over his shoulder. He folded the ladder and leaned it back against the wall. He looked around the room to make sure that he had not left anything out of place. Not that it would matter very shortly, but he didn't want anybody sending out any alerts if they happened to come into the clinic before the blast.

He looked at his watch. It was eight thirty. An hour and a half before the building would explode. The plan was working perfectly. He would have plenty of time to return to Hot Springs before the blast. He would not be anywhere near when the explosion occurred.

Kevin walked the ten feet to the back door, opened it and slipped out. The snow was really coming down now. It was accumulating on the street. Within minutes, Kevin was back in his Bronco. Fifteen minutes later, he was back on Interstate 30 heading west to Hot Springs.

* * * * *

Carla and Marty had taken their time at dinner. With Thomas in Memphis, they had no real reason to rush home. Marty had related the entire story about the baby that he had delivered and Janet had killed. Carla was as horrified as Marty had been.

They were at one of Little Rock's more popular restaurants. Although the service had been good, it had taken quite a while to get their food. The topic of most of their conversation during the evening had been focused on the events that had occurred at work. The events had been unpleasant, but the freedom to discuss it with someone who cared was rewarding. They had become very comfortable with each other.

At 9:15, they finally left the restaurant. Snow was falling on them as they hurried through the parking lot to Carla's car. They got into her car and pulled out into traffic. The dark sedan pulled out right behind them.

"Why don't you drop me off at my place and I'll get my car?" Marty asked. "I might change clothes also. These are getting a little stale."

Carla took the next turn and headed to Marty's.

"While you're doing that, I'm going to stop by the office," Carla said. "I have a form that I need to finish for the incident report today. I'm afraid that I'll forget it if I don't do it now."

"That's fine," Marty replied. "I'll just meet you at your house in about 30 minutes." He looked at the clock on the dashboard. "About 9:45."

Carla pulled the car up in front of Marty's condo. He leaned over and kissed her. He then jumped out of the car and ran through the snow to the door of his condo.

"You better wear a coat!" she called out to him as she drove away.

The dark sedan was trailing behind.

Chapter 36

"Mr. Giovanni?" It was Andy Costello calling.

"Yes, Andy," Ronaldo said.

"We've got the information that you've been waiting for," Andy said.

"That's good news, Andy," he said. "Go ahead. I'm listening"

"The hacker's name is Kevin McLaughlin," Andy said.

"Do you have an address yet?" Ronaldo asked.

"I do," Andy replied. "I would have called you earlier, but we just made a match on his address. He's renting a house in Hot Springs." Andy relayed the address to Giovanni.

"Thank you for this information, Andy," Mr. Giovanni said. "I won't forget your help."

Giovanni immediately terminated the call and found another phone number on his desk. He dialed the number that rang to a cell phone that was currently with its owner in Hot Springs.

"I've got the information," Giovanni said into the phone.

"Good," the voice said, "we've been waiting for it."

Giovanni relayed the information and hung up.

He sat back in his chair and smiled to himself. He was going to win this one. This poor guy, Kevin McLaughlin, would never know what hit him.

* * * * *

Carla wheeled her car into the parking lot at the clinic, surprised to see J.P.'s car still there. This had been such a weird day, who knew why it was still here.

She parked close to the back door and quickly got out of her car and into the clinic. The falling snow coming down through the fluorescent glow of the streetlights gave Carla a surreal feeling about moving around in the parking lot. It spooked her.

She hurried up the back stairs to her office. If J.P. happened to be in the building, she did not want him to know that she was here also. Carla really didn't feel like talking to him tonight. She quietly slipped into the administrative area and then into her office. She sat down behind her desk, turned on a lamp and started to go over the incident report from this afternoon's bad turn of events.

She heard something. Carla froze and listened intently. The sound was gone now, but she was certain that she had heard something. The quietness sent shivers down her spine. She carefully got up to look out of her window. There was nothing to see, except for the falling snow, but she couldn't see her car in the parking lot at the side of the building. She would have to look from the windows in the conference room across the hallway.

Carla quietly moved around the desk toward to her office door. As she was about to move into the doorway, a shadow crossed in front of her. Carla screamed and felt someone grab her arm. It was someone strong and they spun her around and shoved her to the floor. Before she could react, the attacker jumped on her back, pinning both of her arms behind her.

He roughly jerked her up off the floor by her arms. Carla thought that he was going to pull them out of their sockets. He pushed her down into one of the side chairs that sat in front of her desk. With some rope that he pulled out of nowhere, he tied her hands behind the chair. Carla screamed. She saw his hand coming out of the corner of her eye, but she didn't have time to react. The back of his hand caught the side of her face. The large ring that he wore sliced a gash in her cheek.

It was the first time that she had gotten a look at the man who had attacked her. In the dim glow of the light from the lamp on her desk, she saw that he was not an attractive man. His features were large and the shadows created by the light in the room made his appearance that much more sinister.

"Well, Ms. Sharkley," he said, "I'm glad that we finally get to meet. I've been following you all evening. I was afraid that I would have to go home with you. This will be so much more convenient." He had an evil grin on his face. "Thank you for stopping by the office. You've made my evening much more enjoyable."

The pain from the cut on her cheek had caused tears to come to her eyes. The tears were mixing with the blood on her cheek as they ran down her face.

"What do you want?" Carla asked him. "We don't keep money in this building overnight."

He laughed. "Oh, I don't want your money. I bring you greetings from Mr. Giovanni."

"Brad?" Carla was confused.

"That's right," he said. "Brad wanted me to visit with you tonight. It seems that some money is missing out of the company coffers and he wants to know where it is."

"I've already told him," she explained. "I don't know where the money is…"

The sound of his open hand smacking her face created a sharp echo in the quiet office. The force of the blow snapped her head into the back of the chair and she screamed. This time the blood came from the corner of her mouth.

"Listen, lady, let's get the rules established up front," he growled at her. "I'm not here to listen to you babble on. I'm here to get answers to my questions and I don't want you wasting my time."

His face was inches from Carla's. She could smell his bad breath. He had grabbed her chin with his hand and was gripping it tightly, so that she could not look anywhere but in his eyes.

"Do you understand me?" His eyes were sparkling. He was enjoying this.

Carla nodded her head in understanding. She was afraid that she really did understand him. She was very afraid.

* * * * *

Kevin pulled the Bronco into the driveway and stopped it right in front of the house. He breathed a deep sigh of relief. His shoulders were tense from hunching over the steering wheel on the drive back to Hot Springs. The weather had become progressively worse as he got closer to Hot Springs. The accumulation of snow had reached four to five inches along his route home. The driving had become treacherous. If it had not been for the four-wheel drive on his vehicle, he may not have made it back. He had seen many accidents along the way and many abandoned vehicles. The normally one-hour drive had taken an extra half-hour because of the weather. His arms and shoulders ached from the tension of driving through the snow.

Kevin looked at his watch. It was ten o'clock. He smiled in the darkness of his vehicle. Mission complete.

He grabbed the duffel bag and went into the house.

* * * * *

"She doesn't know anything, Brad," Charlie said over the phone. "I've worked her over pretty good. If she would have known something, she would have told me."

"Are you sure?" Brad asked.

"Positive," Charlie replied. "What do you want me to do with her now?"

"Did you use my name?" Brad asked.

"Of course," Charlie said, "how else was I supposed to get to her?"

"Yeah right," Brad said. "Go ahead and get rid of her, don't leave her in the clinic."

Charlie closed up his cell phone.

Carla was still tied to the chair. Her chin was sagging on her chest. Her face was cut and swollen. The blood was still flowing from several of the cuts. Charlie had beaten her to the point that she was almost unrecognizable.

It was now time for him to finish her off.

At that moment, a voice called from the hallway.

"Hey, what's going on in there?" the slurred voice called.

J.P. Straun stumbled through the door carrying an almost empty bottle of rum in one hand. The other hand he used to support himself against the doorframe. He stood there surveying the scene with bleary eyes.

"I must have fallen asleep in my office," he muttered. "I got up to see what time it was and I heard noises up here."

"Hey, who are you?" He directed the question to Charlie. J.P then realized that Carla was sitting in the chair. "Carla, what's going on here? Are you alright?"

Charlie started to move toward J.P.

"Buddy, you're not supposed to be in here," J.P. said, the rum giving him more courage than he should have had. "You better get out of here, before I call the police."

Charlie reached J.P. and swung a backhand that caught J.P. on his left temple. The blow knocked J.P. against the wall and stunned him. The bottle of rum fell from his hand and tumbled to the carpeted floor, spilling its contents.

Charlie stood in the middle of the office, his hands on his hips, admiring his handiwork. An evil grin was permeating his face.

"Well now," he said loudly. "Now that we've shut the drunkard up, we can get down to business. It looks like we're going to have a two-for-one tonight. You guys are letting me have too much fun."

Charlie's laughter bellowed through the quiet hallways of the clinic. The ringing phone on Carla's desk interrupted his enjoyment of the situation.

* * * * *

Something was wrong and Marty knew it. He was in his car heading back to the clinic. He had tried to call Carla on her cell phone and her office phone. She had not responded to either one.

He was worried. He looked at his watch. It was nine fifty-nine. Carla had dropped him off almost 45 minutes ago. He had cleaned up at his condo and driven to Carla's house. He had been waiting there for her for 20 minutes.

She should have been home by now. She was only going to review some paperwork. It was taking too long and now she wasn't answering the phone.

Carla did not live far from the clinic. It would only take Marty a few minutes to get there.

Chapter 37

The digital timer on the bomb turned to ten o'clock.

The explosion was deafening. The initial blast obliterated the back hallway of the clinic. The door to the staff entrance was blown across the parking lot. Because of the placement of the bomb, the main thrust of the blast blew a three-foot wide hole in the wall of OR 1. The concussion of the blast traveled along the crawl space between the two floors of the clinic. This jarred the surgical light that was attached to the ceiling and caused it to crash to the floor of OR 1. It also damaged the PVC pipes that carried the medical gases to the OR's and the recovery room.

A cart filled with medical supplies was toppled over in the hallway between two of the OR's. Every piece of glass on the first floor was shattered. An EKG machine that had been rolled into the hallway was now in the floor in a thousand pieces.

The three people upstairs were all rocked to the floor by the explosion. The chair in which Carla was tied tipped over from the jolt that traveled through the support structures for the second floor.

Charlie, who had been standing in the middle of the office, was bounced against the wall. The collision with the wall left a gash on his forehead and the blood poured down his face. By the looks of it, he had also broken his arm.

J.P. had been struggling to get up when the explosion hit. The force of the blast sent him sprawling again. He hit his head on the corner of the door and lost consciousness.

The rumble from the explosion rattled the windows in buildings for a half-mile radius.

* * * * *

"What was that?" Marty uttered the question aloud as he was driving to the clinic.

Marty was trying to drive fast, but the accumulation of snow on the streets was slowing him down. He heard a tremendous crash. It was difficult for him to determine the direction of the sound.

He had tried continually to reach Carla on her cell phone or her office phone. He had just tried her office number again and got a recorded operator voice, telling him that the line had been disconnected.

His level of concern had heightened now. He pushed the accelerator a little harder to increase his speed. As he came to the next corner, he could feel the car sliding to the edge of the road. He let off on the gas and resisted the temptation to hit the brakes. He turned the wheel of the car toward the direction that the car was sliding. This maneuver allowed him to regain control of the car. He slowed the speed of the car slightly and proceeded on to the clinic.

* * * * *

Kevin had planned for the explosion at the clinic very thoroughly. He had researched the type of explosive necessary to inflict the most damage on the clinic. He had spent a great deal of time studying the placement of the device. He had placed it so that the bomb would cause severe structural damage as well as cosmetic damage.

With all of his planning, there was one thing that he did not take into consideration. Oh, he knew it was there, but he never considered the catalytic impact that it could have on his work.

Three doors down from the dirty linen closet, where he placed the bomb, was a closet that held the heavy, metal cylinders that contained the medical gases used in surgery.

The initial blast had knocked the cylinders over. One of the cylinders contained oxygen. When this cylinder fell, the force of the fall knocked the valve off the top of the cylinder. This caused the oxygen gas to begin spewing out of the cylinder. The small closet slowly filled with the gas.

The explosion had dislodged the ceiling tiles in the entire downstairs portion of the clinic. In the medical gas closet, the tiles were gone. During the first minute after the explosion, quiet settled over the debris that minutes before been a clinic to help women in their time of need. The only sound came from the severed electrical wires in the ceiling between the two floors. The hot wires were shooting sparks from their exposed ends. The sparks were falling from the ceiling down to the first floor.

It took a minute before one of the sparks landed in the medical gas room. The spark ignited the oxygen in the room and caused a second explosion that was significantly more damaging than the first.

Carla was still tied to the chair. She was lying on her side in front of her desk. The explosion had stunned her. She thought that she might be the only one still conscious in the room, but it was hard to tell. She could not see out of her left eye, it was swollen shut from the blows that she had taken from the man who had attacked her. The dust that was swirling in the room hindered the little vision that she still had in her right eye. The explosion had confused her. She wasn't sure if her attacker was responsible for the blast or not. She was having trouble putting coherent thoughts together.

It was the last thought that she had.

The second explosion came with such force in the small closet downstairs that everything in the room became a projectile. In the corner of the room was a spare oxygen cylinder that had not been used. The first explosion had caused this cylinder to fall against the wall. The next explosion sent this cylinder flying, like a rocket, through the ceiling and on through the floor of the second level.

The projectile cylinder came through the floor under Carla and did not stop, killing her instantly. She was the lucky one. When the sparks came in contact with the oxygen, a fire broke out. With the oxygen fueling the fire, it did not take long for the entire structure to be consumed in flames.

Marty turned onto the street in front of the clinic, just as the second explosion hit.

"Nooooo!" he screamed into the emptiness of the night.

He stopped his car on the side of the street. The heat from the fire was already too intense for him to go any closer to the clinic.

He used his cell phone to dial 911, but he knew it was useless. His dreams had just disintegrated in a ball of fire. The clinic that had held his career in chains earlier in the day, now in its destruction held his future in captivity.

Chapter 38

Something was wrong. He knew it the minute that he opened the door.

Kevin could hear the alarm from his computer sounding as soon as he entered the house. He tossed the duffel bag on the kitchen counter and hurried over to his computer in the living room. He had left the desktop computer on while he was gone. It was still crunching through the program when he left.

He quickly moved the mouse to bring the screen back to life. Immediately, Kevin saw that he had received two urgent messages. The first email was from Wheels.

To: KayMac
Sent: Friday, December 10, 1999 8:45 p.m.
From: Wheels
Subject: Discovered!

KayMac,

Get out quick. They found you. I've been monitoring my sources and they have tracked you down. Get out before they get there!

Kevin glanced again at the other unopened message. He realized that it was a message that he had programmed his computer to send if someone got too close. The arrival time of the message indicated that they found him more than two hours ago. He didn't have any time at all.

He grabbed the laptop that was sitting on the desk and crossed the area to the kitchen quickly. He stuffed the laptop into the duffel bag and turned to the stairs that led to the basement.

It was the first time that he had caught a whiff of the smell of gas. It was natural gas. He looked down at the oven and saw that the knob had been turned on to allow gas to escape without starting the oven. He now realized that the smell was heavy in the house. The sound of the computer alarm must have distracted him from noticing it before.

Kevin looked around the house, but he didn't see anything else out of place. As he was turning back to the oven, he caught the reflection of a red light out of the corner of his eye. The red light was coming through the glass panes in the door. He knew it was time to go.

Kevin ducked down and crawled to the basement door. He opened the door and moved to the landing of the stairs. He had almost closed the door, when he heard the glass window in the front door shatter. The friction, of what must have been a bullet, created just enough heat to cause the gas in the house to explode.

The door to the basement had shielded Kevin from the force of the explosion. The explosion flung the door against the wall, knocking Kevin down the stairs. Although he was banged up from the fall, being behind the door probably saved his life.

The gas caught on fire and began to burn the house. Since the door to the basement had been closed, the gas had been contained on the main level of the house. The basement did not immediately catch fire with the rest of the house.

Kevin jumped up and quickly grabbed the backpack off the table in the middle of the basement. He ran down the tunnel to the lake in the dark. He was afraid to turn on any lights for fear of being seen or causing another explosion.

He threw the duffel bag and backpack into the canoe and hurriedly put on the wet suit that was lying there. He groped in the dark to find the handle for the door that led to the lake. He found it and shoved the door open.

He grabbed the front of the canoe with both hands and started dragging the boat to the water. He was facing the house, as his back was toward the lake, hunched over trying to get the canoe down the shore. He hesitated for a second, amazed at the bright illumination that his house was providing to the night sky.

The canoe finally reached the water. He walked around to the rear and shoved once more to get it totally in the water. Kevin jumped into the canoe and crouched down, to stay out of the brilliant light coming from the house.

He paddled vigorously to get out in the bay away from his house. He could already see the lights from the other houses along the shore coming on. The neighbors would be out in their backyards soon, looking at the ball of fire that had once been his house.

Kevin remembered what he had learned about paddling from his time on the lake this past week. He settled into a smooth steady motion with his paddling strokes. Within a few minutes, he was out in the main channel. He turned and headed west. His destination was Blakely Dam. As he made the turn, the glow on the water died down. He could still see a glow in the sky over his left shoulder.

He began to breathe easier now. He felt that he had escaped imminent danger. He knew that he still had a long way to go, but at least he had made it past the first hurdle.

The snow was coming down harder. Visibility on the lake couldn't have been more than 15 feet. The water was a murky gray-green that seemed to be fluorescent under the falling snow. He was thankful that he had taken the time to get a wet suit. He would have frozen to death without it.

He paddled hard and steady for three hours taking an occasional short break. He was making good time.

It was 1:30 a.m., when the bow of the canoe finally touched shore in Stephens Park at the base of Blakely Dam. With the minimal visibility, the dam was just a huge wall of darkness.

Kevin unloaded his equipment on the shore. He took off the wet suit and put it in the canoe. He pulled some dry clothes out of the backpack and quickly dressed. He searched around on the shoreline for some medium sized rocks. He placed all that he could find in the canoe. When he thought that it was sufficiently weighted, he pushed the canoe out into the lake. Kevin stood on the shore watching it slowly sink to the bottom of Lake Hamilton.

Kevin shouldered his backpack and duffel bag. He took a moment to shine a flashlight on the map that he had in the side pocket of the backpack. This had been his destination all along. He knew that he needed an escape route and this had been it. Kevin just didn't expect to get here by canoe.

He reviewed the map briefly and set off to skirt the northern edge of Lake Ouachita. He left the park area and found an old logging road that took him to the edge of the Ouachita National Forest.

There were trails in the forest that would take him all the way to Oklahoma if necessary. He consulted his map once more. He would use the GPS to keep on course.

It was almost daybreak. He had hiked several miles. The snow was no longer falling, but in this area, there were at least eight inches on the ground. It would be several days before Hot Springs would dig out of this.

Kevin readjusted his load and disappeared into the Ouachita National Forest. With the new debit card, issued under his new identity, packed safely in the backpack, he would be able to travel undetected for a long time. Three million dollars of clean Mob money should last for a while.

Chapter 39

The church was quiet on Saturday morning. Bill Roberts had been in his office for 15 minutes, when Mike Hanks came barging in.

"Have you seen the news?" Mike asked, gasping for breath. He had run up the steps to Roberts' office.

"I have," Bill said calmly.

"I can't believe this. This is horrible." Mike was standing in front of Roberts' desk, his distress showing in his voice and on his face. "What are we going to do?"

"Mike, you have a hard time seeing the big picture in all of this, don't you?"

Mike stopped and stared at Brother Bill.

"I couldn't imagine anything that would have given us the kind of attention that we'll receive now," Bill continued. "Everyone will want a piece of this story now. It will be the perfect tool to escalate the attention that we can get from this."

Mike was stunned. "I don't understand. I thought we didn't want anyone else killed."

"Mike, this is bigger than you can imagine. The deaths of these people will allow us to also focus on the extremes that the foes of abortion are willing to go to stop the killing of babies."

"But, killing other people? I thought we wanted to stop the killing."

Bill shrugged his shoulders. "Mike, we can't help it when these terrible tragedies happen. It just makes our position against abortion that much clearer. The legality of abortion has to be stopped to prevent further tragedy from occurring."

Mike was struggling to put the pieces of this ordeal together in his mind.

"Mike, this is the beginning of our crusade. It was a great start, but you need to understand that we just started the journey."

Roberts reached in his desk drawer and pulled out an envelope. Her slid the envelope across the desk toward Mike Hanks.

"I have a new project for you. Can you get in touch with our friend?"

Hanks' face showed his puzzlement. "A new project?"

"Yes, open the envelope."

Hanks reached down and picked up the envelope. He opened it and inside was a key.

"Can you find him? I want him to do another one."

Chapter 40

Marty sat down in his car and let a big sigh of relief escape.

He had just left Thomas. He had been dreading a face-to-face visit with him. Marty wasn't sure that he could endure any more sorrow.

It had taken Marty a week to get to Memphis to see Thomas. The record snow that had fallen on central Arkansas had brought travel to a standstill. Once the streets had cleared, Marty had been required to spend a great deal of time with the police. He told them all about the last day at the clinic. He gave them the details of the murder of the baby that he had delivered.

The clinic had been totally destroyed. Any evidence that the police may have found was gone.

They were still sifting through the debris. Right now, Marty was the closest thing that they had to a lead. He had never been considered a suspect, but he was the only one that the authorities could find with any knowledge of the recent events at the clinic.

Janet Rawls had disappeared and the police were looking for her. Brad was hiding behind an army of lawyers. And Carla was dead.

It was assumed that J.P. Straun was killed in the blast. His Porsche was still in the parking lot – a charred wreck. Marty confirmed that Carla had been in the clinic that evening. Her car was buried under the debris by the back door of the clinic. An abandoned car was found a block from the clinic. With all of the cars that had been left along the side of the road due to the weather, it had taken several days to verify that it was indeed abandoned. The police now had suspicions that the driver of this car might have been in the building also. The license plates on the car indicated that it had been stolen in Jackson, Mississippi.

The final verification of the identities of those killed in the blast would take several more weeks. The police had informed him that it would require matching dental records.

Thomas had responded just as Marty had expected. He was alone now and the pain had already begun. Marty promised Carla's sister that he would help her take care of Carla's affairs in Little Rock, which he had already begun. He found that Carla had a million-dollar life insurance policy, naming Thomas as the beneficiary. His financial needs would be   met.

Two days after the explosion, the sun had come out in Little Rock. It was the first time in almost a month that it had been clear for more than a few days at a time. The bright sunny days had quickly melted the snow and ice away. The weather was perfect, but Marty didn't care. He didn't have anyone to share it with. The dreams that he and Carla had begun to have together were shattered by the blast. His life would be changed forever.

He still found it hard to believe that he and Carla had grown so close in such a short period of time. He could have spent the rest of his life with her.

Marty had crossed over the Mississippi River Bridge leaving Memphis. He was heading back to Little Rock, but was in no particular hurry. Just outside of Memphis, Marty turned off of Interstate 40 and went south on Highway 79. He spent the next hour driving aimlessly through the Arkansas delta.

The ringing of his cell phone snapped him out of his daydream. He picked it up.

"Hello," Marty said into the phone.

"Hey Marty," the caller said. "This is Brad Giovanni. We've been looking for you."

"You have?" Marty replied sarcastically. "Why are you looking for me? I don't work for you anymore."

"Yes, I realize that, Marty," Brad said. "J.P. told me about that unfortunate incident, before his untimely demise. But, that's not why I called you. I wanted to ask you about some money that is missing from the clinic."

"Maybe it was blown up, Brad," Marty said snidely.

"Very funny, Marty," Brad said, not amused. "It appears that someone has made some electronic transfers of funds from the clinic. The money appears to have been transferred randomly. One of the receptionists in the clinic had her home mortgage paid off. One of the nurses had her car loan paid off. There was even a contribution made to the pro-life movement. Can you imagine that? Someone had a lot of nerve."

"So what does this have to do with me, Brad?" Marty asked. "Why don't you just get these people to give the money back?"

"The reason that I'm calling you is that one of the transfers went to pay off the remainder of your student loans," Brad said. He let that sink in with Marty for a moment.

"You're kidding," Marty responded.

"I'm not kidding, Marty," Brad told him. "It was almost $120,000."

Marty was silent.

"There's more missing that we can't find," he said. "I need you to come back to Little Rock and talk to me about it. It's too bad that Carla was killed in the explosion at the clinic. We were talking to her about the money also."

"What does Carla have to do with this?" Marty barked. "Can't you leave her out of it? She's gone."

"Yes," Brad said, "and a little prematurely I might add."

Marty was confused. What was Brad talking about?

"Now, Marty," he started again, "come back to Little Rock and talk to me. You might be able to help me find my money."

Something that Brad said caught his attention.

"How do you know that I'm not in Little Rock?" Marty knew that Brad could be dangerous.

"You mean, how do I know that you are driving around the back roads of the Arkansas delta?" Brad asked tauntingly. "Marty, I know everything about you. You can't escape from me!" Brad was laughing through the phone.

That's when it hit him. Brad was tracing him through his cell phone.

Marty quickly snapped the phone shut and slammed on the brakes to the car. He sat silently in the car with both hands gripped tightly around the steering wheel. His knuckles were white.

He looked around and realized that he had driven to Helena, Arkansas. He was about a mile from the bridge that crossed the Mississippi River into the state of Mississippi. Marty's emotions had been on a roller coaster ride over the last month.

The frustrations he had about his work had closed in on him during that time. He couldn't stand the thought of doing nothing but abortions. Before the bomb had destroyed the clinic, he had reached the point professionally where he could not continue another day. If could not find a job in a regular obstetric practice, he was ready to leave Little Rock, or Arkansas to find something.

If the work itself had not been an emotional issue, then the Mob connection would have surely convinced him that it was time to leave the clinic. At first, he had been afraid of the Mob, but after Carla's death – what did it matter?

Carla's death. Losing Carla still seemed unreal. After growing so close, so fast, the loss was hard to accept. He had never before cared for someone, as much as he had Carla. How would he deal with that? How could he go back to a normal life without her?

An idea came to him and for the first time in a week a smile crossed Marty's face. It was a way for him to put these emotional reminders behind him forever.

He drove his car to the middle of the bridge and stopped. He dialed Brad's number on his cell phone and waited for the answer.

"Hello Marty," Brad said patronizingly. "I knew you would see it my way."

"Brad?"

"Yes, Marty," Brad said.

"Find me now, you son of a bitch!"

Marty took the phone and flung it as far as he could over the side of the bridge. He stood there watching until the phone landed in the muddy waters of the Mississippi and floated away.

Marty stood staring for a few more moments.

"Good riddance," he muttered.

He climbed back into his car and left Arkansas forever.

Made in the USA
Middletown, DE
21 December 2020

29906694R00166